Acknowledgements:

Firstly, thank you to my phenomenal family, who endured all my questions and doubts; to my daughter, Kimberly Glucoft Massari, for her unwavering confidence and in all cases shielding me from pitfalls; to my granddaughter, Madeline, for her brilliant insight into what became my cover art; to my son-in-law, Mark Massari, for suffering an atypical mother-in-law; to my grandson, Joesph Massari, for keeping me laughing; to my ex-husband, Stephen Glucoft, for his undying faith and love; to my partner in crime, mystery writer Darrell James, for his support and encouragement through the entire process of writing and living and so much more.

This book would not have come to pass but for my writers' group: Bill Astrike, Peter Finkle, Francis McCarthy, Colleen Patrick-Riley, and Bob Fisher. Thank you from the bottom of my heart. Special thanks also to former members Lee Baldwin and Dennis Hall.

Thanks also to editors; Indigo Press, Kristin Thiel, Karen Brown and Meredith Phillips. Thank you to Karen Phillips for creating Madeline's vision for my cover.

Lastly, thank you to Kate Dyer-Seeley aka Ellie Alexander whose novel Underneath the Ash gave me courage to write.

D1707602

Dedication:

In memory of my brother, Dale Dehnke, 1948-1971

If Ever Hapless Woman Had a Cause

If ever hapless woman had a cause
   To breathe her plaints into the open air,
And never suffer inward grief to pause.
   Or seek her sorrow-shaken soul's repair;
Then I, for I have lost my only brother,
Whose like this age can scarcely yield another.

Come therefore, mournful Muses, and lament;
   Forsake all wanton pleasing motions;
Bedew your cheeks. Still shall my tears be spent,
   Yet still increased with inundations.
For I must weep, since I have lost my brother,
Whose like this age can scarcely yield another.

The cruel hand of murder cloyed with blood
   Lewdly deprived him of his mortal life.
Woe the death-attended blades that stood
   In opposition 'gainst him in the strife
Wherein he fell, and where I lost a brother,
Whose like this age can scarcely yield another.

Then unto Grief let me a temple make,
   And, mourning, daily enter Sorrow's ports,
Knock on my breast, sweet brother, for thy sake,
   Nature and love will both be my consorts,
And help me aye to wail my only brother,
Whose like this age can scarcely yield another.

–Mary Sidney Herbert, Countess of Pembro

(1561-1621, British)

CONTENTS

Prologue

Leslie

January 1, 2013

I'm beginning to dislike these people, my family. It's getting harder and harder for me to hold on to the better days we once had.
    Or did we?

A Father's Letter on the Birth of His Daughter

July 27, 1944

> *Howdy folks,*
>
> *Well, this is my first letter as a father and the first you will receive as grandparents. I have a daughter, Leslie Mildred, named after Bette's brother and you, Mom. Leslie is certainly the sweetest and cutest gal there ever was. You need only to look at her to tell that she is going to be a champion. No, that's wrong! She is a champion now. July 26, 1944 is truly my lucky day.*
>
> *Tomorrow morning, I check out of Squadron VR-7 for good. Hurray!*
>
> *Love,*
>
> *William*

Chapter One

The Princess

Leslie

December 25, 1951

Grandma Goodman gave me this diary for Christmas. She died in June, a week after I arrived at our new home in Texas. Grandad said she bought this for me while I was living with them, but she wanted to save it for a Christmas present. It's kind of creepy to get a present from someone who is dead. Grandad said she wanted me to write about my life and to remember her.

My family moved to Texas, but I stayed with Grandma and Grandad so I could finish second grade in Detroit. My grandma let me watch Felix the Cat on television, and she let me have a 7 Up, which is a very big treat. Daddy won't let me have soda pop. He says it'll ruin my teeth.

Once Grandma and Auntie Anne—she's Daddy's sister—locked themselves out of the house, and I had to climb in the milk chute and open the side door. I was a little scared, but Auntie Anne said it was a big adventure.

Grandma let me sip her beer. It was disgusting. That's my new word, "disgusting." Auntie Anne sometimes uses that word about things that happen at the hospital. When I grow up, I want to be a nurse like Auntie Anne. She wears a white cap, a white dress, and white shoes. She was a Red Cross nurse during the war.

I knew Grandma was going to die. I heard her talking to Auntie Anne about the scarlet fever she had when she was little and how her heart was hurt and she was weak and afraid. She told Auntie Anne she loved me so much and wanted to see me grow up to be the fine young lady she knew I would become. Grandma said I was a champion, just like Daddy told her I was the day I was born.

2

When I got on the plane to fly to Texas, I waved to Grandma and Auntie Anne through the little round window of the DC-6. I know it's a DC-6 because Daddy told me. Daddy's a pilot. He said he flew a DC-6, and it's a good, solid aircraft, so I was not to be afraid. Mommy is scared to death of flying, but I love flying. It's very exciting to be up in the air, looking down on the world through the clouds.

I was very sad because I knew this would be the last time I would see my grandma. I will always love her and remember her. Grandad says I need to tell my brother, Liam, and sister, Deedee, about her so she will live in their memories too.

January 7, 1952

Today I went back to my new school in Texas. I love my books and pencils and notebooks. The books smell good. Mommy made me some cute new dresses that look just like my Betsy McCall doll's clothes. I met a new friend, Sally. After school Sally came over to play with me, and she stayed for dinner. Sally only has one leg, and she doesn't have very many friends. She said, "Maybe kids are afraid of me because I'm different." I'm not sure what that means. I said, "Let me think about that."

January 9, 1952

This was a very bad day! Daddy got mad about something. I said, "Daddy, please don't be mad. It scares me."

It's been a long time since Daddy got mad. It was when he punched the neighbor in the jaw. It had something to do with the fence in the yard at our house in Detroit.

January 13, 1952

Today was sharing day at school. I took my Mary Hartline doll to share. Everybody liked her red dress with the music on it and her cute little white boots. She was a present from Grandma Goodman. I miss Grandma. I can't go visit her anymore. I heard Mommy and Daddy talking about how sad Grandad is since Grandma died. When Daddy was talking to Mommy, I heard him say, "My dad is drinking too much whiskey." I'm not sure what that is, but I don't think it's good. Daddy says he's flying Grandad out to stay with us for a while. That's really good!

January 17, 1952

It's Daddy's birthday. Grandad is here. Mommy fixed dinner and invited Hetty and Scooter and Chip. They're the boys who play baseball with Liam, and Hetty is their mom. We had cake and ice cream, and after Hetty and the boys left, Daddy let me watch *I Love Lucy* with him and Mommy and Grandad. We're trying really hard to cheer up Grandad. I told him that I miss Grandma too. Mommy said to me, "Don't be sad. Someday you'll forget all about Grandma." I put my hands on my hips and said, "I will never forget my grandma."

January 22, 1952

Deedee is only three months old, but Mommy let me help her take care of Deedee, and then she gave me fifty cents. Grandma Haines—she's Mommy's mom—gave me a savings account. Mommy took me to the bank, and I put my fifty cents in the savings account. I like to see all the stamps in my little black bankbook. I have fifteen dollars in my savings account. Grandma Haines said she is very proud of me and maybe she could borrow some money. She's so funny!

January 27, 1952

Sally and I went on television for the program called *Tricks and Treats*. Sally got to go up on the stage. It was hard for her with the crutches. She got lots of treats and shared them with me. Sally is very nice and very brave. I wonder how she lost her leg. I haven't asked because I don't want to embarrass her. Maybe it's better if she thinks I don't notice. That's my new word, "embarrass." Daddy says Mommy embarrasses easily.

February 1, 1952

I cleaned the house for Mommy. I got another fifty cents to put in my savings. I told Grandma it would be nice if she started a savings account for Liam. When he grows up, he wants to be a lawyer like Uncle Les. Uncle Les told us law school costs a lot of money and Liam should start saving now.

February 14, 1952

It's Valentine's Day. I got to watch *Disneyland* on television. I asked Mommy if we could go to Disneyland. She said, "It's a long way from Texas!"

May 18, 1952

Today Mommy had a party for Liam's sixth birthday. She made him a sponge cake, and it tasted just like an old sponge.

August 12, 1952

Daddy flies airplanes, so he's gone a lot, but he always calls and sends letters. I got this postcard from him today:

> *Hi, Princess,*
>
> *This picture postcard shows where the Alaska Highway is supposed to begin. Tomorrow I fly out into the bush and mountain country. Tell Liam I saw a lot of moose. Be good to Mommy and be sure to take care of everyone while I'm gone.*
>
> *Love, Daddy*

Daddy always tells me to take care of everybody while he's gone. It's a big job.

January 12, 1953

I adore getting mail! That's my new word, "adore." I watch for the mailman and run out to get the mail. I'm always excited to get a letter or a postcard or my new issue of *Jack and Jill* magazine. When Mommy was a model, she would get *Vogue*, but now she gets *Good Housekeeping*. Mommy told me sometimes she misses the fun she had being a model. Now she says she likes being a good wife and mother. She said, "Someday you will grow up to be a good wife and mother too." I told her, "Oh no, Mommy. I'm going to be a famous writer."

June 10, 1953

Mommy took Liam, Deedee, and me to downtown Dallas to go shopping for summer vacation clothes. Liam got some nice new shirts and trousers, a pair of brown Buster Brown shoes, and a bow tie. He looks so grown-up. I got some summer dresses, shorts and blouses, and sandals. Deedee got crabby and wouldn't try on clothes, so Mommy just bought her some real cute outfits. Liam thinks the stork brought Deedee from another planet because she's so cantankerous. "Cantankerous" is my new word, and I taught it to Liam.

June 20, 1953

We're on our summer vacation. Today we arrived in Detroit. It's where Grandad Goodman lives. We went to Woolworth's downtown. I went to the water fountain. Daddy yelled at me, "Don't drink from that fountain. Get a drink from the one next to it." I asked, "Why?" He said, "The signs say 'White' and 'Colored.'" I said, "They're both white." He said, "It doesn't mean the color of the fountain. It means the color of your skin." I said, "Well, my skin is red from my sunburn, so I'm drinking from the right fountain." Daddy said, "'Colored' means people with black skin." I asked him, "Is the water different for people with different colors of skin?" He said,

6

"No, the water is the same." Then I asked, "Why can't I drink from this fountain?" He bent down next to me and said, "I'm frustrated because I don't have an answer. I think people make up these rules because they are afraid of others who don't look like them." I got a drink of water from that fountain. So did Daddy. Then I said, "I have to go to the bathroom." Daddy said, "Oy!" The lady standing behind us said, "I'd be happy to take your daughter to the restroom, sir." She had black skin. Daddy told her thank you. She was nice. I told her my new word was "frustrated."

July 28, 1953

Today we arrived in Caledonia, Wisconsin. We are staying with Grandma and Grandad Haines. We are on our way to California. It's going to be our new home. Daddy can't come with us because he's flying the helicopter to California. Daddy was on the news. Mommy let Liam and me stay up to watch it. Daddy is a very important person. He is flying the first helicopter into California. He will land on the roof of the Santa Monica Hospital. He's going to make an ambulance out of the helicopter and save people's lives, like Auntie Anne. We are all so happy to leave Texas.

Liam and I are happy to be moving to California. We get to go to Disneyland!

This morning Grandma let me go up in the attic of the place they keep beer. It's called a brewery. There's a lot of stuff up in the attic: music, lamps, decorations. I found a box of Nancy Drew books. They're called mysteries. Mommy said she hoped I liked reading them as much as she did.

August 4, 1953

I like our new house in California. It's called a flat, and we live upstairs. The backyard is like a jungle. Will likes to play cowboys and Indians out there. He pretends he's the Lone

Ranger. He wants me to be Tonto. I told him I would be an Indian princess.

I get to have my own room. We can walk to the ocean but only if Mommy or Daddy are with us. When I open my bedroom window at night, I can smell the ocean. It smells heavenly. That's my new word, "heavenly."

September 22, 1953

Daddy flew the helicopter over the school playground while everyone was outside. The helicopter was buzzing, and he was waving. The teachers and kids were jumping up and down and waving. I was so embarrassed I wanted to hide under the flagpole. But everyone said it was very cool, and now I'm the most popular girl in my class.

Liam made a friend his first day at our new school. His name is Tommy. Liam said, "Tommy has a crush on you." I said, "Tommy's too young for me." Liam said, "He's only three years younger." I told him, "That's a very long time."

October 31, 1953

Today Mommy and Daddy took Liam, Deedee, and me trick-or-treating. I was a gypsy. Liam was a cowboy. Deedee was a clown. We saw a lot of friends out trick-or-treating. Their costumes were so cool. We got a lot of candy. I tried to get Liam to do some trading with me, but he would only trade oranges and nuts, none of the good stuff. Mommy said we could only have three pieces of candy before bedtime. Deedee snuck her candy into her room and ate so much she was sick all night. Mommy was really mad and told Deedee, "You better watch out or you'll get fat."

January 5, 1954

It's a new year! Daddy's cousin came to visit us. Her name is Heather, and she's very pretty. She looks just like Deedee.

She picked Deedee up and hugged her and played with her for a long time. Heather asked Mommy a lot of questions about Deedee. She brought us all presents, but she brought more for Deedee. I think that made Deedee feel very special. It's good that she feels special. Maybe she won't be so crabby.

February 2, 1954

Today we moved into a new house. I don't have my own room. Daddy said, "It's Liam's turn to have his own room." I have to share with Deedee.

We live in the big house in the front. There is a smaller house in the back where another family lives. Mommy said, "They're Irish, like my mother's family." They have two little boys I can babysit. We're nine blocks from the beach. We can still smell the ocean, and it's still heavenly. We have a real nice yard to play in. It has a big avocado tree. Mommy said she doesn't know what an avocado is, so Liam and I have to gather them up in boxes and take them out to the alley. It's our new job. Mommy pays us an allowance for it. Liam and I walk to the bank with our allowance money and get more stamps in our little black bankbooks.

I met a new friend who lives next door. Her name is Madge. Her father is a teacher at UCLA. They have a huge piano. It's called a grand. Madge plays all kinds of music. I love to listen to her play. Her mother is a musician. And Madge's uncle is a famous orchestra leader. His name is John Scott. Mommy says she knows who he is because he plays the music for Bing Crosby. Boy! Uncle John is a very important person!

April 10, 1954

Hetty and the boys stayed in Texas when we moved to Santa Monica. But they missed us, so they've moved to Santa Monica too. They stayed with us for two weeks until their new house was ready to move into. It was kind of crowded, but it was fun having them here. However, when they left, Dad went around the house singing, "Are they really, really gone, really gone?" I said, "Daddy, that's mean." And guess what! He apologized!

June 28, 1954

We went to Disneyland! Liam and I drove a car. He was thrilled because he got a driver's license. Fantasyland is so cute. We went on the teacups. Deedee yelled at us, "Stop going fast." We went faster and laughed our heads off. We went to Tomorrowland and rode a rocket ship. We talked on the phone of the future. You can see the person you're talking to. That would not be so good if your hair is in rollers and your boyfriend calls.

July 26, 1954

Today was my birthday. Mommy took us to a place called the Hollywood Farmers Market. There are lots of shops and places to eat. Mommy told Liam and me that we could have whatever we wanted for lunch. I had a piece of pecan pie with vanilla ice cream. It was so good! Liam had a banana split. Mommy had a salad. Deedee didn't get to come with us because Mommy said she's too hard to handle. It was really nice without Deedee crying and having fits.

January 5, 1955

Grandad Goodman is Jewish, but Daddy is an agnostic. Mommy says we should have a religion. Her mother is Catholic, and her father is Episcopalian. Daddy said, "My children will not be raised Catholic," so Mommy decided we'll go to the Episcopal church. I'm in the choir. Liam is in a youth group. Mommy asked Hetty to be Liam's and my godmother. That made Hetty very happy.

May 18, 1955

Today was Liam's birthday. He and Daddy finished the tree fort in the avocado tree. It's so neat. Liam let me climb up and see it. Then he put up a sign, NO GIRLS ALLOWED. Deedee started crying because she couldn't go up and see it. She told Liam, "Mommy said I can," but Mommy heard her and said she was telling a lie, so Deedee had to go sit in the corner.

February 1, 1956

I was reading my Nancy Drew book with a flashlight under the covers. Deedee tattled on me. Mommy said, "It's all right," and gave me a little table and lamp to put by my bed so I don't have to use the flashlight to read under the covers. Deedee stuck out her tongue and said, "I'll get you next time."

I love these Nancy Drew books. I want to be like Nancy Drew and be adventurous and solve mysteries. She has the best car. It's a blue roadster. And she has the nicest boyfriend. His name is Ned, and he's very kind and polite. Nancy Drew is brave, and she helps people. On the back of the book it says she has a feisty spirit. That's my new word, "feisty." Her father is a lawyer like Uncle Les. Her mom died. That is very sad. But she has a housekeeper, Hannah, who acts like a mom for Nancy.

March 20, 1956

Today was the first day of spring. It's so pretty. The sky is a beautiful blue. The air is fresh with the smell of the ocean. If you listen very hard, you can hear the waves crashing on the beach. My friend Patty joined the choir at the church. The choirmaster asked me to just mouth the words. I guess I was singing a little too loudly.

Auntie Anne is visiting us. She was babysitting for Deedee the other day, and Deedee told a lie. Deedee got into trouble and blamed me. Auntie Anne said, "Leslie wasn't even home," and Deedee had to sit in the corner. She just stuck her tongue out at Liam. That little girl spends a lot of time staring at walls. Maybe she'll be a house designer when she grows up. I just hope she doesn't kick the people she works for.

July 26, 1956

It's my birthday, so I asked Daddy, "Can I have a new bike?" He said, "No, you never ride the one you have." I said, "It's old." He said, "It's like brand new." And it is. Before we lived in Texas, we lived in Pensacola, Florida. One day, I was riding my bike on a dirt road and hit a rock. I went over the handlebars and hit my head. I was bleeding and unconscious. A lady from the neighborhood saw me and roused me—that's my new word, "roused"—and took me home in her car. Mommy called Daddy at the navy base. He came home, and they took me to the emergency room, and the doctor sewed up my cut. I don't remember much about it because I was knocked out. After that accident Daddy wanted me to ride again. He took me outside with the bike and told me to get on. I refused. We went on like that for a long time. He finally sent me to my room. The bike wasn't spoken of too much after that. I know Daddy wanted me to ride again so I wouldn't be afraid. Now I'm riding that old bike, and Daddy is very happy.

May 25, 1957

Mommy took me shopping in Beverly Hills today. It's a very fancy place. That's my new word, "fancy." We had lunch at a fancy restaurant. We ordered Cobb salads. Mommy says we have to watch our weight. The salads were very good. The restaurant had pictures of movie stars on the walls. Mommy could name every one of them because when she was a teenager, she was crazy about movie stars. She met a lot of them and collected their autographed pictures. One time we saw a movie with the Marx Brothers. Mommy told me she did some work with them, and one afternoon they babysat me. It was strange to know those men on the screen knew me when I was a baby.

After lunch we went to J. W. Robinson's and bought some new dresses because we're going to meet "I Love Lucy." Daddy has been flying the helicopter for her. I used to beg to stay up to watch the *I Love Lucy* program. Now I'm going to meet her!

May 28, 1957

We met "I Love Lucy." Her real name is Lucy Ball. I went to shake her hand, as I was taught to do, and she shook my hand, but then she gave me a big hug. She was wearing pearls, and she smelled like Chanel perfume. After the filming, there was a party. She introduced Daddy to the crowd of people, and Daddy gave her a little kiss on the cheek. A newspaperman took a picture and said it will be in the morning paper.

June 12, 1957

Daddy took me flying in the helicopter with him for the first time. Well, he said he took me up with him when I was little, but I don't remember. Mommy doesn't like us to go in the airplanes, but Daddy is very careful. He has something called a flight checklist, and he checked everything off before he let me get in. I was very excited. When I looked down at the city from the helicopter, it was like looking at my dollhouse. We flew over the shops in Beverly Hills, my school, the baseball park, the library, the tennis courts, Palisades Park, and the beach, and we landed on what Daddy called the mud flats at Venice Beach. It's an awful place, lots of squishy mud. I had to walk very carefully on some wood planks Daddy put down for us. We walked to an old, abandoned amusement park on the Santa Monica Pier. I told Daddy, "It's sad to see everything closed down and broken." He said, "Yes, it is, but there are plans to renovate it." I asked, "What does 'renovate' mean?" He said, "It means to repair it and make it like new again." I could see, in my mind, how beautiful it was going to be. "Renovate" is my new word. We saw some men fishing, and Daddy spoke to them. I wondered if they take the fish home to their families for dinner. Daddy loves flying. On the way back to Santa Monica Airport, Daddy said, "When I die, I hope I come back as a bird."

July 4, 1957

Tonight Mommy, Daddy, Liam, Deedee, and I walked down to Palisades Park to see the fireworks going off at the beach. It was so pretty to see all the colors of the lights on the water. I love California!

July 26, 1957

Ever since my tenth birthday, Mommy, Liam, and I go to the Hollywood Farmers Market. Mommy always asks me if I wouldn't like to do something different, but I don't. I like going with them to the farmers market. It's our tradition. That's my new word, "tradition." We look around in the shops, and then Liam and I always get the same treat: banana split for him and pecan pie with vanilla ice cream for me. Mommy always gets a salad. Deedee gets left at home because she's naughty. When we go someplace with her, she tries to run away. She says she's an orphan like Little Orphan Annie.

August 17, 1957

Tonight, was just horrible! Daddy got mad. We don't know why. We were just sitting there at the dining room table when suddenly he took his arm and flung all the dishes and food off the table. I was really scared. It reminded me of one of Deedee's tantrums. Deedee started screaming bloody murder. Liam and I crawled under the table. Mommy stood up, shocked, and looked around the room. Daddy stormed off. Liam and I crawled out from under the table and started helping Mommy clean up. She was crying. Liam and I started crying too.

August 1, 1959

I can't believe it's been two years since I wrote in my diary. My last entry was the night Dad threw the dishes all over the kitchen. That was scary. Dad hasn't lost his temper since then. In fact, our home life has been very calm. Mom said that Auntie Anne told her that Dad was an angry child. He had a lot of temper tantrums. Auntie Anne said, "He fancied himself a little Lord Fauntleroy." I guess he was too much for my grandma to handle, so she sent him to her parents for the summers.

At any rate, I'm going to try to be more diligent about writing in my diary. That's my new word, "diligent." It's important to chronicle my life through my diary entries, but writing in my diary also helps me to get my thoughts in order.

September 8, 1959

Today was my first day at Santa Monica High School. It's a beautiful campus. My English class overlooks the ocean. You can see the waves crashing on the sand and the sun reflecting off the water. It's an inspiring setting for writing stories when we get free writing time in English class.

After my classes, I walk over and pick up Liam from school. We race home, change into our swimsuits, and head down to the beach. We rent rubber surf riders and get snow cones. Liam loves the surf rider. He doesn't come out of the water until it's time to go home, and by then his fingers are cold and wrinkly. We can't stay too long on school days because we have to get our homework done before dinner. I like to help Liam with his homework. He's inquisitive and very smart. That's my new word, "inquisitive."

Chapter Two

Enter Miss Dump and Duck

Deedee

December 25, 1959

I got a Barbie doll for Christmas! Barbie dolls are new. All my friends are getting them. And I have been wanting one real bad. Barbie is so pretty. My mommy says I look just like her. Leslie gave me a diary for Christmas. She said, "You're eight years old now. You're smart and you're pretty, but you get angry a lot. Maybe writing in a diary will help you to not be so angry." I like having a secret diary. I can write things that nobody else will know about. I think I'm an orphan. Maybe having a diary will help me find my real parents.

Mommy and Daddy say I'm a handful because I get into trouble all the time. Leslie and Liam never get into trouble. They are goody two-shoes.

I heard my aunt talking about me. She said that when I was born, my daddy was unhappy because I was a girl. He wanted another boy. Leslie is his princess. Liam is his pal. I'm nothing. Liam and Leslie get to go to the beach after school. I have to stay with the neighbors. Mommy says I can't go to the beach because I am bad. I don't do what Leslie tells me to do. I don't do what Leslie says because she's not my boss. One time, I ran away from Leslie, and a bad man grabbed me. I screamed and hollered and kicked and bit that bad man. He dropped me and I ran like hell. The neighbor man uses the "h" word. I got my mouth washed out with soap when I said it. Everybody can do stuff but me.

Leslie

July 27, 1960

I just can't seem to be consistent with writing in my diary. I'm busy with homework and writing for my English class. However, yesterday was a special day. It was my sixteenth birthday. I had a slumber party, and we went to the Aero Theater and saw *Auntie Mame*. I want to be like Auntie Mame. She had an exquisite—that's my new word, "exquisite"—and, at the same time, outlandish wardrobe, and she had such adventures. After the movie, my dad wasn't there to pick us up like he was supposed to be. We waited and waited. Finally, the manager at the movie theater let me come in and call home. My dad forgot that he was supposed to pick us up. He came and got us right away, but it scared me that he forgot me. He said he was sorry and that it would never happen again.

September 2, 1960

Deedee got into trouble for lying about something Liam had done. Liam said "Dee Dee" stood for "Dump" and "Duck" because Deedee always dumps trouble on us and then ducks out of the way.

October 25, 1960

Liam did something naughty. I don't know what. Dad said he was going to get a spanking with the paddle. Unfortunately, the ball fell off the paddle ball, and now that thing is a constant threat. Dad told Liam to bend over his knees on his lap, and then he spanked Liam, but he hit something hard, and Liam and I started laughing. Liam had put a book in his pants. Dad started laughing too, and that was the end of the spanking.

December 2, 1960

Dad flew Santa to the shopping mall in the San Fernando Valley. Santa arriving in a helicopter was very exciting news, so of course it was in all the local papers. There were throngs of people cheering and drinking hot chocolate and carolers singing. Dad let me fly back to the airport with him. I felt like a movie star! I love California!

Deedee

December 19, 1960

I wanted to ride back in the helicopter with Daddy and Leslie after Daddy brought Santa to the stores to see the kids, but Daddy said I wouldn't sit still. I had to be good like Leslie to ride in the plane. I cried and screamed and had a fit. He didn't care. I said, "I don't want to ride in that stupid plane anyway."

Leslie and Liam got to go Christmas shopping. I couldn't go because I might run away. I only ran away one time. That's a lie. It's my diary. I can lie if I want to.

Chapter Three

Date Nights and Dark Turns

Leslie

January 6, 1961

I have a boyfriend. His name is Ted Hansome, and he is very handsome! My parents said it was okay for him to drive me home from school. He has a very old car. There is no floor on the passenger side, so I have to hold my feet up. I'm glad it's a short ride home. My parents let me go out on a date with Ted. It was my first date, and I was very excited. Dad said I had to be home by midnight, and for every minute I was late, I would be grounded for a week. Ted's father let him drive the new Volkswagen he brought back from Germany. It's small and cute, like a bug. We went to a movie in the Palisades, and then we got ice cream at a soda shop. Ted held my hand while we walked back to the car. When we got home, he walked me to the door and gave me a good night kiss. It was all very romantic!

I got a C+ in trigonometry, and Dad is making me take it again. He says, "You need an A+ average to get into a good college." Ugh! Here comes summer school!

Deedee

January 20, 1961

I hate school. Mommy and Daddy say I don't have the brains God gave me. They make me sit at the table with Liam and Leslie to do my homework. If I don't have the brains God gave me, I'll never get the homework right. Leslie and Liam try to help me. I don't understand what they're telling me, so I just get mad. I'd rather be playing with my Barbie. I like it when Leslie goes out with her boyfriend and Daddy takes

Liam to do stuff. I get to be alone with Mommy. Sometimes she pays attention to me. Mostly she bakes cookies.

Leslie

July 26, 1961

For my birthday Ted and I went to Date Nite at Disneyland. There's a band and dancing in Tomorrowland. A whole bunch of our friends met us there, and we danced almost every dance. I was glad I wore my white buck shoes because they're so comfortable. We went on rides, and Ted put his arm around me and held my hand. He's so sweet!

September 5, 1961

Back to school! I'm a senior. I tried out for cheerleader and got in. I've lost ten pounds. I feel so much better with all the exercise and the weight loss. Mother is always telling us how important it is to be thin. She thinks it's terrible that Aunt Rain and Cousin Suzi are so fat, but I think Aunt Rain and Cousin Suzi are lots of fun. They do interesting things, and they laugh a lot. Aunt Rain is an accomplished pianist. She's also a marvelous seamstress and knitter. I'm learning to sew and knit too. Aunt Rain and Suzi love to cook together, and they make delicious meals, unlike Mother, who is the world's worst cook. We have the same repeat dinners every day of the week: Sunday, roast; Monday, stew; Tuesday, pork chops. Those are the worst! I can't even chew them. Liam says we should make shoes out of them. I think he's right. Dad laughs at us. Mother doesn't think we're funny, but she doesn't eat those pork chops.

After getting a C in trigonometry, I took it over in summer school and was just as lost as I had been during the semester. I asked Dad to explain it to me. He hired a college student from Santa Monica City College to tutor me. Johnny is his name. He was quite good at explaining trig in simpler terms, giving me charts and such to help me along the way. I got an A–! I was so excited! Dad was very happy.

Deedee

September 12, 1961

Everyone is so happy that Leslie is a cheerleader. She got skinny. Mommy said that's good because she was fat. I will be like Barbie. I will never get fat.

Leslie got an A in that math class because Daddy got that guy to help her. I asked Daddy if he would get me help because I don't understand nothing. He said Leslie and Liam can help me. Damn! I don't want their help. The neighbor says "damn" all the time, but I can only use it in my diary because I will get my mouth washed out with soap if I say it.

Leslie

September 22, 1961

One of the girls in my math class has a brand-new Thunderbird. Mary is her name. I felt like a movie star, cruising around Hollywood in that beautiful car. Mary took me to her father's drive-in hamburger place in Hollywood. The hamburgers are so good, and you can get extra Z Sauce. Mary smokes cigarettes too, Spring menthols. She is so hip! She's an only child and lives with her mom and dad in a mansion in Beverly Hills. They have live-in maids. Mom would sure like that. Mary told me about tampons. Wow, do they make life easier!

September 28, 1961

Ted and I went to Pacific Ocean Park at the Santa Monica Pier and saw Dick Clark! It was outta sight! Some of our friends saw us dancing on television. They said we looked like movie stars.

Dad tried to teach me how to drive, but I was so nervous trying to please him he told me he couldn't teach me and I'd have to take driver's ed in school. I was so mad at him. I said, "You teach people how to fly airplanes, but you can't teach your own daughter how to drive a car?" He said, "You got that right."

October 5, 1961

My English teacher submitted one of my essays to the student section of the *New Brunswick Magazine*, and it was published. This is so groovy! I'm going to be a famous writer.

I'm taking driver's ed, but I must be making the teacher nervous too, because he keeps slamming his foot on the brakes. I wonder if I'll ever learn to drive.

Deedee

October 22, 1961

For my tenth birthday Mommy made me one of her yummy sponge cakes. I made a wish and blew out all the candles. My wish was that I could be as good as Leslie so Mommy and Daddy would love me and say nice things about me. Mommy let Leslie and Liam and me stay up late to play Monopoly. I got mad because they wouldn't let me win. Liam told me to be patient because eventually I would learn the strategy. Whatever that means. I told Mommy that Leslie's friend smoked. She got real mad at Leslie and said, "I'd better not find you smoking, young lady." They had a big fight when Mommy found out about the tampons. I don't know too much about that. Nobody tells me nothing. I'm just an orphan.

Leslie is getting a lot of attention. Her teacher put one of her stories in a magazine. It was a story about me, so shouldn't I be getting some attention too?

Leslie

October 25, 1961

The worst thing happened today. Dad broke his foot while coaching Liam's Little League team. He's very upset that he can't fly.

November 27, 1961

It's gotten worse. It's been a month, and Dad still can't fly. Flying is everything to him, except of course for Liam, Mom, Deedee, and me. Plus, he's self-employed, so if he's not flying, he's not making money. My poor dad!

December 4, 1961

Tonight, Dad pulled the wall phone out of the wall and threw it on the floor. I was in my room doing my homework, so I don't know what made him do that, but I ran into the kitchen. We all stood there, staring, even Dad. It was as if he was as surprised as the rest of us.

December 14, 1961

I can hardly put these words on paper, but I must. Today I came home from school and found a note Dad had written on the blackboard above the phone. It said, "Call Gates, Kingsley & Gates." That's a funeral home. I didn't understand. Then I realized something was awfully wrong. I ran around the house calling, "Dad! Dad!" I heard a noise and found my brother in his closet, sobbing and shaking. I wrapped my arms around him and held on tight. "It's going to be all right," I told him. "No," he managed to gulp out. "They took Daddy away in the ambulance. I tried to stop them, but he took too many pills, and they had to take him to the hospital to empty his stomach. I love Daddy. I don't want him to die. What are we going to do?" He buried his head in my shoulder; his tears ran down my neck and drenched my blouse. I held him tighter and closed the closet door. I wanted to make us safe. I cried too. I knew things hadn't been good. Mom had had to go to work to help out with finances. I'd heard them talking about using my college fund to pay the bills, and now how would they send me to college? My parents had never raised their voices at each other, but now they argued all the time.

Deedee

November 30, 1961

Bad things are happening. Liam thinks it's all his fault that Daddy can't fly because Daddy broke his foot when he was coaching at Little League. Then Daddy got real sick. An ambulance took him to the hospital. Leslie and Liam are very sad. I don't know why. Nobody tells me nothing. Mommy and Daddy yell a lot. I hide with Barbie and stay out of the way so I don't get into trouble. When Daddy's not home, I yell at Mommy because this is probably all her fault. She's always complaining that we don't have enough money. They say Leslie won't be able to go to college. Damn! I wanted the bedroom by myself.

Chapter Four

Breaking News

Leslie

January 2, 1962

It was a quiet Christmas. Ted spent the afternoon with us. I haven't told anyone about my dad's attempted suicide, not even Ted. Mom and Dad don't talk about it. Deedee knows something is wrong but not what. She's angry that no one will tell her, so she just gets mean, and that's pretty hard on Mom. Liam and I spend a lot of time together, just being near each other. I wish I could take away his memory of that day. My poor baby brother! Why did he have to come home early that afternoon? It should have been me. I do thank God, however, that Dad changed his mind and called the operator for help.

February 18, 1962

Mom's friend, who's a policewoman, got me a job working security at Penney's department store. My friends are teasing me that I'm an undercover agent because my job is to hang out just inside the front door area of Penney's and watch for anyone trying to steal things. Today I caught a woman stuffing clothing in her jacket, right in front of me. Did she think I couldn't see her? Since I look like a kid many years younger than I am, I guess that makes me invisible.

Yet as I watched, I wondered about this woman. She looked shabby, like she might be homeless. A feeling of gratitude came over me. I have a family and a home. I feel fortunate that even though my dad has a temper, he loves us and does his best to protect us and provide a good home. I waved the policewoman over, and together we continued to watch for a few seconds until the policewoman approached the thief and said, "Ma'am, you'll have to come along with me to the manager's office."

Deedee

March 17, 1962

It's Saint Patrick's Day! Barbie and I wore green to school. My Grandma Haines is Irish. Her mother came to America from Ireland when she was sixteen years old. And she was married! Nobody gets married at sixteen. That's gross. She had a baby at seventeen. My great-grandma must have been bad because Mommy says only bad girls have babies at seventeen. She says I better be good. I don't understand. Nobody tells me nothing. The only time they pay attention to me is when I get mad. Maybe it's my fault that all this bad stuff is happening.

After school Leslie is working with Mommy's friend, who works for the police. Leslie is getting a pay stub. She saves her money in a little black book. Maybe she'll go away to college now, and I can have the bedroom by myself.

Leslie

April 10, 1962

Today was opening day of Dodger Stadium. Ted's dad got us tickets—great seats, second bleacher row up, just off first base. I will never forget this day. Ted and I were joking, laughing, and enjoying the game. Ted was looking around for the hot dog vendor when he suddenly looked at me and said, "Isn't that your dad directly behind us, three rows?" I looked back, and there was my dad, sitting next to a lovely-looking lady. He was holding her hand. Then he put his arm around her and gave her a kiss! I was so shocked I literally could not form a word. Ted put his arm around me. "Take a deep breath! Seriously! Breathe! You're turning red. Leslie! Stop holding your breath," he said, patting my back. I gasped and sputtered! People were looking at me. That's when my dad noticed me and sat bolt upright. His face was ashen. When we got home later, Dad did not mention the game, nor did I.

Deedee

April 13, 1962

Mommy has a boyfriend. I don't think Daddy is going to like this. Mommy and Daddy used to go square-dancing together. Daddy hasn't been dancing in a long time because he spends a lot of time at the place where he keeps his airplanes. Mommy still goes dancing, and this man brings her home and comes into the house. I'm supposed to be asleep, but I sneak out of bed and watch what's going on because nobody tells me nothing. Last night they were sitting on the couch, kissing. Gross!

Leslie

April 18, 1962

It is with a sad heart that I write tonight. We all drag around the house. We sit down to dinner, but none of us eat. I've lost five pounds. Liam and Deedee cling to me. Deedee refuses to go to sleep unless I'm home. Liam keeps asking when I'll be back.

Dad had been sleeping in his hanger out in Van Nuys, but now he's bought a house in the Valley and moved out of our home in Santa Monica. Our world has been turned upside down and inside out. Mother is taking Deedee and going to visit her parents during Easter vacation. I'll stay home and take care of Liam when he's not out at the airport with Dad. Hetty is nearby if we need her.

The other night I was talking to Dad, and he said, "Don't love anyone too much because you'll just get hurt."

April 22, 1962

Mom and Deedee are in Caledonia, Wisconsin, with my grandparents. Dad and Liam are at the airport. It's quiet. Ted's family moved out to Anaheim, and Ted got a job at Disneyland, so we rarely see each other. I've gone on some dates with an older man I met working at the theater.

Deedee

April 26, 1962

Mommy and I got on a big airplane and went to see Grandma and Grandad. Barbie got to come too. Mommy was scared. She doesn't like flying. I held her hand. I don't like flying either. It's scary being up there in the air. I don't know how the airplane stays up. Mommy is very sad. Stuff is going on. Nobody tells me nothing. It's very cool that I get to be alone with Mommy. Maybe I did something right. Daddy doesn't live with us anymore. Liam and Leslie are gone a lot, and I get to have Mommy all to myself.

Leslie

June 15, 1962

Last night was my senior prom. Mother made me the most beautiful dress I've ever seen. It has layers and layers of baby-blue chiffon and tiny little spaghetti straps. It looked like something Grace Kelly would wear. I felt like a movie star! Ted brought me a lovely corsage and fumbled putting it on. Mom had to help. I had a boutonniere for him that he pinned to his jacket lapel. We had such a lovely time. We really did dance the night away.

June 16, 1962

I'm shaking and sick to my stomach! We just heard on the news that Ted's sister was killed last night in a car crash, coming home from her junior prom. Their car was hit by a drunk driver. No one survived. I've called and called, but I can't get ahold of Ted. Mom and Liam are just as sick as I am. Thank goodness I have them here with me. Ted must be out of his mind with grief.

August 4, 1962

So much has happened in the past few months. I graduated from high school. Ted and I aren't seeing each other much anymore. He's working at Disneyland, so I drove out there to have lunch with him, but he's shut down. He won't talk to me about much of anything. His grief, and that of his parents, has sucked the life out of him. He's a ghost, a shell of a person. My heart aches for him.

Mom bought a house in the Valley and moved out there with Deedee and Liam. Hetty and the boys decided to move back to Texas. I'm living in our Santa Monica house until it sells. I got a job on the switchboard at the phone company, which can be quite amusing. I've met lots of new friends, and I adore my supervisor. She lets me work a schedule that allows me to attend my classes at Santa Monica City College.

October 27, 1962

I did one of the craziest things a person could do. I don't know what I was thinking. Maybe I just wanted to escape my parents; maybe I wanted to hurt them. I've been seeing the older man quite a bit, and we decided to get married. We even planned a wedding, and I bought a dress. I was afraid to tell my parents, so they didn't know about it. We were standing at the altar of the Catholic Church—I'm not even Catholic—and when it came time for me to say, "I do," I couldn't say it. I just looked at that man and froze. Some of his family were

29

there, and they were all staring at me. Suddenly, I turned and ran out of that church as fast as I could. I never looked back. I haven't seen him since.

November 1, 1962

The marriage story gets worse. I was working the late-night shift on the switchboard last night when my supervisor came up to me and said my dad was outside and wanted to see me. The phone company is very conscious of security; thus, my supervisor and two men from the office accompanied me outside. I was scared to death that something had happened to Mom or Liam or Deedee. I flew out the door, and there was my dad. He looked at me and said, "You little tramp! You ran away and got married. Now you'll never go to a college football game." At which point he drew back his arm, and his fist connected with my jaw. As I fell to the ground and my world went dark, I saw the two men grabbing him and pulling him away. My supervisor was yelling.

I came to shortly after that in an ambulance, where I was taken to the Santa Monica hospital and told I would be kept overnight for observation in case I'd suffered a concussion. As it turned out, I had suffered a concussion and remained in the hospital another day and then spent several days off work. The doctor said I shouldn't be left alone, so Patty came and stayed with me. My supervisor called to check on me every day and asked if I wanted to press charges against my dad. I said no, and when I returned to work, I had to sign a release form for the phone company. I'm so embarrassed, and I feel just awful. The wedding plans must have been leaked to my dad, but I guess he didn't hear the part about me not being able to go through with it.

November 21, 1962

Our Santa Monica house sold, so Patty and I rented a little cottage on 26th Street. She's dating Oliver, a real nice guy she met through a friend. He's in his second year of college. Besides my job and classes, I'm submitting stories and articles to various magazines, and one has been published.

December 1, 1962

One of the girls who sits next to me at the switchboard, Donna, told me she is pregnant. Geez! We're only eighteen with our whole lives ahead of us. She told me, "One night of pleasure is not worth a lifetime of suffering." She can't get a legal abortion, so she's going to perform an abortion on herself using a Coke bottle. That sounds so painful and dangerous. I said, "There are doctors who will perform illegal abortions, and many girls go over the border into Mexico for abortions." Sadly, she said, "I can't afford those options."

December 4, 1962

It was another very sad and disturbing night at work. My supervisor called me into her office and told me that Donna had died. She knew Donna and I were friends, so she wanted to tell me herself how Donna died rather than let me hear about it through the switchboard gossip. She said that Donna bled to death in a botched-up abortion attempt. Donna was dead at eighteen because she didn't want to be pregnant. She should have been able to go to a hospital or clinic. I find it difficult to believe that women vote for laws that take away our right to make decisions about our own bodies, laws that, if they don't kill us, will forever affect our lives.

January 1, 1963

It was a terrible thing I did, thinking I would get married without telling my parents. Mom was furious, but she's gotten over it. She's a "buck up" sort of person. Dad has not been in touch with me since the night he hit me, and I'm too scared to call him.

May 8, 1963

The other night around midnight, Mom was coming home from a date with Hank. She ran out of gas just off the freeway in front of the Veterans Administration building. She walked to a pay phone and called me to bring her a can of gas. So there we were, trying to pour gas into Mom's gas tank at twelve thirty in the morning. A priest pulled up beside us. I was so relieved, someone to help. Well, he didn't even get out of his car. He rolled down the window and said, "You girls should not be out so late at night." I was stunned, and before I could speak, he rolled up his window and drove off. Mom was delighted. "He thought I was your girlfriend!" We laughed and finally got the gas in the tank. I went home and back to bed. I sure was glad it was a Saturday night.

Deedee

October 22, 1963

It's my birthday. I'm twelve. Liam is seventeen. Leslie is older. Mommy and Daddy were really upset about Leslie. There were a lot of big fights. I don't know too much about it. Nobody tells me nothing. But I know Leslie moved into a place of her own with her friend Patty. I finally get to have my own room.

Daddy is getting a divorce from Mommy and is going to marry a witch. Liam and Mommy and me live in a new house in the Valley. Mommy and me drive over to Santa Monica every morning so Mommy can go to work and I can go to school. I don't like school. I wish I could just stay home and watch TV. Liam spends the night with Daddy a lot. I don't go there because I'm afraid of the witch. Mommy says she's a home wrecker. I'm afraid that witch will come and wreck our new house. Mommy says the witch steals husbands. I don't understand. Daddy is too big to steal.

Leslie

February 24, 1964

Well, Patty and Oliver moved in together, and they are very happy. They fixed me up with a guy named Monty. He's nice enough, but he's a sad person. On the way to the world's fair in Seattle he was in a car crash with his family. Monty and his sister survived, although she lost a leg. Their mother and two brothers died. Monty was driving. I don't think he will ever recover.

April 4, 1964

I moved in with Mom, Deedee, and Liam. It was fun sharing the cottage with Patty, but I love being home with my family again. Liam got a job at Sears in the Valley and is going to Pierce College. He's working long hours and taking a full load of classes. Eventually, he'll transfer to a university and begin his legal studies. I love talking to him about his classes. He has such insight into people and subjects. He makes me laugh too.

June 2, 1964

Monty and I didn't date very long. After a few months of not seeing him, he called me and told me he missed me and loved me, but he'd gotten a girl pregnant. I read in the paper yesterday that Monty was killed in a construction accident. The backhoe he was driving went over a cliff in Topanga Canyon. There was a picture, and it wasn't pretty. I was so upset, I called Dad's friend Lou, who owns the local newspaper, and asked him how they can print such horrible photos. I was mad and I was sad, not a good combination. Lou said, "I hate it too, Leslie, but until laws change, those pictures and stories sell papers." Nobody had enough money to pay for a headstone for Monty's grave, so I paid for it out of my savings. Mother's boyfriend, Hank, went with me to the funeral. I hope Mom stays with Hank; he's a good man.

August 16, 1964

I got promoted to a service rep at the phone company and transferred to the business office in Beverly Hills. I love this job. The other day I was working in the front office, and I met Rock Hudson and George Burns. I've met lots of new friends too. We're like a little family, always joking around and having some good laughs. They're teaching me how to play bridge on our lunch hour. After work I head over to SMCC for my classes. I get home around nine and work on my articles for the magazines. I try to be in bed by eleven, but Mom and Liam are addicted to *The Tonight Show Starring Johnny Carson* and wake me up with their laughing. Then, of course, I have to get up and see what's so funny, and I end up staying up much too late, but Johnny Carson is so funny, and time spent with Mom and Liam is very special.

Deedee

October 22, 1964

It's my thirteenth birthday! Mom made me my favorite, sponge cake. Daddy is still not speaking to Leslie. She moved back in with us a few months ago. But I don't have to give up my room. Miss Perfect is sharing with Mom. She has to drive into Santa Monica every day too, but she takes her own car because after work she goes to college. I hate her. I wish she'd be like other kids and go away to college. She's always telling me I need to help Mom more around the house. I don't like cleaning. Barbie would never clean a house. She's too pretty to do that. I told Leslie, "You're not my boss." She said, "Mom is working very hard to make ends meet and needs our help. Even though you're only thirteen, it might be a good idea for you to be more responsible." I don't know what she means, but I don't like it. I just stuck my tongue out at her.

Leslie

November 4, 1964

My friend Cassie, whom I work with at the phone company, fixed me up with a friend of her husband's. His name is Jacob. He's very good-looking. Mom says he looks like Van Johnson. We went out for Italian food. It was raining and very romantic.

Deedee

December 15, 1964

Leslie has a new boyfriend. He went with us to get our Christmas tree, and Leslie's friends came over and helped us decorate the tree. Mom made some real good eggnog and put out her homemade cookies. We sang Christmas songs. Singing makes Barbie and me happy. I'm working on my Christmas gift list. It's pretty long. I hope I get everything I want.

Leslie

February 4, 1965

I can't believe I own a brand-new car, a Ford Mustang! The smell is intoxicating! I saved enough money from my writing to put a nice down payment on it, so my monthly payments are minimal. Hank helped me with the purchase. I hope Mom stays with him.

July 26, 1965

Today is my twenty-first birthday. The present I received from Dad was quite a surprise. He called me. He said he'd like to see me; could he take me to lunch? I said yes. We met at the Broken Drum in Santa Monica. I was so nervous I was shaking and couldn't lift my fork to eat, not even my glass to drink water. Dad said hitting me was the worst thing he'd ever done in his life. He was ashamed and embarrassed and sorry. He asked me to please forgive him. I said yes. He said he loved me and was proud of me, and that nothing like that would ever happen again. I believed him.

When I arrived home, I had a special delivery package waiting for me. Inside was a bankbook in my name and papers for me to sign. For my birthday my father had opened an account for me and put $10,000 in it. I was stunned!

Tonight, Jacob and I and some friends went to the Charter House for dinner. Hank recommended it. It's located right where he moors his boat at the first finger of the Venice Marina project. I've been watching *The Thin Man* and other old movies, and I think it's so cool the way they drink martinis in those beautiful crystal glasses, so I ordered my first martini. It did come in a beautiful crystal glass. It tasted just awful, but I smiled and tried very hard to look sophisticated.

August 7, 1965

Dad called and asked me to come to dinner at his house. He wanted me to meet his new wife, Diane. I agreed but asked whether I could bring Jacob with me. He said that was fine; he'd love to meet him.

It was a lovely, warm Valley evening, so we swam in the pool and barbecued. Diane is a very nice person. She's a good businesswoman, and she has made my father's business prosper. She's only eight years older than I am, which seems a bit strange.

November 5, 1965

I got pregnant! I use two forms of birth control. I told the doctor he must be mistaken, but he wasn't. I told Jacob, "I'm scared. I don't want to get married, and I certainly don't want to be pregnant, not right now anyway." Jacob said he'd heard of a doctor that will perform illegal abortions, so we went to see him; however, the doctor told us that he was no longer performing abortions, but he could recommend a doctor in Tijuana. Jacob made the arrangements, and a few days later we drove down to Tijuana, where I had an abortion. I am so glad that's over and in my past. Mother put the fear of God into Deedee and me about getting pregnant without being married. I'm grateful that we could afford the abortion and that Jacob stood by me. There are so many women who cannot afford illegal abortions, and the men they're with disappear, leaving them alone and devastated.

March 8, 1966

A man sued Dad over a business issue. I don't know the details, but they went to court today, and Dad said, "My attorney told me to say, 'Nolo contendere' any time I was asked a question." I said, "Dad, that's very serious. It means you neither accept nor deny responsibility for the charges." He said, "I know, but I had to follow my attorney's advice, and we ended up settling." Dad said that he found the court system very interesting.

August 6, 1966

The National Organization for Women was formed June 30, and I joined. I heard Betty Friedan speak, and I hung on every word she said about women's rights. Afterward I stood in line to meet her. She's brilliant!

December 24, 1966

Jacob asked me to marry him! I don't want to get married, but I don't want to hurt Jacob and disappoint people. What could I do? I said yes. I wrote a story about my fears of marriage that was published in *Women's Daily*. Thank goodness Jacob doesn't read women's magazines. I told Jacob that I needed time. When you get married, you belong to somebody. Men think they are smarter and need to take care of the little woman. They want to manage your time, your career, your money, and your life. A girlfriend actually asked me if it would be okay with Jacob if I went out to dinner with her and a few friends. I was appalled that she'd think I'd have to ask him. This is not going to be my life. I can't love; it hurts too much.

Chapter Five

Here Come the Wedding Bells

Leslie

January 4, 1967

Well, wasn't our little announcement just the highlight of the season! Now everyone wants to have showers and help plan the wedding. I have put if off until I graduate. Obviously, I'm stalling. How can I possibly tell Jacob I can't get married? What is wrong with me? Why can't I take control of my life and just say no? I don't want to be a wife. I'm going to be a writer. I am a writer. My stories are selling. They don't pay much, but at least they buy groceries. When I told Mother that I didn't want to get married, she said, "That's rather selfish of you."

February 18, 1967

One night while Jacob was driving the car, I was sitting in the passenger seat, staring out the window when I saw this house all lit up and set back in a wooded area. It looked warm and peaceful, a place where a person could live, quietly reading by the fireplace, writing, gardening, cooking. I yearned for that house and that life.

March 7, 1967

Why would my mother say that because I don't want to get married, I'm selfish? I asked her. She said, "Well, it's every woman's duty to get married and have children." I said, "What? Are you serious? These are the '60s, not the '50s. We're not chattel, Mother. We can make choices: to get married or not, to have children or not, to have a career, to have it all."

The choice to have it all stuck with me, and I pondered that thought. I can have it all. I don't have to give up a career to be a wife. I began to see marriage in a different light; it can be a partnership, a sharing, rather than a jail. I spoke to Jacob about these feelings. We decided to write our own wedding vows. We'll both have careers and share the home responsibilities.

July 26, 1967

I bought a Siamese kitten for my birthday, a little girl. I named her Princess. She is so, so cute! She sleeps with me, and she fetches a little ball and brings it back to me as long as I'll keep throwing it. I just love her so much!

Deedee

October 22, 1967

Leslie and Jacob took us all out to dinner for my sixteenth birthday. It's the first time I've been to a nice restaurant. I liked it. I'm going to marry a very rich man so I can go to nice restaurants all the time. Leslie is getting married. I am so happy. Now she'll move out of the house. It will be just Mom and Liam and me. Liam spends a lot of time with Dad, so it will be like it's just Mom and me. Maybe I'll get more attention from Mom. She still bakes a lot of cookies, but she watches TV with me and takes me shopping with her when Miss Perfect isn't around.

Leslie

November 24, 1967

I got married. I feel like I just jumped out of a plane wearing a parachute, slowly drifting and not knowing where I'll land. We chose Thanksgiving weekend so we wouldn't interrupt our college classes. The ceremony was in a small chapel in the Palisades, and the reception was back at Mother's house. It was a small and intimate affair, really quite lovely. We decided to drive down to San Diego for a short honeymoon. Before we left, I changed clothes, and we said good-bye to everyone. Liam hugged me with tears in his eyes.

December 12, 1967

Princess went into heat. She cries all night. Jacob and I take turns walking the floor with her to keep her quiet so we don't get kicked out of our apartment. My vet said we should breed her once before having her neutered. I agreed. He gave us the name of a lady who had a male for hire. I called her, and she came to our house with an extra-large cage holding a monstrous Siamese cat. I was afraid to let him out. The lady said he's really just a big baby. She had to pull him out of the cage, and he made a beeline for under our bed. A day later I had to drag him out and put him in the bathroom with Princess. It worked. She's going to have kittens.

January 8, 1968

Mother broke up with Hank! I'm devastated. I asked her why, and she said, "I think he's been sleeping with another woman." I said, "Oh, Mother, that doesn't sound like Hank. He's devoted to you." She said, "Well, I also met another man who seems to be a much better prospect." "What?" I asked. "A better prospect?" "Yes," she said. "His name is Boone, and he's a retired police officer. He receives a nice pension, and he's starting up his own handyman business." Then she said, "When Hank finally accepted that I was ending the relationship, he sang the song to me, *I Wish You Love.*"

February 11, 1968

Last night I felt something wet and clammy under the covers. I woke up screaming bloody murder. Princess was having her kittens. I felt so bad for scaring her. I made her a warm, cozy bed in the bathroom. She had three kittens, and they are so cute. One is huge, just like the father. We're going to keep him, and the two little girls are going to our mothers.

February 28, 1968

Jacob's college friends Lydia and George came down from Seattle to stay with us. We had so much fun sightseeing and eating out. They sure drink a lot, though. We bought a blender because they like whiskey sours, which are awfully good but very sweet. Personally, I cultivated a taste for martinis on my twenty-first birthday and still favor them. Lydia is pregnant and so happy. It's all she talks about. Her excitement is contagious. I've decided that I'd really like to have a baby too.

May 31, 1968

I thought I'd get pregnant right away. The doctor said everything was just fine with Jacob and me and there was no reason why I couldn't get pregnant. He said to take a vacation. How hard is that? Hawaii, here we come!

September 14, 1968

I'm pregnant! Oh, my God! I'm so sick! I fall asleep eating dinner. But I'm going to have a baby. I'm having trouble keeping up with my classes because I'm so tired, but maternity leave will kick in soon. My pregnancy stories are selling. Hey, it's grocery money.

October 14, 1968

Liam enlisted in the army! I am so upset with him. There is a war going on, for God's sake! He's playing pro ball, he's a pilot, and he's in law school, but he said it's better that he enlist and control his future rather than be drafted.

I think the reason he enlisted is because Mom and Dad are pulling him apart. They are suing each other and battling over property and Dad's business. Our parents are demanding we choose sides, and we told them we won't do that. They need to stop. Look what they have done to my poor baby brother! Goddamn them all to hell!

Deedee

October 22, 1968

I'm seventeen and I'm five months pregnant. I haven't told anyone. At first, I wasn't sure what was happening to me. Then I figured it out. Roy, this boy in my class, doesn't like school either, so we ditch school and go to his house, smoke cigarettes, drink beer, and have sex. Roy loves me. He says I'm beautiful. In May I was a runner-up in a beauty pageant. I wish I wasn't pregnant. I went to live with Dad. I don't like Mom's new boyfriend. She spends all her time with him. He's always at our house, and he drinks too much. Mom is starting to drink too much too. I don't know what to do. It's too late for an abortion. I wouldn't know how to get one anyway. Mom says only bad girls get pregnant before they get married. I don't want to get married. I don't know who to tell. If I tell Dad, he'll kick me out of the house. If I tell Leslie or Liam, they'll tell Mom and Dad. Roy said, "You look like you're putting on weight." I said, "Yeah, I am."

Leslie

November 18, 1968

Miss Dump and Duck is seven months pregnant! We're all shocked. She has hidden it so well. She'd been living with Dad, who began to suspect she was pregnant and finally confronted her. He insists that she give the baby up for adoption, and he's making all the arrangements. She's only seventeen, and she's dropping out of high school. What is wrong with that girl? She said, "I thought it would go away." I hope she was trying to be funny.

Deedee

December 18, 1968

Oh God! Dad is so mad. He said it's all Mom's fault that I'm pregnant because she's too busy with her new boyfriend and not keeping an eye on me. Dad is right. It is all her fault. If she'd paid more attention to me instead of her boyfriend and Leslie and Liam, I wouldn't be pregnant. Nobody ever pays any attention to me. Now they all know I'm really a bad girl. Dad got me an apartment and has Leslie keeping an eye on me. I feel so alone. Dad and I had a big fight. I told him, "Maybe I don't want to give my baby away. Leslie doesn't have to give her baby away." He said, "Your keeping the baby isn't an option. If you would just try to be more like Leslie, you wouldn't be in this mess. After the baby is born, you're going to get back to school; otherwise, you'll always be a high school dropout and never get a decent job." I said, "I don't need to finish school. I'm pretty, like Barbie, and I'm going to marry a rich man."

Leslie

February 20, 1969

Deedee's baby was born today, a little girl, and she went directly to a foster family. Deedee is furious and wants the baby back; the father, Roy, wants to marry Deedee and keep the baby too. Deedee doesn't want to marry him, though. Roy was recently drafted and is stationed at Fort Ord and calls Deedee every day. He must have a large can of change because he has to call from a pay phone. He has to be in love, right?

It's sad and difficult for me to say, but I wish Deedee would just let the baby go to a couple who desperately want a baby and can't have one of their own. They would love her and see that she's well taken care of and educated. Deedee's hormones are all over the place right now, and she's not thinking straight. She can't support a baby. She's a high school dropout, and she's never had a job. Even if she were to marry Roy, they still couldn't support themselves and a baby. Roy barely finished high school and has no job training. Hopefully, he'll learn a skill in the army.

March 12, 1969

Deedee got married and got the baby back. She and Roy seem happy enough. Deedee named the baby Amiala. I mentioned to Mother, "That's an unusual spelling." Mother said, "Deedee can't spell." Mom and Dad want Deedee to finish school, but she said, "I hate school, and I don't need a high school diploma. I'm pretty, like Barbie. That's all I need." Dad washed his hands of Deedee. He won't see her or speak to her, and he refuses to acknowledge Amiala. I'm sure he'll come around eventually. Meanwhile, it's very sad. If he'd supported her decision to keep the baby, maybe she wouldn't have married Roy, and maybe she would get some job training, at least. If she would only get her GED, Mom and I could help her get a job. Why do I feel responsible to make things right for Deedee?

Deedee

March 18, 1969

When Amiala was born everything happened so fast. I wasn't supposed to see her, but the nurse made a mistake and brought her to me. Once I saw my baby, I knew I had to keep her, but they took her away and gave her to a foster family. I was so mad. I didn't want to marry Roy, but I did so I could get my baby back. I can't tell anyone this, but Roy might not be Amiala's father. I was having sex with another guy at the same time as Roy, but that guy went away to college and is engaged to another girl. Maybe I should have told the other guy anyway because I don't like having Roy around all the time. He always wants this or that. I'm not his maid. He's in the army, so he won't be home much, and he'll send his paycheck home, so I won't have to work. I can stay home with the baby and watch TV.

Leslie

April 16, 1969

Deedee got a job working at a nursing home in Santa Monica. She and Roy couldn't afford Santa Monica rentals, so they got a place in Venice Beach. Mother hates that Deedee is living in Venice Beach because it's a slum area and can be pretty scary at night, especially with all the construction going on at the marina. Roy's mother watches Amiala while Deedee is at work. Brenda is her name, and she appears to be a real nice lady and is wholly devoted to Amiala. Roy was shipped out to Vietnam, so Deedee is alone with the baby.

Deedee

May 2, 1969

My dad filed a lawsuit against me. He wanted the money back that he'd paid out for the apartment he got me when I was pregnant. I didn't ask him to do that. I hated that place. I had to go to court yesterday, and Leslie went with me. She looked pretty funny. She's eight months pregnant, and she was madder than hell. She spoke to Dad and his attorney outside the courtroom. I don't know what she said, but Dad agreed to drop the suit. He never even looked at me.

May 20, 1969

My mother married that drinking boyfriend. I hate him. He treats her like shit. He
rattles the ice cubes in his glass when he needs a refill of bourbon, and she comes
running. If I did that, she'd tell me to get it myself. The wedding was all spur-of-the-moment. They invited a few friends over and got married in the yard. My mother is so fucking stupid.

We had an infestation of sand fleas. God, it was awful. The baby and me were eaten alive. Mom said to use calamine lotion, so I put it all over us. We look like zombies. I wish Dad was dead! When I kept the baby, he said, "Deedee, you're ruining yours and your baby's lives. Rather than taking responsibility, you have always made yourself a victim of circumstances, and your child will do the same. You would be better off getting an education, like Leslie, and your child would be better served with parents that can afford to support and educate her." He put a curse on me. Fucker!

Leslie

June 17, 1969

Diane called me and told me Dad was in the hospital; he'd been in an auto accident. She said she didn't know if he'd been injured and she was on her way to Santa Monica Hospital from the Valley. I told her, "I can get there sooner," and ran out the door. I found Dad sitting up in bed, looking a little pale but smiling. He was bruised and sore but otherwise uninjured. He was driving down Pacific Coast Highway, right where Liam and I used to go to the beach, when a guy came out of nowhere and clobbered him. His truck had to be towed away. He's more upset about his truck than himself.

June 19, 1969

This is my week for unpleasant and tragic phone calls. Roy's father called me today. He told me, "Roy has been shot up pretty badly." "How badly?" I asked. He said, "Roy may never regain the use of his right leg." Oh, no! I was shaking. I had to have him hold on while I wrapped myself in a blanket and sat down. He said, "Roy is being shipped stateside, but it will be some weeks before we know when. Will you go see Deedee and tell her what happened?" I replied, "I'll go right now." I had to turn on the bathroom heater and sit there until I stopped shivering. How was Deedee going to take this? I'd freak out. I thought about calling Mom, but she was at work and I didn't need two freaked-out women on my hands. I drove over to Deedee's. When I told her about Roy, she got very angry and shouted, "Isn't that just like him to get himself shot up! Now I have a baby and a crip to take care of! He never thinks about me!"

I was horrified! "What! Deedee, you must be in shock," I replied.

July 21, 1969

I gave birth to a beautiful baby girl June 21! She is one-month old today. We've named her Rachael. Ever since I was a little girl, playing with dolls, I loved that name and knew if I ever had a daughter that's what I would name her.

She was two weeks early, and she was born so quickly. All this nonsense about will it be a boy or a girl—I was in so much pain, I didn't give a damn what I had as long as they got it out of my body. But when the doctor said, "You have a beautiful baby girl," being the intelligent woman I am, I said, "Oh, yeah, it had to be one or the other, right?"

September 15, 1969

Deedee lost her babysitter! I don't mean to be flippant, but Brenda, Roy's mother, shot herself. Roy Senior came home from work and found her dead on the kitchen floor. They had a horrible relationship; they were always putting each other down. However, Roy Senior is very broken up. I can't imagine Brenda doing that. She loved Amiala. I would think she'd want to remain alive to see her granddaughter grow up. Deedee said, "She did it to piss off Roy Senior." I replied, "That's rather drastic!"

October 12, 1969

Miss Dump and Duck and Roy broke up. I know it's been rough on Deedee since Roy came home. Our boys coming home should have some transition period with emotional, as well as physical rehabilitation. Deedee said that Roy got hooked on heroin during the time he was in the hospital in Saigon. Last night Roy woke up, jumped out of bed, grabbed his gun, and began to run around the apartment, screaming and waving his gun. The neighbors called the police, who were able to subdue him. Deedee pressed charges so they would lock Roy up. Then she packed Roy's personal belongings and drove them over to Roy Senior's. I feel sorry

49

for Roy Senior. His wife just killed herself, and now he has a disturbed son to deal with.

Deedee

October 22, 1969

It's my eighteenth fucking birthday! I got married so I could keep my baby. Then I found out how much work she is. I never get any sleep. Then Roy gets himself shot up and comes home, limping around the house and waving guns. I hate him! We separated. Thank God. His mother was watching the baby until she had to go and shoot herself. Why does everything happen to me? I wish I didn't have to work. I hate Leslie. She gets to stay home with Rachael. That would be nice. I could sleep as late as I want and watch TV all day.

October 28, 1969

Amiala fell off the changer and broke her leg. Damn! She never sits still. I didn't have any clean diapers on the changer, so I had to walk over to the closet. It's only a few feet away, but do you think that baby could lay still for a minute? No. Over she goes, screaming her head off so loud that the neighbor came over. I said, "It's nothing. The baby just fell off the changer." She was, like, "Here, let me help you," and took Amiala. That's when we noticed that Amiala's leg was at an odd angle. My neighbor said, "We'd better get her to the emergency room," so we did. The doctor asked, "How did this happen?" I told him, "I never took my hand off the baby. She slipped off the changer right in front of me."

Leslie

November 3, 1969

Rachael is five months old! She is the most amazing baby! We bought a house in Santa Monica. It's small, and I nearly had a heart attack when I heard that our monthly payment would be $350. I'm still writing, but it still only pays for groceries. Jacob thinks I should go back to the phone company or get another job. I told him I would leave him before I would leave my baby with a sitter all day.

Our new house looks like something out of Ozzie and Harriet's neighborhood. I want to be moved in by Thanksgiving because Liam's coming home on leave.

Cassie and her husband, Derek, only live a block away. And we met the nicest couple who live across the street, Bernie and Jake.

November 28, 1969

Liam is home. I am so relieved. He's in the Special Forces, and while I think he probably has more control over his life than a grunt soldier, such as Roy, I worry about him every day.

I made Thanksgiving dinner, and the family came to our house for the holiday. It was warm, so we sat outside for a while. Liam played with the girls, jumping around and making them giggle. Poor Little Ami has this huge cast on her leg from her fall. She's such a brave little tyke; she never complains.

Today we went to Dad and Diane's. Auntie Anne and Uncle Burt flew out to see Liam and spend the holiday with us. It was a wonderful surprise! Dad had lots of friends over too. He is so generous and kind to his mechanics and pilots. I wish he could be as nice to Mother, but then, Mother has not been kind to him. Surely two adults can be capable of getting a divorce and being civil to each other, rather than filing lawsuits and dragging each other through the court system.

December 30, 1969

This was Rachael's first Christmas! It was lovely, but we all missed Liam. We spent the morning at Mother's and the afternoon at Dad's. They're still locked into their lawsuits and fighting over property and money. I wish they would stop. It makes me sad.

Deedee

March 6, 1970

I want a house! Leslie always gets what she wants. Her part-time job pays three times what I make. How come she's so lucky. One of these days, I'll get lucky and marry a rich man. Then we'll see about Miss Perfect, the Princess.

Leslie

May 16, 1970

Jacob's business is not doing well, and he's still nagging me to get a full-time job. I told him I would as soon as Rachael turns two. Meanwhile, I'm still writing, taking one class at UCLA, and working part-time in the legal department at UCLA. Bernie and I are actually sharing the job. I work the morning while she watches Rachael, and she works the afternoon while I watch her little boy.

December 23, 1970

Liam is home for Christmas. He is very unsettled and disturbed. He said this is his last tour; he'll be coming home in May. He looks just awful, and he's drinking a lot. Last night we drank a whole bottle of my homemade Kahlúa. Boy, did I have a headache and upset stomach this morning. He told me he'd be home for a couple of months; he was home on a mental leave for disobeying orders. He was supposed to take out a team when he knew there was no possibility of return, and he refused to do it.

On his way home he'd made a stop in Texas to visit Hetty, Chip, and Scooter. He and Scooter went to a bar. There were some bikers who gave Scooter a bad time. Liam told them, "Let's leave it alone," which they did. But when Scooter and Liam left the bar, the bikers ambushed them, beating them with brass knuckles and kicking them with steel-toe boots. My brother can hold his own in a fight, and so can Scooter, but not against brass knuckles and steel-toe boots. A couple came out of the bar, and the bikers took off. Liam and Scooter were pretty badly beaten up, so the couple drove them to the ER, where the boys got stitched up. Liam came home with a split lip, swollen eye, and limping, but I think his ego was wounded more than anything.

January 21, 1971

Liam is improving every day. But it's been a difficult month. I can't stand to see my brother suffering. I want to pull him back into that childhood closet and hold him and let him cry it out. He should be a happy young man, taking on the law, playing baseball, spending time with his nieces, beginning his own family. I hate this war! At any rate, I've listened and drunk an awful lot of bourbon this month. I think I've helped just by being here and listening when he needs to talk. I sure hope so. I hate to see him return to 'Nam, but he'll be home for good in May.

Miss Dump and Duck has been dating this guy Larry, who spends his days at the gym, all day, every day. He doesn't have a job; his parents support him. Deedee thinks this is very groovy and has quit her job and is living on welfare, food stamps, and handouts from Mom and Boone, and she's spending her day at the gym as well. She has become obsessed with her body, saying, "I have to look like Barbie." I think she's gone off the deep end.

When I picked Ami up from the neighbor in Venice Beach the other day, she smelled like marijuana. Needless to say, I was extremely upset. I told Mom what was going on, and now she's upset as well. She and Boone have a rental in the Valley that they've been fixing up this past month. They told Deedee they would allow her to live there rent-free. Deedee wants the guy, Larry, to come along as well, but Mom told her, "There's no way we're supporting that loser." Liam went to see Larry, and I guess Larry saw the light of day and has broken up with Deedee. Deedee is furious but has no choice but to move into the house in the Valley. She won't even speak to Liam. I'd love to know what he said to Larry.

Deedee

January 22, 1971

Goddamn that brother of mine! I will never again speak to him as long as I live. I wish he hadn't come home. He's doing nothing but causing me problems. Then Leslie went and squealed on me about the sitter smoking dope. Why do those two have to stick their noses into my business? Now Mom is all pissed off at me. I can't have her mad at me because I need to live in that house of theirs. I can't pay rent on the little bit of money I make. Maybe I could learn to type or take in ironing. Then I could stay at home. Leslie said she'd give me a recommendation at the phone company, but I'd have to get my GED, and I'm not doing that. I hate school. They might as well put me on a torture rack.

Leslie

January 30, 1971

Liam returned to 'Nam today. Thank God he'll be home for good in a few months. I tried not to cry when he boarded the plane, but I couldn't help myself.

Yesterday we all got together at Mother's so we could spend Liam's last night at home with him. We barbecued and swam. The girls had a great time bouncing around in the pool with Uncle Liam. I won thirty dollars playing poker, just enough to buy those gold filigree earrings I've had my eyes on at Bullock's. Ami and Rachael put on little Hawaiian grass skirts and performed the hula dance for everyone. Of course, they received a standing ovation, and knowing they were going to be putting on a show, I presented them each with a small bouquet of flowers. They were delighted with all the attention.

February 10, 1971

Yesterday in the early-morning hours, our bed started shaking. The cats ran and hid, books flew off the bookshelves, furniture and dishes rattled. The house felt like it was breaking apart. I thought it was the end of the world. How could I have lived in California all these years and not thought about an earthquake? I flew into Rachael's room to find her safely asleep in her crib. Thank you, God!

We didn't have much damage, and no one we know was hurt. Mom said she couldn't believe what she was seeing when the water in her swimming pool whipped up in the air like a tidal wave and dropped back down into the pool.

Deedee

March 17, 1971

Liam won't be butting into my life because he went back to 'Nam. I wouldn't speak to him at Mother's. I didn't think that was a good idea for Leslie to give the girls flowers because every time they do something, they'll expect a present. Leslie has stupid liberal ideas about raising kids. She lets Rachael eat whatever she wants. God, if I let Amiala eat whatever she wants, she'd eat cake all day. And Leslie lets Rachael talk back to her. Mom is always asking, "Why do you let Rachael talk to you like that?" Sometimes Leslie takes Rachael into another room for a little talk. God! If Amiala talks back to me, I give her a good smack across the face and wash her mouth out with soap.

Chapter Six

Puff the Magic Dragon

Leslie

May 21, 1971

My baby brother is dead. I can barely write. My arm is weak, my hand is shaking, and my tears are blurring the page. I feel like I've been punched in the stomach, and I can't stand up. My body is a sack that I can hardly move from one place to another. I throw up everything, even water. Please, God, this has to be a mistake. He's coming home in two days. Liam died on his birthday. Nobody dies on their birthday. This is some sort of horrific nightmare. I'll wake up and everything will be all right.

It was Dad who called early in the morning. I was feeding Rachael in her highchair, so Jacob answered the phone. When Jacob told me Liam was dead, I dropped Rachael's dish and spoon. Everything in my vision became white. I couldn't speak. I couldn't think. I couldn't cry. I stumbled into the living room, dropped onto the couch, and stared out the window. Then I heard a blood-curdling scream. *"Nooooo!"*

June 2, 1971

It took two weeks for the army to get Liam's body back to us. They said, "You're lucky you got him back." Lucky? Bastards! I wanted to see Liam, but they wouldn't let me. They? It would be too upsetting for me, they said. I screamed, "This is not your decision to make. I have to be sure it's my brother." My mother said, "Let it go."

June 5, 1971

The funeral was yesterday. What a fiasco! I felt like I was walking through cobwebs in a fog. My father planned the whole affair. He had pictures of Liam from baby to toddler to baseball player to college student to war hero. He had the pianist play "Walk on, Little Boy," "Danny Boy," and "Puff the Magic Dragon." He took it highways beyond heartbreak. It was utterly wretched. I understand his grief, but if he would just think about the rest of us, consider us even for a second. He's torturing us with his grief, making it impossible for us to grieve or to help him grieve. I can't think. I can't feel. I'm numb. The inside of my head feels like it's full of air or fog, or like when you're in an airplane and your ears need to pop. I don't hear what people are saying. It's like they're talking in slow motion, and I just want them to shut up and leave me alone. My mom and dad are pulling at me more than ever, blaming each other for Liam's death, demanding I take sides. Diane said, "You can't walk the fence." I said, "Yes, I can."

At the funeral, the family sat off to the side in a little curtained-off room, so I don't know exactly how this began, but things were said between Boone and Dad, and Dad hauled off and hit Boone in the jaw, knocking him to the ground. To say everyone was shocked would be absurd. Boone got himself up and started to take a punch at Dad, but Dad was ready and hit Boone again. Blood splattered everywhere. Boone was holding his jaw. The funeral home personnel were trying to pull Dad off Boone. I wanted to crawl into the coffin with my brother.

Deedee

June 7, 1971

For a year Liam and I went to the same high school, and sometimes he'd let me wear his letterman jacket. I feel bad that I wasn't speaking to him before he left, but he'd been butting into my business. I couldn't go to Dad and Diane's when he was home because I'm being shunned by Dad. So, everybody got to be together but me. What a bunch of crap! Liam came to see me a few times when he was on leave, but mostly he was at Leslie's. He and Leslie had always been tight. They had secrets. At the funeral Dad broke Boone's jaw when he hit him. They're filing lawsuits against each other. I'm living in Mom and Boone's rental, and I hate it. They are constantly on my ass about going back to school. I told them I will never go back to school. Get it? Never. I hate school. I was never good at it. Look where it got me. Pregnant. Last month, I suddenly blew up like a balloon. I'm so fat I don't want to leave the house. Mom and Leslie made me go to the doctor. It's a hormone thing. The doctor gave me some pills and the weight is coming off. I knew it wasn't my fault because I stick my finger down my throat after I eat. I have to stay thin and pretty like Barbie.

Leslie

June 10, 1971

Diane called. She said my dad won't speak to me anymore. She said if I don't take his side, then I'm on my mother's side. I told her that I can't take sides; please get my dad to a psychologist. I can't believe Dad is once again pulling himself away from not only me but also Rachael. He loves Rachael. His grief must be driving him into a cavernous depression for him to separate himself from Rachael.

Jacob took a job with a company in Riverside, so we rented the house in Santa Monica and moved to a lovely house on a golf course. The house is quite large and has a beautiful view of the golf course and surrounding area. I miss being close to Mom, but I drive out to the Valley on Sundays to spend the day with her.

June 19, 1971

We went to my ninth annual high school class reunion last night. A few weeks before, I'd taken Rachael shopping with me for a new dress to wear to the reunion. She was all dressed up, and we went to a fancy restaurant for lunch. People were watching us. A woman came over to our table and told me how sweet it was to see such a beautiful mother and daughter out to lunch together.

I bought a dress that is long, light, and flowing. It's made of chiffon in a floral pattern in blues and pinks. Rachael loves it, and so do I. It's perfect for a hot summer night at the beach.

The reunion was at the Santa Monica Bay Club. The sun setting over the ocean reminded me of living at the beach and how much I miss that. It was nice catching up with old classmates, but it tore me up when people offered their condolences, saying, "I'm sorry to hear about your brother's death. We shouldn't have been in that war. It was useless." Translation: "Your brother died for nothing."

I'm still writing and taking classes. I'm almost done with college, but I'll go on for my graduate degree. I love learning.

Our poor little Ami has had three surgeries on her leg, but the doctor said the damage is such that she will probably always walk with a limp.

Deedee

August 4, 1971

Dad won't speak to Leslie. Now she knows what it feels like to be shunned, Miss Perfect, the princess! I'm surprised because he worships Rachael as much as he did Leslie. He never really cared anything about me. Mother and Leslie are all hyped up about Amiala having a limp. I'm not worried about it. You hardly notice it. At least she didn't lose her leg. Leslie is all pissed off about people thinking Liam died for nothing. I told her to get over it. He did.

Chapter Seven

Murder and Betrayal

Leslie

February 15, 1972

Yesterday was Valentine's Day. I made heart-shaped pancakes for Rachael before I took her to nursery school. After dropping her off, I returned home to clean house and prep our Valentine's Day dinner before going back to pick her up. I had the radio on while I was vacuuming. Suddenly the music stopped, and I heard, "We interrupt this program for breaking news: William Goodman, prominent Santa Monica businessman and owner of the Helicopter Center, was found shot to death on his son's grave. Although there was no note, the police are considering this a suicide."

My father! I dropped to the floor. Oh my God! I should have paid more attention. I should have broken the silence between us, but I selfishly needed a break from the drama and the lawsuits. I thought his not speaking to me would blow over. I wanted to scream at him, "Why did you do that? What about Deedee and me? We're still alive, and we need you."

There was a lot of noise outside, and Jacob came through the front door. He told me there was a bunch of reporters out in front. They wanted a statement. I couldn't make any words come out of my mouth. My mind was quite literally a blank screen. I was swept up into a vortex, "Don't love too much; you'll only get hurt."

February 25, 1972

Robert Overland, owner of Transit Airlines and a friend of Dad's, came to see me. He said, "Leslie, I don't believe that your dad killed himself. He was going to take over the pilot simulator training for Transit, and we were excited about working together again. He told me that Diane was pregnant and had moved out of the house. She'd been having an affair with your dad's business manager. There's a lot of money involved, and I think she may have killed your father." I was stunned. Dad's aunt had called and told me a similar story, but I'd passed it off as more drama; it was too unbelievable. Hearing it now from Robert, though, made it credible. Diane had had Dad buried the day after he was found. She hadn't even called me to tell me, and she'd refused to have any kind of service. I didn't want to think about this. It was too bizarre.

Robert and Dad's aunt thought I, as the next of kin, should go to the sheriff's office and speak to someone. It was the last thing I wanted to do, but maybe we could get some clarity. The sheriff I spoke to happened to have been the first responder on the scene. He told me there were three bullets in the body. He said, "It would have been unusual, but not impossible, for your father to have shot himself three times," and went on to explain why. He said that at one time during the investigation, they'd suspected that the wife might have killed him. I thought, *What? Has everyone gone mad?* Shakily I asked, "If Diane was a suspect, why wasn't she arrested?"

The sheriff said they'd looked carefully at all the evidence, questioned Diane, and interviewed people, and then he said the most astounding thing I've ever heard: "Husbands and wives kill each other every day, and we can't prove it." He continued, "You don't want to reopen this case. The crime scene was a bloody mess. Photos will be dragged out that you do not want to see. We concluded that it was most likely suicide and closed the case." I'd brought Rachael with me, and she was sitting in my lap. The sheriff said, "The best thing you can do is go home and take care of your little girl."

Deedee

February 28, 1972

If I'd been born a boy, maybe Dad wouldn't have killed himself. Fuck! Leslie is all in a stir because she thinks Dad was murdered. She's as dumb as a post. He wanted to die. She said, "It's likely that he didn't kill himself because there were three bullets in his body." I told her, "You have to give him credit because he was one determined motherfucker."

Leslie

March 2, 1972

Last night Jacob didn't come home from work. It was eleven, and I hadn't heard from him. I put Rachael to bed and began to pace the floor. Jacob is sometimes late, but not this late. I always worry about the tule fog out here in Corona. It's impossible to drive in, and there have been numerous accidents. I called Jacob's office. No answer. I paced some more. Finally, I decided to call his boss. It was the middle of the night, but this was an emergency. I told him that I was worried that Jacob hadn't come home; was there a problem at the plant that may have needed his attention? The boss told me, "There's no problem. Have you thought about the fact that Jacob might be having an affair?" I yelled back at him, "Of course not! Jacob would never have an affair! What kind of a thing is that to say to me when I'm worried sick that my husband may be lying in a ditch somewhere off the highway?" Asshole! I slammed the phone down and called the police. There were no reports of accidents. But there must have been. Jacob would call me if he could. He's dead or he's injured. Something is horribly wrong. The police couldn't and wouldn't do anything. I paced and paced, and waited and waited. I was so scared. Finally, at three in the morning, Jacob came through the front door. Thank God! I ran to him. "What happened? Why are you so late? Why didn't you call? I've been sick with worry." I started sobbing and shaking. "Jacob! What is going on?"

He said, "Oh, Leslie, I'm so sorry. I was with my cousin."

"You spent the night with your cousin? What cousin?" I asked.

"My cousin Peggy. We've been sort of having an affair. From the time we were kids, we've had this fantasy about each other. It's only been a few times."

I screamed, "Jesus, Jacob! Are you fucking serious?"

"It's true," he said. "I'm so sorry. It won't happen again."

"What?" I exclaimed. "It won't happen again? Seriously? That makes it okay? I've been pacing the floor all night, worried sick that you'd been in an accident and might be lying dead in a ditch." I've never been so angry or felt so betrayed. I couldn't stop screaming at him.

May 6, 1972

Jacob and I are living together but only going through the motions of our daily lives. My anger subsided and turned to sadness. I'm taking some classes and trying to write, but I feel as though I'm stuck in mud. I'm having difficulty concentrating. Jacob picked a very bad time to have an affair. I'd only just lost Dad and Liam. Now I've lost Jacob too. "Don't love too much; you'll only get hurt."

June 1, 1972

Can I ever forgive Jacob? I don't know. I envy friends like Bernie and Jake who can talk to each other and spend an evening together and not be bored. I wish I had someone to talk to.

Sometimes I feel like I'm in a coma, that none of the horror of the past year really happened. That I can call Dad and he will be right over in his little red truck. That Liam will be home soon, and everything will be all right.

My life is foggy. I have no direction. I sent a piece in to *Readers' Monthly*, and the editor red-marked the whole article. That's never happened before. I threw it in the drawer.

July 26, 1972

This morning I woke up and realized I need help. If I had a broken leg, I would see a doctor. Well, I have a broken heart. All the men in my life are leaving me, rapidly. I have three appointments with three different psychologists. I need to interview them to see whom I can trust. I have my little girl to consider. I must protect her, love her, educate her, make the world make sense for her. In order to do that, I must first do all that for myself.

October 24, 1972

As I watch my daughter sleeping, I think how quickly she'll be grown. I remember the tiny baby lying helplessly in a massive crib. I watch her breathe and worry for her life. I want to hold her close to me and protect her from all the evils of the world. I want time to stand still. When I tucked her into bed tonight, she had her tiny little arms around her Raggedy Andy and said to me, "Don't go yet." She pulled at my hand, and she clutched my heart.

Chapter Eight

Talk of the Town

Leslie

February 12, 1973

Jacob and I separated. I thought we'd be married forever. I'm so scared, and I feel so alone. When Rachael went to bed tonight, she said, "When my daddy gets home, will you tell him to come in and say good night to me?" What have I done? I suddenly wanted to call Jacob and tell him, "Come back. It was all a mistake." Just as suddenly, I realized that Jacob chose to have an affair, and his timing sucked. He hurt me beyond measure, and I don't know if I can ever forgive him. I hurt so much. I wonder if I'll be able to move on. I've lost the three main men in my life in nine months' time. Please, God, make the pain go away.

March 25, 1973

I found a therapist. She is wonderful. I cry until I feel like my insides are coming out and my eyes are so swollen that I can't see. She tells me it's okay to cry, to feel; if we don't feel the pain, we can't feel the joy. All these horrible tragedies are just that: horrific tragedies. They were not my fault.

But I think they were my fault. I should have convinced Liam not to enlist. I should have insisted Dad see a psychologist. I should have paid more attention to Jacob. I was foolishly focused on my own silly life. In a period of nine months my very being was savagely attacked, and my insides were ripped out three times. One was devastating; three were catastrophic. How will I survive such monstrous, unalterable devastation?

Deedee

April 1, 1973

April Fool's Day! And Leslie is the fool. She's going to therapy, and she says I should go too because I have anger issues. I don't have anger issues. I'm beautiful, like Barbie. Leslie's the one with the anger issues. Mom told Leslie she doesn't like her airing our family laundry with strangers. I told Leslie to go get a manicure.

Leslie

June 7, 1973

I got a part-time job as a bookkeeper for a man who owns a slew of orange groves here in the Riverside area. I was surprised I got the job, as math has never been my forte, but this is pretty rudimentary. He's a very kind, older gentleman, and he allows me to work the morning hours while Rachael is at nursery school.

I'm not doing any writing for publication, and oddly, I'm not missing it as much as I thought I would. Journaling has become my outlet, as well as working with my therapist. I'm taking a few classes at UC Riverside.

August 21, 1973

I'm having an affair with one of my professors. I feel so liberated. He's so intellectual. We talk about our love of literature and read passages together. I attend his class one night a week while Jacob babysits for Rachael. One night after class the professor and I were making out in his car when Jacob pulled up in a van with two other people and Rachael. I got out of the professor's car. The people with Jacob pulled me into the van and put Rachael in my lap. The woman, addressing me, said, "You should be ashamed of yourself." I wanted to slap the shit out of the bitch. I was so embarrassed. Jacob was acting like a fucking saint. He must have been following me to know that I was lingering with the professor after class. I kept my mouth shut and held Rachael tight. Not another word was said on the drive home. The next morning, I called Jacob and said, "I want to remind you that we're separated. I love Rachael with all my being and would never put her in harm's way. The rest of my life is none of your business."

October 12, 1973

I broke it off with the professor! It's not like I wanted to set up house with him. Maybe I just wanted to get even with Jacob. At any rate, it was a nice parting. He said he'd always remember me.

December 15, 1973

Since I started seeing a psychologist, my relationships with my mother and sister have begun to deteriorate. Mother wants me to be just like her. I just want to be myself and understand what that means. My emotions are all over the place. One day, I'm happy, laughing and smiling and so very glad to be alive. The next day, I'm dismal and melancholy and scared to death of dying. I'm especially afraid of dying before Rachael grows up. I love her so much. I want to be with her.

Mother said, "You're thinking about the past too much, and I resent that you're discussing family issues with strangers. Jacob has problems, so you think you must have problems too. The past is the past; it's not pertinent today. You're dwelling too much on this psychological stuff. You should bag it and be concerned with what's happening now and think less about yourself and more about other people." I'm scared to death of being a mother like my mother.

Mother must have called Deedee right after hanging up because it was only minutes later when Deedee called and interrupted my writing. She said, "You sit in your house, leading Jacob around by the purse strings and call that living." I explained, "Indeed, Jacob does help with Rachael's expenses, but I'm also working part-time while taking classes. I have an income from our Santa Monica rental, and although Jacob and I are separated, we are determined to remain in a solid relationship for our daughter's sake."

She went on to say, "I'm definitely not jealous of you, but I feel sorry for you. You used to be such a nice person, but you've changed. Other people feel the same way about Jacob and you as I do. I wish I could do something for you." I laughed. She said, "Fuck you," and hung up on me.

Right now, it doesn't matter what my sister and my mother think of me. I don't need their approval, and really, I feel more together, having their disapproval. I don't believe I will ever have the mythical relationship with them that I have been seeking, but that's okay. I will find those relationships elsewhere.

Deedee

January 1, 1974

Leslie is selfish and doesn't care about anyone but herself. Doesn't she know how embarrassing it is for Mom and me that she talks about us with that therapist of hers? The therapist must think we're crazy shits, what with Leslie telling her how bad we are. Leslie laughed at me. That fucking bitch!

Leslie

March 14, 1974

I gave up the house on the golf course and moved into a condo closer to the university. It's peaceful and quiet here, and Rachael and I planted a little garden. At night we cuddle up in bed and read books. I'm attending classes. My mother says I'm addicted to taking classes and a perpetual student, but I've decided to complete my master's and doctorate degrees and teach at the university level. One day I will return to writing.

Rachael is in a nursery school on campus that only takes two children from each ethnic group. It's wonderful to see these children interacting without prejudices and learning so much about other cultures. Liam took a few educational courses in college and encouraged me to educate Rachael in an English Summerhill sort of program, and this is similar.

I needed to increase my income, so I went back to work at the phone company. I was put in the drafting department to work on technical drawings and plans for engineers and architects. I was told that was what my aptitude tests showed was my best fit. I'm scared to death because I can't draft my way out of a toilet! I keep trying to look like I know what I'm doing. I hope it's working. One of the girls I work with is pregnant. I gave her all my beautiful maternity clothes. I know I will never have another child. I just want to give the one I have the best life possible.

May 22, 1974

Wow! I met the greatest guy working at the phone company. He's so sexy! He walks the walk and talks the talk. And his kisses send me down the river of no return. *Whoosh!* He said he was attracted to me because I read the newspaper.

October 1, 1974

I broke up with the very sexy guy from the phone company. I applied for an educational leave and got it. I'm going to return to college full time and concentrate on my graduate studies. Jacob took a job in Long Beach. He wants me to move there and try to make a go of it again with him. I said I would. The sexy guy from the phone company gave me a going-away present, a gold bracelet with the inscription, "To Sunshine, with Love." We had such a gentle breakup. He sang and played the guitar and reminded me of John Denver!

Deedee

October 23, 1974

My sister can't keep a boyfriend. They all ditch her when they find out how weird she is. Now she has to move back in with Jacob. Somehow, she manages to live like she's got a lot of money. She always has a nice place to live, a great car, beautiful clothes. She puts Rachael in fancy schools. That's what's wrong with Rachael. She needs to go to public school and learn to live like the rest of us. I met a real cute guy at a bar last Friday night. His name is Mick, and he's Irish. I think Mom will like him.

Leslie

November 22, 1974

I love living by the ocean again. Jacob and Rachael and I rented a flat in Belmont Shore, half a block from the ocean and half a block from the canal where the boats dock. We open the window at night and fall asleep to the sound of the foghorns and the smell of the ocean air. At five-thirty in the morning I enjoy an exhilarating run along the shore before attending classes at Long Beach State.

My music appreciation class piqued my interest in chamber music, so Rachael and I have been going to a number of local concerts. It's thrilling to sit so close to the musicians while they're playing their instruments, and I love to see Rachael so enchanted. I explained to her that prior to the invention of radio and television, this is what people did in the evenings.

March 7, 1975

I made a roasted chicken for dinner tonight. I dished it up with some vegetables and put a plate in front of Rachael. She took one look at the chicken wing and said, "Mommy, I can't eat the chicken's arm." Put in that manner, I didn't think I could either. This went on for a few weeks until I acknowledged that I would be raising a vegetarian daughter and living that lifestyle as well. Now I'm checking books out of the library, doing research on a vegetarian diet, and shopping in health food stores.

July 5, 1975

Last night Jacob, Rachael, and I watched the fireworks from the *Queen Mary*. What a spectacular sight to see the bursting colors of lights bouncing off the ocean. It was magical and reminded me of when I was a child and we used to go to Palisades Park and watch the fireworks down on the beach.

July 10, 1975

My sister tried to kill herself! She took too many pills, but the guy she is living with, Mick, found her in time to get her to the hospital. My heart was in my stomach. I said to her, "We carry so much loss and abandonment from Dad's suicide. Why would you do such a thing?" She said, "I want to get married, but Mick doesn't. I was just trying to get his attention." This was the first time I'd met Mick, although Deedee had spoken of him. He seems like a real nice guy. I asked him, "What's going on?" He said, "Deedee has a violent temper. She tears up the house, pulling things off walls, out of closets, breaking anything she can get her hands on."

I asked Deedee to please see a psychologist. I set up an appointment for her and paid the bill. When I asked her how it went, she said, "That fucking therapist made me cry. I'm never going back."

Deedee

July 12, 1975

It wasn't a fucking suicide attempt. I was just trying to get Mick's attention. And I don't have a temper. Sometimes I drink too much gin. Gin makes me angry. I need to drink some other kind of alcohol. I wasn't throwing things around either. I was just cleaning out, getting rid of this and that. I had to go see that therapist Leslie paid for because Mick said he was moving out if I didn't. That bitch therapist made me cry. What does she know about anything? I'm never going back. Leslie must be one of those people who likes to torture themselves.

August 30, 1975

I'm pregnant! I'm so happy! Mick said he would marry me. He's Catholic, so abortion is out of the question. My life will be perfect.

Leslie

September 15, 1975

Deedee and Mick got married. It was a small wedding and, to me, a sad one. After the dinner reception, I found Deedee throwing up in the toilet in the ladies' room. I thought it was due to the pregnancy and asked what I could do to help. She said, "I'm fine. I puke all the time because I'm not going to get fat, and you should do the same because you're looking chunky." I looked at her and said, "What? I weigh a hundred and five pounds."

September 21, 1975

Jacob and I are separating again. We did some therapy but decided another separation would be best for now. I love Jacob, but his anger and depression make it difficult to live with him. I want a peaceful, happy life.

Mother has a friend who has earns a very good living as a court reporter; i.e., she bought herself a home in Tiburon in the Bay Area. I decided to put my graduate studies on hold while I go to court reporting college and get licensed. Then I will earn enough money to support myself and Rachael while I return to graduate school. Meanwhile, Rachael and I will live with Mom and Boone out in the Valley because I want to go to court reporting college full time.

Chapter Nine

Just a Little Misunderstanding

Leslie

January 18, 1976

Boone tried to rape me. It was late at night, and he'd been drinking pretty heavily. He came into our room stark naked and got into bed with me. He started to pull at my pajama bottoms. He put his hand over my mouth and told me if I screamed, he'd kill me. All I could think of was Rachael asleep in the bed on the other side of the room. I prayed she wouldn't wake up. I grabbed ahold of his dick and twisted as hard as I could. He grabbed my other hand and began to bend it backward. I grabbed his pinky finger and pulled it back until it snapped. He clamped a hand over his own mouth and ran from the room. Mother remained asleep. I checked on Rachael. She had not stirred. Thank God! I grabbed my brother's Black Betsy baseball bat from under the bed and sat there huddled against the headboard until the sun came up. I heard Mom and Boone stirring and smelled coffee brewing. With Mom awake, I felt safe. I dressed quickly and went into the kitchen for coffee. Mother was in the shower. Boone was drinking coffee. He said, "Good morning. Did you get a good night's sleep?" I was stunned at his nonchalance. Then he went on, "It's nice having you live here with us. You're sexy, and you turn me on. I want to fuck you. I'd take good care of your needs and satisfy you. I've never had a disappointed woman in bed with me. We'd have fun. We could all go camping and fishing together. But, of course, you couldn't tell your mother because if you did, I'd have to kill you."

I couldn't believe what I was hearing. This man has gone off the deep end. He is an ex-cop and has guns in the house. He brags about how many lowlifes he's killed in the name of justice, saving taxpayers hundreds of thousands of dollars. I knew he was a killer. Now I know he's a psycho as well. I have no doubt he could and would kill me. I ran back to my room and waited until I heard his truck pull out of the driveway. He had an all-day kitchen repair job today. I went and told my mother I had a parent-teacher meeting at Rachael's school and wouldn't be leaving right away. The minute she left for work, I bolted all the doors and windows and called Jacob, telling him what had happened. I asked him to please bring his truck and come immediately and help us get out of there. Although I'd put most of our belongings in storage, court reporting college was about a two-year program, so I'd brought quite a bit with us to live at Mom's. I told Rachael I had a surprise for her. We were going to pack our things and go spend the night in a hotel. Rachael loves hotels, especially room service. I left Mom a note in her makeup drawer, where only she would find it, telling her I was so sorry I had to move out in such a hurry and not to worry about us. Something came up with Jacob, and we'll be staying with him. Thankfully, she doesn't have Jacob's number or address.

January 26, 1976

We moved into a lovely townhouse close to my court reporting college, and Rachael is in a school with an experimental program where they've combined Grades K through three. Rachael and I went to the parents' night, and I was surprised to find that the mom of one of Rachael's friends was a gal I'd been a cheerleader with at Santa Monica High School. It was so nice to see her again and catch up.

On another note, I haven't spoken to my mother since we left the house. I got an unlisted telephone number. I haven't told anyone where we're living, except a few very close friends. I'm scared to death that Boone will somehow find me, but I have escape routes out both the front and back of the townhouse, and I have Liam's Black Betsy.

January 30, 1976

Mother called me last night. She got my number from a friend of hers who works at the phone company. Mother was out of her mind with worry and wanted to know what happened that I would just move out so quickly without talking to her about it. I asked if Boone was with her, and she told me he was. I said, "Please don't tell him you're talking to me. I'm going to hang up, but I'll come to your office at noon tomorrow."

January 31, 1976

I was a nervous wreck, but I went to Mom's office at noon, looking over my shoulder the whole time. When I told her what had happened, she said, "Oh no, we just bought a new boat and camper."

What does that have to do with anything? I think my mother has lost her mind too.

"You must have misunderstood," she said.

I said, "Mother, there is no mistaking a naked man with a hard-on in your bed."

Deedee

January 31, 1976

Oh, My God! Mom called me and told me that Miss Perfect says Boone tried to rape her. Give me a fucking break! Boone wouldn't try to rape Leslie. Leslie has quite an imagination. She loves to make up stories. She's always been that way. I feel so sorry for her. I wish I could help her.

Leslie

February 2, 1976

Mother called. I'd changed my number, and she got it again. I should report her friend at the phone company. Mother said, "I spoke to Boone, and this is all just a little misunderstanding." She put Boone on the phone to speak to me. He was so drunk he was slurring his words. I hung up. I have never been so scared! I can't sleep! I sit up all night, trying to read while holding on to Black Betsy.

February 23, 1976

Mother called. Boone went in for back surgery and died in the recovery room. He'd been having back issues. His regular doctor wouldn't perform the surgery because Boone had a heart condition, so Boone found a doctor who would perform the surgery, and as his own doctor had predicted, Boone had a heart attack.

I should feel bad, but I don't. Rather, I have a sense of freedom and newfound safety.

Deedee

February 28, 1976

It's all Leslie's fault that Boone died. I'm sure she gave him a heart attack with all that fuss about rape. Poor Mother. I'm glad she and Mick's mom have become friends.

March 30, 1976

I had another baby girl. She's so cute. We named her Meliza. Mick and I are so much in love. He's doing real good, and we're renting a beautiful house in Laguna Niguel.

Leslie

July 2, 1976

I'd like Rachael to have some sort of religious exposure, so I've been thinking a lot about religion lately. Through the years, I've been drawn to Judaism. My great-grandfather, Mother's paternal grandfather, was Jewish. Although Dad declared himself an agnostic, Grandad Goodman is Jewish. Jacob's father was Jewish, and Jacob's grandfather was a rabbi. I admire Jewish family values, the emphasis on religion and learning. I love the rituals.

I believe that when people die, we keep them alive through our memories and sharing those memories with others.

Chapter Ten

Don't Go Changin' and Rearrangin'

Leslie

January 2, 1977

I've had a long lapse in journal entries. This was the time I needed to write more too, because I have a lot of anger issues that I'm dealing with in therapy. I'm angry that Liam and Dad died. I'm especially angry that Jacob picked that particular time to have an affair. I'm angry at my mother and my sister for always putting me down. Anger stems from hurt. I've been hurt. I've been betrayed, and I've been abandoned.

June 7, 1977

In the past few months, Mother and I seem to be healing the fissure in our relationship. We're spending a lot of time together, and it's nice. We took Rachael and Ami up to the Madonna Inn in San Louis Obispo for a few days. We got all dressed up and went down to the formal dining room for dinner. The girls looked so cute in their beautiful dresses and Mary Janes. There was a band playing soft dancing music from the '40s, and Ami was dying to get out there and dance, but Rachael wouldn't budge. Finally, with much nagging, Rachael relented. They were the only ones on the dance floor, and the band began playing "Thank Heaven for Little Girls." My heart swelled!

I've been checking books out of the library on Jewish religion and history. Rachael is in an after-school program at our local synagogue. I've been sharing these religious thoughts with her and checking out children's books on Judaism to read to her. I've spoken to the rabbi about taking conversion classes. It's a long process.

Deedee

June 17, 1977

We don't have any Jews in our family. Leslie says we do, and she's turning Jewish. Mother told her she was not Jewish. I laughed my head off and said, "It's just another one of Leslie's passing fancies." That girl should go back to writing. She can really make up shit.

Leslie

August 1, 1977

I've read a lot about meditating and the benefits derived therefrom, so I signed Rachael and me up for Transcendental Meditation instruction. We spent about an hour with an instructor. He walked us through relaxing our bodies and then focusing on a mantra for twenty minutes twice a day. I've been practicing for a week now, and I feel great. I can literally feel the tension falling away from my body and my mind.

I miss my brother so much. He had the most amazing, boyish grin. He made me laugh, and we shared all our thoughts and feelings, something I can't do with Mother and Miss Dump and Duck.

Deedee

October 22, 1977

Mick has a good job, but he drinks a little too much. Sometimes he doesn't come home for days. I don't worry because he drinks with his stepdad and stays at his mom's, but I'm mad at him. I tell him it doesn't look very good for us for him to do that.

Amiala is keeping a diary with a key, and she hides it. I'm sure she's making up stories about me. She gets it from

Leslie. I told Amiala she better not be telling tales because if she is and somebody found that diary, it could look very bad for all of us. Now Leslie has taken up meditation. She even got Rachael involved. I swear, what will that bimbo try next?

Chapter Eleven

Moving On Up

Leslie

January 4, 1978

Jacob got a fabulous job offer to be a VP at a company in Northern California. He is as excited as all get-out. Although we haven't been living together, he is reluctant to move without Rachael and me. I told him that I would transfer to a court reporting college in the Bay Area and that we would move up there if the job was working out after three months.

March 28, 1978

I was speaking to Jacob's Aunt Ruth this evening over the phone when she began to laugh and told Uncle Ross to stop kidding around. She said to me, "Oh, Ross is always making with the jokes." Then she started screaming, "Ross! Ross!" There was a lot of commotion. The line went dead. Cousin Rick called me and told me Uncle Ross had had a heart attack and died. Oh, my God! Poor Ruth!

May 20, 1978

Jacob loves his new job; it's all working out quite well. I've made a few trips up to the Bay Area to have a look around. I love it there! San Francisco is such an exciting city!

Deedee

July 1, 1978

Meliza's so cute. We just love her to the moon and back. She's getting a little pudgy. I'll have to keep an eye on that. I can't have fat daughters. How would that make me look! Amiala is nothing but trouble. She gets a lot more spankings than I ever got, and she's constantly getting her mouth washed out with soap.

Leslie

September 1, 1978

Jacob and I moved back in together. We found a charming house to rent in Alameda. Alameda is a beautiful little islet off the Oakland Estuary and close to the Oakland Airport. I love to go running down by the water. The air is brisk and clear. I'm going to a court reporting college in Oakland. Rachael is in a marvelous private school operated on the Summerhill program.

November 1, 1978

I converted to Judaism. I went to the mikvah, which felt like a huge rite of passage. We'd already joined our local synagogue, so I had a small ceremony at a Friday night service. I find Friday night services extremely peaceful. Rachael is considered born of a Jewish mother and thereby Jewish as well. We went to a new members party and met so many wonderful people. Rachael is in Hebrew school and meeting lots of new friends too.

Deedee

December 2, 1978

Mom is real upset that Leslie has moved so far away. I think it's great. Now she's out of my hair. She is the weirdest and most annoying person I know. She's transferring to another court reporting college. She goes to school so she doesn't have to get a real job. And she's got Rachael in another one of those crazy liberal schools. Mother says Leslie is only a Democrat because Jacob is. She's really a Republican like us.

Leslie

January 24, 1979

I've been having the hardest time building up speed to qualify for the state exam for court reporters. I decided to back off a bit and get a job. I'm an interviewer at the Jewish Family Services. It's fun! At noon I go to an exercise class there, which is wonderful, but I'm still running along the bay. This is an engaging place to live, and I'm very happy I moved up here.

July 8, 1979

Jacob read an article in a magazine about Ashland, Oregon, home of the Oregon Shakespeare Festival. Since my major is English Lit, he thought I would like it, and we should make a trip up there. So here we are! What an amazing place! There are three theaters, running all sorts of plays. Bernie and Jake and the children are spending their usual summer traveling the country in their camper, and they've met us here. We went to the July Fourth parade. The temperature was 104 degrees, the hottest day in many, many years. I just could not stand the heat, so I went into the hotel where we are staying, right on the corner where Bernie and the kids were standing watching the parade. I ordered a Bloody Mary, watched the parade, and waved to the kids while sitting on a comfy couch in the air-conditioned lobby.

The next day we all went up to Crater Lake, and we got snowed in. In July! We played bridge while the kids ran around the lobby of the hotel, playing hide-and-seek.

We returned to Ashland and said good-bye to Bernie and Jake, and guess what happened next? Our station wagon broke down. The mechanic said it would take a few weeks to repair. How wonderful! Two more weeks in Ashland! Rachael is excited too. You know how she loves hotels. And this hotel is especially fun. At cocktail hour Rachael and I get our drinks and go up to the mezzanine and play a game. Then we go to dinner and a play. In the mornings, the people at the desk watch Rachael while I go for a run in Lithia Park. Rachael thinks it's just fantastic to hang out with the receptionist and eat her breakfast in the lobby. I wonder if she'll become a hotel manager.

May 18, 1981

It's been a couple of years since I've written. Life happens! Today is the tenth anniversary of Liam's death. Every year on this date I find a beautiful place to sit with a cocktail and raise a toast to my brother's life. I miss him so much. I am fortunate to have grown up with that darling little boy.

June 29, 1981

I've been working hard at trying to pass the court reporting exams. I leave early in the morning for classes, and I spend the afternoons working to build my speed on the court reporting stenotype machine. Then I pick up Rachael from school, Jacob arrives home, and we spend a lovely evening together.

Mom called tonight from Grandma and Grandad Haines's in Wisconsin. I spoke briefly to my grandfather. The conversation left me feeling so sad. I don't want to be old and so near to the end of my life.

August 1, 1981

We finally found a lovely little house in Alameda that we purchased. It's small but perfect for us, and the payments are manageable, $633 a month. I took Rachael out of the private school and put her in the junior high school one block from our new house. I want her to have friends who will be going to high school with her. Rachael loves Hebrew school and will have a bat mitzvah next year.

Deedee

October 18, 1981

How can Leslie afford a house? It's Jacob. He pays for everything. And they all went to Ashland on vacation and spent three weeks watching plays. We spent our vacation moving into this condo. It isn't fair. Mick needs to work harder. I can't work. I have to take care of my girls. Rachael is having a bat mitzvah. That's ridiculous. She isn't even a Jew. That Leslie is dumber than a post.

Leslie

November 23, 1981

We're down at Mom's, and I'm terribly worried about Deedee and the girls. A few days ago, Deedee and I were supposed to take the girls shopping. I arrived at their home and found the door ajar. I knocked and rang the bell to no avail, so I went in. I started calling for everyone, but no one was around. I walked upstairs and could not believe what I was seeing. The hall and both girls' bedrooms were beyond recognition. Books, toys, dolls, clothing, bedding, furniture were strewn all about. It looked like a six-point-something earthquake had hit. My stomach lurched, and I began screaming for the girls. I was scared. I was begging them, "Please, if you're here, come out." The attic ladder came down, and the two sobbing girls jumped into my arms. I held them tight, saying, "Thank God you're safe. I love you girls so much." When the sobbing subsided, I asked, "What happened here? This place is a mess." Ami said, "Mommy said we were very bad. She got real mad because I hid my diary, and then she had a fit and threw everything all over the place." Ami had red marks on her face from where she'd been slapped. I didn't know what to do. Should I call my mother and let her know I was bringing the girls home with me? Would Deedee accuse me of kidnapping? I asked the girls, "Do you know where Mommy went?" They said, "She ran out of the house and drove away in the car in a big hurry." I couldn't think clearly. I knew Deedee had a temper, but this was unconscionable. While I was trying to decide the best course of action, I told the girls, "Let's start cleaning things up." We were in the midst of putting everything away when Deedee walked in the door, smiling and as sweet as syrup. I said, "Deedee, what happened?" She said, "Oh, the girls made a mess of their rooms." I was afraid to contradict her, but I did mention that Ami was bruised. She said, "Oh, Ami's got a mean temper. She's always fighting with the kids."

Deedee

November 30, 1981

That bitch has got to stay out of my business. Those girls messed up that room. I might have thrown a few things. I was mad at Amiala. If she let anyone read that diary, it would look bad for us. It's all a pack of lies. I was trying to find it because I can't stand not knowing what she's making up about me. And Amiala does have a very mean temper. She badmouths everybody but me because she knows I'll slap the shit out of her.

Leslie

December 19, 1981

Grandad Haines died today. It's so hard for me to grasp that a vital human being no longer exists. He was a gentle, kind man. My heart aches for my grandmother. She and my grandfather eloped when they were in high school, but they returned to their respective homes, finishing school before they told everyone they'd gotten married. My grandmother didn't become pregnant with my mother until a few years after graduating from high school, so it wasn't that they had to get married. My grandparents were deeply in love. They were seldom separated. When my grandmother went to help my mother after my birth, my grandfather wrote long letters expressing how much he missed Grandma. Her pain must be unbearable.

December 20, 1981

I just spoke to my grandmother. She sounds so weak and sad. I told her I love her. If you remember, she taught me about makeup and money. I told her how valuable that has been in my life. I no longer have my little black bankbook, but I have a nice savings and retirement plan. And I'm truly nuts about makeup and skin-care products.

Grandfather Goodman called me with tears in his voice. He'd just heard about Grandad Haines's death. Grandfather Goodman truly respected Grandad Haines and regaled me with stories. He admired Grandad Haines for his courage. When Grandad Haines was in his early fifties, he left a secure job at the gas company to open up a beer-distributing business, and he and Grandma relocated from Michigan to Wisconsin. Grandma Haines was a fashionista and a petite little thing, but she threw cases of beer around like they were foam rubber. As it turned out, they were quite successful with that business.

December 23, 1981

I went into Bullock's today to get some skin-care products. While I was waiting to be helped, the woman ahead of me said she was purchasing cologne as a holiday gift for her brother and couldn't decide which scent he might like. I was suddenly overwhelmed with sorrow. I will never again buy gifts for my brother. We will never again spend holidays together. We will never again laugh, and joke, and tease. I burst into tears and fled the store.

Chapter Twelve

If I Had a Hammer . . .

Deedee

January 1, 1982

Mom had to go back to Wisconsin because Grandad Haines died. That kind of put a damper on our Christmas. Without Mom there aren't many gifts and not many cookies either. Grandma Haines used to bake cookies and send them to us, and Mom picked up that habit from Grandma. Now Rachael is the baker. I miss the Christmas cookies, but it's good not to have them because I won't have to stick my finger down my throat so much. Sometimes throwing up gives me a sore throat. Grandma Haines started a bank savings account for Leslie when she was little. She started one for me too, but I don't know what happened to it. Liam had $25,000 in his when he died, enough to buy a house and go to law school. I don't know what happened to it, but I think it got split between Mom and Dad.

Leslie is so stupid. She's celebrating Hanukkah. Mick started drinking more and disappearing for many days. He stays in a hotel near the bar he likes to drink at. We had to move into a smaller condo because Mick's sales have been down because he loses so much time from work. I'm really mad at him. I have to get mad at him to get his attention. I didn't marry him to live like this. I'm very pretty. I can get another husband very easily. In fact, a very rich lawyer that Mom works with told Mom to let him know if something happens to my marriage because he fell in love with me at first sight. And another thing, an eighteen-year-old girl called the other day and claims Mick is her father. Mick listened to what she had to say and said it was possible. He invited her to come to our house. I was very upset, but I took one look at that girl and knew she was Mick's kid. She looks like Meliza with dark hair. I could kill him. And now Meliza is acting up because she thought she was Daddy's little girl. Damn Mick anyway.

Leslie

January 4, 1982

A new year! It did not get off to a very good start. We were down at Mom's and went to a new restaurant in the Valley with Cassie, Derek, Deedee, and Mick. The next day Deedee was furious with me because she thought she and Mick had paid too much for dinner. I'd paid no attention to who paid what, as Jacob took care of the bill, so I was hurt and angry about her getting mad at me. I asked, "Why didn't you say something at dinner last night? Waiting till today and yelling at me doesn't help." I decided the best course of action, however, was to apologize and give her some money in return for her over paying, but when I did, she screamed, "Fuck off! You're a selfish bitch!"

As if that wasn't enough, Mother was angry at me because we went to the Rose Bowl game rather than picking her up at the airport.

Deedee

January 6, 1982

I was so mad about that fucking New Year's Eve dinner. I nearly tore the tablecloth off the table. We didn't have lobster and shit. We can't afford that, but we paid for everyone else. Mick is such a fucking wimp. He should have said something. But no. He doesn't want to look like he can't afford to eat and drink with the best of them. I should have had that fucking lobster.

Leslie

February 1, 1982

I've returned to court reporting college after a long and lovely time off. I'm going to one in the city because the one in Oakland closed down. It's a schlep to the city, but I'm doing extremely well with my speed and hope to qualify to take the state exams this year.

Jacob has been using recreational drugs for years, but I've noticed a big increase in his use of cocaine. I'm finding three or four cocaine vials every day, and they cost $100 each. Where is the money coming from? I'm struggling to keep groceries in the house. I'm also finding empty liquor bottles under the furniture because Jacob is drinking alcohol to come down from the cocaine. I'm extremely resentful about the money he's spending on the coke. I would rather use that money to buy property, pay for my doctorate degree, or send Rachael to college. I confronted Jacob about where the money was coming from, but he got angry and said, "Don't worry about it. The business pays for it. It's the cost of doing business."

Rachael is preparing for her bat mitzvah in the spring, and I have decided to do an adult bat mitzvah with twelve other women from our synagogue. There's a lot to study and a ton of memorization. I meet with the other women two nights a week.

April 2, 1982

Bernie's husband, Jake, has been having an affair with another teacher for seven years! I was shocked when Bernie phoned me. She is devastated. I'm devastated. I thought they had the perfect marriage. Jake the Jerk is moving in with the teacher.

June 2, 1982

Rachael had her bat mitzvah, and she did an amazing job. She led the Shema and read from the Torah and translated. I am so proud of her. I also had my bat mitzvah. It was an incredible experience and one that I am very grateful that I committed to do. We did the Friday night and Saturday morning services. We had a huge kiddush following Saturday services, and Saturday night we all went with our husbands to dinner and dancing at Gallagher's at Jack London Square.

Deedee

June 14, 1982

That stupid bitch had a bat mitzvah. How fucking embarrassing! Mom and I weren't invited. Leslie was afraid we'd embarrass her by saying she's not a Jew. Rachael had a bat mitzvah too. I bet they got a lot of money. With Leslie it's all about money.

Leslie

July 12, 1982

Rachael and I are in Ashland. We've been spending some of the summers here since our first visit. We love the theater, early-morning runs with the smell of baking breads and pastries, the lovely restaurants with their tantalizing menus, the quaint town with all its adorable shops, the peace and quiet. I needed to put life on hold and have this getaway. Jacob's cocaine and alcohol use has taken over his life. He's not mean or abusive, but he's not participating in our marriage, nor is he participating as a father. I can't carry on a conversation with him, and any suggestion I make he takes as extremely stupid. I've asked him to seek help.

August 20, 1982

Rachael and I returned home after our Ashland trip but turned around again and went down to Mother's. Since we have the summer free, we enjoy going and doing, and there's no better place than Mom's. The girls swim and play all day. I'm working on needlepoint and reading. Mom has taken an interest in cooking, and when we visit, she has someone to cook for. She follows recipes and is a fairly competent chef. She's actually putting on weight, but I wouldn't dare mention it.

September 1, 1982

On the way home to Alameda, Rachael and I spent a few nights in Carmel. Running there is incredible. I was so taken by the beauty and smell of the fresh ocean air that I ran ten miles before I realized how long I'd been out. Rachael put on a puppet show out the window of our room at the inn. She drew a crowd, and everyone was laughing and having a good time.

Deedee

September 15, 1982

How does that bitch do it? Leslie went to Ashland for weeks, Mom's for weeks, Carmel. Jacob must be making good money. I wish Mick would drink less and work more. Now he's sending money to that stupid first daughter of his. That just takes away from me and my girls. Leslie is always hanging out at Mother's for summers and holidays. She goes to Mother's because it's cheap and she gets waited on. She doesn't pay for a fucking thing. I never get any time alone with my mother. I'm an orphan!

Leslie

January 25, 1983

Well, I qualified for the state exam and took it. What a horrific experience. Out of two hundred and some people, only three passed. I am so discouraged, but the owner of the court reporting college told me not to give up. I'm qualified to take the exam next June. He told me a woman who owns her own agency was looking for a reporter and that I could report certain cases without a license. He recommended me, and I was to go for an interview. I was excited but nervous too. Guess what! I was hired! I'm working as a reporter! I love it! It's so much fun!

March 25, 1983

After years of asking Mother to go to therapy with me and work through our issues with the Boone situation, she at last agreed. It was pretty powerful for me because I finally felt like she believed me, that it wasn't just a little misunderstanding but something quite serious. During our session, Mother mentioned that Boone told her he'd left LAPD on a medical discharge due to a motorcycle accident, but Mother found out from Boone's sister that he was discharged on mental issues, so I guess that lent credence to my claim.

A therapist once suggested to me that the attempted rape may have occurred because somewhere deep in his subconscious, Boone knew he was going to die and was living out his fantasies. I think he was just plain crazy.

Deedee

October 22, 1983

Mick didn't celebrate my birthday with me this year. He was gone for days, drunk as usual. Mother wanted to come down here and take me out to dinner, but she just bugs me, talking about how wonderful her Miss Perfect is. God, I get sick of hearing about Leslie. I stayed home by myself. When Mick did show up, he gave me just a real nice birthday present. He lost his job, and we're going to have to move to Sacramento because his buddy has a bar there that Mick can manage. If I had any money at all, I'd divorce the bastard, but I'm stuck. And I can't work. I have to stay home and take care of my girls. Leslie's life gets better and better, and mine gets worse and worse. Maybe I should have listened to Dad and finished school, but I don't think I could have. I don't have the brains God gave me. At least I'm pretty.

Chapter Thirteen

I Am Woman; Hear Me Roar

Leslie

January 1, 1984

Happy New Year! What a frolicking, rollicking holiday season! Mom came up for Thanksgiving, and we had a bunch of friends in for dinner. The next day, we took the ferry into the city for lunch and shopping. The city is so beautiful in all her holiday splendor. It's exhilarating to be there with all the shoppers in their festive outfits and splendid spirits. Macy's windows reminded me of Disneyland, and Neiman-Marcus had a tree going from the ground floor up through the mezzanine. Mom and I sat in the mezzanine dining area and had Bloody Marys with large shrimp tucked along the sides of the glasses. They were delicious!

For Christmas we all went down to Mom's, even Miss Dump and Duck and Mick and the girls. The day after Christmas, all us gals hit the sales at the mall, and you'll never guess what happened! We saw Diane looking through a rack of dresses in Macy's. It's been over ten years since I'd last seen her, just before Dad died, and I wouldn't have recognized her in a million years—she'd put on a ton of weight. But Deedee knew who she was straight away and started after her, mumbling, "I'm going to slap the shit out of that bitch." I was looking for a place to hide when I heard Mother pleading with Deedee to stop. I whipped around and grabbed the back of Deedee's button-down-the-front dress in an attempt to pull her back to us, but I must have pulled a bit too hard because suddenly I was holding the dress, and Deedee was standing just inside the entrance to Macy's, wearing a very sexy bra and matching thong panties! I ran up to her and attempted to drape the dress around her, but she was madder than a wet hen and grabbed it away from me. I thought she was going to kill me right then and there, and that's when I started laughing hysterically. Deedee held the dress up to herself, and turning to walk toward the dressing room, she flipped her head back and said, "I think I'll just go try this on!" There were a number of people who had stopped to gape at us, but Diane wasn't in sight.

Deedee

February 20, 1984

God, I hate Sacramento. What a miserable place. We rented a house, but it's a dump. It's in a trashy neighborhood. Leslie and Mom and Rachael came up here to celebrate Mom's birthday. Leslie brought some casseroles she'd made ahead and some salad stuff and other things to cook here. She said, "I know how you hate to cook." It's true. I think Leslie did that because she knows we don't have any money. She lords it over me that she's got money and I don't. She even brought a birthday cake from Mother's favorite bakery. For once Mick didn't go out drinking and disappear. Amiala and Meliza fought all the time. Even Rachael asked them why they fight so much.

June 4, 1984

God, this place is so fucking hot. We couldn't afford the rental, so we moved out of town into a trailer that Mick's boss owns up here. We don't have to pay rent, so maybe we can save some money and get the fuck out of this hellhole. The plumbing is all screwed up in the trailer. The toilet is broken, so we have to use the woods around us to go to the bathroom. We can't get too much water and we have to use a butane tank, so we do a lot of cooking in the firepit outside. I never thought my life would come to this. I hate Mick. I need to find another man, but I never meet any and I look like hell. I can't even find a decent mirror to put on makeup and my clothes are dirty and ragged, and getting showered is a real problem. When we get a little ahead, Mick says we can get a motel room once a week. Fuck!

Leslie

July 27, 1984

I passed the state exam! I'm an official reporter! I got the letter yesterday, which just happened to be my birthday! What a present! Jacob, Rachael, and I went to Helene's, a fancy restaurant on a rooftop in downtown Oakland, to celebrate. This weekend, I'm taking Rachael to this darling little bed-and-breakfast in Napa to continue celebrating. I'm so elated my feet aren't touching the ground.

Deedee

October 22, 1984

Jacob asked Mick to go into a business with him, and we moved down to San Diego. We're in a house again. A nice house. With plumbing. Mom took my girls miniature-golfing, and Meliza went to the bathroom behind a tree at the golf course. Mother was beside herself. Mick hasn't been drinking so much. I hope he can do good in this business.

Leslie

November 18, 1984

I love being a reporter! I worked the federal court for a few weeks, but decided to take a chance on freelancing with depositions. My first depo was at a law firm in their conference room overlooking San Francisco Bay. Sitting there, taking down testimony, I thought, "I'm getting paid for this!" I'm making so much money! I opened a retirement account to be managed by my cousin Dani, who's a financial advisor. I'm in the process of having the garage converted into a family room and office. It's an attached garage with access through the kitchen, so it will be quite convenient.

Jacob finally realized he has a problem and is at a rehab center in St. Louis, along with his friend Richard. I'm glad that they are there together, supporting each other through recovery.

It was a real mitzvah that he asked Mick to go into business with him. He really likes Mick and has a lot of confidence in him.

Chapter Fourteen

Here We Go Again, But Love is Here to Stay

Deedee

January 3, 1985

Mick is working a lot, and he's not drinking so much. This is good, but he wants me to help him at the office and I don't want to. It sounds boring. I have to keep an eye on my girls. Amiala's sixteen and there's no telling what kind of trouble she could get into. Meliza is nine and I have to watch her every minute. She's a troublemaker and a liar.

Leslie

March 3, 1985

Jacob's rehab program is six months, so he has a few more months to go. He's says they're doing very well, and that makes me happy.

The garage conversion is fabulous. It makes the house into a tri-level. Rachael loves having the family room, and I love my office. I'm working with a consultant who is helping me decorate and purchase new furniture.

It's rather sad, but without Jacob's issues looming over our lives, Rachael and I have begun to settle into a quiet, peaceful existence. We go for runs, work out at the club, shop at the farmers' market. We enjoy cooking together and sitting by the fireplace, reading our books. Life is good, and I'm so very grateful.

July 12, 1985

Jacob has been home for two months. He's going to AA meetings as a follow-up to rehab, so our lives now revolve around AA meetings. Somehow, they always happen at dinnertime, so we're either eating very early or very late. Jacob is more at peace, though, and easier to be with. He's going to Friday night services with us, and he's on the board of directors for the synagogue.

Deedee

October 22, 1985

For my thirty-fourth birthday Mick left me! Just like that he walked out! The bastard was having an affair and wants a divorce so he can marry the bitch. He wants custody of Meliza, and Meliza is constantly whining, "Please let me go live with Dad," but I said no. As long as I have Meliza, he has to help with support. I've never had a job except that short time at the old folks' home in Santa Monica. I don't know what I'm going to do. Mom said, "I'll call the attorney who fell in love with you at first sight and ask him for a recommendation for a good divorce attorney." I found Amiala smoking dope, and I know she's using other drugs. So I said, "You need to go live with your dad. Since he gives you the shit, let him put up with it." I found her diary. I had to break it open because it was locked. I can't believe the lies she tells about me. I was so mad I tore the damn thing up and threw it in the trash, and I said, "Amiala, I am done with you. I will never speak to you again." Between her and Mick I'm a basket case. I'm drinking too many martinis and I'm crying! I never cry. Mom said, "There's no sense in crying, just buck up and get over it." She's right.

October 24, 1985

Johnson, Mom's attorney friend, called me yesterday afternoon right after hanging up from speaking to Mom. He said, "I have a friend who is going to handle your divorce, and I'll pick you up at five for dinner." And just like that he hung up. Then the doorbell rang and a deliveryman was standing there with a dozen red roses. Johnson picked me up and drove to the airport. I thought he was taking me to a restaurant there, but we flew in his private jet to San Francisco and had dinner at the Fisherman's Wharf. Now I'm the princess. We got back to my apartment so late I suggested he stay over. Johnson is not handsome or sexy, but I could really get used to living this life.

November 18, 1985

I always knew I was pretty and could hook a rich man. Johnson asked me to marry him, and I moved into his house. It's a beautiful place in the heart of Beverly Hills. He has a dozen red roses sent to me every week. My engagement ring is a huge six-carat diamond. I have unlimited use of credit cards for shopping. He bought me a brand-new Porsche. The other day Leslie told me, "Since you never had a proper wedding, I think you should go all out on this one." So I am. We're having showers and getting beautiful gifts. The attorney Johnson got me is getting me a quick divorce, so we're having a December wedding and getting married at the Jewish temple in Hollywood. I'm finally the princess.

December 16, 1985

God! A week before the wedding, and Amiala tells mother that her dad raped her. Of course, Mom and I don't believe a word she says. She's so much drama. She just wants attention. She moved in with her boyfriend's family. I wonder how long that will last. The boyfriend's parents are members of some Christian religious group. No smoking, no drinking, no drugs, no sex. They have Bible study every night. I give it a week. I'm glad I'm not speaking to her so I don't have to get involved with her temper tantrums. Now that Meliza has seen Johnson's house, she wants to move in with us. For sure I don't need the child support from Mick, but it will put him in his place to know she picked me instead of him, so I told her maybe after the wedding. I'm going to let Leslie be my matron of honor. Mother said, "You have to have your sister be your matron of honor and the girls be your bridesmaids. You don't have any girlfriends." She's right. I've put all my attention into my marriages. And other women are afraid of me because I'm so beautiful.

Leslie

January 1, 1986

What a wonderful holiday season! Deedee got married! It was a beautiful wedding, enchanting really. Deedee wore a designer wedding dress that was white and flouncy. I wore an emerald-green crepe maid of honor dress. Yes, Deedee asked me to be her maid of honor! Rachael, Ami, and Mel were bridesmaids and wore gold crepe dresses. There were over five hundred people in attendance. Johnson insisted that Deedee convert to Judaism, and she did, after all her nasty comments to me about being Jewish. The conversion took place in about a week. Deedee didn't study or even go to a mikvah. It seems that Johnson can make anything happen. Deedee is the happiest I've ever seen her, though. She glows!

Deedee was right, Ami didn't last a week staying with her religious boyfriend's family. She moved back in with her dad.

April 4, 1986

Ami's father shot himself to death! I can't believe it. His mother and now him. Roy Senior must be going crazy. Poor Ami found her dad. In a zombie sort of manner, she recounted the situation: "When I walked into the apartment, I tossed my purse on the kitchen counter and grabbed a soda out of the fridge. I made a sandwich to take to my room. I thought Dad was out. When I went into my room, I smelled a funny odor and followed it down the hall to Dad's room. I couldn't believe what I was seeing—blood and guts all over the bed and walls. Half of Dad's head was gone. I threw the sandwich down like it bit me. I screamed and screamed and threw up all over the place as I ran through the apartment to the front door. People had come out of their apartments. I couldn't stop screaming. Someone wrapped me in a blanket, gave me a glass of water, and sat me down on the steps. Sirens were approaching. An officer asked me what happened. I opened my mouth, but no words came out. Instead, I threw up again."

Somehow, they managed to get Mother's number and call her. She collected Ami and took her home with her. I can't even imagine innocently walking in and finding such a scene. I haven't seen Ami cry, and she hasn't said much about it, other than he was a loser. That's what Deedee always calls Roy, a loser.

June 4, 1986

Deedee and Johnson bought a new house. Deedee said the other one was too small. However, she confided in me, "I signed a prenup that would leave me homeless should we get a divorce. I heard that if we purchase various properties and move a few times, my position might be stronger."

Mick's girlfriend, Bonnie, is a lovely woman from Sausalito. She and Mel get along quite well, but Mel wants to move in with Deedee and Johnson because they live in Beverly Hills with many movie stars as neighbors.

August 5, 1986

Ami moved in with my mother. She told Rachael that she'd gotten pregnant and had had an abortion. So much for the "no sex" in boyfriend's religion. I'd hoped that living with Mother would give Ami some stability, but the two of them fight horribly. Ami has a temper, like her mom. She's also pretty controlling and doesn't appreciate Grandma's advice. I have to admit, the advice, while well intended, can be quite wearing. Rachael said she's glad we live in Alameda and don't have to be involved with the trauma/drama. I concur!

Deedee

October 22, 1986

Today is my birthday, and I'm the princess. Johnson gave me a palomino horse. We bought a ranch. Meliza is living with us, and she's a pain in the ass. She told me that Mom and Amiala fight all the time. I'm glad I'm not speaking to them. I told Mother not to take Amiala in. Amiala has a mean temper.

Chapter Fifteen

Everyday People

Leslie

July 10, 1987

I haven't written in my journal for almost a year. Time just seems to fly by! I get so engaged with living, it's difficult to find time to write, but then I miss writing and come back to it. Since my life is so busy, I'm going to start carrying my journal with me so that when I have a few minutes here and there, I can write.

Rachael and I went down to Mom's for the July Fourth weekend. Jacob was supposed to come with us, but he got angry about one thing or another, I'm never really sure what, and decided not to come along. Which, truth be told, is somewhat of a relief. Rachael and I got up early on the Fourth and went for a run, and then I sat in a float in the pool and read. It was so quiet and peaceful with the warm sun beating down and just the slight sound of the water on my float. I nearly fell asleep in the pool. Later we went to Johnson and Deedee's for a barbecue. If it's even possible, Deedee is a worse cook than Mom used to be, maybe because she's so obsessed with remaining thin. She keeps her Barbie doll on display as a reminder of what she wants to look like.

Mel is at odds with Deedee and Johnson, so she came back to stay with us until we return to Mom's in a couple of weeks. It's two-thirty in the morning. I'm so tired from the long hours I've been working, but I love the money. I've been finishing work on my transcripts at about one in the morning, and Mel and I have been going for walks at that hour. Mel is a voracious reader and has interesting insights on what she's reading, so our walks are quite pleasantly filled with literary commentary. The fresh air and the ocean smells are an intoxicating addition.

I often wonder what my life would have been like if Liam had had a family. What would his wife and children have been like? Whoever you might have been, I miss you!

July 29, 1987

We arrived at Mom's on the twenty-third. I picked up my new Volvo before we left, and I absolutely love it. There is nothing quite like the smell of a new car.

Mom had a surprise birthday party for me. I was floating around in the pool when about thirty friends jumped out the door and yelled, "Surprise!" The big bombshell, though, was that Deedee and Ami began speaking again after two years of silence. That came out of nowhere.

Deedee

August 3, 1987

It feels so good to be better than Leslie. Mother still goes on about how wonderful Leslie is. That's okay because I know I'm better. I have a huge ranch, a dozen horses, designer clothes, four expensive cars. I had a facelift and breast implants. I work out four hours every day. I drink martinis and eat salads. I don't like food. I don't need it. The important thing is staying thin and looking beautiful. Johnson loves the way I look. When I walk into a room, people stop and stare. I've learned to walk like a model on a runway, and I know I'm a showstopper.

Leslie

September 18, 1987

Jacob and I separated again. I'm sad and disappointed because I do love him, but even though he's not snorting cocaine or drinking alcohol, he's still so depressed and angry it's impossible to live with him. At this time neither of us want a divorce; it's too much to think about.

Rachael is going to a local junior college and will go on to one of the universities when she finishes next year. I'm already dreading not having my baby at home with me. I hope she doesn't go too far away.

The house is beautiful with all the new furniture, paint, and rugs. It should be in *Cottage Journal*.

Mom came to Ashland with us this summer and loved it as much as we do. The hotel was going downhill, so we found a lovely bed-and-breakfast, the Queen Anne. It's owned by a retired professor and his wife.

Chapter Sixteen

There Were Never Such Devoted Sisters!

Deedee

January 2, 1988

Johnson and I spent Christmas in New York. We flew in our own private jet. No lines. No nasty crowds. We saw a play. I fell asleep. Plays are so boring, but it's important to be seen. We went for a ride in Central Park, and I was nice and warm because Johnson bought me a mink coat!

Leslie

February 8, 1988

I bought a piano! Rachael and I are taking lessons! I love the feel of the keys and learning to read the music. I'm sitting by the fireplace, writing. I feel so fortunate to have this amazing home. While it's just a two-bedroom cottage, only Rachael and I live here. In impoverished countries, five or six families would live in a house this size. I count my blessings!

May 1, 1988

Mel ran away from Deedee and Johnson's and is living on the streets with an eighteen-year-old boy. She is only thirteen years old! She's a child. Mick called me. He is beside himself with worry. He can't get any information out of Deedee, so I immediately called her and asked, "What the heck is going on?" She said, "You need to mind your own business. Johnson has this under control." Mel isn't getting along with Deedee and Johnson and wants to live with Mick, but Deedee will not relent. The issue is further complicated by the fact that Johnson has a record for consorting with a minor. Mick is really upset about that, and I don't blame him.

May 8, 1988

The police picked up Mel and the boy. It's been arranged that I will have temporary custody of Mel because she is up in the Bunnysville area, just north of us. I've made arrangements for her to fly into San Francisco, where I will meet her as she gets off the plane. Charges have been filed against the boy, as he's an adult harboring a minor.

May 9, 1988

I met Mel at the airport this afternoon. When I saw her, I cried. It wasn't the thing to do, but the tears just came. She was black from head to foot. Her clothes were filthy and hanging on her. She'd dyed her beautiful blonde hair black. Her skin and fingernails were crusted with dirt. I hugged her close to me and tried to stop crying. She didn't cry and said very little. I asked no questions. I took her hand and led her out of the airport.

Deedee

May 10, 1988

I am so mad I could kill Leslie! Johnson is furious! He went out in the field and shot at cans. I threw things around Meliza's room and went shopping. Johnson had things under control, but Leslie had to butt in. Goddamn her! She fucked up Johnson's plan to get full custody of Meliza. I want to call Leslie, but Johnson said, "No! Leslie could be recording the conversation, and you wouldn't be able to control your temper." Fuck!

Leslie

May 13, 1988

It's been a three-day whirlwind! Mel had to take three showers to get clean. We threw out the clothes she was wearing, and she borrowed some of Rachael's. We went into the city and shopped for new clothes, and we had lunch at the Top of the Mark. That seemed to cheer her up. Since the length of time she's to be here is as yet undetermined, I got her enrolled in school. She's in a program for troubled teens, led by a man who is truly gifted at helping kids make sense of their lives and their families. Mel adores him and seems to be settling in. She loves playing the piano and, quite to my surprise, can play anything if she just hears it once.

May 20, 1988

This is unbelievable! Today Mel asked me if Flint, the boy she was living with on the streets, could spend a few nights with us. "Absolutely not!" was my reaction. I could just picture this kid moving in and taking over my house. My mind leaped to him doing drugs and smoking grass in my home, Mel dropping out of school, becoming pregnant, working at a Dairy Queen. I had to think fast. I explained, "Flint staying here would be a violation of his probation, not to mention that both your mother and father would kill me. It would be against the law for me to allow him to stay here. There are very strict rules of conduct that we have to abide by." She argued her case for a while but finally petered out, electing to watch TV. I decided it probably wasn't a good time to ask about her homework.

May 22, 1988

I woke up this morning to find Mel gone. I was so scared. She had to have taken off with Flint. I immediately called the police. Since Flint is on probation, they will be picked up. I called Mick and told him what happened. I felt sick; I knew I'd let him down. He said, "Don't blame yourself, Leslie. It was inevitable."

It was only a matter of hours before Mel and Flint were picked up. I was asked if I wanted to press charges against Flint, and I said yes. He won't get off with probation this time; he'll serve a jail sentence. Deedee won't take my calls. I called Mick, who'd spoken to the judge. Mel will now be a temporary ward of the court, but Mick was able to get her into an extremely expensive and exclusive girls' school. The girls are not allowed off campus unless they are signed out to a legal guardian. The curriculum at the school is the highest of any educational institution in Southern California. Mel is one of the most intelligent children I have ever met. I truly hope she will do well there.

Deedee

May 24, 1988

Meliza wouldn't stay at Leslie's either. That proves it's not my fault. The girl is just an impossible little liar. I agreed to put her in the private school. She needs some discipline. What she really needs is a good smacking!

Leslie

August 23, 1988

Mick has filed for full custody of Mel, and that is what Mel wants as well. I feel so bad for Deedee; she must really be hurting. But she says some of the craziest things. She called last night at eleven-thirty. She was crying and in a very bad state. She said, "It's different with Meliza than with Amiala. I never loved Amiala, but I really love Meliza."

114

Oh, Dad, I wish you were here to help Deedee. She needs to know that you loved her. Couldn't you send her some sort of a message?

I felt like a traitor when I talked to Deedee, knowing that I've been speaking to Mick and not mentioning that to her. I love my sister, but in my heart, I know that Mel is better off with Mick right now. Mel is smart and deserves an opportunity to thrive. She also appears to have the resilience to overcome her misplaced mothering. I'm anxious to see what happens at the next court hearing.

Deedee

September 23, 1988

Fuck! The judge ordered counseling! It sounds just like Leslie and her fucking therapy. Mother even thinks it's a good idea. It pisses me off that everyone thinks I'm a shitty mother. It isn't my fault. Both my girls had loser fathers. And they were problem kids from the time they were born. Leslie got the easy kid. I'm not talking about my family's problems with a stranger. That's for damn sure. Fuck it!

Leslie

October 4, 1988

Mick wants me to testify that Deedee is an unfit mother. I told him I could not possibly do that. No matter how horrible a mother she is, she is still my sister. He said he has to protect Mel and keep her from running away again. He begged me. I've always known that Deedee was an abusive and neglectful mother. She has very real anger issues that she takes out on her daughters. Maybe it's time I took a stand.

October 10, 1988

Well, I spoke to the psychologist working with Mel and the court, making a decision as to who shall have custody of Mel. I liked the psychologist very much and felt that he was genuinely concerned for Mel. Deedee and Johnson have claimed that Mel is a liar, which just hurts me to the core. Mel does not lie.

The questioning went something like this:

Psychologist: "Has your sister ever physically abused her children?"

Me: "Yes, she's hit them in angry fits of temper. They've had bruises. She's torn their bedrooms apart so badly that it looked like an earthquake hit. She's yelled at them, using abusive language, such things as, 'You're a fucking liar,' 'You don't have the brains God gave you,' 'How did I get such stupid girls,' 'You're fat,' 'I'm going to slap the shit out of you.'"

The dam broke. I began crying. The questioning went on.

Psychologist: "Do you think your sister is an unfit mother?"

Me: "Yes."

I felt dirty. I'd betrayed my sister. But she is an irresponsible and inattentive mother. At thirteen, Mel was living on the streets. At nineteen, Ami has a history of drugs, she's had several abortions, and she claims her father raped her. She and my mother fought bitterly, so now she's moved in with another boyfriend.

I felt like one side of me was cheering today when the psychologist gave his report in favor of Mel, but the other side of me was grieving for Deedee. I know Deedee feels like I betrayed her. I did, and I'm sure she hates me right now. My heart aches for her, and I pray that she'll get into therapy. I hope I will see the day we can all be together again. I love my sister very much. This has really cost me.

Jacob and Rachael have been so supportive of me through this situation. After I testified, I was sobbing. Rachael hugged me and let me cry on her shoulder.

Deedee

October 22, 1988

For my birthday this year that fucking bitch Leslie testified that I'm an unfit mother. Johnson is furious. He could kill her, so could I. My sister betrayed me. I'll never forgive her. She called me. She told me how sorry she is and what a difficult thing it was for her to do. She did it for Meliza and hoped I could understand and could we do some therapy. I said, "Fuck off. I'll see you in court." Johnson is filing a lawsuit against her. Mother said, "Leslie butted into your business. She shouldn't have done that, but she was doing what she believed was the right thing to do because she loves Meliza." I yelled, "She's my daughter. You all need to stay the fuck out of my business. If you're going to side with Leslie, I'll never speak to you again." Amiala moved back in with Mother, so I'm not speaking to Amiala either. I hate them all! Mick has full custody of Meliza, and my visits must be supervised. Fuck! Why does everything always happen to me? They can't tell me I can only have supervised visits with my daughter. She's mine. She belongs to me. I was the one that pushed that baby out of my body. Nobody can tell me what to do. Fuckers!

Leslie

November 10, 1988

Well, Election Day is finally over, and Bush will be our new president, although Jacob and Rachael and I voted for Dukakis.

I worked so hard this week that I am taking three days off. Rachael and I picked up Mel at the airport tonight, then we met Jacob for sushi, and Rachael and Mel and I went to see Whoopi Goldberg's new movie.

December 31, 1988

We had a lovely holiday season, although Mother and I had a terrible argument yesterday. I get so angry and frustrated. She still thinks Mel is a liar and a brat, and she says she will never understand why I butted in. I asked her to see my therapist with me, but she refused, stating, "Once was enough." I've admitted that Deedee is not a good mother. Now I have to admit that my mother is not a good mother. She has always thwarted and balked at my enthusiasm and efforts for joy in my life, for learning, loving, and trusting. She hates that I go to therapy. She says I need to forget the past, that Liam reenlisted four times, it's his fault he died, he didn't have to be there; that Dad wanted to die and was finally successful; that I married an asshole, so why was I surprised when he had an affair? Even though she knows that Boone had mental health issues, she still claims that his attempt to rape me was just a little misunderstanding. It's not like she has to take sides on this Miss Dump and Duck issue; I just wish she would understand me. I wish she would accept me for who I am, rather than so desperately wanting me be like her.

Chapter Seventeen

Shake, Rattle, and Roll

Leslie

January 1, 1989

I started out the year with a ten-mile run and then went for a walk with Mother. We have so many contradictions in our lives, and our relationship waxes and wanes, but she is my mother. I love her, and I know she loves me.

Deedee

February 1, 1989

I was so upset about the custody issue that Johnson let me spend three weeks at our condo in Honolulu. I have a beautiful tan. I got facials, massages, manicures, and pedicures. I shopped till I dropped right into a bar for a martini. Johnson flew over for Christmas. He gave me boxes and boxes of sexy lingerie from Victoria's Secret.

Leslie

February 14, 1989

Today is Valentine's Day, and it also marks the anniversary of my father's death seventeen years ago. I miss my dad and think about him a lot. He was smart and had an incredible career. He broke the ground for all the uses of helicopters today. I wish he had known his worth.

Jacob doesn't realize his worth either. Did I marry my dad? Jacob has become an AA sponsor and is helping so many people deal with alcoholism, yet he says, "I'm such a failure." I tell him, "No, you're not! You're touching so many

119

lives. If you help one person overcome their addiction, it has a snowball effect, helping their families and friends." I asked him to come over for dinner and was reminded of how peaceful it is without him here. Depression drives his life.

I've been working hard and keeping busy, attending book groups and going to the theater, so I'm only getting three or four hours of sleep a night. I must stop because I'm feeling very run down.

Mel is coming up for the weekend.

February 22, 1989

I was asked to report a big ongoing case in Milwaukee. I'm staying with Uncle Les and Aunt Etta. Uncle Les and I get up early and go for a run, clean up, and I drive to work with him. The law firm I'm working for is right across the street from his law office, so after work I walk over there and we drive home together. I brought wool suits because the weather here is brutal, but the offices are kept so warm that I'm quite literally dripping in sweat. When I walked out of the building tonight, I was so hot that I didn't put on my coat, and the wind hitting me felt like flames lapping at my body.

Deedee

May 5, 1989

Cinco de Mayo! We had a big barbecue. Lots of our neighbors from Beverly Hills came. We had it catered and we hired guitar players, singers, and dancers. I'm exhausted! I'm sitting in the hot tub with a martini and enjoying our beautiful view. I've been too busy to spend time with Meliza. I know she's gone up to Leslie's with Mother several times. The little liar started this mess and Leslie finished it. Fuck 'em!

Leslie

June 2, 1989

Even though Jacob and I are not living together, as always through the years and our separations, we want to maintain a healthy relationship and some sort of family unity for Rachael. I hated that my parents fought, sued each other, and demanded that Liam and I choose sides. I will never be like that. I try to be sure that Jacob spends at least one evening a week with us. Last night he came for dinner, and he and I watched *Dear America: Letters Home from Vietnam*. It touched my heart about the uselessness of war; however, I can't bear to think that my brother died for nothing. He believed in what he was doing. Rachael refused to watch the movie, but then this is the kid who wouldn't watch *Bambi*!

June 16, 1989

It's Friday. Mom came up on Wednesday and is staying for a week. Yesterday she slipped and told Rachael that Johnson and Miss Dump and Duck had purchased a larger ranch property and are moving to Canyon Country. My feelings were hurt that she never said anything to me about it, but then I guess she has to play the game. I just wish she wouldn't. Am I asking my mother to choose sides? No. I would never ask anyone to choose sides. But she has. She chose Deedee. She thinks I'm the bad one for betraying my sister. I want her to know and acknowledge that I made the best decision I could with the information I had at the time. That's all anyone can do, and I shouldn't be punished for it. It's sad that Deedee won't speak to me, especially with all our losses. She must know somewhere in her heart that she's a horrible mother. I'd like her to be able to confront me with her hurt and anger.

Mel's been doing well in school. She's living on campus and spending the weekends with Mick. She went to stay with Deedee today. I didn't get to talk to her before she left. I hope she'll be all right, not just with this visit but with her life.

121

She's so smart, and so beautiful, and she has so much potential.

June 21, 1989

Twenty years ago today, I had a beautiful baby girl! It's as if I snapped my fingers and the years disappeared. She's always been so kind and considerate, always coming from her heart. She's full of love and compassion. When she was a little girl, I took her to the Oaks Mall to go shopping. She'd been incredibly patient with me. We saw a big table full of stuffed animals, which I knew she loved, so I told her to pick out one she'd like to adopt and take home. She looked around the table and picked out a yellow stuffed duck that was torn. When I pointed out the tear, she said that was why she picked it, because it was torn and nobody else would take it. We took the stuffed duck home and put a bandage on it. Later we performed surgery. She still has that yellow stuffed duck today.

June 24, 1989

Jacob, Rachael, and I, and a friend of Rachael's who shares her birthday, are spending the weekend at the Highlands Inn near Carmel to celebrate their birthdays. This is an incredibly beautiful place with astonishing views. This morning we went for a run down to Point Lobos Park. I was completely enchanted with the fresh smell of the woods and the ocean air. We went horseback riding. I wanted to reach up and touch the leaves and branches.

Since I saw the movie *Letters Home from Vietnam*, I've been thinking about how Liam died so young and so full of life. I've felt that I've had to live twice as hard and enjoy life twice as much for both of us. When I look out and see this beautiful view, it almost hurts. I'm overwhelmed with the beauty. I'm seeing it for two people because he's always with me.

Deedee

July 5, 1989

We had a big wingding at the ranch for the Fourth. Everyone was so impressed with me and my ranch. It makes me feel good to know that people are jealous of my beauty and wealth. Meliza came to visit and that didn't work out. She sucked me in with, "I know a secret. Do you want to know what it is?" Of course! She blurted out, "Johnson is a child molester, and Daddy doesn't want me to stay here." I said, "Where did you hear that fucking lie?" She said her dad or maybe Leslie or Grandma. Fuck!

Leslie

July 15, 1989

Mom, Jacob, Rachael, and I are in Ashland at the Queen Anne bed-and-breakfast. At the moment, Mom and I are enjoying manhattans in the gazebo; Mom is reading and I am writing. We're seeing enlightening new theater productions, and Mom is trying foods she's never heard of at fabulous local restaurants. She has her limits, though, like sushi. She's also put on a few more pounds and hasn't said a word about it. Rachael and I run in Lithia Park in the mornings, soaking in the rich smells of wet earth and the sounds of the water tumbling down the rocks. Then we go shopping with Mom at all the darling boutiques and enjoy being pampered at the spa. It's a wonderfully relaxing vacation.

August 15, 1989

Soon after returning from Ashland, Mom, Rachael, and I flew to Caledonia to spend some time with Uncle Les and Aunt Etta. I've taken my manhattan out on the patio to write; everyone else is inside with their manhattans and gabbing away. We have shopped our pocketbooks into oblivion! My cousin Lana knows every shop, boutique, and otherwise for miles around. We went to a baseball game at the beautiful Milwaukee County Stadium and ate bratwurst instead of the traditional hot dogs. Uncle Les, Rachael, and I run together every morning, laughing at ourselves and trading outrageous running stories.

I'm being called in to play poker. More later.

September 17, 1989

Mother called from West Palm Beach, where she's visiting her aunt. She was supposed to stay for a month but said she has had some vaginal bleeding and thinks she should come home and see her doctor. I concurred.

Work was slow this week, so I had some breathing space, so to speak, time to think about what I want, where I'm going. I'm not sure that I will go back to pursuing my doctorate degree. I love reporting. It's different every day. It's challenging and exciting. I have money in the bank, a new car, furniture. I love my home. It's the foundation for my life, the base from which I go out into the world. It's a setting for family and friends to gather and make memories. It's my safe place.

I want to be a writer, and I never write. I haven't written an article for publication since Dad died and Jacob had his affair. I have every excuse there is; there are always so many other things to do. I love journaling, so maybe it's time I moved writing up on the list of priorities.

Deedee

September 18, 1989

Mother spends all her time with Leslie. I haven't seen her once this summer. I told her that she's my mother too and I'd like to spend time with her. She said, "Leslie includes me in everything she's doing, and we always have so much fun. It's hard on me with you and Leslie not speaking." Fuck it! I'm an orphan!

Leslie

September 23, 1989

Mother called and told me she has cervical, uterine, and vaginal cancers. She's going to have a hysterectomy on Tuesday. Her doctor believes that they've caught the cancer in the very early stage. I know that Mother will be okay. I'm positive. Yet I'm scared. I can't imagine anything happening to my mother, not for many years to come. I've assumed that she would live to be a very old age and be healthy along the way. I love her so much, and I know she knows that.

Jacob, Rachael, and I are in Newport Beach for Mick and Bonnie's wedding reception. It's a beautiful affair. There is a view of the ocean, champagne is flowing, music fills the air, and the dance floor is a maze of cheerful people. Mick and Bonnie are so happy that we came down to be with them for the celebration. It was important for me to be here to support Mel, to show her that her mother and father's divorce and remarriages need not be filled with strife and anger, but can and should be crafted on love, joy, and family unity.

Deedee

September 24, 1989

Fuck! My mother has cancer and it's all Leslie's fault. She has brought so much drama on our family. She's stressed out Mother. That's why she has cancer. Everyone says cancer is caused from stress. Then the bitch goes to Mick's wedding. She's betraying our family. She has no business going to his wedding.

Leslie

September 24, 1989

Mother says that Miss Dump and Duck may speak to me again since she, Mother, is sick. Should I be excited? Grateful? Shall I say, "Thank you, dear sister"? Maybe I don't want to speak to her. I bet that thought never crossed her mind. Is Mom working this to get Deedee and me on a better playing field? Can I forgive Deedee for the devastation she has imparted on all of us? I betrayed Deedee, and I know the pain her inner self suffers from that betrayal and others. It's gut-wrenching, nauseating.

Jacob thinks I envy Deedee for marrying a rich man, being taken care of, and having all that money. I think this is his assumption of what women want. Of course, women live with the Prince Charming Syndrome. However, Deedee has a 24-7 job. I do not. I'm quite happy with my choice and would not trade places. It's been a rough road for me emotionally, and I want to go forward, not backward. It's been eighteen years since ruin fell on my family and I decided to dig myself out of the rubble. I want to continue to grow in understanding myself, my emotions, what makes me do the things I do, feel the way I feel. I've spent some years now, opening up, awakening, and coming into an existence I'm only just beginning to understand. I'm excited about what the future holds for me on this path.

September 28, 1989

Mother's surgery went very, very well. Thank goodness. She won't even need to have radiation. Since Miss Dump and Duck still refuses to speak to me, she has been with Mom in the hospital, and I will be taking Mom home and caring for her until she gets back on her feet. It's eleven at night, and I am really beat. After landing at the Hollywood-Burbank Airport, I went directly to the hospital. Deedee was there, and so was Betsy, our neighbor. I was so thankful that Betsy was there. She was our buffer. I said hello to everyone, and we proceeded to make small talk. I tried to look at Deedee when I spoke but found it too difficult, and I guess she did as well. When Betsy left, so did Deedee.

Deedee

September 29, 1989

Now that mother's surgery is over, I can get back to my real life with Johnson and the horses. I was at the hospital when that betraying bitch arrived yesterday. I left when Betsy did because if I'd been alone with the bitch, I'd have slapped the shit out of her. Johnson would like to kill her for all the trouble she's caused us. I'm glad he wasn't with me yesterday.

Leslie

September 30, 1989

I need to collect my thoughts. I'm scared. I'm sitting in my car in the parking lot of the hospital, afraid to go in because Deedee and Johnson may be there. I believe I almost parked next to their car. Why am I so scared? I'm afraid of confrontation. Johnson and Deedee scare me because they just erupt into violent fits of anger without notice or provocation. They know I'm coming to the hospital today, so why are they here? Maybe they want a confrontation. Johnson boasts about how he likes to put people down and make them squirm. If they're provoking an angry confrontation, it's poor timing because Mother will just get upset. I'm finding it difficult to write because I'm shaking. I can't go in there, shaking and looking scared to death. Maybe I should see whether their car is still there. If it is, what should I do? Go to the mall for a while? Go to the gift shop in the hospital? Perhaps they're prepared to remain the entire evening. Oh well, here I go!

October 1, 1989

Well, they weren't there. I was so relieved. I brought Mom home yesterday. It was quite a busy day. She's doing remarkably well. I thought I'd be here a few weeks, but it will probably be more like a week.

Back to Miss Dump and Duck. Mother said Deedee can't just put the issue aside and pretend it doesn't exist; she needs to deal with it within herself to feel good. I was quite impressed with Mother's insight. In thinking about Mother and the years that have passed, though she hasn't done any therapy, she has grown and changed. I've re-mothered myself through the years I've spent with Rachael. I think Mother's viewing that has changed her as well.

At any rate, back to Deedee again, I must say something that bothers me. Had there not been this incident involving Mel, I have a gut feeling there would have been something else that would have caused Deedee not to speak to me. I almost think it was destined to happen, a catalyst so that those of us involved would work out our various issues. My dad, Grandfather Goodman, Jacob's brother, Deedee, Ami, Mel, and many other people have an attitude that if you cross them or you don't agree with them, they will just cut you out of their lives. Why is that?

October 18, 1989

San Francisco suffered a devastating earthquake yesterday. I was just finishing up a depo at Becks & West at the Embarcadero. We were in a huge conference room on the twenty-eighth floor. There were twelve of us, some attorneys from Texas. We felt the tremor, and the attorney for B & W said, "Oh, we're having a little earthquake for you Texans." The next thing I knew I was under the table with the witness, who happened to be on a breathing machine and was huffing and puffing, his eyes bugging out of his head. I did the best I could to calm him, telling him we have little earthquakes like this all the time. When the tremor seemed to subside, we came out from under the table. People were gathering in the hall. The offices along the windows looked like little boxes that someone had shaken up and turned upside down. Bookcases, books, and files were thrown everywhere. Chairs were tipped over. I was unnerved and realized just how serious this earthquake was. An employee, obviously trained to handle emergency situations, was doing an incredible job. She was calm and explained that we would have to use the stairs to exit the building. My equipment was already packed, so I grabbed it and joined the solemn group going down the stairs, all twenty-eight floors of them, in my three-inch stilettos. Everyone was so orderly and so kind to one another. I thought we would never reach the bottom, though, and I was beginning to get dizzy going round and round, down the hot and stuffy stairwell. My stilettos were slingbacks, and I was having trouble keeping them on because I was sweating so much. I should have been scared, but some sort of calm came over me, and I just moved.

When we got down to the lobby, I realized that I couldn't use the elevator to get to the underground parking, so I trotted down the up ramp three floors to my car. When I reached the floor I'd parked on, I was the only person around, and there was a cacophony of car alarms. It was spooky. It was dark too, but there was a tiny bit of light, so they must have had an emergency generator. I was extremely anxious to get out of there. I jumped in my car and headed to the gate, only to be confronted by the ticket taker. I was surprised that there would be someone checking tickets and collecting money moments after a major earthquake. I found myself asking him, "Do you know whether the Bay Bridge is down?" He didn't know. I felt like an idiot for asking, yet as I approached the ramp for the Bay Bridge, a feeling just came over me that this might not be the best route home. Then I noticed that vehicles were at a standstill on the bridge, and people were getting out of their cars and walking around. I had to make a decision because it was getting more and more difficult to move off the ramp and back onto the freeway. I had my radio on, but there was little to no information. It was too soon. The last thing I wanted was to sit here all night, smashed in between a mass of cars. I turned my steering wheel sharply to the right, bounced over the ramp and onto I-101, heading for the San Mateo-Hayward Bridge, which connects the City of San Mateo to Hayward in the East Bay. People were honking at me like I was crazy. It was a wild decision that I made in a split second, and I began to doubt that I'd done the right thing. But later I was so happy I'd gotten off that ramp and felt so sorry for the others who did not and were stuck there most of the night.

I was the third person to reach the San Mateo-Hayward Bridge. I was immensely lucky that I got out of the city, the building, and the parking as quickly as I did. I was probably among the first to get out. At the bridge, the officers wouldn't let us across until the Port Authority could assess the bridge for damage. Great! Back in the car, I headed for the Dumbarton Bridge, a bit further down the 101. By then, it was dark. People had begun to leave Candlestick Park, so traffic was bumper to bumper, moving about five mph, and I had to go to the bathroom so badly I was in horrible pain and wishing I could jump out of the car and pee on the side of the freeway, like many men were doing. There were no lights anywhere, in the city or on the freeway; it was pitch black. All I could do was follow the string of car lights ahead of me. When I finally exited the freeway to make my way to the Dumbarton Bridge, I discovered that all that traffic was being directed by one officer. I was astounded. It was so dark I was afraid I would lose the taillights of the car ahead of me and go off the bridge, but in no time at all, I'd zoomed across the Dumbarton and was headed for home.

On the Oakland side of the bay, the lights were on, and there was no traffic. Everything looked normal. I was so thankful. I hadn't known what to expect. Rachael had been attending classes at UC Berkeley, and I was sure she would be fine, but would our house be standing? I really didn't think it would fall. I just prayed the plumbing worked. Finally, I pulled up in front of my beautiful home, standing straight and erect. Rachael ran out to greet me. I hugged her really tight and sent up a thank-you to the universe that my world was well.

October 20, 1989

Nobody is returning to work, at least as far as depositions in the legal world are concerned. I'm catching up on transcripts, working out at the club, and keeping Rachael really close. Some people are trapped under a collapsed bypass, the Cypress Freeway, in Oakland. My heart goes out to them. We're glued to our radios, praying they will be safely evacuated.

Deedee

October 22, 1989

Fuck, I'm getting old. I'm thirty-eight today. There was a bad earthquake up north. Too bad Leslie didn't lose her house. It would serve her right. Lying bitch! I went to lunch with Mom, and all she talked about was how glad she was that Leslie and Rachael were safe. I asked her, "What is the point in going to lunch if all you talk about is Leslie? I'm just a fucking orphan!" I paid the bill and left.

Leslie

October 24, 1989

I love this month! The air is crisp, the colors are changing into vibrant hues, Halloween arrives, and the holidays are approaching. I feel a sense of renewal and gratefulness. It's time to make my New Year's resolutions. I know for sure I need to get more sleep, seven to eight hours. I'm going to start taking piano lessons again. I also want to get back to meditating on a more regular basis and be more diligent about writing. I'm signing myself and Rachael up to take a quilting class. I'll continue the opera classes with Claudia.

November 8, 1989

We're settling into post-earthquake mode. The Bay Bridge, of course, is down, but the ferries are running a hyped-up schedule, and it's fun to take them into the city. I get a latte in the morning, and in the evening, I get a glass of wine and enjoy the sights of the beautiful San Francisco Bay. I'm living the life!

Tomorrow I go back on the case I was working on when the earthquake hit. We were supposed to resume on Monday but didn't, so I was there only briefly. It was eerie, being back in that same room.

Chapter Eighteen

The Sounds of Silence

Leslie

January 1, 1990

New Year's Day! Mom and Mel have been here. Mom is beginning to patch up her relationship with Mel after the custody battle. I'm hoping that Mom sees that Mel didn't do anything wrong but was just reacting to the circumstances thrown at her by extremely dysfunctional people. Mel was a pawn in a chess game, a position that children should not be subjected to.

I threw a Hanukkah party in mid-December. I made latkes, and we played games. The house was bursting with the wild laughter of children and adults.

This was the first Christmas we've spent at home in eleven years. I wonder if people think I'm strange for celebrating both Hanukkah and Christmas. My religion is Judaism, but Christmas is a beautiful holiday season. I love the lights, music, decorations, festivities, and holiday spirit. We decorated a tree, read books, cuddled up by the fireplace, played duets on the piano, and watched sappy holiday movies on TV. Since Deedee isn't speaking to me, Mother divided her holiday time between the two of us; otherwise, we'd have been at Mom's and missed this perfect day. I ought to send Deedee a thank-you note!

Deedee

January 3, 1990

Mom was with us for Christmas but went up to Leslie's the next day, so we couldn't shop the sales together. Not that I ever buy anything on sale. The only things that are on sale are the things nobody wants. I hated that Mother had to rush up to Leslie's. Everything is always about Leslie. Since I hate to cook, Mom did most of the cooking at our house. It was a good dinner, but I ate too much and had to stick my finger down my throat, and my throat is sore. Meliza was at Mick's. Amiala did her usual complaining about how I got her gifts all wrong. Nothing makes that girl happy.

Leslie

February 5, 1990

I feel like I can't do anything right. And I'm tired of being blamed for everything. I blame myself, like a lot of kids, for my parents' divorce. Then I blame myself for Liam's death. Grandad Goodman blames me for Dad's death. He said if I'd been speaking to Dad, he wouldn't have killed himself. He forgot that Dad was the one who wasn't speaking to me. Besides, we still don't know the circumstances under which Dad died. What was he doing at the cemetery on Liam's grave in the middle of the night? I suppose it will always remain a mystery. More recently, we have Mom blaming me for Miss Dump and Duck's problems with Mel, and for Deedee not speaking to me. And, of course, Deedee blames me for all her problems. Jacob blames me for not being more supportive of him. When Rachael feels like she can't do anything right, she says I tell her, "Everyone feels that way at times." That's not helping me right now. Rachael says, "At least you keep trying." I'm not sure that's an asset.

March 3, 1990

Rachael moved into the sorority. My heart is aching, and I've been crying my eyes out. The years since her birth have been rolling through my mind: my little newborn baby, my toddler stumbling along the path to walking, preschool pigtail days where every adventure was a new delight, grammar school and high school with their many challenges—math, tennis, friends, boys. I love her so much. It's so hard to comprehend that she won't be living with me anymore. This is a major life change, an ending and a beginning.

At least she's going to UC Berkeley rather than UCLA down in Southern California.

May 2, 1990

This year is speeding by! Our health club started up a racewalking group, so I decided to take a break from running and give racewalking a try. It's a wonderful group of like-minded people who value health and exercise. They've decided they want to do a marathon, so now I'm training to racewalk the Honolulu Marathon on December 9 with Pearl and the others. I love the camaraderie. I did a half-marathon a few weeks ago, and it was a piece of cake.

Rachael is finding it difficult to eat a vegetarian diet at the sorority, so she's begun eating some fish and chicken. With all the lovely restaurants I go to in the city, I've also begun to try some fish dishes. I feel like a kid in a candy store.

June 21, 1990

Today is Rachael's twenty-first birthday! It doesn't seem possible that it's been twenty-one years since I gave birth to that beautiful baby girl. When I would take her to Dad's and be changing her diaper or feeding her, Dad would say that it reminded him of when I was a little girl and played with my baby dolls. He was so happy to be a grandfather. He had very special memories of his grandfather, and he wanted Rachael to have those too. I wish he'd chosen to live to fulfill that desire. Although Rachael doesn't remember Dad and Liam, per se, she has my memories that I've shared with her, plus tons of pictures of them with her when she was little. She has a strong sense of the adventurous man Dad was and the playful, sensitive boy Liam was. Rachael once mentioned something about Uncle Liam to Ami, and Ami didn't know whom Rachael was talking about. The next time the three girls were together, I regaled them with stories and pictures of my beautiful baby brother.

When I think of Ami and Mel, I think of newborn ponies trying so very hard to stand up on those brand-new, wobbly, little legs, curious about the world, eager to learn, and then being beaten into submission. Those wondrous little faces turning to frowns, wondering what they've done wrong. Perhaps Deedee punished them just for being born, as she felt she was punished just for being born.

Deedee

October 22, 1990

Another birthday. Mother and apparently Leslie and Rachael are after Amiala to go to college. They say she has to go to college and they'll pay for it. How can Leslie afford to do these things? They need to leave Amiala alone about it. If the girl doesn't want to go to college, so be it. I didn't go to college and I'm fine. I'm better than fine. I'm up to my eyeballs in money. I did better than Leslie with all her education. As usual, Mother talks about nothing but what a great time she had with Leslie in Ashland. She did bring back some good wine.

Leslie

December 4, 1990

My sister called tonight after not speaking to me for two years. It was an uneventful conversation. I leave for Honolulu in the morning to racewalk the Honolulu Marathon, so we spoke a bit about that but nothing about the issues causing the rift. I wondered why she bothered to call. Maybe Mother threatened her. My life has been much more peaceful without

Deedee in it. I'm not eager to begin a relationship with her again. People who turn on you once will most likely turn on you again, so why bother to put in the energy to have a relationship with them?

December 25, 1990

Rachael, Jacob, and I have spent a lovely day together, playing games, reading, and cooking scrumptious meals. Friends stopped by. Mom arrives tomorrow.

I finished the marathon, just barely. The humidity got to me, plus the Gatorade I drank at mile fifteen. I was reluctant to drink it because I'd been training only with water, but I thought it might give me a pickup. Around mile nineteen, I started feeling sick. My skin was hot, and I felt nauseous and lightheaded. I could hardly walk. If a cab had come along, I'd have taken it. Pearl was all excited about getting our T-shirts. I was so miserable, I told her to get mine for me.

Chapter Nineteen

It is Not Unusual

Leslie

February 7, 1991

I had bunion surgery last Thursday. My feet hurt, but it's so nice to remain at home for a while. I love puttering around the house, reading, and sewing.

Mom came up to help me out. When Ami was living with Mom, Mom would always leave lots of food in the refrigerator for Ami when we went to Ashland, but when Mom got home, the food would be rotten and she'd have to throw it away. When Mom was telling me this, she said, "Ami just wants to open the refrigerator and have dinner pop out!" I thought for a moment and replied, "I want that too!" When Mom went home yesterday, she left plates of meals in the refrigerator. When she got home, she called me, and I told her, "The most remarkable thing happened tonight. I opened my refrigerator, and my dinner popped out!"

I started a quilting group, and we had our first meeting at my house last night. We have a wonderful new wine shop in town, and everyone was quite impressed when the owner delivered a couple of cases of wine because I'm not able to drive yet.

April 12, 1991

Mom and I are in Florida. We began our trip in West Palm Beach, visiting Aunt Cal, Mom's aunt. She loves to cook and prepared meals in the style of the 1930s and '40s: meat cooked to death, unrecognizable vegetables, and potatoes loaded with sauces. She must have been my mother's early cooking teacher. Mom still cooks pretty simply—meat loaf, casseroles, and such—but she's branched out over the years, experimenting with vegetarian dishes for Rachael and me before we gave up the vegetarian diet. It warmed my heart that she'd finally accepted our being vegetarians and tried to please us. At the beginning of our vegetarian lifestyle, she thought I'd gone off the deep end.

After about four days, Mom and I rented a car and drove over to Port Saint Lucie to visit Auntie Anne, who, being a dedicated nurse, made us a healthy dinner of a lovely roasted chicken with recognizable vegetables and roasted potatoes served with herbs from her garden. She also opened a bottle of lovely German wine. I listened to stories of her and Mom's sorority years until late into the night. I finally went to bed to read one of my newest mysteries, but Mom and Auntie Anne were up gabbing until the wee hours of the morning.

After a few days we drove over to Clearwater to visit Cousin Dani, who is doing a fantastic job with my retirement account. We went shopping at the Old Cigar Factory, where I was reminded of Grandad Goodman, who was never seen without a cigar in his mouth. I love the smell of cigars because it brings up memories of him, home, family, and fun.

Deedee

May 5, 1991

Mother and Leslie do everything together. They made a trip to Florida to visit some family. I wonder what terrible things Leslie says about me to these people that I don't even know. She loves to talk shit about me. It makes me look bad and her look good. I called Leslie the night before she left for Hawaii. I don't know why. Pressure from Mom, I guess. I don't have any friends, so sometimes I think it would be nice to have a sister different from Leslie. Leslie makes it so hard to be a sister.

Leslie

June 26, 1991

Rachael, Mom, and I arrived at the Queen Anne bed-and-breakfast in Ashland to find that the owners, David and Loni, had passed away. We'd found out last year that David had AIDS and his health was rapidly going downhill. Loni nursed him and then went to live with her sister up the coast, and, of course, Loni died too. David was Loni's professor in college. When they got married, he'd neglected to tell her that he was bisexual and had AIDS. Loni was only my age, with a son Rachael's age. God, I can't even imagine! I feel like I should hate David, but I felt so sorry for him. Last year he held my hand and told me how sorry he was and how happy he was to have known Mom, Rachael, and me. I can't hate him. Poor Loni. We named her garden at the bed-and-breakfast Loni's Legacy.

On a happier note, a lovely woman bought the Queen Anne. Her name is Ellie. We're having the best time getting to know her.

July 5, 1991

Ellie is dating a man who invited us to watch fireworks at a friend's home up the hill. I sat with him and began chatting, asking him, "So what sort of business are you in?" He answered, "I work as a gigolo for a cruise line." "Oh, that's different," I replied. "Yeah," he said, "I love my job!" I don't think there is a future here for Ellie!

July 22, 1991

A very interesting lady bought the property next to the QA. She's a retired English teacher. The house is a bed-and-breakfast called Russell House. Mom and I had looked at it when the previous owner had it, but we found the room with the dolls too creepy. Alice, the new owner, is renovating it.

Deedee

August 1, 1991

I thought I'd get more attention from Mother if I broke down and called Leslie, but it didn't work. She still spends all her time with Leslie. They never invite me to do anything with them. Well, one time they did, but I didn't go. I didn't think I would fit in because, although I'm beautiful, I don't have the brains God gave me.

Leslie

September 5, 1991

Rachael is finishing up her last year at UC Berkeley. My baby! I'm so glad she's close by. We do fun runs on Sunday mornings. Then we get lattes and go to farmers' market. During the week, we meet at five-thirty in the morning for spin-cycle class. That's brutal!

A few days ago, I went to Black Oak Books in Berkeley and met Carolyn Hart, who writes the Death on Demand mystery series. I think Carolyn is a brilliant writer, so I was very excited to have an opportunity to speak to her. I have all her books in hardback, first edition, signed. I wonder if I could write a mystery. I sure have read enough of them.

November 30, 1991

I got braces on my teeth last week. Although it looks a bit odd to have braces at forty-seven years of age, I feel like a teenager.

Deedee

December 2, 1991

Johnson and me spent Thanksgiving alone. Leslie is at Mother's with her entourage, so, of course, my girls went there. Mother always caters to Leslie. She says she loves us all equally, but Leslie is her favorite. Mother likes to say that Leslie was her firstborn baby chick. After Leslie was born Dad was stationed in Oakland and flying transports overseas. Mother and Leslie had an apartment in San Francisco, and it was a very special time for mother because she was alone with her baby girl. I think they bonded in a way that Mother and me never have.

Chapter Twenty

What a Wonderful World

Leslie

January 1, 1992

What a wonderful New Year's Eve! Mom, Jacob, our friend Winifred, and I went to the Herbst Theatre in the city and saw a performance of Rodgers and Hammerstein's music. Afterward we were served a late, light supper and danced. It was nice to dress up and go out on the town. It's so Myrna Loy in *The Thin Man*!

February 19, 1992

Mom came up, and she, I, and Winifred went into the city and attended a mystery readers' and writers' conference called Left Coast Crime. I was like a kid in a candy store again. What fun, meeting authors whose books I've read. Afterward we went to dinner at a restaurant nearby, and we just couldn't stop talking about the conference, all the books, and all the people we met. Mom won a life-size poster of a middle-aged male author, and she looked pretty funny holding that thing in the back seat of the car.

August 5, 1992

My friend Georgi came to Ashland with us this year, as did Mom's friend Caroline. We've been having a great time with Caroline. We went to the costume shop where Mom and Caroline dressed up, and I took pictures. They were really getting into the posing, waving their hats around and laughing at each other. My mother must have been a terrific model.

Georgi, on the other hand, is being a bit of a pain; she doesn't like any of the plays or any of the restaurants. She's going to go up to Portland to see an old boyfriend. They met working at the same law firm and dated for several years, but he married another woman. Georgi was devastated and married someone else on the rebound. She's spent years pining for the man. He's widowed now, so she's set up a time to meet with him and see how she feels. Why is it that we always want the one who got away?

We took the tour of the Catalogue House in Jacksonville. I can't imagine buying a house from a catalogue in the late 1800s, especially this house. It's huge and has hand-carved woodwork, hardwood floors. It was manufactured back East, shipped out West, and assembled. It's so magnificent it's hard to believe it was an early prefab. We went on the half-day Rogue River Rafting Trip. I loved being on the cool water; it's been so hot here. Caroline and Mom were spraying people in the other boats and laughing their heads off like two teenagers.

We're enjoying spending time with Tina and Joe, a couple we met staying at the QA, and now we coordinate our vacation with them. Joe likes to sit on the porch before breakfast. When I go running, he says, "Will ya run a few miles for me?" When Mom comes back from the beauty shop, he says, "Look at you, all fluffed and buffed!" We've done a lot of laughing, which is so good for the soul.

August 22, 1992

We're back home, and I went to my thirtieth high school class reunion. It seems like only yesterday that Rachael and I went shopping for that filmy dress I wore to my tenth reunion. This year I wore a little black dress, and I got loads of compliments on how great I looked, which is always nice for the ego. I really did look pretty snazzy; however, the colorful bands of the braces on my teeth may have hampered the sophisticated look a bit!

Deedee

September 8, 1992

Leslie was here for her high school class reunion. There's some sort of a reunion almost every year, so I decided to go to mine too. It's the first one I've been to, and I wanted to show off because I look really hot, and I'm rich, and my husband is a very important attorney. Nobody even noticed that I didn't graduate. I was a showstopper in a tight gold lame dress with lots of cleavage showing. And when I flashed my six-carat diamond ring around, I could see the women turning green with envy. Johnson worked the crowd for business. We didn't stay too long. We were bored.

Leslie

November 30, 1992

Rachael moved into a darling apartment in Lafayette. It's on a street right behind the main downtown area, so it's close to restaurants and shops and a beautiful running trail. Since she was born, at whatever age she is, I've always said, "This is the best age." Well, this is the best age. It's incredibly fabulous, having an adult daughter to go running with, shopping with, or just sitting with and reading.

Although we're separated, Jacob and I celebrated our twenty-sixth wedding anniversary by going out to dinner and to a cute little puppet show in the city. My friend Franny, whom I met when her daughter, Drea, and Rachael were in high school together, said, "Leslie, people don't usually go out to dinner with their estranged husbands, but then you're an extraordinary woman." I think that was a compliment.

Chapter Twenty-One

It Was a Very Good Year

Deedee

January 1, 1993

Well, Fucking Happy New Year! I just found out I'm going to be a grandmother! Meliza is just 17, and she's five months pregnant! God! What the fuck is wrong with her? It's all Mick's fault. He broke her heart when he admitted he had another daughter. She has been a big problem ever since. Johnson is actually happy about this baby! He didn't get to be a hands-on dad when his son was a baby. Now he gets to be around to help raise this baby because Meliza doesn't want to marry the boy, although he'd like to marry her. She will be living here with us. Ugh! I don't have enough to do?

Johnson was worried about my workouts and my staying in shape. He thought four hours a day on the treadmill, watching soaps, wasn't a good idea, so he bought me a gym. Now I own a business, and I have a place to work out other than our home gym. In order to run this business, I had to have a license as a personal trainer. It was the hardest thing I've ever done. In fact, I paid a gal to give me the answers on the physical anatomy part of it. I run the place. Why do I need a personal trainer license? The gym doesn't make any money, but Johnson is okay with that. He says it's a good write-off. I think he means on his income tax. So now we're going to have a baby. I told Meliza I will *not* be called grandma.

Leslie

January 1, 1993

It's a beautiful New Year's Day in Alameda! We had a lovely holiday season, going to parties and all sorts of theater. We went to Club Fugazi in North Beach. "Beach Blanket Babylon" is famous for their costumes with outrageously tall hats and headpieces, and they really hit on politics and keep the audience in stitches, laughing. We went to a mystery dinner on the *Hornblower* yacht down at Pier 39. We dressed in the costume of the 1940s, which I adore because women's fashion was so elegant then, with hats, purses, and shoes to match their outfits.

Last night I had a depo that went until nine o'clock. The attorneys were from out of town. I asked if they had New Year's Eve plans with their wives, and they said this depo was more important. I'm glad I hadn't made any specific plans, and I'm glad I'm not married to any of them. There is a custom in the city that on New Year's Eve when the offices close, everyone throws shredded paper out their windows. It's thrilling to see all that shredded paper sailing around, blowing in the wind downtown. I got home around ten, and Mom and I made appetizers and manhattans and watched *Three Men and a Baby*. When they sang the words, "Good night, sweetheart; it's time to say good night," I suddenly had this picture of my mother, old and dying, with me sitting next to her, holding her hand and singing that song. It scared me. Aside from that dreadful thought, it was a very special time to spend with Mother.

Today Mom, Rachael, and I took down the Christmas tree. It's always sad, putting away my beautiful decorations, some of which are from when Rachael was a baby and a toddler and then a little girl. Our decorations, our homes, and what we choose to put in them tell a story of who we are, what we do, and what we value in life.

January 19, 1993

It's been a long two weeks, with lots of all-day, expedited jobs. It's been exhausting but tons of fun, and I've made bushels of money. Mom stayed through the first week of the month. She was so sweet, making nice dinners, having a cocktail on the ready when I walked through the door, a fire in the fireplace. She's spoiling me. I said, "When you leave, I'll have to find a Jeeves!"

Rachael and I signed up to run the San Diego Half Marathon. We've been building up our miles in preparation. Today we did twelve miles. That will be our last run before the marathon, which is coming up next week.

January 24, 1993

We finished the San Diego Half Marathon. Mom walked the four-mile race. I'm so proud of her! She never exercises. She used to walk with some of the neighborhood ladies, but never when it was too hot, too cold, windy, or rainy. I'd like to think that this could be the beginning of an exercise routine for Mom, but I actually think she just wanted to be with us and involved. We're going to stay on another day to do some shopping and check out some of San Diego's highly recommended restaurants.

Deedee

January 27, 1993

Mother could hardly wait to tell me all about finishing the four-mile walk at the San Diego Half Marathon. She's so out of shape it's embarrassing. She's always hated exercise and would rather just starve herself to stay thin. She went on and on about how wonderful Leslie and Rachael are. Yuck! Little Miss Perfect is so refined with all her opera, classical music and theater. She's stuck up, is what she is. I wish Mom would say nice things about me.

Meliza is a real pain in the ass. You'd think she was the only woman who was ever pregnant. She's living with me. Girls always want their moms when they're pregnant. And Mick's new wife is expecting a baby and doesn't want to be upstaged by Meliza. Johnson and I are waiting on Meliza hand and foot. I love shopping for the baby's nursery.

Leslie

April 26, 1993

Jacob and I have gone back to couples counseling, but it seems to me as though he's just going through the motions, which makes me wonder if we're not wasting our time and money. It's hard for me to give up on our relationship. It's hard for me to give up on anything. As an example, I took tennis lessons for seven years and never got out of the beginning group. I took bridge lessons and never did get the strategy. Well, maybe I could have if I'd kept at it. That's just what I'm talking about. I don't know when to quit. But that can be a good thing because I didn't give up on court reporting college, and now I have an amazing career. How do you know when to give up on something?

Work has been very slow lately, and I have thoroughly enjoyed being home, puttering around the house, getting things done. Rachael and I went to a quaint little bed-and-breakfast in Mendocino and had a fantastic R & R. She'll be leaving in two weeks to travel Europe for a month. It hurts my heart to think of her being so far away.

June 15, 1993

Mom was here for a week. We planted flowers in the yard. I bought some new yard furniture. We sat outside with our cocktails and talked and read, then had our dinners outside too.

I had a wine-tasting birthday party for Pearl that was lots of fun and very different. We have a mutual friend who is quite a wine connoisseur and enjoys hosting wine parties in people's homes. He brings in a variety of wines and explains the method for growing the grapes and producing the wines. The wines are delicious, and it's nice to learn so much about what we're drinking.

Deedee

May 28, 1993

Meliza had a baby boy! He is so cute! I love him to the moon and back! Johnson took a month off work to be home with him. Unfortunately, the father's family is involved as per Meliza's wishes. God! That girl doesn't have the brains God gave her! The father thinks he owns Meliza, even though they're not married. His mother is a fat slob who owns a beauty shop in downtown LA. It's all I can do to let them in the house without throwing up. Mom wasn't here when the baby was born because, of course, she was up at Little Miss Perfect's. We're going to have the baby call me Deedee.

Chapter Twenty-Two

Uptight, Everything Is Alright

Deedee

January 2, 1994

What a wonderful Christmas! Mom was here! The baby was the center of attention. The gifts overflowed under the tree and filled the whole room. I had the maids take them out and bring them in a few at a time. Fortunately, the father's family wasn't involved. Unlike us, they're very strict Jews.

Leslie

May 31, 1994

I just love my book groups. One group reads mainstream books, and the other three read mysteries. It's so nice to be around people who like to read. It's exciting to be exposed to new authors and books that I probably wouldn't have picked up on my own.

Tonight, my friends Claudia and Helene and I are going to the opera. This will be the first time the three of us have been together since we went down to Mom's and we all went to see Placido Domingo. It was right after the Northridge earthquake, and it was quite disconcerting. The earth was still moving, so when I went to bed at night, I felt as though I was sleeping on a waterbed.

June 6, 1994

A young man, Tony, has been calling and leaving messages for Rachael, but she hasn't been calling him back. I didn't think much about it, but earlier today the phone rang, and I answered. It was the young man, asking for Rachael. She was waving at me and saying, "Tell him I'm not home." I was mouthing, "But he sounds so nice." I could tell she was wavering, and this guy had been trying so hard to get a date with her, so I said, "Oh, she's right here" and proceeded to hand her the phone. He must be one heck of a persuasive guy because they have a date!

June 14, 1994

Well, the date went quite well. For a gal who didn't want to talk to the guy, Rachael sure is smitten. He took her on a picnic at the Presidio, and he brought champagne and roses. The guy persevered and was successful. I admire that!

June 24, 1994

Mom is visiting, and for Rachael's birthday she, Franny, Drea, and I went to Chez Panisse in Berkeley for dinner. We had a lovely conversation with Alice Waters. I was so embarrassed, though, because Mom thought the garlic soup was too weird and commented on that to Alice.

I gave Rachael a darling card that had a picture of a little girl holding a baby duck. One day last week while we were running, we saw some baby ducks and Rachael said, "I wish I could hold one in my hand," so the card was perfect.

August 18, 1994

We've been in Ashland for the past month, and we're leaving tomorrow. I feel like I blinked and the time was up. We've had such a wonderful time, and I'm so sad to leave.

Rachael got a teaching position at one of our local grammar schools. Tony, the fellow Rachael is smitten with, got an assistant coaching position at a small college in Minnesota. Rachael is teaching year-round, so she has six weeks off at a time when she can go stay with him. She's on cloud nine!

August 28, 1994

Rachael and I are at Mom's. I always feel like I'm at a resort when I come here. We went running a little before eight in the morning, but it was oppressively hot, so we came home and jumped in the pool.

We had a 3.3 earthquake last night! Ugh! I spent a very nice morning, sitting out on the patio in the shade with a facial mask and hair-conditioning treatment on while I read. I just got cleaned up, and I feel great. I'm getting a massage this afternoon.

Ami came by and is sitting out in the sun. She was commenting on what a jerk her father was, and I wanted to comment, "Your mother has a natural bent for picking unusual husbands," and then ask how the wicked witch from horse country is doing, but I was a good girl and kept my mouth shut. However, Miss Dump and Duck goes to the same woman I do for massages, so if the subject comes up, I'm going to be a real little devil and tell the masseuse that Deedee is older than I am because Deedee goes bonkers when people think she is the older sister.

Deedee is so mean! Before I arrived, she took Ami and Mel to dinner and a movie and purposely didn't ask Mom. When Mom asked her about it, Deedee said, "I just wanted to be with my own little family." I wonder why she wants to hurt Mother's feelings.

Deedee

August 30, 1994

That bitch Leslie went and told my massage person that I'm older than she is, and the stupid woman believed her. I am so going to get even with Leslie. She's a troublemaker. Leslie and her entourage are at Mom's again. I can't even go see my mother without that bitch being around. I'm sick of it. I want private time with my mother.

Leslie

August 30, 1994

I hate my sister! I think she's the all-time bitch of the century. She just won't forgive me for testifying for Mel. I know I hurt her deeply and that she feels terribly abandoned, but for God's sake, I wish she'd quit beating me up and go to therapy with me so we can talk this thing out. She complains about everything, and she's making my life a living hell. To top it off Ami had to go and make a comment: "Oh, Mother and Johnson are so in love!" Pleeease! Miss Dump and Duck is a fucking trophy wife! Anyway, that comment really hurt since Jacob and I have been separated for four years and I still can't give up on the relationship. And then Mother soon forgets how mean Deedee is to her and thinks the bitch is a shining star. And Ami sings her mother's praises, forgetting how her mother abused and abandoned her, beat the crap out of her, and tossed her room.

On a happier note, Ami renounced her mother's non-educational beliefs and signed up for classes at Pierce College. I think it was Rachael's influence.

November 24, 1994

Jacob and I were married on November 23. It was always difficult to spend a quiet, romantic anniversary alone because it fell on Thanksgiving weekend. This year was different. I got up early, went for a run, got cleaned up, went and got a latte—I'm addicted to them—and then I caught a flight up to Portland. Jacob picked me up, and we went to the Columbia Gorge Hotel, where we dressed up and went to the most incredible Thanksgiving dinner, very early-American complete with singers strolling about and comedians walking among the tables. Jacob is my rock. Even with his depression and anger, he's always there for me. How can I quit on that?

Deedee

December 29, 1994

Even Amiala loves being an aunt. Our cute little guy, Denzel, is walking and talking. The house is filled with toys and things for him. We bought him a pony. Life is perfect! I'm beautiful and rich, and I have a wonderful husband and sweet daughters. We're going to Hawaii for New Year's and taking our cute little guy. Meliza wants to spend New Year's with her friends.

Chapter Twenty-Three

Let the Good Years Roll . . .

Leslie

January 17, 1995

My father, had he not done himself in, would be seventy-three years old today. I wonder what he would look like. Pretty much the same, I imagine, but with age. Dad always remained fit and would probably be running marathons with me. He embraced change and was many years ahead of his peers in his thinking. In 1954 he was advocating for heliports because that was the future. He didn't allow smoking in his home, car, or offices. During the war, he never drank with the other pilots. They joked that he would go to the bar and order milk. When he had a new interest, he jumped in all the way, learning all he could. He was an extraordinary man.

Enough about Dad! The holidays were magical once again. For Jacob's birthday we took the Napa Valley Wine Train ride, which included a champagne lunch. It was a beautiful train, very lavish inside and out. I was transported back to the late 1800s as a sophisticated lady, all dressed up and traveling in elegance and opulence.

For New Year's Eve, Mom, Rachael, Jacob, and I went to Meadowood in Napa, which is extremely posh. In order to play croquet, one must wear white. We stayed in a lovely two-bedroom cottage on the property. The New Year's Eve dinner was a gourmet's delight. There were vintners from all over the valley, bringing their special bottles of wine. There was dancing, and balloons fell at midnight. I was so happy to spend this very special New Year's Eve with my three favorite people!

Pamela Dehnke

April 15, 1995

Although Deedee called me that one time a few years back, she never called again, nor did I make the effort to call her. Now, suddenly, she's talking to me again. She called and said she figured Mick pressured me, and my testifying in the custody case was all his fault. She said now that her life is so wonderful and mine is so shitty, she can forgive me.

Stunned, I asked, "What's wrong with my life?"

She said, "Oh, you have to work so hard, and you live in that dumpy little cottage all alone. You can't find a man to marry you. I don't know how you live under the conditions you do. I feel so sorry for you. I wish I could help."

I told her, "I'm happy! I love my home and my career, and I don't want to get married. I haven't even gotten divorced, and I enjoy living alone."

She ignored me and said she's a much better mother now. She loves the baby and having Meliza live with them. I suggested that we do some counseling, but she said, "Oh, I don't need it, but you go ahead. I know you do."

Whatever!

I had a huge Seder dinner. I love the ritual, the singing and games, and the food. Rachael invited Tony, who really got into the spirit of the occasion. We played the game where you draw a letter and you have to think of something beginning with that letter that you will take with you out of Egypt. Tony drew "R" and said he'd take Rachael.

May 26, 1995

I'm sitting on a step in the Imperial Garden of Beijing Forbidden City in China. I can hardly believe it! A friend booked this tour but broke her leg skiing and had to cancel, so she asked me if I would like to take her place. What an opportunity! We've seen and done so much on this trip, but the most memorable was seeing the Terracotta Army in Xian. I saw this exhibit at the de Young Museum in the city, and I remember thinking how fantastic it would be to see the actual site, and I did. It was amazing! I thought about the people and their everyday lives, how they married and had children, how they loved or hated, what their relationships were like, what made them sad, and what made them happy.

I saw paintings of the four seasons, and was completely washed over with thoughts, feelings, and emotions about myself and my family. I'm fifty-one years old; the seasons of my life are getting shorter. I thought my family was normal, that we were a good, solid unit, and then the men bailed out and our lives came crashing down around us. I was left with the suffocating responsibility of keeping the women together, but I can't keep them from making horrible decisions and beating the crap out of one another. I can't even keep my own marriage together. Thirty years ago, we were all so young and full of love and life.

Deedee

June 26, 1995

I'm talking to Leslie again. I feel so sorry for her. God only knows how she can live the way she does. My horse stalls are bigger than that shed she lives in. And how she can even speak to Jacob is beyond me. I would never speak to any of my ex-husbands. They're all assholes. And she's still married to Jacob and dates. What's that about? Shit or get off the pot. She needs to get a divorce if she's ever going to move on. She's dating a lawyer. Hopefully she can hang on to him and move her status up in life.

Leslie

August 5, 1996

Another year has gone by without my writing in my journal. I'm so busy living life it's difficult to find the time to write. Jacob and I have been doing therapy with an excellent psychologist. Jacob, however, doesn't seem to want to face his depression. Do some things never change?

September 14, 1996

A couple of months ago, Claudia talked me into taking Italian language classes with her. I have a real thing about "languages aren't for me." I took four years of Spanish in high school and couldn't speak it, although I could read it and I was a whiz at conjugating verbs. Well, Claudia nagged and nagged me about signing up to take Italian, so I thought, okay, I won't sign up, but I'll go with her to the first class. Of course, the class will be full, and I'll go get a latte and wait for her. We walked into the classroom, and the instructor said, "*Benvenuto!*" Seven weeks later, Claudia dropped out, and here I am, plugging along. I have to say, though, that I absolutely love it. The people in my class are so interesting. They speak other languages, enjoy the opera and theater, and they read. I've made a lot of new friends. Thank you, Claudia!

Ami was dating a really nice guy, but she broke up with him. When I asked her why, she said, "He lives too close to the trailer park." I didn't understand what she meant, so I asked, "What does where he lives have to do with your relationship?" She laughed and said, "He's a little too trailer-trash." Now she's dating another nice guy. We'll see how that goes.

I've gotten myself season tickets, a box seat, for the San Francisco Ballet. It was an indulgence, but it's such a thrill! The ballerinas are graceful and their movements so ethereal. They're truly athletes. It's causing me to pay more attention to my body, how I move and how I work out at the gym.

I don't think I mentioned that I went crazy and leased a brand-new Jaguar. I love this car. It's beautiful, it smells divine, and what a car to drive; it hugs the road.

I bought a book in which I write about the things that I'm grateful for. Here's a few: Rachael, Mom, Jacob, the Jag, books, wine, my career, my cats, my friends, Ashland summers, my garden, my piano, laughter, my home, newspapers, opera, ballet, theater, good food, money, Italian classes, five hours of sleep, my religion, rain, shopping, lattes, my fireplace, my health.

October 15, 1996

I'm studying piano at the San Francisco Conservatory of Music. At the first class the instructor asked us why we're studying piano. Everyone recounted their reasons. When my turn came, what popped out of my mouth was, "So I can play the piano at Nordstrom's when I retire." Nordstrom's is my favorite store, and I love that they have live piano music. It's so calming. Who knows, maybe someday!

Deedee

October 22, 1996

It's my birthday and we're in New York doing our holiday shopping. We've bought so much for our cute little boy. Johnson just loves him to the moon and back. I'm so happy. It's freezing here, so I'm getting a lot of wear out of my mink coat. We've gone to some very famous restaurants. I've gotten to be real good at throwing up. I can almost think myself into tossing up nice and clean. I'm a pro. People ask me, "How do you stay so thin?"

Leslie

January 3, 1997

Another bright new year! In between Christmas and New Year's, I went with some friends on a London theater tour with American Conservatory Theater. We saw seven plays in one week. We went to Stratford-on-Avon. We toured castles. It's fascinating to think about the people who lived in them, what their lives were like, the many people who supported their lives in various ways, and how they felt about that. Did they envy the royals? Were they content? The tour included a New Year's Eve party at the hotel: dinner, dancing, champagne, and noisemakers. We all dressed to the nines and cheered the old year out and the new one in with all its many possibilities.

January 6, 1997

I'm thinking about my sister and wondering what will become of my relationship with her this year. I hope it will heal and grow, but I just don't feel any depth with Deedee; she comes off as being superficial and phony. What a terrible thing for me to say. I feel like I have to walk on eggshells with her. I have to be careful about everything I say and do, even my intonations and the volume of my voice. My movements have to be slow and thought through. And I shut down when the conversation drifts toward Johnson or Mel. This relationship is going to take a lot of energy. I intended to call her and wish her a Happy New Year, but I haven't done it yet because even that seems difficult. However, I will keep trying.

February 7, 1997

I called Mom tonight because our phones had been out due to the huge rainstorm we've undergone the past few weeks and I didn't want her to worry. I spoke to Mel. She sounded so cold, so distant, so superficial, so Deedee.

I called Deedee too. I feel guilty because, being seven years older, I got the best of our parents' relationship, and she got the worst. She grew up at a time when they were fighting and suing each other and devoted no time to her. She has no cognizance of what a healthy family unit might look like. She had horrible parenting, and it's clear from everything she says and does that rather than learning from that experience, she embraced it. Talking to her leaves me feeling empty.

February 14, 1997

Twenty-five years ago today, my father took his own life. That's profound, and I'm not into feeling profound at the moment. I'm at the Left Coast Crime conference in Seattle. I went for an amazing run this morning down by the water, past the Edgewater Hotel, where the Beatles stayed in 1964 at the height of Beatlemania. I followed one of my favorite runs into the park and along the water and took pleasure in the peace and quiet. I ran back through the Pike Place Public Market, up some hills and back to the hotel, just as it was beginning to drizzle. Life is good!

February 21, 1997

Today I went to a luncheon where I met the author Joanna Trollope. What an inspiring woman! I'm in awe! Every time I talk to an author, I want to begin seriously writing again. Time! Would that there were more of it in a day!

March 1, 1997

I met the most interesting woman at my friends' Flora and Nick's anniversary party. Her name is Iris, and she's a nurse. She has a son and a daughter, and she's as crazy about them as I am about Rachael. Her daughter is a nurse too, and Iris talks to her several times a day. Rachael would tell me I'm making her crazy if I even called her once a day. Iris had breast cancer but has been in remission for five years now.

Iris and Flora and I went to see the author Ursula Hegi speak at the Herbst Theatre. It took her seven years to write her book. I haven't even begun my novel. Will it take me seven years to write it? What would I write about? I've thought about a mystery. Maybe a collection of essays on life. Short stories?

May 14, 1997

Rachael gave me the sweetest Mother's Day card. It's in Italian. We spent a lovely day together, going for a run and then shopping, checking out a new restaurant, and seeing a play at Berkeley Repertory Theatre. I love my beautiful baby girl!

Ami has been complaining about Deedee and how mean she is. I have to agree with her on that score; however, perhaps Ami misinterprets what Deedee says. Knowing Deedee, though, I doubt it. What about me? Does Deedee's being mean make me look better? Do I get satisfaction from that? I want Deedee to be understanding and supportive of Ami and undo some of the harm that's been done. Ami can certainly tax your energy and she can be extremely unkind, but she can also be sweet, and she's very bright. My biggest wish in the world would be for Ami and Mel to be whole, to be emotionally stable, to be comfortable with themselves and confident.

I'm hard on myself with everything I do. I want to do it all, and I want to be a champion at all I do. When I was born, Dad said I was a champion. Did he set me up to always strive to be perfect?

July 24, 1997

I'm sitting on Ellie's porch in Ashland, writing and watching a lovely little fawn on the lawn in front of me. Mindy, the homeless cat we rescued from the motel in McMinnville, is sitting on the couch next to me. Ellie's dog is lying at my feet, and my beautiful mother is sitting in the chair next to me, engrossed in a new mystery. It's so peaceful.

I'm learning that I can't do everything I want to do in one day, so I might as well let go, do what I can, enjoy what I do, and be in the moment.

I felt good about performing my piano recital before I left home. I overcame my fear of playing in front of people.

Mother was an accomplished pianist, but she was too nervous to play for anyone.

I've been thinking about leisure and how I spend my leisure time. I'm on a fast track with it, always trying to fit in more things to do. Leisure is a precious gift.

Chapter Twenty-Four

Raindrops Keep Falling on My Head

Leslie

December 22, 1997

Mel's little boy pulled a pot of boiling water over on himself! That poor little fellow! He's horribly burned and will be scarred. Mel said she only left the room for a minute.

Deedee

December 24, 1997

It's Christmas Eve, and our poor little boy is hurting so much. Meliza is so fucking stupid! She left him alone in the kitchen with water boiling on the stove. I called Johnson and he met me at the hospital. He was so upset and angry at the staff there that he called his friend, who is a doctor who specializes in burn victims at a hospital in New York. We got little Denzel stable and then flew him to New York. We're making weekly trips there and talking about skin grafting. Meliza is so irresponsible!

Leslie

February 14, 1998

Valentine's Day! I picked out a bunch of beautiful Valentine cards and sent them to all my girlfriends. I had so much fun doing it. Everyone loved them. And I actually forgot that it was the anniversary of my father's death.

Rachael and I are going to culinary school. We go Tuesday and Thursday nights and all day on Saturday. The couple who own the school bring in guest chefs, so we've met some of the top chefs in the city and Napa. They cook; we eat and drink!

July 26, 1998

I'm fifty-four years old today! How can that be? Yikes! We are having a great time in Ashland. We celebrated Rachael's birthday here too. I finished the quilt for her that she'd started when we began quilting lessons. I wrapped it up and gave it to her for her birthday. She was so surprised! It was fun and worth all the work to see the look on her face when she opened it.

August 20, 1998

Last night I read an article in a magazine about being present when someone is born and when they die. I was there when Liam was brought home from the hospital. I was with a neighbor across the street. She was looking out the window and said, "There's your mom and dad with your new baby brother." I was so excited. I ran to the window and saw Dad helping Mom out of the car with a little bundle in her arms. I said, "Please, can I go home now to see my new baby?" Just then I saw my dad walking across the street and waving to me. He took me home. Mom had a bassinet set up in the living room. I whispered, "Mommy, can I see?" She got my little stool for me to stand on. With great anticipation, I looked over the side of the bassinet and saw my baby brother for the first time. I was in awe. He was all red and wrinkled, and so cute.

I didn't see Liam when they brought him home from Vietnam. They said it would upset me and it was better that I have the memory of him being alive. Maybe they were right; maybe they were wrong. Just because someone says he's dead, doesn't mean he's dead. Maybe they made a mistake.

Tomorrow we head for home. I hate to leave Ashland.

September 29, 1998

Uncle Les died. It's nearly impossible to believe. He was so active and seemingly healthy. He came home from a bike ride, hopped in the shower, and had a heart attack. He's always been in my life. It's difficult to comprehend that I'll never see him again. If I ever remarried, he was going to walk me down the aisle. He lived with us while he went to law school, and he babysat for Liam and me. Liam was so much like Uncle Les, a gentleman and a scholar with a fantastic sense of humor. Mom and I flew to Milwaukee for the funeral. My heart ached for my aunt and cousins, and for myself too. My cousin's little boy came up to me and said, "Why doesn't my grandpa get out of that box?

Chapter Twenty-Five

Arrivederci Roma

Leslie

April 18, 1999

I'm in Italy with my Italian study group. We're staying at a
lovely spa resort in Viterbo. This place is far too romantic to
be here with a study group. Next time, I'm bringing a lover.
I've been getting up real early and running in the countryside
before we go to classes. The views are breathtaking! People
wave and greet me with *"Buon giorno!"* The classes seem
advanced for me, even though we are divided into two levels.
The books are all in Italian, and I'm struggling. It's quite an
interesting experience, though. We break from class by ten
o'clock and go sightseeing. We went to a small village, and
while everyone else was in a ceramic studio, I went shopping
on my own. No one spoke English, and the village was laid
out like a maze. I was afraid I would get lost, but I persevered.
It was scary, but thrilling and challenging. I bought a
Wodehouse book in Italian, a gold braided bracelet, and some
beautiful Italian printed fabric for quilting. I was so proud of
myself for making purchases in Italian and finding my way
back to the group.

The highlight of my trip, though, was my day in Rome.
We had a free day, and I wanted to go to Rome. I told our
instructor that I would manage transportation and so forth, but
she insisted on making arrangements and got me on a busload
of nuns going to Rome for a Catholic holiday. Two other
women from the group decided that they wanted to go too. So
off we went. It was about an hour-and-a-half ride, and I was
excited to practice my Italian. As it turned out, the monsignor
sat next to me and wanted to practice his English because he
was preparing to take his pilot's test in English. When we
arrived in Rome, we proceeded to make arrangements for a

tour guide. The person I spoke to asked me if we wanted an English-speaking guide or a guide who only spoke Italian. I quickly said, "We want a guide who only speaks Italian." Now I would be forced to practice my Italian. At first, we could barely understand anything he said, but as the day progressed, our ears adjusted and we caught on.

Walking up the steps of the Colosseum was one of the most thrilling things I have ever done. I thought of all the hundreds of thousands of people who had walked those steps before me. I was suddenly transported back almost two thousand years ago. I was a beautiful Roman lady, walking up these steps and wondering what my day would bring: What will I order to eat and drink? Will the lines to the toilets be long? Will the show be exciting? Will it be too hot? Will I get laid tonight?

May 2, 1999

I don't know if I previously wrote about the man, Maurice, in the wheelchair whom I see on the running path. He would always wave and say hello to me. After a few months of waving and greeting each other, we'd begun to stop and chat. The stopping and chatting were beginning to eat into my running time, and I was getting the feeling that he'd like to get to know me better, so today I asked him if he'd like to get a coffee and talk for a bit. His eyes lit up and he got a big smile on his face, so I was pretty sure that was a good idea. He's very nice, quite the gentleman, and extremely handsome in a Sean Connery sort of way. He's a psychiatrist. He lives on Bay Farm Island off Alameda and loves cats. He is as much a theater, symphony, and opera fan as I am. He asked me if I'd like to go to dinner and the symphony next Saturday night. I really enjoy our chats, so of course I said yes.

June 7, 1999

Ami is a college graduate! This was a momentous event in all of our lives. Mom and Rachael and I nagged, begged, pleaded, and bribed this girl through college, and the day finally came when she received that degree. Even Deedee gave up her non-educational protests and reluctantly added some encouragement. Ami was radiant and wanting so much to please her mother. I saw that Mom-please-approve-of-me look in her eye. I sat between Deedee and Rachael. When Ami received her diploma, Deedee and I jumped up and down and screamed and hollered like two young girls. I miss having a sister! Maybe having a college-educated daughter has softened Deedee. Could she be changing?

July 24, 1999

Mom and I arrived in Ashland yesterday. It was just like coming home. We stopped in the Tudor Guild Gift Shop, which is full of books and all sorts of things Shakespeare- and theater-related. I thought to myself how fun it would be to be one of these charming ladies who wear the little black aprons and volunteer their time in the shop, helping people find and make decisions about what they want to purchase.

July 26, 1999

Buon compleano! I'm fifty-five years old! I ran six miles this morning and then stayed at the Queen Anne with Mom all day, studying my Italian. What a luxury to take that time for something I enjoy so much. In the evening, a bunch of us gals took a picnic and went to see Ballet in the Park. Ellie had a pedicure today, so I took a picture of her feet, which led to taking a group foot photo, which made us all giggle like silly girls. Sometimes my life feels so good, it's scary. I don't want these special moments to end.

170

September 14, 1999

I'm at Mom's. Aunt Etta and Cousin Lana's daughter are here. We went over to Catalina for the day. It was beautiful and cool. Rachael and I used to go over to Catalina in the summers with Bernie and Jake and the kids. The beach is lovely, the water clear. Horseback riding provides views of amazing vistas. I remember the year we were here when Ami and Rachael were about eight years old. Rachael had had swimming lessons since she was about a month old, but flatly refused to swim. I wasn't aware that Ami could swim when I saw her in the water heading toward the floating dock. I panicked, ran into the water and began swimming after her, only to see her arrive at the dock and pull herself up. That girl! She was so courageous and full of adventure.

My summer in Ashland gave me pause for thought about my life. I'm hurtling through life like a jet, wanting to do everything and afraid I might miss something. I want to slow down and take my time. I don't want to feel responsible for my family anymore, and I don't want to be the brunt of their emotional game playing. I don't want trauma and drama. I want peace and tranquility.

Chapter Twenty-Six

Welcome to the New Century

Leslie

January 24, 2000

I'm going through a very angry period with my family. Deedee called me yesterday, and during the course of the uneventful conversation and quite out of the blue, she said, "You know, I don't like you. If it weren't for Mother, I would never see you again." What sort of a person says something like that? I'm tired of being weighed down with the responsibility of trying to hold my family together. When I was a little girl and Dad would go on a job flying for a period of time, he would say to me, "Now, you be sure to take good care of everyone while I'm gone." I was so proud of being the eldest and taking on that responsibility, but then Dad bailed out of the plane of life, and the responsibility he imparted on me is negatively impacting my life. These people that I call family are nefarious nincompoops. I'm finding it impossible to guide them or even be an example for them to follow. They refuse to get out of their victim positions and join me in life. My father's committing suicide was an egregious thing to do. No matter my age, I was his child, yet he abandoned me and left me with the responsibility of caring for a dysfunctional family.

I hate Johnson, and I think my sister is a lily-livered, gutless wonder who sold herself into slavery instead of getting herself educated so she didn't have to be a trophy wife. My mother is also gutless. She won't stand up to Deedee and give her a piece of her mind. I can't hate my mother, though. Amiala is also lily-livered and gutless. She won't stand up to Deedee either because she desperately wants her approval. I have to wonder if there is any hope for her. At least she got an education. Meliza is gutless, selfish, and mean. I find little to like about her these days. She does everything to be like her mother and is angry because her mother doesn't recognize that. In short, they all suck! There is no hope for meaningful relationships with any of them, and I can't stand the shallow relationships we have. They are pointless and a waste of time. They drain my energy and emotions. I need to let go!

March 2, 2000

Howard, Liam's childhood friend, named his son after Liam. When his son turned twenty-three, Liam's age when he died, Howard decided he wanted to find out more about Liam's death and what he was doing in 'Nam. He began tracking people down on the Internet who might have known Liam. Howard also put Mom, Deedee, and me in touch with these people. The Internet is incredible. I don't know much about it, since I use my computer primarily for getting my transcripts out, but I'm learning. These men have a reunion in Cripple Creek, Colorado, every year, and Mom, Deedee, and I have been invited to attend. They will be honoring Liam.

May 16, 2000

The reunion in Cripple Creek opened my heart to feelings I'd pretty much left behind. They made a beautiful tribute to Liam. I was honored and proud to be a part of it. I met a woman who belongs to a group of brothers and sisters whose siblings died in Vietnam. I couldn't believe such an organization could exist. This was a group of people like me. I could find solace with them. They would understand my loss. I decided to attend a conference they were holding in Washington, DC. One of Liam's war buddies met me there and attended the conference with me. It was nice to have his support. I met so many people who shared their stories. I wasn't alone. One woman met her husband through this organization, so she said, "The war took away, and the war gave back."

May 18, 2000

The anniversary of my brother's birth and death. I'd never visited the Vietnam Veterans Memorial, nor had I even seen a traveling reproduction, probably because I didn't want to see my brother's name on that wall. It took all my strength, but I signed up for a sightseeing bus tour, of which one of the stops was at the wall. I wanted to go alone, so I pulled away from the others. It was one of the hardest things I've ever done. My legs were wobbly when I exited the bus. My stomach was churning. My heart hurt, and I was on the verge of tears. I haltingly approached this wall that I had never wanted to see. Finding Liam's name brought the reality jolting through me like a lightning bolt. *"Noooo!"* I dropped to my knees and sobbed. This is a mistake. He survived. He's safe somewhere, having lost his identity. He will remember and find us. But, no, this is the reality. I tried to stand, but I was too shaky. I looked around me to see people leaving gifts and mementos. They didn't approach one another. There seemed to be a mutual respect for one another's privacy and grief. The sweet and vibrant scent of flowers on this beautiful spring day seemed so out of context with the tragedy this wall represented to me. This wall! Why do I hate it so when it's a tribute to these brave men and women who lost their lives? I saw people tenderly touching the names of their loved ones. Families were crying and holding one another. Pain permeated the air.

June 6, 2000

The man who joined me in Washington invited me to visit him in New York, so I did. He's a dreamy-looking guy, which didn't hurt any. I clearly thought he had intentions, and I was all set for a long-distance relationship. I have a habit of jumping ahead of myself. He has a lovely home in Long Island. He put me up in the guest room, but I was pretty sure I wouldn't spend the entire weekend sleeping there. After arriving and getting settled, he took me to a seafood restaurant. We had a window table with an ocean view. The lyrics from the song "Old Cape Cod" were playing through my head. I didn't have lobster stew, but I did see the moonlight on the bay. The next day I woke up early and went for a beautiful run. When I returned to the house, he asked me what I'd like to do today, and I said, "I'd like to take a walk on the boardwalk," so we did. The sun and the salty air were intoxicating. That night he made us a lovely lobster dinner. However, I not only remained in the guest room but also didn't even receive a good night kiss! Sunday, we spent a whirlwind day in New York City. We walked and talked, laughed, and joked. I felt like I was the star in a romantic comedy, but alas he was not on board with that idea, although he played the part well.

July 15, 2000

A man and his wife, whom I'd met at the reunion in Las Vegas, invited me to attend a Vietnam Helicopter Pilots Association event in DC, and I did. I met only a few men who had known my brother, but life can sometimes throw us off balance, and in this instance it quite literally did. I held a door for an elderly couple walking through, and as they cleared the doorway, I let go of the door and turned around, colliding with Brent Goldbarb, a childhood friend of Liam's. I lost my balance, but he grabbed my arm. Dad had taught Brent how to fly helicopters, and Brent flew them in Vietnam. We greeted each other, hugged, and decided to go into the bar for a drink and quick catch-up. Brent told me the story of how he went on a rescue mission and picked up Liam. They couldn't believe it when they saw each other, two young guys from Santa Monica meeting in the jungles of Vietnam. Brent is still living in Santa Monica, is happily married to his high school sweetheart, and has a son attending UCLA. We enjoyed our chat, and as we parted, we promised to stay in touch.

The man I visited in New York attended the conference with me. I was accepting our friendly, platonic relationship. Another man I met has devoted much of his life to working with the Montagnard people, who have relocated in this country. The Montagnard people are from the central highlands of Vietnam. On Liam's last leave he'd told me how he'd been invited to dinner at the home of a Montagnard family. Knowing he enjoyed beer, they'd had a beer for him. That beer had cost that family one week's salary.

On the shuttle back to the airport, I sat next to a woman who looked like someone I'd like to know, so I started up a conversation with her. Her name is Paula, and she told me she was attending the conference because she'd written a book about the loss of her husband in Vietnam and the effect it'd had on her life and that of her children. She gave me a copy, and we promised to be in touch.

July 28, 2000

For my birthday I had fifty people crowded into my little cottage to hear Paula talk about her book, her husband, and the impact the Vietnam War had had on her family and community. Fifty-eight thousand U.S. men and women died in Vietnam, and they were heroes, but the women they left behind are heroines. We had to grieve and still pick up the pieces of our lives. We had to explain to our children why Daddy or Grandad or Uncle Liam had come home in a box. Alone, women who lost husbands had to support and educate their children.

Definition of a heroine: a woman admired or idealized for her courage, outstanding achievements, or noble qualities.

August 16, 2000

It's our Ashland summertime again, and this year, something totally incredible happened. While Jacob and I have a good, solid relationship, I have come to terms with the fact that we will never be a couple again. I do love living alone, but I miss romance and would dearly love to have a romantic adventure. Two nights ago, we were at a performance of classical music at the outdoor Britt Music & Arts Festival, and I made a wish upon a star. I wished for a man who loved all the things I do and who was warm and compassionate. The next night I met Norm. He's staying here at the Queen Anne. We have so much in common. He loves the theater, opera, chamber music. He lives not far from me in the Bay Area. He's leaving tomorrow, so we've arranged to get together when I return. Rachael thinks he looks ridiculous because he wears a fanny pack. I have to admit, it isn't the best look.

September 1, 2000

Paula took me to a writers' group. One of the attendees was Maxine Hong Kingston, who wrote *The Woman Warrior*. I was almost rendered speechless, being in the company of such a famous woman! My mind became a blank when it came to the writing exercises. Other than my journals, I haven't written since Dad died. We walked in the woods in silence as an exercise to clear our minds. I felt like I was back in the '20s at a meeting of the Algonquin Round Table. I want to write again!

September 15, 2000

Mom, Deedee, and I are here again at the reunion of the Vietnam vets. At the first reunion, people were friendly and very nice, but now that they've gotten to know us, they're really opening up. Men who knew my brother tell us wonderful stories of their memories of Liam. One man told me that Liam returned to camp one night from a harrowing mission. He went into the bar to order a drink, and the bartender told him the bar was closed. Liam proceeded to tell him if he didn't get his drink, he would start shooting the bottles off the shelves. Needless to say, he promptly got his drink, and on the house. I couldn't imagine my brother doing something like that. He was such a gentle soul. Shortly before he enlisted in the army, he nursed a wounded bird back to health. Liam was so young. Thinking about all this made me angry, so I guess I could see myself shooting those bottles off the shelves too.

Another man told us that he was on the team that went in and rescued my brother's body. Liam didn't have to go on this mission. He'd been due to leave for home in a few days, but he'd wanted to accompany the new guys on this last undertaking. The two other soldiers were killed as well. The son of one of those men is attending the reunion with his fiancée. I just met the son of the man who died with my brother. This young man has spent and will spend his life without a father, and I without a brother. Why? I was shocked when I heard my sister say, "We should just drop a bomb on those fucking countries." I said, "But there are innocent women and children." Deedee replied, "Oh, grow up, Leslie. Those women and children are killing our soldiers. The children are growing up to be ruthless killers like their parents." To my surprise, several of the others in the conversation agreed with her.

September 17, 2000

A man who was one of Liam's commanding officers is following me around like a puppy. He's smitten! But he's twenty years older than I am, which makes him a better candidate for Mother. When I hinted at that to her, she said, "He's too old." He took me gambling last night. He played blackjack with a stack of one-hundred-dollar bills! All I could think of was how much I could do with that money.

I was sitting at the bar, chatting casually with one of the men, who kept eyeing me with sad eyes and shaking his head a bit. Finally, he looked me in the eye and said, "Leslie, you're truly an extraordinary woman. Not many people could have survived all the devastation you've suffered: your brother being killed in 'Nam, your father committing suicide on Liam's grave, your husband's affair, all in a nine-month period." I didn't know what to say because I don't know how I survived it, but I did know that I had to survive. Did I accept it as normal? Thinking about it now, I realize that those nine months altered my life forever. As we went our separate ways and exited the bar, I wondered how that man knew so much about me. Deedee and Mother love to gossip; they love to tell the stories and receive the sympathy they garner.

Deedee has developed a bit of class, or shall we call it manipulation, being exposed to the rich and famous. She sashayed into the room at cocktail hour like a model on a runway. Every head in the room turned. People just stared, quite unable to look away. She knows how to capture a crowd without saying a word. At dinner a man by the name of Conrad Foreman sat at our table. He was under Deedee's spell. It was something to watch. That girl's got style! Conrad wanted to take Deedee to the airport in the morning, but she'd made arrangements for a driver. Since I detest Johnson, the thought occurred to me: What if Deedee became smitten with Conrad? The devil in me went into overdrive, and I told Conrad to go ahead and take her. I'd unmake the arrangements for the driver!

Deedee

October 22, 2000

For my birthday present this year, Johnson informed me that he is getting a divorce! He got his ugly whore secretary pregnant and wants to be a hands-on dad! Fuck! I wish someone had told me about dick-tation! That fucking bitch was out here a few weeks ago, looking in every nook and cranny in my house. She knew she'd be taking over my home, my life. The bitch! God, I can't stand it! I want to kill her. That fucking bastard Johnson is going to pay for this. I'll go after his law firm. Me, with my Barbie Doll looks, replaced by a fat ugly whore! Un-fucking-believable! I'm beautiful! How can he insult me by replacing me with that ugly bitch?

November 19, 2000

I've moved out of the ranch. I'm in an apartment, which I have totally redecorated. It's nice but small and only temporary. Johnson is buying me a townhouse. It's in a new development and won't be ready for six months. The gym has never made money, so Johnson is closing it down. I asked him to give me more time, but he said no. However, so that I don't go after the law firm he has given me a settlement proposal. It's a fifteen-year plan. He will pay cash for the townhouse and put it in my name, give me the Mercedes sports car, the SUV, and a truck and trailer for the horses. He will pay all the expenses for the horses for five years. He will give me unlimited use of two credit cards for five years and one for the following five years. He will pay all insurance policies for ten years. He will send me a check each month for $10,000 for five years, $7000 for three years, $5000 for two years, $2000 for three years, and $1000 for two years. And he will pay any educational expenses in the next fifteen years so that I can train myself to be in a position to earn an income that I have become accustomed to. My attorney told me to take it. I don't know.

Chapter Twenty-Seven

So Many Men, So Little Time

Deedee

January 1, 2001

Happy Fucking New Year! Why does everything always happen to me? Fuck! I took the settlement offer. I know Leslie is jealous. She would just love to have some fucking Prince Un-Charming pay for her doctorate degree. She told me to get my butt back in school, this was the offer of a lifetime, I can do anything I want, fifteen years is a long time. I'm too depressed to think about it. I'm five foot seven and I weigh ninety-five pounds. I live on prepackaged salads and martinis. I beat both Mom and Leslie on the lowest weight. Neither of them has ever weighed that little. The lowest either of them ever got to was ninety-seven. It feels good to beat them at something. Maybe the divorce was worth it. I thought about another suicide attempt to get Johnson's attention but even that and the guilt he'd feel wouldn't budge him from taking on this baby.

Leslie

February 28, 2001

Why do I surround myself with so many books? Is it an obsession? I remember a night years ago in my little apartment in Santa Monica when I had nothing to read. I had a feeling of emptiness, fearfulness, and loss. Could that be why I buy so many books, the fear of running out? I spend so much money on books. I could go to the library. I buy books that take me years to get around to reading. I certainly will have plenty to read when I retire. I think there's something to the saying that when we buy books, we're really buying the time to read them. I like to see books around me. They're like old friends. I love the smell of books and the feel of books and wondering what new delights await me within the pages. I read to relax, to escape pain and reality. It's my go-to comfort.

March 12, 2001

I arrived home from a deposition last week to find a note on my door saying that someone would like to buy my house. I thought it was one of those scams, but when none of the neighbors I checked with said they'd received such a note, I investigated. I'm glad I did. I found out that Jacob had forged my name on loans he'd taken out against the property. He had not paid on the loans for a year, and my house was about to be foreclosed on. I called him and said, "What the hell is going on?" He replied, "I was desperate to save my business." I said, "Why didn't you talk to me?" He answered, "I didn't want you to see me as a failure. I thought I could get the loans paid up before you found out."

March 19, 2001

I called my mother and told her what Jacob had done. I said, "I am so angry I could kill him." She said, "Oh, honey, don't do that. The wife is always the first one they suspect."

Jacob and I have had some long discussions about how best to handle this situation. We decided it's time to get a divorce to separate me from his financial disaster. I've also contacted my lender and am refinancing the house.

Thinking about all this, I realized how desperately Jacob wanted to succeed, not only for himself but also for me. I'm still angry at him, and I certainly can't trust him with money, but I do love him and feel bad for him. I know he's devastated.

Deedee

April 15, 2001

Tax day! That is being handled for me like everything else in my life. I've moved into my new townhouse. It's three levels. I spent a fortune on decorating and it's beautiful. I brought Jeffie, my three-legged dog from the ranch, with me, but he was peeing all over my new carpets so I gave him to Mom. I've had a few dates, but nothing really came of them. Leslie let Conrad know that I was available, and he has been calling me. On our first date we both got slammed and sex was really bad, but we're working that out.

Leslie

May 1, 2001

My beautiful baby girl is engaged to be married! Tony and Rachael have been dating for six years, but still it's difficult to face the reality that my daughter will move on in new and different ways that I will not always be sharing with her.

May 25, 2001

Well, the guy I met at the Queen Anne, Norm, didn't last long, although we did have a good time. We went to a lot of performances of chamber music, theater, and opera. We even went on an opera retreat. And we went to Hawaii. That was interesting, not terribly romantic or as fun as I thought it might be. He introduced me to women's basketball; he had season tickets. He was a runner too, which is always nice, since I'm devoted to my running.

Ellie sold the QA, so Norm and I went up and helped her move down the alley into an adorable little house. That was a good trip but bittersweet. I stayed there the first year it was a bed-and-breakfast. Now it would be a private residence once again.

Norm and I spent a nice Christmas Eve at my home with my mother, playing card games and drinking eggnog. It was cozy and sweet. I felt my mother's love and joy in sharing this special occasion with me.

Mom returned home a few days after Christmas, and for New Year's Eve Norm and I went to a jazz club in the city. Armistead Maupin, the author of *Tales of the City*, sat next to me. I was starstruck! I told him how much my daughter, niece, and I love his books. He introduced us to his friend, and we enjoyed a lively conversation about the city and writing while waiting for the festivities to begin. His books began as a serial in the *San Francisco Chronicle*. It would be fun to write a serial novel. They were quite the rage in the nineteenth century. Maybe I could write a serial novel about my crazy family. Oh, good grief! Who'd read that?

It was a good year all in all, although I drove to Norm's much more often than he came up to Alameda. He suggested I sell my home and buy something closer to him. There were clues foreshadowing the end of the relationship. He has two daughters, but he's leaving all his money to the symphony so there will be a plaque with his name placed in a prominent location. The clincher happened one day when we were running. We were laughing about something, and I playfully patted his butt. OMG! He went bonkers, running ahead of me and screaming, "Don't touch me like that! Don't come near me!" He became belligerent and withdrawn, and wouldn't speak to me. Later I found out that as a child he'd been sexually abused by his brother.

July 4, 2001

I went to a lovely Fourth of July party at my friend Pearl's place on the estuary. The lights over the water were so beautiful. It reminded me of Fourth of Julys in Santa Monica and Long Beach. There must have been fifty people there, so there was no lack of great conversation. I felt rather lonely, though. Well, not lonely really. I love living alone, on my own. Okay! Here's the deal! I miss sex! It's been quite a while since I've met a man who, well, turned me on. Gave me those butterflies. Made me hot and bothered. Did I mention that Pearl is a professional escort? Yeah, she's just your regular girl next door. I was telling Pearl about this movie I saw where a woman hired a male masseuse for her birthday present to herself and how it led to really hot sex. I told her it's my new fantasy, and as my birthday is coming up, how can I go about accomplishing this? She suggested advertising in some of the trade newspapers. I had no idea such a thing existed. I asked her if she thought Manny, whom I'd met at some of her soirees, might take cash for the task. Manny is an attorney who is really cute and quite charming. He's a straight guy but likes to cross-dress at the soirees, which is quite a hoot and makes him sort of endearing. I wouldn't want to date him, but he'd be perfect for fulfilling my fantasy. She said she'd approach him.

July 10, 2001

Maurice, the psychiatrist, and I have been friends for several years. I truly enjoy his company and look forward to our dates. I feel elegant when I'm with him, like a goddess. We have the most wonderful discussions about everything and anything; there is no lack of subjects to discuss. Maurice also validates and values my intelligence and mental health.

Maurice has never invited me to his house. His son was living with him, and they had cats that misbehaved, so he said it was quite a mess. He rarely spoke about it, and it had been several years. The other night, during intermission at the symphony, he asked me if I'd like to come back to his house for a late-night supper. I know I looked surprised because I was. He just said, "I've gotten the house cleaned up a bit, and it's ready for company." When we arrived back at his place, I walked in and was instantly taken back. This wasn't just cleaned up a bit; this was a designer showcase. Everything was new and remodeled. And I do mean everything: hardwood flooring, oriental carpets, beautiful furniture and window treatments, remodeled kitchen and baths. It was stunning! And he'd prepared a delicious meal accompanied by astounding wines. Later, when I arrived back home, upon reflection, I realized he'd done all that work on his house for me.

July 20, 2001

The Sex in the City Over Fifty gals met in the city for dinner tonight. Pearl had us in stitches, laughing over her latest sexual escapades. Franny's face never left the bright-red stage, and Beatrice had to excuse herself three times to go to the restroom and throw cold water on her face. The ladies at the next table were quite literally leaning our way to capture every word we were saying, while the couple at the other table near us were stone-cold sober and staring down their noses at us. It was an elegant restaurant, and we should have comported ourselves in a like manner, but we are quite incorrigible. We like sex, we enjoy talking about it, and we love to laugh.

I told them about going to Maurice's home and how totally stunning it is. The first thing Beatrice said was, "He did that for you." I told her I could not believe a man would go to that much trouble to bring a woman home, especially me. I felt so undeserving. Yet I felt like the most important woman in the world, like I'd just walked a red carpet of rose petals in my bare feet, wearing a sleek, slinky dress. I felt like Grace Kelly. I told them how the kissing in the car when he brought me home was getting quite heavy, and I didn't know how to handle the sexual part of our relationship. They said I should go for it.

July 22, 2001

Oh, my gosh! I met the best-looking man, Parker, at Friday-night services last week. I could not take my eyes off him. Maybe the Orthodox Jews know what they're doing by separating the men and women. He introduced himself to me at the Oneg Shabbat after the service, and we chatted until we were the only people left. We decided to walk over to the restaurant across from the synagogue and get a glass of wine. We talked until the bar closed and then exchanged numbers. He's been calling me every day since, and we've met for dinner twice.

July 27, 2001

You will never guess what I did for my birthday! Actually, to back up, Pearl called and told me Manny was up for helping me fulfill my fantasy and didn't want to be paid. I was quite flattered, but I told Pearl that I didn't think I would be in need of Manny, as I'd met a very nice prospect and decided to give myself that gift. So, Parker, the man I met at Friday-night services, had tickets to see a very popular jazz singer. When he found out it was my birthday, he tried to get another ticket, but they were sold out. So, I said, "Why don't you come by for a drink after the performance?" and he did. Well, one thing led to another, which led to bed. Wow, that guy is built! I feel fantastic! I think he just moved up to number one as the best-ever sex!

Earlier in the evening Franny had called to ask me what I was doing for my birthday. When I said, "Oh, not much, just relaxing at home," she said, "You can't be alone on your birthday. Come over here. I'll make martinis." I said, "No, really, it's what I want to do." She said, "No, you can't be alone; I'll be right over with a pitcher of martinis." I thought, "Oh no, here goes my birthday present to myself." I said, "Really, Franny, it's okay." Well, she was pretty insistent, so I had to confess my plans. I could feel her face get red through the phone wires. When we have our Sex in the City

Over Fifty get-togethers, she's quite open about sex, but she still gets beet red and is a bit shocked at some of the tales.

Did I mention that Parker is fourteen years younger than I am?

August 21, 2001

Mom and I are back in Ashland. We took a knife class at the cooking store, and I met yet another man. He asked me if I'd like to go to dinner with him, and I said yes. It was a lovely evening. The next morning, we met at his house to go for a walk. His house is my dream home! The shower in the master bath has a view of the valley! The pantry in the kitchen would fit a dozen people quite comfortably. There's a fireplace in almost every room. You go up a spiral staircase to an office with a surrounding view of the valley and city. I would marry this man for his house alone. However, in the short time we spent together, I found him to be extremely arrogant and harsh. He's not for me.

Rachael and Tony found a lovely location for the wedding and set a date, June 22, 2002. We'll go shopping for her dress when I return home. Franny is having a shower for her. What a very special time in our lives!

September 11, 2001

This morning our country suffered the worst terrorist attack on US soil, three hours of terror and chaos. Two hijacked airliners were flown into the twin towers of the World Trade Center in New York, a third hit the Pentagon, and a fourth crashed into some fields just north of Somerset County Airport in Pennsylvania. I have been in a stupefied state all day. I have been glued to the television set and on and off the phone with Mother and Rachael. Fear is rampant. I have been trembling and unable to focus. I turned off the television, took a hot shower, and am sitting by the fireplace in the living room with a manhattan, classical music, and a cozy mystery. I had to escape.

September 29, 2001

Just two weeks after our country was attacked, I'm attending another conference of the Vietnam Special Forces vets. I was asked to make a transcript of their official meeting. Having been given a special pass to get in, I set up my stenotype machine and off we went with the meeting. It was extremely boring.

Deedee and Conrad are an item now, and they are here, having a great time. I met up with the man who accompanied me to the brothers and sisters conference. Henry's his name. We were deep in conversation when he looked across the room and was rendered speechless. I followed his glance. He was staring at another man. Suddenly they both ran and hugged each other, sobbing.

When they got themselves composed, they related this story to me: While in 'Nam, Henry had gotten tangled up in a parachute that then caught on fire. Men were jumping in trying to pull him out. One of them shouted, "We can't get him out; we've got to get out of here. The helicopters are hovering." Another man yelled, "I'm going to try one more time." He ran into the burning parachute and by some miracle he was able to pull Henry out. Henry was brutally injured and bleeding, trying desperately not to pass out. The man, Jim, grabbed him and dragged him to a helicopter ladder, pulling Henry up on it behind himself. Jim was shouting, "Hang on." Henry was bleeding profusely and slipping in the blood as he cried, "Please, for God's sake, don't let go of me!"

Chills ran up and down my spine at the sight of these two men meeting for the first time since that day.

Deedee

October 22, 2001

Another fucking birthday! God! I'm fifty! Conrad is taking me out to dinner. I'll have to throw up and that always gives me a sore throat. I'd rather eat a salad at home. Mother and Leslie are on me about furthering my education so I can support myself, but I don't need to. I'm sure Conrad will pop the question and I'll soon be married again. Leslie is so insistent about education, which of course she should be since she can't find a man to marry her. Rachael graduated from college and got another degree. She's teaching. Amiala graduated too, but she can't find a job. Amiala was very lucky. Due to her disability, she got state aid to help pay for her education. See? That limp isn't such a bad thing. It's not very noticeable. Amiala is still living with Mom. Meliza is living with some rich guy she met at a bar and having a great time. My grandson spends a lot of time with his dad, who managed to get one-half custody. I enrolled in court reporting college, but I dropped out. It was too hard. You're supposed to have gone to a four-year college first. I hadn't, so the classes were way over my head. And that little machine is a bore! Leslie tells me to at least get my GED. She told me Meliza did, but Meliza didn't. She lied to Leslie and Mother.

Leslie

October 28, 2001

Rachael and I went shopping for her wedding dress, and we found one that is perfect. It's a white brocade fabric, floor length with two small spaghetti straps. It's simple yet stunning and fits her like a glove. I took loads of pictures. Rachael should be a model. She looks fantastic in anything she puts on. It was exciting, watching her try on dresses. Sitting there, I wondered how this day had come so fast.

Time! It's so elusive and yet so seductive. It seduces you with its hint of years to come and then slips away.

Chapter Twenty-Eight

Memories are Made of This

Leslie

January 1, 2002

Happy New Year! Parker and I spent a lovely New Year's Eve at Davies Symphony Hall. We got box seats, drank champagne, and listened to beautiful music performed by the symphony. Then the stage was cleared, and it became a dance floor. We danced, and at midnight balloons fell from the ceiling as we celebrated the grand entrance of a brand-new year. Parker and I blew our horns, and jiggled our noisemakers, and enjoyed a very sexy kiss. It was an extraordinary New Year's Eve! I wonder if I could see a future with Parker.

February 12, 2002

Rachael and I went shopping in the city to try to find a mother-of-the-bride dress. We found a stunning, strapless, slinky, navy blue, sequined dress. I love it! We also went to various stores and registered Rachael and Tony for wedding gifts. She picked out china, silver, and crystal. How exciting to be embarking on a new chapter in her life with all its many possibilities!

April 4, 2002

Franny had an extraordinary shower for Rachael here in Alameda. Mother and Ami came up, and some of Rachael's sorority sisters flew in from various parts of the country. Franny is an amazing cook and had all sorts of lovely tea sandwiches and pastries. The house was festive with wedding shower decorations. The day was sunny and warm. Everyone was dressed in beautiful spring attire. Rachael was glowing! I am so happy and so proud. Life is good!

June 23, 2002

Rachael got married! It doesn't seem possible. Looking back at my journal entries, she truly was just a little girl only yesterday.

She was the most beautiful bride in the world. Tony cried! Jacob cried! I cried! Ami was her maid of honor; Mel and her sorority sisters were her bridesmaids. Deedee, Mom, and Conrad flew up from the Valley, and their plane was late. Fortunately, though, they arrived before the wedding, in plenty of time to change clothes and have pictures taken. I was getting in the car to drive Rachael to the wedding and telling her, "You can't possibly get married without your grandma here," when I saw their taxi pull up. I stopped the car and jumped out to tell them to hurry, that we were on our way. While I was doing that, an older gentleman saw Rachael in the car and said, "Oh my, you look quite lovely! Do you have a date?"

The food was mouthwatering and plentiful. The DJ was a hoot, and the dancing was so much fun that it was hard to take a break and sit down. The speeches were heartwarming. Tony's family and mine and all our friends greeted one another with warmth and sincerity. It was a memorable wedding. And now my beautiful baby girl is off on a new adventure.

Deedee

July 4, 2002

I've been having stomach pains and a sore throat. I sound like an old smoker, but I haven't smoked in years. It could be from throwing up, but it's probably a case of the flu. At Rachael's wedding I felt like I was part of the family. Everybody loves

Conrad. I've always felt like an orphan and that Leslie and mother have no respect for me. They think I'm stupid because I refuse to finish school. But since Conrad's been in my life, I think mother and Leslie have some respect for me.

Leslie

September 16, 2002

I didn't go to the vets' reunion this year, but Deedee and Conrad did. Deedee called me and told me that a man by the name of Dan Rosseau had come up to her in the bar and said, "I'm so glad to see you. Is your sister here also? I've been wanting to meet you two." Deedee said no, and Dan said something that caused Deedee to drop her drink and almost fall over, herself. He said, "I was there the night your father died." When Deedee told me, I felt like I'd been kicked in the stomach. It was like finding out about Dad's death all over again. Why was Dan there on the night Dad died? Deedee proceeded to tell me that Dan was Dad's backup in case he couldn't go through with shooting himself. I couldn't believe what I was hearing. Then I became outraged. How could this man have known this and not told our family? Didn't he have a moral obligation to inform us of Dad's state of mind? If one of my girlfriend's mothers told me she was going to commit suicide, I would immediately tell my friend. What kind of a sick individual was this man?

Deedee gave me Dan's phone number, and I called him. He was so nonchalant, chatting like he could hardly wait to tell me the story. It seemed as though he thought I would be very happy to hear it, like now we would be best friends. He basically confirmed what Deedee had said. If I'd been in the same room with him, I would have slapped the shit out of him, as Deedee would say. It was all I could do not to scream. Then I hit him with a good punch! I said, "Well, Dan, since you were there, then you know that there were three bullets in my father's body, and the likelihood of him firing three shots

194

into himself is slim to none. It sounds to me like you must have fired that third shot, if not all three." He hung up on me.

I was so incensed I couldn't let go of this. I called a friend who is a detective and a Vietnam vet. I wanted to get his take. He said some kind things, but the gist was he told me to let it be; it would be impossible to produce evidence. I called a friend who is an attorney and asked if we couldn't sue Dan and bring him to justice on the grounds that he had a moral obligation to inform the family. My friend said yes, but it would be godawful, and it would come down to Dan's word against ours as to whether he really said those things. I was contemplating the conversation with the attorney when Deedee called. She knew I was investigating legal avenues to bring justice to our father's death, but she said, "You need to drop it. Conrad is as mad as hell that you're getting involved." I said, "What? Of course, I'm involved. This was my father. He didn't have to die. This asshole Dan took him away from us by not telling us that Dad was thinking about suicide. Dan is a murderer." Deedee's reply was, "Conrad says these guys do this every day. You'll be targeted for opening this up." I asked her, "What the hell does that mean?" She said, "Leslie, they're a brotherhood, and they will stick together. You'll look like a fool. You need to drop it."

October 1, 2002

I've thought of nothing else for two weeks but Asshole Dan. I don't know how to come to terms with this. Maybe I can't; maybe I never will. I'm angry, sad, and extremely frustrated. There's an underbelly of life that I don't know anything about. In my mind, Asshole Dan took my father from me, and I want justice. To bring someone to justice: "If a criminal is brought to justice, he or she is punished for a crime by being arrested and tried in a court of law." We can't always get what we want.

October 12, 2002

One of the ladies in my book group, Jane, said that her brother-in-law will be coming here to spend Christmas and that I should meet him. I said fine. She said, "Meanwhile, could I give him your email so you can get to know each other?" I said sure, like I know something about email. Well, a few weeks ago, I got an email from mountainman! Really? I asked Rachael, "Do you think this is safe to open?" You hear so much about computer fraud and weird men. Rachael said, "Sure, give it a try." What an email! I'm in love! I need to find the email, but it was along the lines of "Do you think love could blossom in the Oakland Hills?" And it goes on from there. We have been emailing every day since. I can hardly wait to get home and check my emails at night. What an interesting and very sexy guy!

November 29, 2002

Maurice and I fixed a fabulous Thanksgiving dinner at his house. We had twelve people for a sit-down dinner. It was a delightful evening. Maurice is probably the best cook I've ever known. I think it might have to do with all the chemistry classes he took in med school.

Today Mom and I went to the Great Dickens Christmas Fair in the city. A man stopped Mom and asked her if she'd seen Mr. Dickens. She got the biggest kick out of that. I am so fortunate to have such a loving relationship with my mom. She's my best friend. After the Dickens Fair we went to Maurice's house for leftovers and told him all about our afternoon adventure. I wonder if I could make a life with Maurice.

December 10, 2002

Jacob came over and helped me put the lights on the tree last night. This morning he called to tell me that the twinkling lights were like the twinkling in his heart. That was so sweet and so unlike Jacob. I sure am juggling an awful lot of suitors at the moment.

I can't believe how intrigued I am about mountainman. He'll probably turn out to be some beer-bellied cowboy with a Stetson and boots. Maybe it's the anonymity of email. He seems to have a quick mind and a great sense of humor, and he certainly has brought out my sexual devilishness.

December 16, 2002

After months of emailing and so much anticipation and sexual buildup, the time finally came for me to meet mountainman, which is his moniker for what he loves, climbing mountains. His name is Ken. He'd be arriving December 15. I was nervous and terribly excited. I suggested that since Jane and her husband will be picking Ken up at the Oakland Airport around five that they come to my house for dinner, as I'm only ten minutes from the airport. I thought about what to make for dinner that would be impressive but simple. I decided on a roasted chicken. Franny helped me plan the menu. I thought about what to wear. First impressions are so important. We had not exchanged pictures. I chose skinny black pants; stilettos, which have become my norm since *Sex in the City* became so popular; and a camisole with a matching, short-cropped, black-and-gray blouse.

As luck would have it, the Bay Area got hit by a huge rainstorm. Streets were flooded. Ken's plane was late. Dinner was beyond ready. The anticipation for this meeting was something I'd never experienced. The buildup of emailing for months was making me crazy, sexually and emotionally. I was at a place where I was ready to meet the love of my life. I pictured him moving in with me and living an amazing and incredible life. We would be bonded and support each other in our endeavors, and sex would be over the top. I would have a loving family; I adored his sister-in-law and knew we would be close, spending holidays and such together. He would be handsome; we would make a winning couple.

Since I was such a nervous wreck, I decided to relax by playing the piano. With the loudness of the storm and piano, I didn't hear the knock on the door. I was startled when I realized they'd arrived. I opened the door and greeted them. I'd never met Mario, Jane's husband, so I wasn't sure which of the two men was Ken, and no one clued me in. There weren't introductions because I imagine they assumed I'd met Mario previously, and I didn't dispel that assumption. A bit into dinner I realized who was whom. Ken was definitely the cuter of the two, but what a dingbat. I mean, really, he had nothing to add to the conversation and just nodded and stared dumbly around at us. It was then that I realized that this man was long into his cups; he began to talk about flying first class and having all the drinks he wanted. Oh boy! I could hardly wait to get rid of them. What a major disappointment. Ugh! How could I have been so foolish?

While I was out shopping today, Ken called and asked if I would like to go to Muir Woods with them tomorrow. I begged off, claiming I had a lot of work to do, when in reality I'd cleaned my slate workwise in anticipation of spending the holidays in bliss with the love of my life. Yes, I know it's enough to make one puke! Ken was persistent. Finally, I relented, thinking a day with Jane and Mario in Muir Woods might be enjoyable.

So today I met them at the Market Place in Berkeley. When I hopped in the car, dressed in jeans and boots, I noted that Ken was dressed in a shirt and tie. They all began to laugh, explaining that I'd said dress last night would be casual, and they thought I was dressed to the nines. Interesting! They should only see me dressed to the nines!

Well, at least Ken was sober and none the worse for wear. The day was pleasant. Jane and Mario live in a million-dollar-plus home in the Oakland Hills and drive a Mercedes. Jane tried to impress me with the fact that Ken also drives a Mercedes. I said, "That's nice." Since I drive a Jaguar, I wasn't terribly impressed.

On the drive back, I was looking forward to getting home and relaxing in front of the fireplace with a martini and a good book when Ken began patting my thigh. The patting turned to rubbing. The rubbing was getting sexy, then extremely sexy. I thought I'd have an orgasm, calmly sitting there! I gently removed his hand, but the feeling remained. Then Jane suggested I join them for dinner at their home, and they would run me back to my car after. I thought, "Why not?" It was a lovely evening. Ken drove me back to my car where the necking began, and I thought I would go bonkers with lust.

December 25, 2002

What a whirlwind ten days this has been! Ken and I have been inseparable, and needless to say, he turned out not to be a dingbat. We spent a lot of time with Jane and Mario, but we managed to spend time with my friends too. In fact, maybe too much, as Mario commented that he'd invited his brother for Christmas and Ken was spending all his time with me and my friends.

I took Ken to Flora's birthday dinner party. Upon arriving back at my place, we were incredibly hot and bothered and immediately ended up on the bed. Before I knew what was happening, Ken was done. We didn't even have our clothes off. All this anticipation for naught. A premature ejaculator! Great! However, in the end it worked out rather well.

We spent romantic nights in the city, taking in the holiday atmosphere, enjoying unique boutique city restaurants. We went to hear the Gay Men's Chorus holiday musical. One night after a lovely day and evening in the city, as they were dropping me off at my house, Ken suddenly told Jane and Mario that I was afraid of the dark and perhaps he should spend the night!

We went to a holiday party at the home of a neighbor of Mario and Jane's; it was a very posh affair. I was asked to play the piano, and I played what holiday tunes I could remember. The hosts asked Ken if we were engaged; Ken said, "Not yet; perhaps next year," which sent thrills of excitement running through me.

199

Since Rachael was spending Christmas Eve with Tony's family and Mom was with Deedee, I went with Ken to Mario and Jane's. It was a lovely evening, filled with beautiful memories and a lot of sexual tension.

This morning Rachael and Tony were here opening gifts. Tony kept eyeing a small package and nudging it toward me. I finally opened it to discover an Italian charm that read "Gma." I have a friend who has no grandchildren, but she has a granddog, so I thought, "This is a little over-the-top to be grandma to their adorable golden lab, Woody!" Then it hit me! Oh my God! I'm going to be a grandmother! This is the most exciting thing that has ever happened to me! I'll buy a crib and a highchair. I'll make baby clothes, and quilts, and knit little sweaters. I'll need a stroller too. I'll spend every weekend with the baby!

December 30, 2002

Ken left to spend New Year's in Chicago and then head for home, Beverly Hills, Texas. I've done nothing but cry. I really got locked into the last fifteen days. I can't quite believe it's all over. It was truly an amazingly romantic holiday season, something from a Hallmark holiday film: the lights, the decorations, the music, the romance, the laughter. I wish it could go on forever!

The day after Christmas, Ken and I spent the day together, and Ken told me that for Christmas dinner they went to the home of a friend of Mario's. Ken said, "I think my brother is gay!" I said, "What makes you think that?" He said, "He kissed this guy on the mouth." I responded, "That doesn't necessarily mean he's gay." Ken said, "It was a very sexy, tongue, deep-throat kiss!" I said, "Oh! Well, so what if he is gay? He's a great guy, and he does a lot for the gay community." Ken just grunted.

Chapter Twenty-Nine

I'm a Believer

Leslie

January 1, 2003

I did have a lovely New Year's Eve, but I missed Ken and wished he'd invited me to go with him to Chicago. It would have been so incredibly romantic to spend New Year's with him. I have to pull myself back into the real world, so I went to the symphony New Year's Eve gala with Parker. Parker is a sweetie, but my heart belongs to Ken!

Deedee

January 1, 2003

Conrad and I went to a party at the Stafford Hotel for New Year's Eve. I've been putting on weight. That's not a good thing. We've had extended happy hours with too many bar snacks and then a full-on dinner. Still, heads turned when I walked into the room last night. It's a wonderful feeling to walk into a room and have all conversation stop and heads turn as you walk by. You know you've done it right! I'm still having stomachaches and a sore throat, so it's been hard to throw up, but I'll get back to it. I will not get fat.

Everybody likes Conrad. Mother has always said, "Everybody loves Leslie." Then it was, "Everybody loves Rachael." She's never said, "Everyone loves Deedee," but then it's a given that I'm the prettiest. Leslie is cute and petite, but she's not beautiful and she certainly does not command the attention of a room when she walks in. She is so wrapped up in her job and saving money, and yet she's always crying poor. She can't find a husband. I wish I could help her. Maybe I'll fix her up with one of Conrad's friends. I think it's

201

time Conrad and I moved in together, but he says he isn't ready. You'd think he'd be dying to have me live with him. I mean just look at me! He's been a bachelor all his life. Well, he was married when he was very young, but she was a crazy bitch and the marriage didn't last two years. He has a son who is as screwed up as his mother. He's been in and out of jail. My daughters have problems, and it's all their fathers' faults. I married two real losers, but at least the girls haven't been in jail. Actually, Meliza has been in the drunk tank more times than I can count. Conrad and I had a nice brunch with Bloody Marys! Now I'm off to hit the New Year's Day sales, although I've never bought anything on sale in my life.

Leslie

May 23, 2003

Ken and I talk almost every day and email several times a day. Although he hasn't returned to Alameda, I've been back to stay with him. He has an eight-to-five job, where my schedule is my own. He lives in a nice community, but I'm struck by the whiteness, the many churches, and how the homes all look the same. It feels creepy. When I go out running, nobody looks at me, waves, or says hello. I feel isolated, alone in a mass of humanity. There are a couple of live theaters that I enjoy, and I love going to their upscale market to purchase ingredients for the recipes I like experimenting with.

July 7, 2003

I'm in Texas with Ken. I'm crazy about him! He's so easy to be with. If he asked me to marry him, I would do so in a New York minute. If he just wanted me to move here and live with him, I don't know. It's pretty hard to give up my home of twenty-five years to go live with him without a commitment.

The traveling back and forth is costing me a bloody fortune. It would be nice if Ken offered to help out with the cost.

My granddaughter, Taylor, will be born in a month. I am so excited about being a grandmother. I told Rachael that I wanted to see her pregnancy progress, so we've been meeting at Russell House in Ashland every month. Rachael is radiant. There's a lamppost in the front of Russell House that reminds me of Gene Kelly in *Singin' in the Rain*. I took a picture of Rachael swinging around the lamppost, and she looks so sweet.

July 10, 2003

Ken comes home from work, makes himself a highball in a gallon-size mug, and goes out to the garage and does woodworking until eleven at night or maybe even as late as one in the morning. And we eat dinner after that. I sit out there with him and read or sew. It's relaxing, but it's weird at the same time, sitting in a garage in the middle of the night. Still, he's so attentive and really appreciates that I'm out there with him.

September 3, 2003

I'm on a plane, flying home from Dallas. I was fifty-nine years old in July. My granddaughter was born August 21. I was staying at Russell House in Ashland and called Rachael, thinking I might go on up to Eugene, where they'd moved a few months ago. Taylor was overdue, and Rachael was going to call me when she went into labor, but I decided since I was so close, I'd go on up before heading back home, if only to give her a hug. I arrived on the evening of the twentieth, and Rachael went into labor in the early morning hours of the twenty-first. She said Taylor waited for me. I was present for the birth. Just saying that takes my breath away. I felt a bit as though I was intruding on Rachael and Tony's special time, but then I was in awe of Taylor being born, three generations of women together. Taylor was born with her hand coming out first, as if she was waving to the world. I thought, "This is a sign of this child's future!" It was the most amazing thing I have ever witnessed and probably ever will. I admire my daughter beyond any other woman in the world.

November 3, 2003

I'm at a court reporting conference in the city. I bought new software that I'm very excited about. I also bought a new rolling bag to carry my equipment in and a tilting tripod. I can hardly wait to use it all.

Ami married Lil's son, Marvin. Lil is Mother's niece by marriage, so Ami and Marvin have known each other since they were children. Lil and I have been close friends for years. She's joined Mom and me at book conferences, Ashland summer vacations, and holidays.

Mom and I really liked the last fellow Ami was in a relationship with. He was mature and sensible and would have been a good match for Ami, but Ami wanted to get married and he wasn't moving fast enough for her. Marvin is spoiled and childish and a real womanizer, but he's what Ami wants. They got married in Las Vegas, and we're having a reception at Mom's today. Jacob flew down, and we shared a ride from the airport.

I'm scared about the possibility of moving to Texas, but one step at a time. I'll be seeing Rachael and Taylor on Friday, and I can hardly wait.

I was in Texas for the High Holy Days, so I went to a local conservative synagogue by myself. Ken is not Jewish. When I arrived at the entrance, there were heavily armed and very serious-looking security guards swarming around—not just one or two old fellows, but six to eight bodybuilder types. My stomach swung up into my throat, and my knees rattled. Had they been having problems here? All I could think of was some crazy redneck coming in and shooting everyone, so I left early. Added to my anxiety was the fact that nobody even acknowledged me. Again, I was completely alone in a mass of people. My own people, I might add!

November 20, 2003

I'm at Mom's. I came down because I was supposed to have training on my new court reporting software, but it was canceled at the last minute. I decided to come anyway because I didn't want to disappoint Mom. She's having cataract surgery, and I wanted to be with her.

I met Ken at LAX for a few hours. He was traveling for work and was on a layover between Taipei and Dallas. I am so besotted! I've lost time from work, home, and family to be with him. The flights are still costing me a fortune and Ken has still not offered to help out with the cost, and I have not asked him to, as I'd like it to be something he'd offer. He says he loves me and wants to spend the rest of his life with me, but I think I'm more committed to the relationship than he is. I keep hoping he'll ask me to marry him, maybe at Christmas.

Chapter Thirty

All I Want For Christmas...

Leslie

January 3, 2004

Ken came here for Christmas, and it was another romantic whirlwind holiday season. I wore the sexiest outfit I could find with stilettos, of course, to pick him up at the airport. We're talking about living together, but Ken can't come here because of his job, so that would mean I would have to move to Texas. I could put everything in storage and rent my house, but he wants me to move bag and baggage. He says it's a lifetime commitment, although he has not asked me to marry him. He checked, and I can get reciprocity in Texas to court report. It's a big move. I've lived in California since I was ten years old. I never did like Texas, but Beverly Hills, Texas, is a pretty nice place. And there's Ken! I am head over heels in love with the guy! A future with him sounds marvelous. And we can move back to California when he retires in seven years.

April 4, 2004

Ken has still not asked me to marry him, and I'm still infatuated. However, I love my life in California, and I love my career. I wonder if Ken would be supportive and understanding or selfish and passive. He watches a lot of television and even eats dinner at the coffee table while watching some horribly violent movie. We've never had a meal together at the dining room table. Ken doesn't go to live theater or restaurants; in fact, he doesn't get out much at all. He doesn't read or exercise, although he used to be a bodybuilder and still looks like a hunk. I do like just being at home with him. However, perhaps that's because it's a respite from my whirlwind life.

July 15, 2004

I was thirty-one years old when I left my graduate studies to go to court reporting college. Rachael was in kindergarten. I was younger than Rachael is now. Where does the time go?

Franny and I saw our last ACT performance for the season. It was Eve Ensler's *The Good Body*. It was a very enlightening story about accepting our bodies; however, I still want to get some nips and tucks and lose this dreadful ten pounds. Not too long ago, Mom confided to me that Deedee was having stomach issues and always had a sore throat. On the way home, Franny and I were talking about the play, and I was reminded of Cassie's daughter, Maura, who had stomach and throat issues as a result of bulimia. Deedee has been throwing up all her life. Could she be bulimic?

August 21, 2004

We celebrated Taylor's first birthday at the Ashland brewery. Tony's family came down, and we had a wonderful party. At the Russell House, Taylor is pulling herself up holding on to Alice's coffee table and walking around it. She is the most astonishing child in the world! I love her so much! I can't get enough of hugging her, and I just want to seize every moment with her.

September 14, 2004

I'm in Texas. Ken still says he loves me, and he wants us to be together, but he doesn't want things to change—that is, he doesn't want to get married. I don't think he loves me enough to make a place for me in his life. I need a commitment. For the past few years, traveling back and forth,

I've left a lot of clothes, etc., at his home. Today I packed up eight boxes and shipped them home. I can't afford this relationship and way of life financially or emotionally. As painful as it is, I need to move on.

October 20, 2004

Rachael, Taylor, Mom, and I met in Ashland to go to the closing of the outdoor theater. I walked Taylor around Ashland for four days, but she would not let go of my hand and walk on her own. On Rachael's way home, she stopped at a Starbucks for a latte, and Taylor got out of the car and walked into Starbucks! I was a bit disappointed not to see her take her first steps on her own, but I shall never forget holding that precious little hand and walking all around Ashland.

Chapter Thirty-One

I'm Still in Love with You

Leslie

January 14, 2005

Moving to Dallas seems less desirable now. I started taking Italian language classes again, and I purchased season tickets to the San Francisco Ballet. Ken says he loves me and that he made a commitment two years ago. He talks in circles. So do I! I made a last-minute decision to fly to Dallas. As Iris suggested, I gave Ken the shit-or-get-off-the-pot lecture. He said he couldn't be forced into making a decision, but he doesn't want me to leave him. I'm going home tomorrow.

February 15, 2005

Ken has been calling me nearly every day since I was last there. One of his hobbies is glassblowing, and yesterday I received a beautiful red glass heart for Valentine's Day. It's a perfume holder with a little glass stick in it for applying perfume. It was wrapped in yards and yards and yards of bubble wrap. I thought about the love and care it took to not only create this astounding piece of artwork but also wrap it to ensure it arrived unharmed. It gave me pause for thought about why I want to remarry. It's a beginning and an ending. Marriage puts an end to one way of living and a beginning to another. It's an important ritual. It's a commitment to each other. It can also be a strengthening of financial ties, making a couple stronger together financially than independently. Marriage brings two families together. Maybe I just want to know that marriage can work. My marriage to Jacob was so fraught with trauma and drama, depression and anger. Is it possible to be in a healthy and happy marriage? I believe so. I have to ask myself, do I just want to be taken care of by a

209

man? Maybe I'm tired of the struggle of taking care of myself. I know I'm tired of trying to take care of my mother, sister, and nieces. Taking care of them hasn't been so much of a financial drain as an emotional one. It's a responsibility I've felt since Dad would go on a flying trip and ask me to take care of everyone while he was gone. Oh, I know now that it was just his way of making me feel important, to perhaps begin to make me aware of responsibility, but, as any child might do, I took it quite seriously, and then I dragged that responsibility with me through life like a heavy backpack.

I've deviated from the subject at hand, Ken and marriage. It's a huge undertaking to give up my home of twenty-eight years and move to a state I'm not terribly fond of.

April 1, 2005

It's April Fool's Day. Am I the fool? I have the opportunity to embark on a great adventure, and I'm hung up on marriage. People say it's only a piece of paper. But in fact, it's actually a legally binding contract. Do I need to be legally bound to this man? Do I really want to be legally bound to this man?

May 2, 2005

Ken shocked me by taking time off work and coming to California to see me. He called me from the Dallas Airport and said, "I'm arriving at the Oakland Airport at five. Will you pick me up?" Will I! Oh, my goodness! My heart was beating on overtime! We spent a marvelous ten days together, talking about our future and how to go about creating a life that works for both of us. Ken has been married three times and is scared to death to try it again. I can understand that. Perhaps after we've been living together for a while, he will feel safe and secure enough to consider marriage, or perhaps I will feel safe and secure enough to not be so concerned about getting married. I read somewhere that, above all else, a woman needs to feel safe.

Deedee

May 11, 2005

It's Mother's Day! I moved in with Conrad a month ago. He finally gave in. I sold my townhouse and spent almost all the money from the sale remodeling his condo. It was unlivable. He hadn't done anything to upgrade it since he moved in in the '70s. It's beautiful now, but he thinks it's crowded. And I got rid of half his crap. He's still working as a potato chip salesman, and I got a job working sales at a clothing store. It's boring. Conrad and I meet after work, go to the club to work out, and then have drinks and dinner. Conrad has a lot of friends that we meet up with, very rich people. I told Leslie that I would put her in touch with one of the girls I met because she also speaks Italian, but Leslie speaks Italian like a stupid American and I don't want to embarrass myself.

Mother went to Alameda to spend Mother's Day with Leslie. They drove up to Rachael's. Mother called me to wish me a Happy Mother's Day. I feel left out. They never ask me to come along. I've never been to Ashland, and I haven't been to Rachael's either. But I'd rather be with Conrad anyway. Leslie spends a lot of time with Mom and Rachael because she can't get a man.

Leslie

June 12, 2005

I arrived home tonight after spending a long and lovely weekend with Ken. It was quiet and peaceful. We went to see a play at a small theater in Dallas, which was quite entertaining. Afterward, we went to a restaurant and bar for a delicious and relaxing meal. I decided to take the leap and move to Texas. He will fly to California on July Fourth weekend. We'll pack up my belongings and drive my car back to Texas. If I don't do this, I will never know what could have been.

211

July 15, 2005

Here I am! I rented my house and moved to Texas. I'm settled in, and life is pretty darn good. Ken and I love being together. We stay up half the night, cooking and then watching movies on his extremely large television screen. He's very into tech. He loves to cook, and it's so much fun to have someone to cook with. As I alluded to previously, we eat on the coffee table every night while watching movies, something I've seldom done before, so this is an adjustment. Rachael and I ate our meals at the dining room table, cleaned up, and then watched movies or read.

The actual move wasn't the best experience. While I wanted to hire movers, Ken insisted that he could handle the move himself, which turned out to be a disaster. Most of my beautiful furniture was damaged. It broke my heart. I lived so long with hand-me-downs and worked so hard to purchase all this lovely furniture. I know Ken meant well. He didn't have the money to help me finance the move, so moving me on his own was his way of helping. However, things were not packed well in the truck, and he literally dropped several things while unloading. Needless to say, I was upset. I spent pretty much a whole day crying and mourning the damage. My heart felt broken along with the furniture. Ken felt so bad he took another day off work to spend with me. He said he would repair everything. I tried to tell myself it's only furniture and Ken is a terrific guy.

August 22, 2005

I'm in Ashland! Yesterday we celebrated Taylor's second birthday with a party in Alice's garden at Russell House, and I found out that I'm going to be a grandmother again. I'm so excited! Rachael is expecting a baby boy the first of March. Taylor will know the joy of having a baby brother!

Deedee

August 25, 2005

Leslie finally got a man! I have to admit he's handsome. Now that she'll be so far away I'll get more of Mom's attention. I went to the doctor about my stomachaches and sore throat. They ran tests. I don't have an infection or a virus. They want to run more tests, but I said, "Let's wait for a while." I think I may know what the problem is.

Leslie

September 5, 2005

As it turned out, I could not get reciprocity to report in Texas; they don't accept Californians based, more or less, on the fact that they hate us. Meanwhile, in order to continue earning a living, I fly to the Bay Area or Los Angeles. I stay at Iris's for a couple of weeks and report, and I fly to LA and stay with Mom for a couple of weeks and report. Then I go back to Texas and process my transcripts. Every other working trip, I go to Eugene to see Rachael and the children. I feel like I'm in a three-ring circus. It's fun, though. I love airports, and I love flying! I often think of Dad and wonder if he's returned as a bird, flying around and watching over for me.

At the moment I'm on a plane, returning to Texas after spending two weeks working in LA and two weeks vacationing in Ashland. Mom and I drove up from LA, spending a night at Franny's in the Bay Area. We spent lots of time with Alice from Russell House and Ellie. Rachael, Tony, and Taylor came down from Eugene. Taylor is adorable! Every day brings something new, and she is talking up a storm. She warms my heart! I could sit and watch her all day.

Flora joined us in Ashland. We all had dinner in Jacksonville last night and toasted one another by saying cheers and clicking glasses. This morning when Flora came to the breakfast table, Taylor held up her orange juice class and said, "Cheers."

I will be working in the Bay Area September 25 through October 15 and am looking forward to seeing all my friends and going to the theater and all the spectacular restaurants. Right now, I am just looking forward to seeing Ken. Thinking about him brings a smile to my face, and when I see him, I want to jump in his arms, I get so excited.

Deedee

October 22, 2005

Conrad proposed to me on my birthday! He gave me his mother's wedding ring. It's very sweet, but it's so small. I tried very hard not to look disappointed. Conrad said we'll add some diamonds to it. We're planning an April wedding. Conrad is retiring the first of the year and wants to move to the Carolinas. It's his retirement dream. We can get a three-thousand-square-foot house there, right on the lake and off a golf course, for $350,000. I can't believe it! I've lived in California too long! I'm not going to get a job there. I would make so little money it's not worth my time. In celebration of all this we each bought a new Mercedes. Conrad got the sports car and I got the sedan.

Leslie

November 1, 2005

Yesterday was Halloween! It was so much fun to see all the children in costumes, trick-or-treating, and we sure had a lot of them. We ran out of candy. Ken's not too keen on handing out candy, but I love it.

I found a piano teacher I enjoy working with and am learning a lot from her. I visited the local quilting store, and I joined a book club. I joined the Y. It's quite large and has a running track, which is nice because it's so bloody hot here.

Ken doesn't have too many friends; he's more of a loner, but there are two couples we socialize with, so I've had a few small dinner parties. Scooter passed away a few years ago, but my dear Hetty lives in Arlington with her son Chip. Of course, I looked them up on my first trip here to visit Ken. Hetty hasn't changed a bit; neither has Chip. He's as goofy and sweet as ever. I feel like I have family here. Hetty, Chip, and I drove over to our old Arlington neighborhood. Our beautiful homes are now dreadful messes, very white trash. I hate to use that term, but sometimes it just fits. Broken-down cars and trucks scattered on lawns; driveways crowded with junk; liquor bottles lying about; women in bathrobes, smoking cigarettes; guys hanging about, drinking from whiskey bottles. The beautiful grass that I had to water in the horrible heat of the summer was now mud, littered with debris. I took pictures to send to Mom. When I got home that day, I felt so dirty, I poured a glass of wine and took a shower.

November 5, 2005

Mother called me, very upset. Mel has been missing for two weeks. Deedee didn't know where she was but was sure she'd just gone off with some guy for a holiday. Mother was beside herself and asked me what I thought we should do. Mel is an adult; however, young, beautiful women go missing all the time, and that could easily happen to Mel. I got information from Mom about when she had last seen and heard from Mel, the name and number of a girlfriend, and the name of the last guy she'd been living with. I started out by calling her dad, but he hadn't heard from her in about a month and didn't know where she was living. She does have a habit of disappearing, but she usually checks in with Mom or Rachael or me.

215

November 9, 2005

It took me a couple of days, but I finally found Mel at a resort in Las Vegas. She was fine and having a great time with a new guy she'd hooked up with and was sorry she hadn't checked in with us. Mother was very relieved and thanked me profusely. Then she called Deedee to let her know we'd tracked Mel down. Miss Dump and Duck called me, yelling and spouting obscenities. "You have no right to be butting into my business and tracking Meliza down. She is not your daughter. She's mine, and I can handle her." I tried to explain, saying, "Mother was beside herself with worry, so I took action," but she wouldn't listen, and when she wore down, she said a pleasant, "Fuck you!" and slammed the phone down.

Deedee

November 12, 2005

I am so pissed at Leslie! She stuck her nose in where it doesn't belong again. Meliza is always disappearing when she meets some stud in a bar. It's none of our business. She's a grown woman. I'd rather she find a guy and get married, but she doesn't want to get married. I swear she takes after Leslie. It's like our children got mixed up at birth. Rachael is so much like me, calm and level-headed. So Mom called Leslie, and Leslie took over. She found Meliza holed up at the Bellagio Hotel in Las Vegas. Meliza obviously picked a rich one this time. I was so embarrassed. People will think I'm a bad mother because Leslie took over and found my daughter. I told Leslie to stay out of my fucking business with my daughters!

Leslie

November 26, 2005

A fog of depression has dropped over me. I think it's the major change and stress I have been under, getting settled here in Texas. The move didn't seem to bother me, but seeing my furniture destroyed was extremely disturbing. Four months have gone by, and Ken has still not even begun to repair anything, which adds to my distress. I feel damaged along with my furniture. Perhaps I need repairing as well.

I wanted to do some painting, a little redecorating, just to add my personality to the home, and even though I offered to use my own money, Ken said no. I assumed that we would share financial responsibility, with me paying half the mortgage and utilities, but Ken doesn't want me to be financially involved with his house.

I am constantly getting my feelings hurt. Ken can be selfish and controlling, but he can also be kind and loving. He gets depressed and grouchy, causing me to believe I did something wrong. I'm afraid of losing his love. And there are so many rules: I can't have a cat because he doesn't like cats. I can't read in bed because he can't sleep with the light on. I can't knit while we watch movies because the light detracts from the movie screen. He won't play a game with me, or take a walk, or even eat at the dining room table. I've spoken to Iris, who tells me that Ken should step up to the plate and marry me. Franny admires me for taking the chance and moving to Texas, but she's worried about me being swallowed up in this relationship. Have I made a colossal error in judgment by moving here?

December 24, 2005

Christmas was so unusual. Ken and I spent the morning together, opening gifts, then enjoying Bloody Marys and a lovely brunch. Midafternoon I caught a plane to Burbank to have Christmas dinner with Mom and the girls, while Ken caught a plane to Denver to meet up with a friend and go on a mountain-climbing trip. I couldn't believe I'd had breakfast in Texas and dinner in California. Mother served dinner buffet style because she had so many people. She wanted everyone to be able to visit with me. I missed Ken and wished he were here with me and my family; however, I put that behind me because Mother had gone to so much trouble to make this a special occasion. We were all visiting and having a lovely time when all of a sudden we heard, "You fucking little prick!" I looked up to see Miss Dump and Duck draw back her right arm and hit Ami's husband smack in the jaw. He dropped to the floor, splattering his drink all over. Deedee had a plate of food in her left hand that did not even wobble. That girl has great balance. And she's strong as an ox. Deedee was yelling, "Get the fuck out of here!" Lil, Ami's mother-in-law, was backed into the corner, cowering and crying, "Please don't hit him again!" The poor guy was bleeding all over the place. Ami was crying, "Mother, for God's sake! What have you done?" The rest of us were stunned and speechless. Deedee turned around in high heels, walked across the room, and sat down to commence eating her dinner. Conrad was beside her, asking her to please calm down. Ami and Lil took Marvin over to the ER, where it turned out his jaw was dislocated. It hurts to think about it. Meanwhile, I and the other guests sat or stood, gaping and taking in the drama unfolding before us. Mother recovered first and began to apologize and clean up the blood and spilled drink. My poor mother! I jumped up and began to help her. We went around, calming people down, and soon everything was back to normal. Deedee didn't say a word but continued to sit on the couch, eating and drinking. Conrad began to apologize to people, saying that Deedee had been under a lot of strain lately. I guess so! Mother told me later Deedee was having financial issues, which I found hard to believe, what with that amazing settlement from her ex, Johnson. And we all know that Deedee hates Marvin. She's hated him since he was a little boy. I have to admit, he is abysmally obnoxious. But he's Ami's choice. And for Deedee to hit him! Good grief! I think I'll stay out of her way!

Chapter Thirty-Two

Stand by Your Man

Leslie

January 1, 2006

Here I am on New Year's Day in Beverly Hills, Texas. I just came back from a walk by the creek where all my hopes and dreams for coming here and being with Ken first began. Now I am sitting in my rocker on the patio—if you can call this small slab of cement a patio—looking out on this mess of a yard. Last night was one of the worst New Year's Eves I have ever spent. I was alone. Ken went to bed. Last night he told me he would never get married again. Maybe I'm making too much of marriage. There's nothing wrong with just living together; however, in this case it doesn't feel like a commitment. Am I sliding backward in life?

February 1, 2006

I'm in the Bay Area, working and housesitting for Iris. Ken joined me for the weekend, and we had a fabulous time. From here I'll go back to Texas for a week and then to Eugene for the birth of Baby Boy, who is as yet unnamed. I'm having horrible stomach issues. It started after Franny and I had dinner in the city one night. I asked her how she felt, and she was fine. I thought maybe it was a case of food poisoning.

Deedee

February 19, 2006

Conrad and me took Mom to a fancy restaurant downtown for her birthday. The girls wanted to come, but Conrad thought it would be quieter with just the three of us.

219

At Christmas dinner I punched that idiot husband of Ami's right in the jaw. I can't stand that little asshole. And his mother, Lil, is just a fat, gray-haired old lady. She's the same age as Leslie, but people think she's ten years older. One Thanksgiving, Lil and Leslie had us all read poetry. I laughed my head off. Mother told me I was rude, and someone kicked me under the table. I was embarrassed about hitting Marvin. It isn't ladylike or sophisticated. I'm trying so hard not to lose my temper. I just sat down and ate. I didn't know what else to do. That little prick had it coming.

Leslie

February 28, 2006

The stomach issues have gotten worse. I went to the doctor and was told it's just a case of the flu, but I'm not buying it. It's been a couple of weeks. I can't keep any food down, and I've lost ten pounds. I'm so weak I can't even blow my hair dry without sitting down a few times before I'm done. I'm flying into Portland tomorrow, and I let Rachael know that I want to go directly to the Kaiser medical facility in Salem. I'm going to insist they run tests.

March 3, 2006

Rachael had a baby boy yesterday! They named him Joshua Jacob. Josh is adorable! He's lying in my lap, sleeping as I'm writing, and he fits just the length of my thighs. Rachael called yesterday after he was born. When she spoke to Taylor, the first thing Taylor said was, "Woody is in big trouble, Mommy! She chewed up your wooden flute." Rachael had had that flute since she was just a bit older than Taylor, but Woody is Rachael's first child, so it's a moot point.

I had tests run at Kaiser, and the outcome is that I had giardia, which was quite a surprise as I don't drink from streams, which is the first question you're always asked.

However, I did sample arugula at the farmers' market at Jack London Square while I was at Iris's. I learned that tasting lettuces and berries at the open markets is not a good thing to do as they are often not washed well. After taking the medicine they gave me, I felt better within hours. The good thing that came out of it is that I lost twelve pounds and I feel great.

June 6, 2006

I'm back in Texas, and Mom is here, visiting. I asked Hetty to stay with us too, so they could spend time together. They are like young girls again, chattering away all day. I've been taking them sightseeing, and I've been cooking meals that they've raved about. I've really enjoyed having them here. I did have an issue that stopped me in my tracks: Ken has a room that he uses for storage. Since we have the garage and the attic, I suggested maybe we could clean it out so the ladies could have a room, but he answered with an emphatic no. So I said, "Well, then we'll give them our room, of course, and we'll manage with a camping futon in my office," which is very small. Ken answered once again with a very loud no. I couldn't put the ladies in my office on a futon; they'd never get off the floor. I rented two single fold-up beds, and set the room up as best I could, resulting in Mom and Hetty having to crawl to the ends of their beds to get up and down. I heard them giggling about it the other night. Ken can be selfish, but to be deliberately mean to two older ladies is a side of him I have not seen.

June 19, 2006

It's Rachael's birthday in two days! I'm flying to Eugene to celebrate with her.
I decided it would be a good idea to take the Texas Certified Shorthand Reporters Exam, so I'm taking an online course in

a live classroom situation three nights a week. I've met a lot of new friends, and I love the class. We're working on speed, which is quite challenging.

June 25, 2006

Taylor calls me Aunie! How or where she came up with that name, we have no clue, but I love it. She gave me my own personalized grandma name. Nothing could be more special.

When Rachael picked me up at the airport, she and Taylor were standing in the waiting area just as I exited the plane. The picture of them standing there, waiting for me, was so beautiful and loving, my eyes began to tear up. I was overwhelmed, knowing the effort it took for Rachael to park the car, unload Taylor, and find my gate to be here to greet me as I came off the plane.

June 30, 2006

I'm back in Texas, preparing to fly to the Bay Area to work. Ken is extremely happy. He decided to retire early to go into business with a couple he's worked with for several years who he believes are very business savvy. They both have MBAs, so I hope he's right. Ken has no education beyond high school, but he's smart and a hard worker. His excitement over this has taken the strain off our relationship. The other night when he got home from work, he surprised the heck out of me by asking if I'd like to go for a walk. We walked down to the park and along the stream. It was a perfect evening!

August 16, 2006

Here comes summer! The fellow at the wine shop sings that when Mom and I come into the store. We're in Ashland and staying at Main Street Inn across from Alice's. Taylor is three, and Josh is five months. What a precious time. Taylor will have her birthday party in Alice's garden again this year. We spend a lot of time at Alice's. Mom rocked Josh in

Alice's rocking chair, and I got some amazing pictures. Mother is so happy. Rocking Josh takes her back to a memory of rocking my baby brother. When she closes her eyes and rocks, she's back there. I was able to capture that in my photos.

Ken has never been to Ashland. I wish I could get him to join us, but he's working very hard at helping to put the new business into operation. Hopefully, it will be up and running in a few months.

Chapter Thirty-Three

I Fall to Pieces

Leslie

January 1, 2007

I spent the first day of the New Year putting away Christmas decorations and packing for my trip to the Bay Area. Ken wouldn't allow me to put up a fresh tree. He thinks they are a fire hazard. He has a fake tree that I decorated. He refused to help me. It's an awful-looking fake tree, but the decorations looked great. Ken worked all day, arriving home after eight. I prepared a new recipe, and we ate in front of the television.

February 2, 2007

Deedee's wedding is coming up soon, and Ken won't go with me. He says he's too busy with the new business. I said, "It's really important to me that you attend my sister's wedding with me, and it's only a weekend," but he wouldn't budge. I don't understand his moods or why he won't participate with me and my family. He's never even met Rachael. At first when he refused to go to the wedding, I was angry, and then I just got sad. The Christmas holidays of 2002 were so amazing. I thought our lives would be like that, but Ken doesn't know how to be in a relationship. He has no concept of the word "compromise." He's been saying some incredibly mean things lately, like: "This is not your home; it's mine." "You're a guest in my house." "You're a horrible person." "My friends tell me to run away." I know I can't stay in this relationship and that I must begin to think about how to go about moving back home. It's going to be so expensive, replacing some of the furniture and appliances I got rid of when I moved to Texas. Plus, the house will need painting and some repairs. The move itself will be very expensive. I made a monstrous mistake.

Deedee

February 10, 2007

My wedding was beautiful! We got married at the Bonaventure downtown and had a sit-down dinner and dancing for 30 people. My dress was to die for! Rachael and Tony brought little Taylor and Josh and came down from Eugene. Ami was there with baby Lily. Did I mention that I was a grandmother again? Amiala and the prick had a baby girl. Do you think they could name her after me? No. They named her after fat, gray-haired old Lil because she pays the bills. Meliza came to the wedding alone but worked the room for men. My friend Jessica was my maid of honor. I let Leslie be a bridesmaid, but I wish I hadn't because she ruined my wedding pictures. She wouldn't smile, probably because Ken didn't come with her. We sold the condo and bought an enormous house in the Carolinas. I've been buying new furniture and having it shipped ahead. The movers packed our stuff, and we leave tomorrow. I'm so excited! My life is going to be perfect!

Leslie

February 15, 2007

Deedee's wedding was an impressive affair. She looked absolutely stunning. For me the highlight was my little Taylor. When I walked down the aisle, she stared at me, openmouthed. As I walked by her, she whispered, "Aunie, you look like a princess!" I took her hand, and she walked with me. She is the most captivating child. She stayed at my side all night. Well, except for some whirlwind dances with her daddy.

I'd hoped this would be an opportunity for Ken and me to spend some carefree vacation time together, but he continued to belligerently refuse to attend the wedding, exhibiting anger and insolence. I was crushed.

I felt so bad for Deedee too, because on the morning of her wedding day, she found out that Conrad had entrusted her beautiful six-carat diamond ring to a jeweler without obtaining a receipt. I can't even imagine. How could one be so foolish! Apparently, they were going to have some of the diamonds from that ring put into Conrad's mother's ring to sparkle it up a bit. When Conrad went to pick up the rings, the jeweler denied ever having been given Deedee's ring, claiming he was only to clean and size Conrad's mother's ring. So here was Deedee on her wedding day, furious with Conrad for being so utterly stupid and negligent, and despondent over the loss of her gorgeous diamond ring.

Deedee

February 17, 2007

I love the new house and all the new furniture. I'm taking golf lessons. My golf instructor is a hottie! We bought golf clubs and a golf cart, and I went a bit crazy on a golf wardrobe. I keep finding the cutest outfits, and of course they have to have matching shoes, but now I have to sneak everything in the house because Conrad gets mad at me for spending so much money. He says I spend a lot on groceries and the refrigerator is always empty. That's because I throw out all the leftovers so I won't be tempted to eat them. Now he's doing the shopping and the cooking, which is fine by me. My alimony checks from Johnson have dropped down, but I still have eight years. That's a long time. Conrad asked me what I do with the money. I said, "It just goes." He said, "Why don't you let me handle it for you." I said, "No!" That's my money. The nerve of him!

Leslie

February 18, 2007

I'm in the Bay Area, staying at Iris's. Mom is here with me to celebrate her birthday. We went to Biscuits and Blues in the city, saw a comedian, and got stomachaches from laughing so hard. Mom can't stop talking about what a great time she had. Today we're relaxing. Mom told me that Deedee and Conrad had a horrible argument because Deedee found out that they owed $75,000 in taxes and had to make payment arrangements. Wow! I would have had a heart attack. She also told me that the girls wanted to go to Deedee's for Christmas, but Conrad said no, they couldn't afford to fly everyone out and there was too much drama when they all got together. Boy! Is he a fast learner! Mom flies home tonight, and I go back to reporting depos tomorrow for one more week, then home to Texas.

Ken's new business endeavor looks like it will fail, and our relationship has been slowly deteriorating as well. I asked if we could do some couples counseling, but he steadfastly declined. He was so excited about the new business that his malaise seemed to remedy itself. However, even then he seemed to distance himself from me. He acts so strangely, like there is something wrong with me that he can't tolerate and has to look the other way. I keep wondering if I have a huge hair sticking out of my chin. I've gone back into therapy to see if I can figure out what part I've played in the decline of the relationship. I felt so bad for Ken, with the failure of the business and all, that I told him I'd be happy to help with expenses. He said, "I don't want a trail of your financial involvement in his property." He explained that the reason for this was that if the relationship broke up, I could then claim ownership of a portion of his house. I nearly laughed out loud but held it back due to the seriousness in which he was speaking. Owning a $200,000 property in Texas is not on my bucket list. The last time I broached the subject of marriage, he said he doesn't want to get married because he doesn't want to take on the responsibility of my property. I didn't comprehend that logic. Then I heard him saying to his friend, "I'm just letting her live with me," as if I were homeless. When I confronted him about that, he reiterated, "You're just a guest in my house." I nearly flipped my lid! I said, "I have a beautiful home in the Bay Area. I didn't move to Texas because I needed a roof over my head, and I've never considered myself a guest. You didn't bring that up when we made the decision for me to relocate here." Asshole! Iris said, "Darlin', you've got to come home. Moving to Texas was not one of the better decisions you've ever made." She's right.

April 9, 2007

Mom and I are in Eugene, spending time with Rachael and the children. Ken surprised me by calling several times just to tell me he loves me and misses me. This is a change of tone. It was so sweet; it gave me hope.

July 27, 2007

This relationship is like a seesaw. Ken didn't acknowledge my birthday in any way. I went shopping. I'm a big fan of retail therapy. Ken is miserable. He barely speaks to me. They had to close the business. The couple Ken went into business with lost a neat $1 million. Ken lost a tidy sum as well. I know he's very worried about his financial situation. I suggested we rent his house and move back to California. I thought being near his brother and sister-in-law would be good for him. And I miss California, my home, my Jewish community, my friends and colleagues. While I've made friends in Texas and enjoyed aspects of the community here, I've felt forsaken with this despondency hanging over Ken. When I recommended we move back to California, Ken looked at me with pure hate in his eyes and hissed, "I will never move to that land of Jews, Blacks, and queers." I nearly fell off my chair. I couldn't believe what I was hearing. What has happened to this man? I couldn't keep my mouth shut. I said, "I'm Jewish, Iris is Black, and your own brother is gay, as are two of your nephews." He said, "You and Iris are different, and my brother is not gay."

November 7, 2007

You'll never believe all that has happened in the past few months. The first week in October, I was at Mom's, reporting. I'd just arrived home from a particularly stressful day when Ken called. He'd been very attentive the past few weeks, calling me several times a day, asking where I was, what I was doing. What he said shook my world. He'd moved all my furniture—piano, clothing, jewelry, library, wine collection—into a storage unit in Texas and was sending me the keys via FedEx. I was stunned! I couldn't believe what I was hearing. Shouldn't we have discussed this? I could have moved myself if he'd just told me that's what he wanted. I was furious! I caught the next plane back to Texas. He did pick me up, and I did stay at the house; it could have been worse. The next day I went to the storage unit and nearly threw up. All my beautiful things were crammed into a very small storage space. The hallway was so narrow that I don't know how he and his friends had managed to move things in here. I felt violated, having these men go through my personal belongings: journals, jewelry, lingerie. There was no way I could sort through things in that hallway and get them moved back to California. He'd packed my checkbook, my computers, my clothing, my court reporting files, backup equipment, even my car keys. I couldn't do without these things for the sixty days or so it would take to give my tenant notice and move back home. I was sick to my stomach and shaking at the realization of this atrocity. I sat on the cement in that hot hallway and cried.

The next day while Ken was at work, I hired some local movers and had everything moved back into the house. He was devastated when he arrived home that night. It was his birthday. I thought, "Happy fucking birthday, bastard." We spent a few days pretty much in silence, but then he began to act quite normal, as if nothing out of the ordinary had taken place. However, I took action. I gave my tenant notice, but Mother asked me to please come and stay with her for a while. She argued her case with the facts that she needed help due to her blindness and that my tenant's boys were in school and shouldn't be disrupted. She had a valid point. And it would be good to be in the comfort of my mother's presence. So I made a decision to put some things I wouldn't be needing in storage with the moving company, put some things I wanted close at hand in a storage unit near Mother, and take some things with me to Mother's. I sorted through everything Ken had packed, trying to control my anguish and anger. He'd tossed $100,000 worth of jewelry haphazardly into boxes, packed lamps using cashmere sweaters as wrapping material. I was appalled! What causes someone to do something like this?

After several very long days, I had my three groupings in order and had the professional packers come to pack, labeling everything carefully. Iris's ex-husband offered to come to Texas and drive my car back to California, which was a kindness I shall never forget, but I had the movers take my car as well. I'd been faithfully working with my psychologist to move through this demolition of my life and decided that in between moving from Texas to California I would spend a week at a spa and resort on the coast as a transition period. Through all this, Ken continued to act as though nothing untoward had happened. When it came time for me to leave, Ken took me to the airport, as if I were going to California to work. I arrived at the airport early, went to my gate, sat down, and with the comprehension that everything was said, and done, and behind me, all arrangements had been made, I had a complete and total breakdown. The realization of what Ken had done, the manner in which he'd violated my love and trust, and the hazardous disrespect he'd had for my beautiful furniture and personal property became reality. The pain took over my mind and body.

The week at the resort truly was a blessing. I cried. I journaled. I tried to make sense of what had happened. I read, went to lovely restaurants, and pampered myself at the spa. I realized that I wouldn't heal in a week, but it was a beginning.

December 7, 2007

The move went smoothly. Mother was so sweet in blending me into the household, even making room for my piano, my rocking chairs, my office equipment, and cooking and sewing supplies. I knew it was important to have possessions around me that comforted me and made me feel at home. I am comfortable, and I do feel safe. The way Ken moved me out was devastating. With one phone call, just a few words, I was without a home. My therapist tells me that I'm suffering from Post-Traumatic Stress Syndrome. I've taken a lot of time to rest and recuperate. Mom and I have been watching movies, sewing, shopping. I found a piano teacher and am studying with him. We've been out to lunch and dinner with friends. I'm so fortunate to have Bernie and Cassie here. I've known Cassie since I was eighteen and Bernie since I was twenty-five. They're family now. Claudia is here also. She married a gentleman from Venice Beach and relocated.

I'm not able to sleep at night. I have horrible nightmares about being homeless or living in some crazy house. It frightens me, and then I can't go back to sleep, so I allow myself to sleep in in the mornings. I must get back to work, but if I'm not able to sleep, it's going to be quite difficult.

Mom and I flew to Deedee's for Thanksgiving. I'd invited Auntie Anne and Uncle Burt to join us, so they came from Florida. When I told Deedee that I'd invited them, she went off on me, screaming, "You had no right to do that. You're always butting in. It's my home, not yours. You can't just invite people here. I don't want any more guests. I have enough to do as it is." She was wild with anger. She was right: it was her home, and I hadn't thought that through. I'm just so used to Auntie Anne being with us for Thanksgiving;

it's something we do almost every year. Mother was upset and called Deedee and told her that it had been her idea to invite Auntie Anne. Auntie Anne was Dad's sister, but she and Mom have been friends since they were teenagers. It was very kind of Mother to defend me and take that on. Miss Dump and Duck did calm down after Mother's call, and Thanksgiving turned out to be a wonderful weekend. I was comforted, being with Auntie Anne.

December 10, 2007

Tonight, I took Mom to the supermarket. She was taking her good old time, looking things over, and I was getting extremely impatient. She must have been deliberating over pastries for ten minutes when she picked up a small cake, walked over to me, and with her eyes twinkling, said, "Doesn't this just look delicious?" as she handed me the cake. Her sweet smile, and bright eyes, and the kindness with which she brought that cake to me—a flash of seconds in time—is a memory I shall never forget. I love my mom so much!

December 17, 2007

A lady came to drop off some cosmetic products that Mom had ordered at a home party. The two of them were in the office, and I overheard the woman, Jana, telling Mother that she wouldn't be selling these products any longer because she was pursuing her passion and opening up a hypnotherapy practice. I immediately went into the office and said, "I think I need to see you!" I've had two sessions with Jana, and my sleep pattern is improving. I'm going back to work next week.

Ami called and was furious with me. She said, "You have no business going to see Jana. She's my friend, and you're interfering." I explained, "I'm seeing Jana in a professional capacity. The hypnotherapy sessions with her are really helping me sleep and deal in a positive way with all the trauma I've been through in the past few months." But nothing would appease Ami. It occurred to me that Ami is having difficulty with my living here. She used to take Mother to the market, and Mother would buy Ami's groceries. Now I'm taking Mother to the market, and Ami has had to take on the expense of her own groceries. I think perhaps I need to let Ami take Mother to the market occasionally. Ami also used to take Mom to the mall, and Mother would buy whatever Ami needed for herself and Lily. Now I'm taking Mother to the mall, and Ami is losing out on that benefit as well. There are so many resentments I don't even know about.

December 24, 2007

Today is Christmas Eve. I'm embarking on a new chapter in my life. I became an unwanted guest in Ken's home, and now I'm living with Mom. I don't know where I want to go next in my life, but I do know that I want another exciting adventure, minus the trauma and drama. For now, I will grieve, and heal, and see where life takes me. I'm spending the holidays with Rachael, the children, and Tony. Jacob joined us today. Mom and Miss Dump and Duck have criticized me for being too eager to be in a relationship. This from my mother, who was so hurt by men that she allowed them to take her power, and my sister, who attempts suicide to get a man to marry her. They are right, though, I am eager to be in a relationship with a wonderful man, to share my life, to have a hand to hold for the duration. My feelings for love and life are deep. Something good will come out of the Texas debacle.

Chapter Thirty-Four

A Moment Changes Everything

Leslie

January 1, 2008

Today was a perfect New Year's Day. I never got out of my PJs! I read books, cooked, worked on my recipe file. Tommy, our childhood friend, came down to spend New Year's with us, and the three of us went to Moonshadows in Malibu. I haven't been there in years, and it was lovely to spend an evening enjoying the ocean air. It was also very nice to get dressed up. What does 2008 hold in store for me? Will I find new love, old love, home?

Deedee

January 1, 2008

Conrad makes me crazy! He's too friendly. He sees people out on the street and starts talking, and the next thing I know they're in my house having cocktails. I told him this has to stop. Leslie is living with Mother. Next thing I know she'll be stealing from Mother. As a belated wedding gift and my birthday present and Christmas gift, she sent us a $300 gift certificate to play golf at Bridgeport. I know that was Mother's money she used. That bitch! She's always crying poor. Amiala is upset with Leslie living there too. She'd like to visit with her grandmother without Leslie hanging around. Leslie's either home with Mother or taking Mother out somewhere or having friends in. And you know who's paying for everything! Mother! Leslie is not giving Mother any rent money. I'm furious! I want to live rent-free. Mother said she would never think of taking money from any of us. I'm going out there to see what the fuck is going on.

Leslie

January 10, 2008

I thought I would just get on with my life, but that is not the case. I am grieving my life and relationship with Ken. He won't return my calls or my emails. That really hurts, but I must quit blaming myself. It's okay to grieve and feel sad; this has been a tremendous loss. Even his family has turned their backs on me.

January 16, 2008

I had a session with my therapist today, and this is what came out of it: I have no room for disruption in my life right now; I need order. I am feeling lonely and displaced, and I have a lot of anxiety. I am untethered.

Working on hypnosis and positive affirmations is really helping. I slept all night last night without experiencing nightmares.

March 8, 2008

Miss Dump and Duck came for a visit. Mother assumed she would stay with us, but Miss Dump and Duck said, "I'm going to stay with Ami. I need to bond with her." This is the first time that Deedee has not stayed with Mother, and Mother's feelings were hurt. I felt so bad for Mom. Then Deedee, Ami, and Mel came over to spend an evening. We were all sitting around chatting when Deedee suddenly looked at me and pugnaciously said, "When are you leaving Mother's house? You need to go back to your own house."

I was a bit dumbfounded and wasn't too quick to respond, when Mother said, "Leslie will stay here as long as she wants. This really isn't any of your business, Deedee."

The subject was dropped. However, later Miss Dump and Duck looked at me and very contentiously asked, "Where did you get that ring? It looks like one of Mother's."

While it may not seem like much, Deedee's outbursts scare me. She can be cheerfully having a conversation with someone and suddenly out of the blue, with seemingly no justification, become hostile and confrontational, shouting profanities, frightening anyone in her path. And I'm not good at dealing with these outbursts; I freeze up and my mind goes blank. Again, Mother stepped in and said, "That's Leslie's ring."

Where is all this animosity coming from?

Deedee

March 20, 2008

I went to see what the hell is going on at Mother's. I was too mad at Mother to stay at her house, and I knew if I saw Leslie, I'd probably slap the shit out of her. The fact that Leslie is there and getting a free ride makes me madder than hell. I want to kill the bitch so I will be the only child and get all the attention. I stayed at Ami's and it was crowded. Lily is cute, but she bothers me. I'm much too young to be a grandmother. When I went to Mother's, I was shocked to see Leslie's crap all over the place. She even brought her piano. I don't think she plans on leaving soon. Fuck! I wish I'd have thought about living with Mother and getting a free ride. I never would have gotten married. Leslie is always in the right place at the right time. It's not fair. I have to work so hard for everything. Conrad is angry about my spending habits and keeps bugging me to death about where all my alimony money goes. It's none of his fucking business. Then he said I needed to get a job, and the only job I could find in this town was at the local department store as a stock clerk. Me, a stock clerk! It's only temporary. I told them I wanted to be a department store manager. They said they require a high school diploma and at least two years of college, but maybe I could work my way up.

Leslie has stolen Mother's jewelry. I know that was Mother's ring she was wearing when I was there. Mother said it wasn't, but she's blind and wouldn't know. I couldn't get into the office or Leslie's bedroom to check things out because she never left us alone. That really made me mad. I told her I wanted some alone time with my mother, and she suggested I take Mother shopping and out to lunch. I told her I wanted to be alone in the house with Mother. She said that was good. She'd be in the office, working, and let her know if we needed anything. Need anything! What I need is for her to get the fuck out of my mother's house.

April 15, 2008

My stomach pains have gotten worse. And I always have a sore throat. I think it might be from throwing up. I went back to the doctor, and they ran some more tests. He said I have stomach ulcers. I have some sores in my throat too. He asked me if I was throwing up. Was I suffering from bulimia? I said, "God, no! It's stress. I'm totally stressed out about my sister living with my mother and stealing from her." He gave me some medicine.

Leslie

May 19, 2008

I spent the weekend with Rachael and the children in San Luis Obispo. We went wine- tasting at a beautiful winery, where we relaxed, sampling wine and eating cheese. I bought a case of chardonnay so that our lovely afternoon would linger on back at home and I could share the wine with Mother.

I'm still sad about Ken and sometimes call or email him. He was abusive. Why do I want to be in touch with him? Franny told me I should take golf lessons because that's where all the men hang out. Beatrice said I should buy a secondhand black Chanel suit and go to funerals in Beverly Hills so that I could meet a nice, wealthy widower.

Tonight, I took Jeffie for a walk. He is such a sweet dog. I love his tenacity to move forward on three legs. I was enjoying our walk so much that I'd walked about a mile before I realized it. When I turned around to head home, Jeffie sat down and refused to take a step. I thought maybe he was being stubborn because he wasn't ready to go back. I got him to begin walking, but he stopped again. This went on for a bit, and then I wondered if perhaps he was in some distress, so I picked him up, all fifty pounds of him, and carried him, stopping a number of times along the way. When I finally got home, I set him down on the living room floor, and he just lay there. I was worried, so I told Mom we should take him to the emergency vet. As it turns out, he has a stomach tumor, and we're having him operated on.

June 15, 2008

I decided that I need to put Ken in my rearview mirror and begin dating again, so I'm going to try Match.com. I needed a picture, so Claudia and I went up to the Ronald Reagan Library to take pictures. She is an excellent photographer, so we got some great shots. I went home and navigated the site, filling out my info and uploading the pictures. I have had numerous one-hour-or-less glasses of wine and some humorous conversations with various men. I met one gentleman at Maggiano's Little Italy restaurant at the mall, and he asked, "Do you always go to such expensive restaurants?" I was a bit surprised, as Mom and I go there frequently. It gave me pause for thought: Is my value system skewed? No, I work very long hours to have spending money and to ensure my future. This fellow lived in an apartment in a not-so-great area of LA and didn't work.

Then I met another man at Maggiano's. I pick Maggiano's because it's close to home, and I usually have to get back and get jobs out. This guy was very dapper, a little rotund, but he didn't complain about meeting at Maggiano's. However, he asked, "Are you into group sex?" For a moment all I could do was stare at him, wide-eyed and contemplating. Then I said, "That's a great fantasy, but it's not really on my bucket list!"

August 20, 2008

We've been in Ashland a month. We rented a flat again, and various friends stayed with us for some periods of time. One night, Mom was asleep and I was reading. Iris and Flora called and asked me to join them at Liquid Assets for a late-night snack. We were enjoying some decadent desserts and chatting away. As usual, the discussion led to the upcoming election. We're all voting for Obama, of course, but Iris said something interesting I hadn't thought about. She said, "When white people get into the voting booth, they are not going to vote for a Black man." I was speechless for a moment, and then I said, "Darlin', you're going to eat those words."

October 1, 2008

Mom is visiting Deedee. I called her several times because I was terribly worried about Jeffie. He wouldn't eat, and he was suffering from diarrhea. I took him to the vet and called Mom from there because they said there was nothing further we could do for him, it was time to let him go. I was sobbing and did not want to make that decision without her consent. She agreed that it was the best thing to do at this point; we had given him extra time with the surgery. I stayed with him and held him while they gave him the shot. I was overwhelmed with sadness and grief for this poor, sweet little dog.

Later Deedee said, "You had my dog put down because you didn't want to be bothered with him."

October 15, 2008

Cassie's daughter, Maura, died! The poor girl had suffered from complications of bulimia for many years; still, it came as quite a shock. My memories of Maura's childhood are many. Cassie and I were pregnant at the same time. Maura was the cutest little girl, and she and Rachael were best pals. I can't even imagine Cassie's pain.

October 19, 2008

My friends Franny and Beatrice came to visit from the Bay Area. We did some sightseeing and spent time reminiscing and laughing over the retelling of stories of our San Francisco Sex in the City Over Fifty group. I invited some of my LA friends over to meet them, and we had a fabulous dinner and a lovely evening. Mother and I were sorry to see them return home.

 Mom and I love to shop the farmers' markets. I'm doing all the meal preparation, as Mother's eyesight is truly gone. In fact, I'm now realizing that when I do move, she cannot live alone. I asked Mother how much she was able to see and what it looked like. She told me that she could see me as a grayish mask, but she couldn't make out details. She said it broke her heart to know she would never again see her daughter's beautiful face. I was glad she couldn't see the tears flowing down my cheeks. What a brave, brave woman!

October 21, 2008

Cooking is creative and relaxing, and Mother loves entertaining friends, so about once a month we have a dinner party. I started a book group. We read only books that are available in audio so that Mother can participate. We also put together a small Sunday afternoon Scrabble group. Mother can't see well enough to play, but she sits with us and enjoys the ladies' visits and the general Scrabble conversation. I'm so fortunate to have these special times with my mother.

Deedee

October 22, 2008

Another fucking birthday! I use moisturizers and scrubs and all sorts of things on my face, and I still have deep lines and creases. I hate it. Mother and Leslie say it's because I've spent too much time out in the sun working on a tan, so in the last few years I've been using the tanning booth. No one told me I would get wrinkled from the sun. Leslie is just lucky. She hates the hot weather so she doesn't sit out in the sun. I got new boobs and a little facelift after my ex Johnson dumped me for his whore secretary, but the facelift didn't last. I got a promotion to senior stock clerk. It won't be long before I'm the manager. I guess Leslie is dating again. Good fucking luck. Maybe she'll meet someone and move out of my mother's house. She just needs to settle. She says if she can't find the right guy, she'd rather be alone and she enjoys being alone. Un-fucking-believable! It was sad and scary that Cassie's daughter died. I've been sticking my finger down my throat since I was fourteen, but I'm not bulimic. I'm just keeping my weight under control in a healthy way. Mother says Leslie's friends came to visit, and she had a wonderful time. I don't like Leslie's friends staying at my mother's house. That's what the fuck hotels are for. I told Mother that Leslie shouldn't be inviting her friends to stay there. It isn't her house. Mother said they're her friends too. Yeah! Right! Leslie has taken control of my mother's life with her dinner parties and book clubs and stuff. She needs to stop.

Leslie

November 30, 2008

Mother flew out to spend Thanksgiving weekend with Deedee and Conrad, so once again I got my four-day pajama weekend: cooking, sewing, reading, getting my transcripts out. Mel begged me to make Thanksgiving dinner for her and

Denzel, but I stuck to my guns and said no, multiple times. She thought she could wear me down with guilt.

I brought home Gabby and Max on Friday. They are the cutest little kittens. I don't think I mentioned that someone had left a box of newborn kittens in our neighbor Bertha's yard. She'd taken them to the vet to be checked and gotten the tiniest little bottles to feed them. It was quite a chore, and Bertha was more than thankful when the mother cat showed up. She quarantined her with her kittens for six weeks. She was ready to find homes for them, and I missed having cats. The time I spent with Ken was the longest I've ever been without a cat. Pets bring love and joy into our lives, and I'm ready for love and joy. Gabby and Max kept me amused all weekend with their adorable antics!

Chapter Thirty-Five

Imagine!

Leslie

February 20, 2009

I had a birthday party for Mother. Friends came from all over. We only have one guest room here, so I blocked out a group of rooms at the Hilton, about five minutes from the house. We had just over seventy-five people. I had the party catered and hired a bartender. We decorated in a combination birthday and Valentine theme. Mother wore a pretty pink beaded dress. She was radiant! I asked everyone who wished to, to tell a bit about themselves and their relationship with Mother. What astonishing stories! We laughed and carried on until two in the morning! It's a good thing we love our neighbors and invited them all!

There was a bitter note that happened while I was planning the party. Ami phoned saying that I needed to cancel the party, that Grandma didn't want one. This wasn't a surprise, Mother and I had discussed it, and she'd been quite excited. I explained that to Ami, but she wouldn't hear it. She kept saying, "La, la, la, la," while I was trying to talk. Finally, she screamed obscenities at me and hung up. I was shocked and could only think, "What the heck is going on?" I told Mother about the call, and we both agreed that Ami is facing some tough issues about me living here. She is also having job difficulties and problems with Marvin, who is now her ex-husband. We decided to give her a wide berth and to be patient, and that I would offer to do therapy with her. We were still in the middle of this conversation when Deedee called me. She, too, was screaming obscenities and yelled, "I'm calling everyone and canceling this fucking party. You cannot have parties in my mother's house." I couldn't believe what I was hearing. What right does she have to cancel an event I've planned? I was furious with her and began to give her a piece of my mind when Mother intervened and asked to speak with her. When they were done talking, Mother said it was all settled and Deedee wanted to speak to me again. Hoping that after speaking to Mother, she would apologize for her rash behavior, I took the phone only to find Deedee was continuing to shout at me. She said, "You're a fucking controlling bitch! You always have to have your entourage around you. Someday I'm going to be in control, and you'd better watch out."

Deedee

April 1, 2009

Conrad said we couldn't afford to fly to LA for that stupid birthday party. I am so fucking mad. That bitch has no right to plan parties at my mother's house. I asked Mother to give me a list of who Leslie invited and I would call them and cancel the party, but she said no. She always says no to me and yes to Leslie. God! I hate that bitch Leslie. I need to get rid of her.

Mom spent Thanksgiving with us. It was nice without Leslie and Aunt Anne. But while my mother was out of town Leslie snuck two cats into my mother's house. Shit! She's never going to leave. That bitch knows that Mother doesn't want cats. Then the bitch wouldn't even have Mel over for Thanksgiving dinner. I'm sure she had her friends over. She needs to go.

Leslie

June 10, 2009

Mel lost her apartment and had been living in her car with Denzel. Mother and I were shocked. Mother told her to come to the house immediately, that she and Denzel would use the spare room. I cannot tell you what a nightmare this has been.

Mel stays up all night, drinking. She takes Denzel to school in her pajamas, comes home, and goes back to bed until she has to pick him up. She fixes meals for herself, using my expensive pots and pans, and then leaves them in the sink stuck with muck. When I arrive home at night, the house is a mess, she and Mom are looped, and the more they drink, the louder the television becomes. It's never off. The noise is making me crazy. When I get home from a job, I have to spend a few hours getting out transcripts and preparing for the next day. One night when I said I couldn't drink with them because I had work to do, Mother came into the office and told me, "You're being very rude not to come out and have a drink with us."

Although the house has three full baths, Mel uses my bathroom and my cosmetics and leaves it all in a mess, and I can't stand my surroundings to be in a state of disaster. Then I discovered Mel was wearing my clothes. That really infuriated me! I spend a lot of money on my clothes, and I'm very particular about them. I can't sleep because Mel stays up all night drinking and talking on the phone with the television blaring. I'm exhausted. I've lost all patience, and I'm ready to bop somebody over the head!

June 30, 2009

I'd become a total wreck! I never had a moment's peace unless I was sitting in my car on the freeway. I'd begun going to the library and Starbucks to get my transcripts out and sometimes just to read and relax. I was faithfully working out at the gym, which helped with the stress. I'd begun to think about renting a house, moving out and leaving Mother and Mel to their drunkenness. I was desperate for sleep, peace, and quiet. Then everything came to a head. Mother was taking us all out to a lovely new restaurant on Ventura Boulevard: Ami, Lily, Mel, Denzel, and me. While we were getting dressed, Mel began drinking martinis. I wasn't counting, but looking back, I think she had two or three before we even left the house, and she was becoming belligerent. When we arrived at the restaurant, Mel continued to drink martinis and became louder and more cantankerous. Finally, she said, "We didn't want to come to this fucking restaurant. It was your choice, Aunt Leslie. It's crappy, and I'm leaving," which she did. She went and sat in the bar and continued drinking. When we'd finished our dinner and were ready to leave, we nearly had to drag her to the car. Back at home Mother looked Denzel in the eyes and said, "I feel sorry for you because you have a shitty mother." That's when I lost it. I told Mel she was leaving, put some clothes in a bag. I booked a room for her and Denzel at the Hilton and called a cab. She left, screaming profanities. The next morning, I told Mother, "*Basta!*" She was very contrite and ashamed of her words to Denzel. Mel found an apartment, and Mother is paying the rent. The house is quiet, and I'm sleeping. In fact, I took a few days off to enjoy the tranquility.

August 20, 2009

Iris has been walking stiffly lately. She said her legs are sore, like she overexerted herself with exercise, which can't possibly be the case. She and my mother are in agreement that exercise should be a limited activity. When we're in Ashland, Iris and Mom get coffee and pastries while Flora and I go for long hikes.

The Match.com dating got overwhelming. It's like a second job. And I've met some of the strangest men. One man lived in a boarding house out in Bakersfield. He rented one room and lived there with three dogs. Another man was rather interesting. He enjoyed chamber music and theater, and we went on quite a few rather pleasant dates. I did, however, notice that the back seat of his car was a junk pile. He said he loved to shop at the Salvation Army. My first thought was "Neiman Marcus just met the Salvation Army." I was talking to him on the phone one day when he said, "I smell smoke," and then yelled, "The back of my house is on fire!" Yes, indeed, the back of his house burned down. When I saw the damage later, I could understand how this happened. I could scarcely walk through the house due to all the clothes, magazines, newspapers, items of all sorts, strewn about. I could not in my wildest imagination think of living in such a manner. He made a trip to Ashland with me, and while there, his mood suddenly changed; he became withdrawn, short-tempered, and grumpy. When I asked if something was bothering him, he said, "No, nothing." The drive up was horrendous. He is the worst driver I have ever encountered. He talks with his hands, which causes him to swerve all over the road, and he drives with one of those radar speed detectors. That was a major clue! We stopped for lunch, and he wanted to eat the food while driving, and I replied with an emphatic "No!" He was to drive my car back to LA. I was going up to Eugene to visit Rachael and would fly home the following week. I was absolutely sure he would wreck the car, so I called my insurance agent and told him to max out my auto insurance. As it turned out, the fellow and my car arrived home safely. I couldn't get his mood-swing attack off my mind, as Jacob suffers from depression and Ken was all over the map; thus, I can affirm, depression and mood swings are not a pleasant thing to live with. I'd decided to tell him I wouldn't be seeing him anymore when he called and asked if I would do therapy with him and pay for half of it.

Another guy I dated for quite a while seemed to be such a nice man, but as it turned out, he was dating me, his ex-wife, and his ex-girlfriend. How he kept up with it I'll never know.

I'd had quite enough of Match.com. It's extremely time-consuming to squander one's evenings going through messages from potential dates, so I decided to spend some money and save my evenings. I hired a professional matchmaking service. One guy I met in a bar had flaming-red hair and very little of it. It was sticking up all over the place. He wore a biker's jacket, though he wasn't a biker. The encounter ended very early when I walked into the bar and saw that he had a beer in each hand and one was clearly not for me.

Another guy rode a huge Harley. He seemed to be a very kind man looking for company, and he wanted me to go riding with him. I was giving it some thought when he called and told me he'd been in an accident and was in the hospital.

There was another guy whom I'd only spoken to briefly on the phone. One evening I was speaking to him while driving home from a job. I was tired and having difficulty following his conversation. He seemed to be out of breath, almost a panting sound, then groaning. I asked, "Are you all right?" He replied, "Yes, but I need to get off the phone." When I got home, Mel was there, and I mentioned this strange call to her. She started laughing hysterically and said, "Aunt Leslie, the guy was getting it off!"

I signed up for another service, which was extremely expensive—$4,000—and I received an extensive interview and professional photos, so I was confident I would meet some outstanding gentlemen. When my first date called me, I was excited. He told me he drove a cab. I thought, "Oh, he's being modest; he must own the company." But no, he did not own the company. However, he was outrageously sexy! What's a girl to do? We spent quite a few dazzling nights together. One morning my neighbor Bertha came over and said, "Did you know there was a cab parked in your driveway all night?"

Deedee

October 2, 2009

That fucking bitch kicked Meliza out of my mother's house. How dare she! I am so going to get even with that bitch. Then Leslie told Amiala she needs to clean up after herself when she visits because she leaves the house in a mess and Leslie is tired of cleaning up after her. Fuck that bitch. I won't have her bossing my daughters. She's got to go.

December 10, 2009

Fuck! I have bleeding ulcers and I need to have surgery. This is all Leslie's fault! She's causing me so much stress. She needs to move out of my mother's house.

Chapter Thirty-Six

Bad Vibrations

Leslie

January 1, 2010

Happy New Year! It's going to be a great year! Mom went to Deedee's for Thanksgiving again, and I got my four-day pajama weekend to myself with my darling little boys, Gabby and Max. The other day when I put out their food, they began tumbling over each other to get to their dishes. Gabby likes to fetch his ball. I throw it down the hallway, and he brings it back to me. In the mornings, he drops the ball on my chest and pats my check to wake me up to play with him. What a blessing these guys are!

Deedee had to have surgery for bleeding ulcers. She claims it's because she's under a great deal of stress, but I suspect it's bulimia. I can't think of anything that Deedee has to be stressed about. Mom wanted to fly back to be with her when she had the surgery, but Deedee said no, probably because she doesn't want Mom to find out about the bulimia.

Mom and I flew up to spend Christmas with Rachael. It was a perfect holiday. Taylor and I slept in the guest room together, and with her tiny little hand, she held my hand while we fell asleep. Mother slept in Taylor's room, and when it was time to go to bed, Taylor went in to say good night to Mom and said, "Good night! Sleep tight, and don't let those bedbugs in my room!"

February 18, 2010

Mom's birthday was quiet this year. She wanted to go to the Camarillo outlet stores, so I took the day off work, and we went shopping. When we'd worn ourselves out, we went home and changed, and I took her to Ruth's Chris Steak

House for dinner. The steaks truly did melt in our mouths. They brought us a huge piece of decadent chocolate cake with a candle in it and took our picture. It was a day I shall not soon forget.

February 28, 2010

Iris's cancer has returned. It's in her bones, thus, the sore legs. I don't want to believe this is happening. She's suffered so much already. I'm going to remain cheerful and hopeful, and try to help lift her spirits. I don't want to lose my dear friend. She is a fighter. She could outlive all the rest of us. I'm praying!

March 4, 2010

A boy cat has been living on our patio. He is such a charmer! I bought him a heating pad and put it on the patio chair for chilly nights. I bought him an Igloo too, but he doesn't seem to care for that. I've been calling him Papa Cat because he looks so much like my Maxie, I think he could be the boys' father. What a happy guy he is. He bounces around the yard, chasing leaves. Of course, I can't help but feed him on demand.

May 18, 2010

Another anniversary of the birth and death of my baby brother. This year I cried. I miss him so much. Mother was surprised that I stop and make a toast to Liam every year on this day. I made manhattans, and we sat by the pool, drinking them. I told her how much I miss Liam and how often I think about how very different our lives would have been had he lived. Dad wouldn't have killed himself. I would most likely have a sister-in-law and nieces and/or nephews. Liam would have been a calming influence in our family. I would have had a like-minded pal to assist and advise me. Mother said,

"Leslie, you dwell too much on the past. What's done is done. Buck up."

June 4, 2010

There are a couple of law firms that always ask for me, and they do large, ongoing cases with lots of depos, so work has been terrific. I'm always up for a challenge and the money that comes with it. I can actually see myself retiring one day, or at least cutting back on work.

I've been talking to Mom about building an addition over the garage for a caretaker. I might meet someone and want to get married again, and I want to know that she is safe and well cared for; however, she gets upset when I broach the subject. She tells me how grateful she is to have me here and how happy I've made her with all the things I plan, not to mention going to our book conferences and summers in Ashland. It makes her sad to think of my leaving.

I'm training for the Mount Ashland half marathon for my sixty-fifth birthday celebration. I've decided to give up running as a statement that I want to slow down my life, so I'll be racewalking the half marathon; however, it's all uphill, so my training is rugged. I enjoy walking the hills behind Pierce College because the views at the top are fantastic. Cassie has been joining me a couple of times a week, and her companionship really helps the agony of climbing those hills.

Deedee

July 4, 2010

I just hung up from talking to Mom. She's in Ashland with the bitch and her friends. When their friend Ellie was at Mom's, I heard her call my mother, "Mom." I got right in her face and told her, "She is not your mother!"

I got promoted to supervisor of the stock clerks. I got a small raise. I need it. My alimony checks are getting smaller and smaller. God! It's so unfair. Leslie has all the luck. I don't have any luck. Leslie says you have to think positive and make your own luck. I don't understand what she's talking about. You're either lucky or you're not.

Leslie

July 5, 2010

What a glorious summer in Ashland! The sun is shining! It's warm but not unbearably so. We're staying at Alice's, and friends are coming and going, using the spare room. It feels like home or maybe Grandma's house for the summer. I completed the Mount Ashland Hillclimb Run. I do believe I was the last person to the top, but, hey, I made it. When I got back to Alice's, everyone was congratulating me for finishing. They treated me to drinks and dinner at Kobe. We sat on their beautiful patio, right next to the creek, and chatted away happily for hours.

Iris and I went to see a gospel singer. Everyone began clapping, including me, but I'm not a very good clapper. I kept watching Iris's hands and trying to copy her. Finally, she looked at me and said, "Girl, you can't clap!" I replied, "Well, if I'm embarrassing you, just pretend you don't know me." Then we got the giggles, which were impossible to control, and people were shushing us.

Taylor saw her first play this year, *The Imaginary Invalid* by Molière. She loved it so much we saw it three times. It warms my heart to see Taylor's eyes so enthusiastically glued to the stage. It reminds me of the first time we took her on the "It's a Small World" ride at Disneyland. Her eyes were trying so desperately to take in all the action, and her sweet little face wore a look of awe and wonder!

August 24, 2010

We're at Harris Ranch, our usual stop on our way home from Ashland. We just got back to our room from sharing a delicious steak and lobster dinner. Mom is really tired. I reminded her that she's always tired at the end of our Ashland summers because she's walking and on the go all the time. She agreed and said with a little rest she'd be ready to rock and roll again. The drive here is brutal for me, eight straight hours, but then I only have three and a half hours to drive tomorrow. And I love to relax here with Mother, drinking manhattans and eating a lovely dinner. Tonight, we had drinks in the bar before dinner. There was a marvelous guitarist, and we didn't want to leave, so we had two manhattans. Some nights call for that!

August 27, 2010

Mother is in the hospital! I am beside myself! When we arrived home, Mom was complaining of being tired and she looked flushed, so I told her to just relax, I'd get the car unloaded. She insisted on helping but finally gave in and let me do it. After I got everything in the house, we went out to eat, as we always do our first night home because we have no food in the house, and honestly, we just want to prolong our vacation mood.

The next morning Mom said that her back was sore and asked if I would take her to our chiropractor for an adjustment, so of course I said yes and called for an appointment. At the chiropractor's, Mom put on a gown. I hadn't noticed the sores on her torso. Our chiropractor took one look at her and said she has shingles. I couldn't believe it. This was my fault. I was supposed to have taken her for her shingles shot before we left for Ashland, but I'd been too busy to make the time, thinking we'd do it when we returned home. I immediately took her to Kaiser, where they confirmed the diagnosis of shingles and put her on meds. Mom was in good spirits, though, and we had a lovely evening, having a late dinner at Maggiano's.

In the middle of the night, Mom woke me up, gasping for air and telling me she couldn't breathe. We threw on some clothes, and I rushed her to Kaiser. They gave her oxygen, and she was doing much better. They wanted her to stay another day or two for observation. I thought I should let Deedee and the girls know, but Mom asked me not to because she didn't want to worry them. It was eleven in the morning. I'd been up all night and all morning. I was so tired I couldn't even think. I went home, and crawled into bed, and didn't wake up until ten that night. I grabbed my keys and flew out the door to Kaiser. I ran into Mom's room and found her fast asleep. The nurse told me she was doing much better and could probably go home tomorrow. I sat in her room, not wanting to wake her, but hoping she would wake up. I fell asleep in the chair and woke up to the light of a new day streaming through the windows. Mom was propped up, smiling, and said, "I didn't want to wake you." I told her I'd gotten there about ten-thirty last night and hadn't wanted to wake her either. We laughed, and that felt wonderful. I told her she could probably come home tomorrow. She said, "Go home, feed the kitties, take a shower, and put on some clean clothes." It was then that I realized what a disheveled mess I was, so I went home to do as she suggested.

At home there was a message from my tenant saying that she was going to have to move because she needed to downsize financially. I love this gal and knew she hated to leave. She loves the house as much as I do. However, the timing is extremely bad. I'm going to have to make a trip up there and assess the situation before I can get a new tenant.

There were also messages from Deedee and Ami. I realized that I would have to let them know what had happened in spite of Mom asking me not to bother them. I knew they would both be at work, so I sent them an email, including Mel and Rachael, letting them know that Grandma had contracted shingles and would be in the hospital a few days, but all was well and she should be home tomorrow. I got an email back from Ami saying, "Thanks for letting me know," and one from Rachael saying, "Take care and give Grandma a hug." Then I got one from Miss Dump and Duck: "She is not my grandmother! You pick up the goddamned phone and call me! I don't care if it is in the middle of the night!" She said a number of other very classy things as well. I chose to ignore it since I would be bringing Mom home tomorrow, but I did decide that when I got back to the hospital, I would have Mom give Deedee a call.

Early this morning I got a call from a nurse at Kaiser saying that Mom had been hallucinating, and they'd moved her to ICU. Again, I threw on clothes and ran out the door. It's nine at night. I've been here all day except for a quick run home midday to check on things, feed the kitties, and grab a snack. Mother's doctor told me she's doing well, that I shouldn't worry, she'll be home in a few days. I called Deedee an hour ago to relay this message, even though it was eleven at night her time, and I knew she had to get up at five to get to her department store job. Conrad didn't want to wake her, but I said she'd insisted quite vehemently that I was to call her. She answered the phone in a sleepy fog but quickly began to let me have it, "You need to stop lying. I don't believe anything you're telling me." I said, "Deedee, I'm so sorry you feel that way. I think it would be best if you speak to the doctor yourself. Please give him a call." She said, "I'll do better than that. I'll be arriving at ten in the morning," and slammed the phone down.

Deedee

August 28, 2010

I'm on the plane on my way to LA. I can't believe a word that stupid bitch says. Imagine taking my mother to the chiropractor when she has shingles. How stupid can you be, and she thinks she is so fucking smart. I'm the smart one. I'm going to show them all.

Leslie

August 29, 2010

What a day! Mom is doing well and will come home tomorrow. At the hospital this morning I went down to get a latte and saw Miss Dump and Duck walking huffily up to the elevators. I made a hasty decision to ignore her. I'm tired and irritable; the last thing I need is to deal with Miss Dump and Duck's nonsense. I got my latte and began to walk reluctantly back up to ICU. When I got to Mom's room, Deedee was calm and collected. Thank goodness! She said that since Mom was doing so well, she was going to head down to San Marino to visit Jessica, her one and only friend. I know it's catty of me, but they're two peas in a pod. Almost! Jessica is extremely wealthy, has a huge diamond ring and income property. Deedee is envious and strives to be exactly like her. Deedee took off almost immediately, much to my relief. I stayed with Mom the rest of the day and into the evening, then went home to a well-deserved glass of wine and sushi takeout. Around midnight I headed for bed. I'd no sooner gotten tucked in with my darlings when the phone rang. It was the nurse in ICU. Mom was worse. I threw on clothes and ran out the door. At the hospital, the doctor told me that Mom had gotten a staph infection, but they were treating it. Meanwhile, however, she needed to be put on a ventilator. Did I think she would want to do that? I went into Mom's room and asked her if she wanted to go on the ventilator—the alternative being she'd die. She said she wanted to live and gave permission to be put on the ventilator, so that's what we did. When Mom was comfortable, I gave her a hug and went on home to bed.

August 31, 2010

Iris called this morning to see how Mom was doing. She loves Mom dearly and is very concerned about her. Being a nurse, she's been of great help to me. When I told her about my tenant and what horrible timing this is, she said, "Darlin', I don't want you to worry about a thing. I'll take care of the house. You take care of Mom." An enormous load was lifted off my shoulders. At the same time, I was overwhelmed with love for this woman. At a time when she is in so much pain from the cancer, she is finding the energy to help me by getting my house ready for another tenant.

Mom is still on the ventilator and fighting the staph infection. We haven't heard from Deedee. I'd rather thought she'd return yesterday. Then around dinnertime she came waltzing in and did a double take when she saw Mom on the ventilator. "Who the hell gave permission for this?" she shouted, looking at me. She and I are supposed to make joint decisions about Mom's health care, if Mom is incapable. Mom heard Deedee, and while she couldn't talk, she pointed to herself; however, Deedee was seething and didn't see her because she had her eyes locked on me. She finally noticed Mom and calmed down. About an hour later Deedee said she was meeting Ami for dinner and staying at her place tonight and left. The tension in the room went from ten to zero!

Deedee

September 5, 2010

Mom is doing well, so I returned home. I had a wonderful time with Jessica. I wish she was my sister. My golf game is really improving. I love working with that really cute pro.

Leslie

September 18, 2010

Mom is still in the hospital and has contracted several staph infections that she's been fighting and winning, but her doctor told me that she'd been on the ventilator too long and needed a tracheotomy. She'd have a tube in her throat, but it can be taken out, so she can talk. The doctor explained the procedure to Mom, which he said takes only a few minutes to perform, and asked if that's what she'd like to do, to which she indicated yes with a nod of her head. It was early afternoon, and Mom was falling asleep, so I told her I was going to go work out and get a little lunch, I'd be back in a few hours.

When I returned, Ami was leaning over Mother's bed, holding her hand, and crying, "Grandma, are you sure you want to have this surgery?" I panicked! I'd only been gone a couple of hours; no one had called me. "What surgery?"

Ami looked at me and exploded with anger, "You can't okay surgery without my mother's permission."

"What surgery?" I repeated.

"The tracheotomy," Ami screamed. "My mother is going to be furious with you."

What a relief! I explained that it was a procedure that only took a few minutes to perform and that Grandma had given her permission. Ami would not be assuaged; she was lit up like fire. She was screaming at me. The nurse came in and asked her to please calm down, but Ami was on a roll. Mother was getting visibly upset, and I was about to cry. The nurse returned and, taking Ami's arm, said that she was going to escort her out of ICU, but she could return when she calmed down.

It gets worse! Within a few minutes Miss Dump and Duck was on the phone at the nurses' station, asking to speak to me, so I took the phone. She was yelling so loudly, everyone around me could hear. I tried to explain, but she wouldn't listen. She continued screaming that I had no right to okay surgery, that I'd be hearing from her attorney, and that she and Conrad were catching the next plane to LA; whereupon, she slammed the phone down.

It gets even worse! That night after arriving home, I was so worn out from the mental and emotional exhaustion, I called the nurses' station and asked one of the nurses to let Mom know that I would be late arriving in the morning, but I'd be there. I wanted to sleep in, play with my kitties, do a little journaling, and relax with my morning coffee and papers. It was eleven when I arrived at the hospital the next morning. While I felt refreshed, I was nowhere near ready to meet with Miss Dump and Duck's hostility; however, she does keep herself in check when Conrad is about. I was stalling and took my time walking to Mom's room, stopping in the gift shop and greeting all the staff I came across, but when I got to Mom's room, Miss Dump and Duck wasn't there. I wondered what had happened and asked Mom, but she shrugged, indicating she didn't know. I sat down with my stack of magazines and filled Mom in on the latest antics of our darling kitties.

Around three, as Mom and I were both drifting off for a nap, Deedee called my cell phone. Acting as if nothing untoward had taken place the day before, she said she and Conrad were at Jessica's in San Marino but would be driving up, arriving around eight. They would stop to check on Mom and would be spending the night with me at her mother's house. My stomach lurched! Oh no, I couldn't have them staying with me, not as angry as she was. Just the thought caused my body to go into panic mode. I said, "Now that you've hired an attorney, not only should you not be staying with me but we should not even be conversing." She said, "What attorney?" I replied, "The one you told me would be calling me." She said, "You need to stop lying. I didn't say anything about an attorney." I was astounded. I said, "Deedee, I'm not going to play this game. You've been staying at Ami's because you wanted to bond with her, so you stay with her again and do some more bonding." Then she screamed, "We'll be staying at my mother's house," and hung up on me.

I'd been seeing a very nice man who would on occasion pick me up at the hospital and take me out to dinner, returning me to the hospital where I could check on Mom again before returning home. This happened to be one of those nights. While we were out to dinner, the house security company called me, telling me we'd had an attempted break-in by someone claiming to be Mother's daughter; could I confirm that Deedee was, in fact, a daughter of the homeowner, to which I answered yes, although I would love to have denied it. We'd had all the locks changed on the house last summer, so when Deedee's key wouldn't secure access, Deedee and Conrad had tried windows, and the security system went off. I was appalled and a bit frightened. Why was Deedee so bent on getting into the house?

Deedee

September 25, 2010

Conrad is really angry about all these expensive trips to Los Angeles. He says Leslie is a good businesswoman and I should let her handle things. I try to tell him that she lies and makes decisions without talking to me, but he doesn't understand. I could have killed that bitch when I found out she'd had the locks on the house changed. That's my house as much as it is hers. She can't keep me out. I need to get in there and see what's going on. I was so embarrassed when the police showed up. Fuck! She just won't stop harassing me. It was a wasted trip except that I had a good time with Jessica. I know Leslie is paying Mom's bills. She's on my mother's account. I'm not. That's not fair. I should be on those accounts too. I'm sure she's paying her own bills with my mother's money. Fuck! I'd like free rent, groceries, and all my bills paid. Why her? Why not me?

Leslie

September 30, 2010

My poor mother! She's overcome most of the staph infections, but she can't get off the ventilator. She's been at Kaiser a month, and they're moving her to a subacute nursing facility. I was speechless when I was told it would cost $25,000 a month. Kaiser will pay the first three months, then the director of the facility told me that we need to get her on Medi-Cal. I told her that Mother had enough money to pay out-of-pocket for a while. At $25,000 a month, I thought this place would be like somewhere the president would stay. When I walked in the door, I broke down crying. It was old and crappy, and it stank of urine and cleaners. There was no way I was going to leave my mother here. I'd find another facility. The only other place I located was in Santa Monica, and it was about as bad as the facility in the Valley. I did some research and found out that I could bring Mother home on the ventilator, but we'd have to upgrade the electrical in the house. I talked to Mother about it, and she said she just wanted to come home, do whatever was necessary.

Having taken most of the summer off and now this month with Mom's illness, I'm a bit concerned about my own finances and need to get back to work.

November 16, 2010

What a month! I'm working on some great cases and catching up financially, but my hours are very long. I go to see Mom before I hit the freeway in the morning and then again on my way home at night. She's struggling but in good spirits.

I got some estimates on upgrading the electrical and they'd begun work, but they ran into some asbestos, so they had to stop work and get that handled.

The director of the facility is constantly bugging me to get Mom on Medi-Cal. She recommended three attorneys who specialize in this area, and she arranged for me to meet them at the facility. We met in Mom's room so she could participate. Although her responses are primarily nonverbal gestures or writing on a chalkboard, the nurse does on occasion take her off the ventilator to give her a break so she is able to talk, which she did in this case. After meeting with them, Mother wrote on the chalkboard, "Sleazy!" I laughed and agreed, saying, "Their suggesting we can hide money seems a bit corrupt, and I don't want to get into any trouble." At Deedee's wedding, we'd met a friend of Conrad's who is an attorney. He's done some will and trust work for both Mom and me, and we have great respect for him, so I said,

"Why don't we call Stephanos." Mother answered, "Stephanos's wife is quite ill, and he has retired in order to care for her. Check with Bertha, our neighbor. She used someone she really liked for her mother's estate." I got the name of Bertha's attorney and set up an appointment with her and Mother. When I went to see Mother the night after her appointment, she said, "I really like this attorney." The nurse had taken Mom off the ventilator for a time so that we could talk. Mom told me she was putting the house in my name because she wanted me to have it. She said, "Anything I've ever given Deedee, she's sold or given away, and I don't want to lose the house." She told me in order for the house to be titled to me alone, I needed to refinance and pay Deedee her fair share. I agreed to do that.

Chapter Thirty-Seven

There's No Place Like Home

Leslie

January 1, 2011

I spent Thanksgiving Day and Christmas Day with Mom at the facility. The day after Christmas I went to Rachael's for a much-needed break. The drive along the coast thrills me and reminds me of my childhood in Santa Monica. While I was gone, I arranged for Bernie and Cassie to visit Mom a couple of times a day, and they said they really enjoyed their time with her. I'm truly blessed to have such amazing friends.

Miss Dump and Duck constantly sends emails advising, "You're lying and not telling me everything. You'd better not be using my mother's money on yourself." I try to remain calm, sending her notes back with synopses of doctors' reports and Mother's progress. I suggested that she call and talk to the facility personnel herself, which she did, but she got into an argument with one of the director's assistants and had the poor girl in tears, so now they won't take her calls, and, of course, it's all my fault.

We haven't made much progress on the house due to the holiday season, but we're picking up now. Since the house is in my name, I've decided to spend some of my money for upgrades that I would like: French doors in Mom's room, crown molding, new tile in my bathroom.

February 18, 2011

Yesterday was Mom's birthday. I bought a cake at her favorite bakery and invited a bunch of friends, as well as some of the other ladies at the facility, to join us for a little party. When I walked into Mom's room, I was surprised to see Deedee and Ami hunched over the bed, holding Mom's hands and cooing. I had no idea Miss Dump and Duck would be here. Ami and Mel have only visited Mother once, which was a few days before Christmas, to complain that I hadn't sent them as much money for Christmas as she does.

My family has been deteriorating, and it breaks my heart. What is wrong with us? We should be sticking together through this terrible time with Mother. We've suffered enough pain with the loss of Dad and Liam; we do not need any more. I went back to doing some therapy because I want to understand what triggered all this hostility. I've been overwhelmed with Mother's illness, all that involves, and working on top of it. I'm usually up at five in the morning, stop to see Mom before I hit the freeway. I leave my jobs around five-thirty and get to the facility around seven so I can check in on Mom again and hear about her day. I finally get back home around eight-thirty and work on transcripts until ten. To top it off, the house is a disaster with all the work going on. It leaves me feeling unsettled and irritable.

Deedee

April 1, 2011

Leslie says this nursing home she put my mother in costs $25,000 a month, plus other expenses. She's lying. I worked in an old age home. It does not cost that much. If she's going to lie, she should have picked a believable amount, like $5000. Then the bitch tells me she hates the place Mother is at and is going to bring her home on the ventilator, but the house has to be rewired first. Does she think I'm stupid? I know that she just wants to fix up the house because she's living there and she can use my mother's money. Mother inherited $1 million from her aunt. That's my money too. Maybe I don't want to use it to fix up that house. It's just a shitty old tract house. I'd rather use the money on myself. Now the bitch is talking to an attorney about getting my mother on Medi-Cal. I told her I know an attorney she can call, but she said my mother already decided on an attorney that the neighbor recommended. Oh, yeah! Right! The bitch got her own attorney to do her dirty work for her. My mother can't even talk. She can't make decisions about Medi-Cal. I'm so fucking pissed off. I want to fly out there and take over, but I can't get any more time off work and Conrad says Leslie can handle it. Bull-fucking-shit! I couldn't take it anymore. I told my supervisor at work that my mother had a relapse and wasn't expected to live. I had to go back. It was an emergency. I went back and surprised my mother for her birthday. When I saw that place, I knew Leslie had been lying about how much it cost. What a fucking dump! For Christmas I wanted to have the girls come here, but Conrad said, "No! When you get together with your girls, there's nothing but drama."

Leslie

May 1, 2011

Thankfully, the work has come to an end, and the house is beyond beautiful. Mother is going to love it. The French doors in her room bring in so much light, and they offer a lovely view of the yard and pool. I can hardly wait to bring her home.

June 2, 2011

Mother and I have gotten friendly with other, shall we say, inmates at the facility. I noticed that Grace, in the next room, would be off the ventilator, talking, eating, and such; the next day she'd be nearly comatose and back on the ventilator. With the huge push from the director to get Mom on Medi-Cal, which I wish I'd never gotten into because dealing with the government is never a good experience, and the way people seemed to get better, then worse, I began asking some of the family members of the other inmates what they thought about their relatives' progress. What I got back were blank stares and "I don't know" responses. I made a mental note to ask the director about it.

Jacob called me and said that Rachael was worn out and disheartened over all the text messages she's been receiving from Deedee, Ami, and Mel. She's been calling it "tattletale texting." I knew she was receiving these, as I was, but I hadn't known to what extent they were affecting her. I'm sure she hadn't wanted to mention it to me because she didn't want to burden me, knowing the stress I was under. I told Jacob I'd handle it. Those women can mess with me, but when they start messing with my baby, it's over. I sent them all an email, and using Taylor's term, I told them they are on time-out, no more texting or emailing Rachael or me. They could talk to doctors and nurses themselves to check on Mother's progress. *Basta!*

June 22, 2011

As Mother had asked me to do, I had the house appraised and sent a check off to Miss Dump and Duck for her share, $250,000. Mother told me that she'd talked to Deedee about this, so I was surprised when Deedee called me and left a scathing message: "You fucking bitch! I tore up your fucking check. You can't buy me off! I'm part of this family too, and that house is mine. I've hired an attorney. I'm going to get that house back. You better watch out, you fucking liar!"

July 28, 2011

I spent my birthday with Rachael and the children. Rachael took us to a darling teashop in Santa Barbara for tea, sandwiches, and pastries. Rachael is my reality check. When I get off track in life, I think of my daughter and get right back on.
I saw the facility director this evening. We were chatting, and I mentioned that some of the ladies are off the ventilators for

some period of time, and then they are suddenly back on them. I know from taking depositions involving some of these subacute nursing facilities that they can be quite corrupt. I'd been wondering if patients are kept on ventilators so the subacute nursing facilities can collect Medi-Cal funds, so I asked her. She got very indignant, made some excuses, and we parted company.

August 25, 2011

Mother is doing so well. After being told she would never get off the ventilator, she is now off and even doing some physical therapy. I wonder if her amazing recovery has something to do with my little chat with the director.

September 22, 2011

After a long, painful year of struggling to get well, Mother is finally back home. The joy radiating from her beautiful face warms my heart. I was told she would need twenty-four-hour care, so I hired a caretaker to be here with her while I'm at work, although I took this week off to be here while she settles in. We've had a lot of medical assistance. Kaiser is very thorough, to say the least. They sent out a social worker, who, after speaking to Mother, was frazzled and wished me good luck and on her way out the door suggested I get in a support group. A physical therapist worked with Mom for an hour, telling her she would need to use a walker. She told him that was nonsense, she could walk just fine. He suggested exercises, and she told him she hated to exercise. Kaiser sent out someone to go over the meds with us, and a nurse will be coming out twice a week to do blood draws in order to monitor meds. It's been an exasperating week.

Deedee

October 10, 2011

It took Leslie a year to bring my mother home because she didn't want her peace and quiet disrupted. Selfish bitch! And she had the nerve to put me and my girls on time out. Fuck! She's going to be on permanent time out when I get done with her. My attorney says I'm over the top and I can't really sue the bitch for anything. Leslie says she's going crazy with Mother's care, the caretaker, her long work hours. She doesn't work long hours. She meets guys and goes out drinking just like Meliza. They call that long hours. I should have such long hours. Leslie said, "Could we please just stop with the angry texts, emails, and phone calls." I told her, "I'm not angry. I just want the facts, as they used to say on that TV program. I want you to stop lying and spending my mother's money on yourself." I told her I'd come out for a month and help her. She said no. I try to help, but she won't let me. I want to be part of what's going on. I have a right to make decisions too. I want to take care of my mother and her money. I want my mother to love me as much as she loves Leslie. I tell Mother I'm the orphan. She says she doesn't have favorites with her children, but I know that's not true. When I prove to my mother that Miss Perfect is a lying, stealing bitch, my mother will love me.

Leslie

October 21, 2011

I still grieve over Ken and sometimes call just to hear his voice on the answering machine. That's really sick! If a girlfriend told me she did that, I'd tell her, for her own health and well-being, she needs to let it go. I was emailing him, but eventually I let go of that, so I will put this phone-calling in my rearview mirror as well. What's wrong with me that it's taking me so long to get past this abusive relationship?

I think about that miraculous holiday season we spent together. It would make a great love story: the tension and anticipation, the smell of rain in the air, the chill off San Francisco Bay, the holiday season with all its jollity and frivolity, the lights and decorations, the new sex, family and friends, belonging. Maybe I'll write a romance novel!

November 1, 2011

I'm going absolutely insane! I feel like I'm living in the lobby at Kaiser. I get up at four- thirty in the morning, make Mom's breakfast, lunch, and dinner, try to get ready for work, but the caretaker comes at six and has all sorts of questions. People are in and out all morning, checking Mom's meds, taking blood draws. When I finally get out of the house, I'm completely frazzled. I can't live like this. I'm working on a case in downtown LA that has been going on for months. It's great money, but the days are far too long. I get home around eight, after sitting in all the traffic. Then I have to get my transcripts out before I can relax, but again the caretaker has to tell me this and that. She is so sweet and goes out of her way to help us, even cleaning the house when Mom is sleeping. She takes Mom to the beauty shop, the mall, and the senior center. I couldn't ask for a better caretaker, but when I get home, I'm exhausted. I need some time alone, peace, and tranquility.

November 8, 2011

I have absolutely no patience anymore, and I must remember to lock the screen door. I go out to retrieve the newspapers, water the lawn, put my equipment in my car, and I don't lock the door. The other morning, I was getting ready for work. Mom was sleeping. The caretaker hadn't arrived yet. I was walking down the hall with a cup of hot coffee, wearing only my bra and panties. I was right at the front door when a woman opened the screen door and walked right in the house.

I was so startled I dropped my mug, spilling hot coffee all over everything and splattering some on myself. The woman was the nurse from Kaiser here to do a blood draw. I was so angry, I yelled, "Get the fuck out of the house! This is a private home. You have no right to just walk in without ringing the bell. I don't want you coming back here anymore. The caretaker will take Mom over to Kaiser for blood draws." I couldn't believe how angry I was. I sat down, shaking and crying.

November 10, 2011

Miss Dump and Duck has been offering to come out for a month and help me. She called yesterday, quite insistent on coming here. I panicked! You never know when she'll lose it, so to speak, and she's been a real witch lately. I hesitated only a moment before I said, "No. The caretaker has things under control, and really, another person in the house would just add another level of stress. There's a lot of commotion, and every spare part of the house is taken up with medical equipment."

As it turns out, it's a good thing I said no because it gets worse. Of course, Miss Dump and Duck and Ami would call and want to talk to Mom. They should, and it's good for Mom to talk to them. However, we're having an issue with Mom's hearing aids. She doesn't want to wear them. She says they're annoying. As a result, when Deedee calls, we have to put the phone on speaker so Mom can hear, but Deedee yells at the caretaker or me, "Get off the fucking phone. This is a private conversation." Then I try to explain to Miss Dump and Duck that Mother can't hear if the phone isn't on speaker and that I have other things to do, I don't have time to sit and listen to their silly conversations, so it is private. Deedee wouldn't hear me, though. She just kept screaming over my voice. So I put the phone off speaker, gave it back to Mom and left the room. The next thing I know, Mom is calling me, "Please put the phone back on speaker because I can't hear Deedee." Deedee is still screaming "fuck this" and "fuck that" while

Mother is now trying to tell her that she can't hear if the phone isn't on speaker and that I am not listening in on the call. By now I am certain that I am being filmed by some psycho reality TV show.

November 13, 2011

It gets even worse! Yes, it is possible! That stupid phone was fairly new, so I decided to return it and get something for a hearing-impaired person. I put it in the car, thinking I would stop at Best Buy on the way home, but I had some late work nights and was anxious to get home and too tired to deal with it. Mind you, the caretaker and I both have cell phones, and Miss Dump and Duck has our numbers. However, rather than call our cell phones, she called the police and said, "I'm very concerned about my mother because I can't get ahold of her by phone. Would you send an officer out to check to be sure she's okay?" I was at work, so the poor caretaker had to deal with this. I was furious when I got home and heard this tale. What is wrong with that girl? This is deliberate meanness.

And then it gets even worse! Yep! I'd returned the phone but hadn't yet had time to get one for the hearing impaired, although I should have made that a priority because Miss Dump and Duck sent me a scathing email saying she would have the police come out every day until I got that fucking phone back in the house. The police came out on two more occasions. The last time they came out, one of the officers asked, "Is your sister crazy?"

November 18, 2011

Last night I'd actually gotten home at a rather normal time. The caretaker left. My jobs were out. I had dinner prepped. Mom was listening to the news on TV, and I was enjoying a glass of wine and reading my newspaper when the doorbell rang. It was a handsome gentleman who introduced himself as a detective for the Valley police department. I let him in, and he explained that he was here to check on Mother and wrap up the case of Deedee's complaints. He chatted with Mother and me for a few minutes and said he'd be on his way. He said he was sorry about all the harassment from Mrs. Foreman. I leaped on the word "harassment" and asked him, "What can I do to protect myself against Mrs. Foreman's abuse?" He suggested I take pictures of Mother every day and send them to Deedee so she would know Mother is well, that I send her statements of how money is being spent because that would surely be her next complaint, and that I should file a restraining order.

December 1, 2011

I finally got some peace and quiet! Mother went to Ami's for Thanksgiving weekend. I spent a blissful four days doing the things I love to do. I thought I'd died and gone to heaven. When Ami picked up Mom, she was fumbling through Mom's purse and said, "I can't find Grandma's ATM card. Where is it?" With all the people in and out of the house, I'd locked up banking records and credit cards. I just said, "Grandma doesn't see well enough to use it."

I took the detective's advice and filed for a restraining order. We go to court on the seventeenth of the month.

December 18, 2011

I went to court yesterday for the restraining order and was shocked to see Miss Dump and Duck there with an attorney. She'd hired an attorney and flown out from the Carolinas for a restraining order. Her attorney came over to talk to me. I'd brought the documents showing that I was the legal owner of the property and the records from the police department of the calls and visits to the house. I'd brought an extra copy, so I gave that to her. I explained to her that I was at my wit's end on how to resolve these issues with Deedee. I told her I'd sent Deedee a check for her share of the property, and she'd torn it up, but I said, "I have another check here for $300,000, an additional $50,000, because with the upgrades to the house, I feel the value has increased." Deedee's attorney took the check and lit up. She was quite excited and said, "Give me a minute to speak to my client." I watched them. It didn't look promising. Deedee was raising her voice and waving her hands around. She grabbed the check, tore it into pieces, and threw it into the air. Tiny pieces of paper were floating down in their hair and onto their clothes. The attorney returned, saying, "I'm sorry, but my client has declined your offer." I lost the restraining order because the judge said that since Deedee was Mother's daughter as well, and Mother was living with me, Deedee had a right to call and speak to her, and visitations could be worked out so they didn't have to take place on the property. I felt so tainted, so sad. How had we come to this? This was our family home. We should all be gathered there together. I cried all the way home. Deedee did not try to see Mother while she was here, nor did she call.

Deedee

December 21, 2011

Fuck! I am so pissed! That bitch listens in on my conversations with my mother. She's harassing me. Then the bitch files for a restraining order against me. She can't do that. It's my house and my mother. She even offered to pay me. I told my attorney to tell her to fuck off. She can't buy me out of this family. I paid that stupid attorney for nothing, and Conrad is real mad that I spent more money to fly out there. Now the bitch is sending me pictures of my mother every day. She sends me financial statements too, but I know she lies about them. They can't be right. She claims she's paying all the bills because my mother's money goes to the caretaker. Amiala wanted to use my mother's ATM card to buy groceries for Thanksgiving weekend. I thought that was a good idea because I want that account number, but the bitch wouldn't give Amiala the card. I wanted to go be with my girls for Christmas, but Conrad said we're spending too much money on last-minute flights. I want to scream! I used to be able to afford anything I wanted. Fuck my ex Johnson for fucking his whore! I should have held out and married another rich man. I can't stand being poor and told what I can and can't do. Fuck Conrad! I've got credit cards that he doesn't know about.

Chapter Thirty-Eight

Little Orphan . . .

Deedee

January 1, 2012

Conrad and I had a quiet Christmas at home. Conrad made dinner, but I didn't eat much. I'm trying real hard not to throw up so much. I know I'm not bulimic, but the doctor keeps asking me about it and I don't want to get those bleeding ulcers again. So, I just try not to eat. Conrad gave me one of those DNA testing kits for Christmas. I spit in it and sent it in. I know I'm mostly Irish. I don't know what else I am, though. We'll see.

Leslie

January 1, 2012

New Year's Day! The doorbell rang this afternoon. I answered the door, and Ami pushed right past me into the living room. I was working on my recipe file project and had papers spread all over the living room floor. I didn't want to abandon my project and leave a mess, so here I was, listening to Ami talk to Mom. What a phony bitch! I hate her, and Miss Dump and Duck, and Mel. I'm sick to death of them. When I'm home, I don't have the caretaker come, which means I help Mom with her personal hygiene and all that entails. I won't go into the details, but there's a good reason I didn't follow in Auntie Anne's footsteps and become a nurse. Those women have no idea what it's like to take care of Mother. Mother's doctor says Mother needs to be in a board and care. I thought I could handle her care, and I wanted to do that. That's why I brought her home, but those three malicious women have made my life a living hell, which makes them happy. When they see me angry and frustrated, they give me this tight little score-one-for-me smile. I'd like to smack them! And Mom sticks up for them. I'm beginning to agree with the doctor that Mom needs to go to a board and care. I'm tired of those vicious game players.

January 5, 2012

Another year has come and gone. My New Year's Day entry was rather harsh, but last year was a nightmare. This year will be good. No, it will be fantastic! Mom went to Ami's again for Christmas, so I went to Rachael's and was surrounded by love. Jacob was there too. He has been so supportive. I gave Taylor a diary for Christmas. I told her someday she will be very grateful that she kept diaries. It's important to record your history and your feelings. When I read entries recorded through the years, I'm surprised and enlightened by what I wrote. I see not only how I've grown and changed but also how my family and friends have reshaped their lives as well. I see how a phone call can alter one's life forever. I see how tragedy and love have woven their way through my life. Maybe someday I'll turn my diaries into a novel.

January 10, 2012

Last night I arrived home to find a business card from a representative of Adult Protective Services stuck in the screen door. My stomach did a flop. I thought, "What now?" I immediately went in and gave them a call and was told that a Mrs. Deedee Foreman had called and filed a complaint, asking them to go out to see her mother. She'd said, "I'm worried about my mother's care. I believe my sister is abusing her." Tears began streaming down my eyes. I had to ask the gentleman to hold on a minute. I wanted to let loose with a good cry, but this wasn't the time. After drying my eyes, I set up an appointment for two days hence. I'd have to take myself off the reporting calendar, but this was a priority.

January 12, 2012

Mr. Patel from APS came to the house tonight. I had butterflies in my stomach, but I remained calm. The caretaker and I were taking good care of Mother. The house was immaculate, and Mother was happy, even with all the stress of the infighting, which I didn't discuss with her unless absolutely necessary. She, however, would say, "Deedee has issues, and you need to be kinder and more patient." Patience was a virtue I'd completely lost, and I hated to be reminded of it.

Mr. Patel spoke to both of us. I showed him around the house. He said he could see my mother was getting a lot of love and excellent care. He commended me for my patience and apologized for the intrusion. He said he would be filing a highly complimentary report, and we would have no more visits from APS. He continued, "I consider Mrs. Foreman's calls harassing not only to you but also to APS. I have a lot of seriously abused seniors who need my help. Your mother is certainly not one of them."

January 16, 2012

Mother has been falling a lot. She even fell right in front of Rachael, Taylor, and me. However, she usually falls during the night because she has to get up to use the bathroom and gets disoriented. I was getting her up off the floor and back to bed myself, but I hurt my back and can't do it anymore. One night I called our neighbor, a big strapping guy, but he couldn't get her up, so I've had to call 911 ever since. We're getting to know them on a personal basis.

I've been trying to get our lives back to some normalcy with book group, Scrabble, dinners and such. Mom's spirits are up, but she's weak. I keep trying to get her to do her exercises, and I've had some success. Kaiser tested her for her Activities of Daily Living, or ADLs, and they said she should be in a board and care situation. Mother is so upset about that report she refuses to go back to Kaiser. While I hate to see

Mother go to a board and care, I have to get myself out of this caretaker position I've fallen into. I can't keep this up forever. I'm desperate to get my life back. Miss Dump and Duck told Mother they could do some remodeling, and she could come and live with them, to which Mother told me, "Guess who'd be paying for their remodeling?"

February 1, 2012

Mother fell last week and crushed some vertebrae in her spine. She went back to Kaiser. The doctor said that she must go to a board and care. I said, "Good luck!" He said, "She has no choice. She's flat on her back, and I'm ordering the transfer." I knew they'd send her to another horrible place, so I asked, "Could you give me a couple of hours? There is a facility I like extremely well. I'll give them a call to see if they have availability." They did. I was delighted. This place is the epitome of luxury. It would take all Mother's monthly income to pay for it, but so did the caretaker, and I'd continue to subsidize Mother's other expenses: beauty shop, cosmetics, clothes, books on CD, dinners out, etc. I went with her when they transferred her to the board and care. I put my hand on her arm to comfort her as well as myself, and she slapped my hand away, saying, "You finally got what you wanted. You got rid of me. Now you can have your peace and quiet." She turned her head away from me. OMG! Her words stung! Tears streamed down my cheeks. I'm always crying lately. One of the female paramedics gave me a hug and told me this was normal behavior; my mother must love me very much to feel safe in taking this out on me. I knew she was right, but it crushed me to the core and still does. I tried to hug Mom and said, "You know that isn't true. When we don't have Deedee and her girls screaming at us, we do have a peaceful life together." Then she said the operative words that stung with meanness and spite, "Deedee says you put me here on purpose to get rid of me so you could have my house to yourself. She said you never gave her, her share of the money for the house, and that's not fair. She says you got everything, and she got nothing."

Deedee

March 2, 2012

That man from APS is an idiot! He didn't do a fucking thing! He said he'd rarely seen a woman getting as good care as my mother. I know that's not true. Leslie is abusing her. My mother is falling a lot, and I'm sure Leslie is giving her a push. Mother says she doesn't have much appetite because the meds are affecting her taste buds, but they're working on adjusting her meds. I bet Leslie is working on adjusting the meds! Mother broke some vertebra in her back and has been transferred to a board and care. Another fucking setup by that bitch Leslie! She's been dying to get rid of my mother. She took her to get her old age activities checked. The doctors told them that my mother needs to go into a board and care. But good for Mother. She refused to go. Leslie set that up. She knows a lot of those stupid Kaiser doctors, and I'm sure they lied for her. Leslie gets everything she wants. Everybody loves Leslie. Now my mother is in a board and care that's eating up all her money. My mother hates it there. She wants to go home, and the bitch won't let her. I had Amiala take my mother to the bank to get her name on the checking account, but the bank manager called Leslie and security. Amiala said it was very embarrassing and she wouldn't do it again. She said I'd have to do it if I wanted it done. So now I have to schedule another trip out there. Fuck! Conrad is going to be ready to kill me!

April 1, 2012

OMG! I am a fucking orphan. That DNA thing came back. My parents aren't who I thought they were. I called mother immediately and asked, "What the fuck?" She said they'd never dreamed I would find out. She said my real mother was Dad's cousin, who got pregnant at seventeen and gave me up for adoption. Mother had just had a miscarriage and was told she probably would not be able to have any more children. Dad's aunt asked if they wouldn't take the baby because Dad's cousin was beside herself at giving me away. They said, "If you take the baby, she'll stay in the family. We'll be able to stay in touch and know she is well taken care of." My real father never knew about me and died in the Korean War. My real mother never got over giving me up and losing her boyfriend in the war. She committed suicide after visiting us in Santa Monica in 1954.

I asked Mother, "Where are my adoption papers?" She said, "We never got around to doing anything legally. Your birth certificate is a fake. I've been so embarrassed, I've never said a word to anyone, and I never will. I'm ashamed that we never legally adopted you. Time just moved on, and then it seemed too late to file for adoption. Your birth parents were dead, and your mother's mother had passed away. I haven't wanted anyone to know how foolish we were. I don't know what we were thinking. But, Deedee, you are my daughter, and everyone thinks you are my daughter. We'd moved away from Detroit. I'd lost a baby, but I brought you home shortly thereafter, so nobody suspected a thing. I've been burdened with the guilt, and that's why I've always wanted things to be fair between you, and Liam, and Leslie."

April 23, 2012

I'm sixty-one years old and just found out I really am an orphan. My mother lied to me and cheated me out of a life I should have had. My birth mother shouldn't have been forced to give me up. Maybe she wouldn't have killed herself. I should have known my real grandmother and my real father's family. I'm madder than hell and more determined than ever to destroy Leslie. That fucking bitch has been the real daughter, and I've been the fake. I'm never telling anyone about this and I know my mother won't either. My mother? I'm going to get even with Leslie. They owe me!

Leslie

May 1, 2012

Mother and I seem to be growing further apart. I go to see her every morning and evening. On the weekends, I take food I've prepared that I know she likes. I take my knitting and sit with her. Mom talks nonstop about coming home. I can understand that because as lovely as this place is, it's not home. She told me that Deedee says she can come home, that I'm keeping her a prisoner in this place because I don't want to be burdened with her. Deedee says I'm mean and vindictive, that I'm using Mother's money for myself. I've tried to explain the finances to her, what things cost, etc. She knows I pay for her beauty shop appointments and anything else she needs or wants. I've even had the owner of the board and care talk to her, but she won't listen to either of us. I feel so bad. I've begun to go see her less; I just get so beat up with "Deedee this" and "Deedee that."

Deedee

June 2, 2012

Conrad and Amiala and Meliza were bugging me about my DNA results. I told them it's just what you'd expect. I'm mostly Irish and that was about it. But now Amiala wants to have her DNA done. Shit!

Leslie

June 30, 2012

Other than my visits to Mother, life is quiet and peaceful once again. When I talk to her on the phone or go visit her, I try to schedule going for a workout right after. It gets my mind off all the hurtful things Mother says and relieves some of the stress.

Mother likes the other ladies and gentlemen at the board and care. She's passionate about gossip, so she's in the right place. She can hardly wait for me to get there to tell me all about it. If Miss Dump and Duck weren't feeding her so much craziness, I think Mother would really enjoy living there. They take her to her doctor appointments, the beauty shop, and the senior center. She's getting so much more social interaction. Bernie was in a tap dance program at the senior center, and Mother was thrilled to let everyone know that was her friend up on the stage. I have our book group meet at the board and care, which has turned out to be nice for the other people there who want to participate. I've played a piano concert a few times, making up little programs and bringing cookies and soda for the intermission. Cousin Robert has come to entertain them by playing the ukulele and telling jokes. I think these events help Mother to feel grounded and at home, and very much a VIP.

Deedee

July 26, 2012

My mother had to call me today and remind me that it's the bitch's birthday. She said "Oh, I remember the day she was born. Your dad and I were so happy. What a beautiful child. She never gave us any problems. Everybody loves Leslie!" Well, I hate the bitch, and I'm sick of hearing about her! All my life everything has been about Leslie and how good she is and why can't I be more like her. I don't want to be like her.

283

She listens to that screechy opera music, and she's always going to school. She's not a sexy dresser. She knits like an old lady. She certainly can't get a husband. Why would I want to be like her? I told my mother that Leslie and that attorney had her sign the house over when she was on drugs. Mother said, "I was never out of it. And Leslie has tried to pay you several times, but you tore the checks up." I said, "My lawyer told me that Leslie didn't have to pay me." My mother said, "She certainly does. She signed an agreement." I said, "No, she doesn't, and she hasn't paid me. I'm just a goddamned orphan. You don't love me because you left everything to Leslie. It just isn't fair. My attorney can get your house back and arrange for me to take care of everything, and the first thing I'll do is take you home. You don't need to have your old age actions checked." Mother gets real excited when I tell her I'll take her home. She wants to go home so bad. I told her, "I'll come and stay with you for a month, and then you'll be ready to live on your own again." She said, "I don't think I can live completely on my own. I'll probably need a little help." I told her, "You'll be fine." She likes to hear that. I told her she needs to get her bank statements and jewelry from Leslie. She said, "Leslie said no, a board and care was not a good place for bank records. She did bring some of my jewelry." I told her we'd have her address changed. That way her mail will come to the board and care. She thought that was a good idea. She could have the people at the board and care read it to her. I told her I'd make an appointment for my attorney to come and see her. I'm going to get even with that bitch! She stole $1 million from my mother and wants to give me $300,000 for the house alone. Where's the million in cash? How stupid does she think I am? I'll have her ass thrown out in the street.

Leslie

August 15, 2012

I'm in Ashland for our summer vacation. Friends are coming and going, but I miss my mother; Ashland is her place too. I see her everywhere I go and in everything I do. I arranged for friends to take shifts visiting Mom, and all the reports are good. She revels in the attention, especially from the men.

August 24, 2012

Upon arriving home and unpacking the car, I went immediately to see Mom. She told me how nice it was that all these people came to visit while I was away, and they enjoyed themselves so much that they promised to continue visiting. Jana was so impressed with the facility that she's transferring her mother here as soon as they have an opening.

Mother repeated her desire to have her banking records with her. I reiterated that a board and care facility is not a place to retain financial documents. She was quite upset and said she had a right to see her banking statements. I said, "Yes, you certainly do, and I will bring them and go over them with you as I always do." Then I reminded her that she couldn't read them anyway, something I hate to bring up because it's painful, but she said she could with her overhead enlargement machine and would I please bring it to her. Oops! When Mother first bought the machine, she could read a page at a time; however, her eyesight has deteriorated to the point where she can barely manage to read a word at a time. Thinking that we would never again have need for the machine and also that part of it had broken, I'd donated it to an organization for the sight impaired. I told her this, and she came a bit undone, saying, "You had no right to do that." I agreed and said, "I'll look into purchasing a new machine, but I will not leave financial records at a board and care."

Jewelry! Financial records! I was beginning to smell a rat, and I knew just who that rat was.

Deedee

August 30, 2012

Amiala got the DNA results back. Roy was not her father. It was Liam's friend Howard. Howard was the one who got us in touch with the veterans' group. He was the one I was having sex with at the same time as Roy. Howard died of an embolism last year. Amiala is very angry at me. She said, "How could you not tell me?" I said, "I didn't know. We didn't have DNA testing back then. I assumed it was Roy." Howard had gone away to college and met a girl that he fell head over heels in love with and married. I know that they were very happy together and had a nice family. Amiala said, "But if you'd told me you weren't sure who my father was, I could have been tested earlier and had time to spend with my real dad. Now it's too late. You took him away from me. You've ruined my life. You're just a selfish bitch!" I told her it never occurred to me to tell her. It wasn't important. Now Amiala wants to be in touch with Howard's family. I told her, "You need to leave it alone. You'll only bring drama into their lives."

Leslie

September 12, 2012

Iris died today. I've spoken to her many times over the past few months. I told her how much I loved her and valued our friendship, and that I would keep her memory alive. I was able to say good-bye. That doesn't help. I hurt. I can't write any more right now.

Deedee

October 22, 2012

Another birthday, and all I get is more wrinkles! I get facials every week, but it doesn't help. I flew out to see my mother. We couldn't take Leslie's name off the account so we opened a new account for me and my mother and we changed her retirement funds to be deposited in our account. I thought I finally had control, but Leslie went crazy when she couldn't pay the board and care, and she threatened the people at the bank. She must have had a good tantrum because they closed our account and sent me a letter saying I could never open another account with them. That made me furious! Leslie got one up on me, but I'll get even. I'm going to make her pay for stealing that $1 million. I took my mother to the house. I really want to see what Leslie did to the house. But she wouldn't let us in. She pretended she wasn't home. The fucking bitch! I walked around and looked in all the windows. She did a really fucked-up job of decorating.

Leslie

October 24, 2012

It's October and time to make New Year's resolutions. In an effort to get into a renewable spirit, I went to the spa, where I sat in the hot tub, got a massage, took a shower, and washed my hair. Now I'm sitting out by the pool in my comfy-but-stylish sweatpants and sweatshirt, drinking a lovely glass of wine and pondering my New Year's resolutions. They are, as always, a long list. Here it is: lose ten pounds, get in better shape, be on time, be patient, and spend more time playing the piano, studying Italian, reading, and writing.

November 1, 2012

Auntie Anne had a stroke and died. I flew to Michigan for the memorial service. I actually flew there and returned in twenty-four hours. I couldn't believe I did that. I just felt so sad that I didn't want to drive around to see other family; I wanted to come home. I miss her so much. She was always my go-to person. I know she loved me, and I truly loved her.

November 24, 2012

I spent Thanksgiving with Mom, taking her a turkey dinner using all her recipes. She was delighted! Ami had come to visit her the day before, and Mother bent my ears with all the goings-on with Ami and how she comes faithfully to visit her every week. I doubted very much the "every week" visits; according to the sign-in records, it's twice a month, but at least it's that. Mel has never been here. Deedee visited once recently. She also calls several times a week, and according to the director, the calls are getting more frequent.
Mother began her diatribe about wanting to come home so she can put pictures in her albums and knit. I knew she couldn't see to put pictures in albums, but I hit on the knitting because even without sight, one can still knit. I said I'd bring her knitting here and knit with her. She said, "No, I want to knit at home. Deedee says I can come home, and if she were in charge, she'd bring me home." That hit me like a brick wall. Deedee must be vying to take over Mother's care. I signed an agreement that even though the house was titled to me, it would always be Mother's home. I just about threw up at the thought of Deedee taking over, bringing Mother home, and staying for a month, maybe months. Who knew what that girl had in mind, but I can tell you for sure, she would not hire a caretaker. She thought that was a waste of money. Maybe she was going to leave Conrad and stay forever. She'd be invading my privacy, allowing her girls to come in unannounced, destroying my home and worse, my sanity. It would be devastating. It made living in the lobby of Kaiser

look like a Caribbean vacation! And much worse than the time Mel spent with us! Maybe I could move out and let Deedee have at it. But then I'd have to pay two mortgages because there's no way Deedee would pay the mortgage. I couldn't afford that. I said, "Okay, Mom, let me give this some serious thought to see what we can do. We'll have to have your ADLs redone to see what issues we are facing with your care." She absolutely refused to consider that, citing, "Deedee said it was completely unnecessary. She would know. She used to work at a home for the aged in Santa Monica." OMG! That was forty-five years ago, and she only cleaned. That makes her an expert in this field? I was getting nauseated.

Chapter Thirty-Nine

It Was a Very Good Year, and It Was a Very Bad Year

Leslie

January 1, 2013

Where do the years go? I will be sixty-nine years old in July. I'm determined to have only joyful days. Okay, I know that's not always possible, but I can maintain that attitude.

I had a Hanukkah party out in the yard. I set up games for the children and adults. We had a cookie-decorating table and a coloring table. Bernie brought gifts for everyone. Rachael brought the children and came down. Josh is so cute; he put a linen napkin over his arm and began to wipe people's glasses before I refilled the sparkling wines and sodas. The party was a smashing success! I'm absolutely passionate about getting friends together!

Mother went back to Ami's for Christmas. I hired a caretaker to go along. Ami was very upset about that and refused to allow her in. Great! I pictured Mother falling and killing herself. Plus, did Ami want to wipe her Grandma's bottom and bathe and dress her? I was furious with her. She has no clue what Mother's care entails. Miss Dump and Duck doesn't have a clue either. She only knows how to throw gasoline on the fire to keep the flames up high, causing explosions. I'm beginning to dislike these people, my family. It's getting harder and harder for me to hold on to the better days we once had.

Or did we?

April 1, 2013

I went on our annual trip to Left Coast Crime. Mom, Flora, Iris, and I have been going to this mystery readers' and writers' conference for twenty-plus years. This year it was held in Colorado Springs. I missed Iris terribly, as always, but I did not miss Mother. I was at my wit's end with her telling me "Deedee says I can come home," and "Deedee this" and "Deedee that."

At any rate, I had a fabulous time with Flora. It was wonderful to see all my reading-and-writing friends, and it wasn't long before my mind was off my troubles and I was relaxing. Our first night there, I was sitting in the lounge of the bar, talking to a friend about Ashland, when a very handsome gentleman sitting on the sofa across from us said, "Why don't you come over here and tell me about Ashland?" so I did. He is charming! His name is Darwin, and he writes a mystery series, lives in Nevada, and is a widower. We spent a lot of time together. He gave me a quick kiss as I was catching my ride to the airport and said he would be coming to LA next week for a writers' conference—would I like to join him for lunch? I assured him that I would be delighted, that I had a guest room he was welcome to use, and that as long as he would be there, I would host an author at-home evening, which consists of inviting friends to come and hear him talk and serving wine and cheese. We had twenty-one people out by the pool, drinking wine and listening to Darwin talk about his books. He'll be returning next week.

May 16, 2013

Flora arrived yesterday. We're going to go to Bristol for CrimeFest, another mystery readers' and writers' conference. Reading mysteries is my escape, and I enjoy meeting the authors whose books I read. I am actually thinking about writing a mystery myself. Flora and I are friends with the fellow who puts on CrimeFest, and we've been wanting to visit a bit of England, so off we go. We spent a busy day getting me ready for the trip. Flora helped with all the chores. I finished up my deposition transcripts and got them turned in.

We ran errands, got money exchanged, and were finally ready when the shuttle picked us up.
May 18, 2013

We spent a long night on the plane, partaking of the usual tasteless plane food. Going through customs went quite well. I was exhausted from a fitful night of napping on the plane. We settled into this lovely two-bedroom apartment, centrally located in London, that Flora arranged for us. Her cousin Dina had filled the refrigerator for us and even included a bottle of wine. She'll be joining us for a few adventures too. Tonight, we went to an Italian restaurant and had martinis and toasted to the memory of my baby brother.

May 20, 2013

Today we quite literally walked all over London. And it rained, and rained some more. I wore UGG boots because they are the most comfortable and look nice, but that was a huge mistake. They got soaked. The insides of my boots were a swimming pool, and my ankles were getting chafed, plus I was chilled to the bone from being so wet. We were going on to dinner and a play, and I knew I wouldn't be able to tolerate the evening and the walk back slugging along in those boots, so I dragged Flora back to the UGG store we'd passed earlier in the day. I bought a pair of waterproof boots. I will not even contemplate the exchange rate and what those boots cost me. I know it's a bloody fortune, but I simply do not care. These boots are warm and comfy, and my feet are very happy, and so am I.

First thing this morning we went to the British Museum and saw the Pompeii Exhibit. It was horrifying to see men, women, children, a baby, and even a dog with fear and pain etched on their faces as the molten lava melted their bodies and cast them in stone for eternity. It seemed like such a violation to look at them.

May 21, 2013

We went to Hampton Court. The history was so interesting, and the gardens were astonishing. We walked around Westminster and stopped in a pub, and I ordered a martini, which turned out to be a gin and tonic, which I declined and instead ordered gin neat, which even then came on ice with a slice of lime. The smoked bar nuts, though, were heavenly. When I asked for two olives for my gin, I got two bowls of olives.

May 23, 2013

Today Cousin Dina met us, and we went to Bletchley Park, where the decoding took place during World War II. It was a day that there happened to be a reenactment of those years. People were dressed in the clothing of the '40s, which I think is timelessly gorgeous. We had lunch in the commissary, where the food that was served was a reenactment from the war days as well. Dina, who was born and raised in England, commented that only the English could prepare such disagreeable food.

May 24, 2013

Today we went to Cambridge. I imagined myself attending college there. How exciting that must be! We went to the Eagle, a pub where, during WWII, the soldiers burned their names in the ceiling with their cigarette lighters. We took a walking tour, and Flora got lost, but she found the group again. Thank goodness! I would not want to be the one to tell her husband that she got lost in Cambridge. We took a train back to our apartment, arriving well after midnight, where we are now enjoying a nightcap and noshing on crisps while we write in our journals.

May 27, 2013

The day after Cambridge, we met Dina for lunch and went to the British Library. I got completely lost in the literature and music, all the original manuscripts of Shakespeare, Johnson, Boswell, and Shubert.

Yesterday we arrived in Bristol. We got settled into our hotel, which is elegant. My old UGG boots I wore in the rain are still wet, even after I attempted to dry them with the hairdryer, which I blew out in the process. We went down to the bar and met up with old friends and new, and we all went to dinner.

The conference is fantastic! I'm meeting so many interesting international authors that I would not have met but for coming here.

Today we went to Bath and once again walked in the rain all day; however, my feet are dry and happy thanks to my outrageously expensive new boots. Bath is charming! I felt like I just stepped into *Victoria* Magazine. We are now back at our hotel enjoying martinis in the bar.

June 4, 2013

We're homeward bound! What an incredible trip! I hate to see it end! Although it will be nice to see Darwin again, and I miss my kitties.

September 13, 2013

After spending another lovely summer in Ashland, I returned home and rushed over to see Mother. Again, she was delighted with all her visits with friends. There was one, however, that I had not scheduled. Knowing that I would be in Ashland, Miss Dump and Duck scheduled a visit by a doctor her attorney hired. This was a complete setup. He wrote a glowing report about Mother's health and mental capacity, citing that she was quite capable of living alone, preparing her own meals, and all sorts of other things that she could not possibly do. According to him, she could even drive a car. He never mentioned that she is legally blind. The director told me that he did not do a physical exam and that the mental exam consisted of speaking to Mother about literally nothing at all. I was appalled!

September 20, 2013

Deedee's attorney met with Mom and me at the board and care. He wanted me to sign the house back over to my mother, with Deedee as trustee. I thought for a minute, because I truly had had it and was ready to be done with this chapter in my life, so I said, "I'll do that if you'll just return the $100,000 that I put into the property." Her attorney said, "No, we're not giving you $100,000. You didn't have to spend that money, and for all we know it was your mother's money you spent, claiming now it was yours." I was irate and explained that Mother's intention had been that I keep the house. I'd planned on retiring and staying there. I needed to be returned the funds I'd in good faith put into the property because I could not afford to give away $100,000, and it was only fair, as they would now be getting the benefit. Again, he said no. I said no, as well, and if looks could kill, that man would be dead. As he left, he asked Mother, "Is it okay to leave you alone with Leslie?" I wanted to jump up and scream, "Get the fuck out of here!" But I felt like I'd just been punched in the stomach. I couldn't form words. I ran out and sobbed hysterically all the way home.

September 29, 2013

I was concerned because when I called the board and care, no one was answering the phone. I called and called, and got so upset that something might be wrong, I went directly over there. The director said, "Deedee called me yesterday and told me that her attorney said we're not to allow you to speak to your mother because you upset her." This is crazy! I went into

295

Mom's room and asked, "What the heck is going on?" She said, "I don't know anything about it. You don't upset me, except when you don't come to see me more often." Mom and I spoke to the director, Mom assuring her that I did not upset her, while I assured her that this was just my sister stirring up a little more drama. If she's ignored, she'll likely stop.

October 1, 2013

Darwin has moved in with me, bringing his two beautiful girl cats with him. He passed all thirty-two items on my "I'd Rather Be Alone Than Be with a Man Who . . ." list! In April I'd attended a course on understanding men. One of our assignments had been to write down what we needed in a relationship. I put it in the form of "I'd rather be alone than be with a man who ...," for example, has to have the TV on 24-7, or who doesn't like cats, or who can't sit and read a book. It's an interesting undertaking, and I took it quite seriously after my jail time with Ken.

I took Darwin to meet my mom, and she was delighted to have such a charming man give her so much attention. She's been more subdued of late, and I haven't been hearing much about Deedee. I think maybe just getting the approval from the doctor Deedee bought, $1,200 for fifty minutes of chatting, might have satisfied her; he told her exactly what she wanted to hear. For such an independent woman, it was devastating to have her doctor tell her that she can no longer live on her own and take care of herself. That prognosis would crush me. I assured her that if she would just go back to Kaiser for a checkup and testing by her doctors, who have treated her nearly all her life, we might be able to bring her home. I'd been looking into twenty-four-hour home care, thinking that anything would be better than living with Miss Dump and Duck. Mother refused to go back to Kaiser even to have her meds checked, and prescriptions were running out. The director informed her that she wasn't sure she could keep her there if she didn't see her doctor again soon, and she told me Mother's behavior was becoming erratic, that she'd actually pooped in the shower, thinking it was the toilet. Mother said she liked her new doctor that Deedee found, so the director called him to have him refill the prescriptions, but he refused to do so, citing that wasn't his specialty. Asshole!

October 10, 2013

I needed a time-out! I went to the mall and shopped. It's relaxing to walk around and visit salespeople I've known through many years of purchasing from them. I went to Nordstrom's and bought pajamas and cosmetics. I bought candy at Godiva and some charms at Brighton. Then I came home and sat out by the pool in my comfy clothes and wrote out my New Year's resolutions. This year I'm going to focus on being on time, making more time for me, writing, losing ten pounds, being a fashionista, studying Italian and piano, and letting go of people who don't add goodness to my life.

October 19, 2013

The director called me in the middle of the night. Mom couldn't breathe and had been sent to the nearest hospital. She refused to go to Kaiser. I rushed over there to find her breathing on a small machine. She could go back to the board and care tomorrow, but the machine had to go with her. They adjusted her meds and said she must see her regular doctor. I returned the next day to accompany her back to the facility. How the heck could I get her to go to Kaiser? She loves the attention of handsome men. Maybe I could have Darwin talk to her.

October 21, 2013

It worked! Darwin told Mother that he would accompany her to Kaiser and make sure they didn't tell her things she didn't want to hear. As it turned out, we had to schedule the ADL testing for some weeks out, but she got her meds regulated.

Her breathing is better, so she doesn't need the machine. Tonight, we're taking her out to dinner with Bernie and Bernie's husband, Andy, trying a new restaurant with Mexican cuisine, Mother's favorite!

October 22, 2013

I used to think of this day as my sister's birthday, but from now on it will always be known as the day my mother sued me. I'm in shock. Mothers don't sue their daughters. I got home from work about six and found the papers tucked in the screen door. I cried all evening. I'm inconsolable. My mother has accused me of elder abuse and wants her house back plus $1 million. They're not claiming physical abuse but financial abuse. Financial abuse? I've been subsidizing her financial care. How can this be? And I don't have $1 million to give them. I know my mother isn't behind this. This is Deedee's doing. Still, I cannot believe my mother has known about this and not said a word. We had a lovely time at dinner last night. It's shocking that she knew this was going to happen yet acted as if nothing untoward were in the air, even telling me she loves me and thanking us for dinner.

October 23, 2013

I went to see Mother today. She said, "It took me two years to make this decision." I asked her, "Why didn't you talk to me? If you'd told me you were going to sue me, we'd have worked something out." She said, "I want everything to be fair between you and Deedee, and my attorney told me that you didn't have to pay Deedee." I told her, "As you know, I signed a legal agreement to pay Deedee and have offered her money on three occasions. Deedee refused to take it, and now we know why. You're suing me for elder abuse and not only asking for the property back but also one million dollars." She said, "That's ridiculous! I never claimed elder abuse, physically or financially, and I certainly don't want you to give me a million dollars. I told my attorney this was just a little misunderstanding." I said, "Mother, your naked husband crawling into bed with me in an attempt to rape me was not a little misunderstanding, and neither is this. These allegations are very serious."

Deedee and her attorney are lying to my mother and having her sign documents she never would have signed could she have read them. After seeing Mother, I met with my attorney. We'll make an offer to give them the house back, but we cannot give them a million dollars.

Deedee

October 25, 2013

Leslie got the lawsuit papers on my birthday! OMG! What a wonderful gift! My mother loves me. She said she wants everything to be equal. And it will be because Leslie stole a million from my mother and we're going to get the million back as well as the house. Mother doesn't exactly know about the million dollars. She told my attorney this wasn't a major case. It was just a little mother-daughter misunderstanding. Fuck a little misunderstanding. I told my mother, "You owe me for taking my real life away from me. I'm entitled. Leslie is not. If you don't do exactly as I say, I might have to mention that I was kidnapped as a newborn, torn from the arms of my real mother." My attorney sued my mother's other attorney too. He said her insurance company will settle and that should cover his bill. Leslie's going to be kicked out on her fucking ass!

Leslie

October 29, 2013

I can't work. I can't think. I'm so cried out, I'm exhausted. Deedee's attorney refused to accept the house back without the million as well. My attorney suggested mediation. We have a date for two weeks hence.

November 30, 2013

Deedee's attorney refused any offers in mediation. Deedee claims I stole $1 million from my mother, and she wants it back. Mother said she had $300,000 when I took over her accounts. I suggested Deedee and her attorney do the math; $25,000 a month for one year of subacute care is $300,000.

We're going to begin taking depositions and try to settle.

Chapter Forty

Being Strong When Everything Seems To Be Going Wrong

Deedee

January 1, 2014

Settle for the house! What a joke. I'm getting my million and the house. I'm finally going to show Leslie and my mother that I'm smarter than Leslie. I'm going to get my mother all to myself. She's going to love me when I show her how Leslie stole all her money. I wanted to fly out for the mediation, but Conrad said, "No, we can't afford it." I am so tired of him telling me what I can afford. I know what I can afford. I used to be very rich, and I'm going to be very rich again, and I'm not going to let him handle my money. I used my credit card to pay for my ticket out there. This was too good to miss. Leslie looked like shit. My attorney refused any offers they made. The attorney for the insurance company representing my mother's other attorney said my attorney was such an asshole that he would personally see to it that the insurance company never paid out a dime. And my attorney was real pissed when he heard the judge had called him a scumbag. I told him that was a compliment. A scumbag attorney gets things done. My ex Johnson recommended him.

Leslie

January 1, 2014

Darwin and I spent a lovely Christmas at Rachael's. It was a beautiful day and evening filled with lots of love, which I so desperately need right now. Mother's suing me feels like she stopped loving me. It was her idea to put the house in my name. Why is she changing her mind now? She says she loves me, and she just wants things to be equal between Deedee and me. Then why didn't she just tell me that? I don't understand, and it hurts to think my mother would do this.

In spite of all this horror, the first day of the new year has been peaceful and luxurious. I am strong, and I will prevail in this lawsuit.

January 15, 2014

They brought Mother in to take her deposition. Her eyesight has gotten so bad she didn't even know I was in the room. I was sure I was going to throw up. It was surreal, Mother and me sitting across the table from each other while painful questions were being asked and lies were being told. I wanted to scream, "Stop!" I wanted to run from the room. Ami's mother-in-law, Lil, came to handle Mother's personal needs, going to the restroom, etc. I was crushed. That's my job!

March 15, 2014

Darwin and I went to Ashland for the opening of the theater season. He looked at the real estate office windows, checking out prices of property, and saw a condo for $150,000. I jokingly said I could credit-card that amount. I'd been credit-carding my attorney's fees, $5,000 here, and $10,000 there, and even $20,000. I'd gotten my savings too low to use it anymore. When Darwin and I got home, the property sticker prices stuck in our heads, and we began to talk about buying property in Ashland. I go up there so often and spend a fortune on places to stay, I might as well put my money into a property, especially with Rachael and the children coming up several times a year as well.

March 21, 2014

On the advice of my counsel, I relinquished my trustee position to Deedee. I call Mother many times a week but rarely go to see her. I feel so betrayed and abandoned. I can't believe she has done this. She continues to say, "It's just a little misunderstanding." My mother has a very sick idea of what constitutes a little misunderstanding. Perhaps she and Deedee think that suing family members is a normal thing to do. My dad sued my mother; my mother sued my dad; Dad sued Deedee. Deedee didn't have any basis for which to sue me, so she's concocted this lawsuit and talked Mother into suing me. However, Mother has the capability of saying no. I've noticed that Mother's tone has changed. She's more assertive and confident. I think she's feeling important because she's getting lots of attention, and the attention is a huge motivating factor. She was lonely. What could I have done differently?

April 4, 2014

Darwin and I made another quick trip up to Ashland to see a couple of plays and to look at property. We're working with a charming real estate woman Alice recommended. My head is beginning to spin; I've seen so many properties, and I haven't really fallen in love with any of them.

May 5, 2014

I spent a lovely day with Rachael and Taylor. We did a Mom's Day fun run. Taylor and I held hands and ran and walked the race together. We love our shirts that say GIRL POWER. It reminds me that I can't give up my power.

June 8, 2014

The lawsuit drags on. I'm still pleading with Mother to please drop the suit, but my pleas fall on deaf ears. Friends have gone to see Mom, asking her to please stop this nonsense, but she tells them the same things she tells me, and they get frustrated and don't go back. She says, "Tell Leslie I love her," and they reply, "Suing your daughter is not a loving thing to do."

July 12, 2014

I will soon be seventy years old. Where is life going so quickly? I must live every moment to the fullest. My blessings are abundant; this incredible man who wandered into my life, my amazing daughter, and son-in-law, and grandchildren, my darling cats, my home, my health, and my way of life.

    I have nearly always celebrated my birthdays with my mother. I should be with her on this, one of my milestone years.

July 18, 2014

Darwin and I are in Ashland. We saw a townhouse that we fell in love with and made an offer on it. We're staying at Russell House, and we have the house all to ourselves. Alice's health has deteriorated, so she's moved into an assisted living facility. Years ago, Alice and I were standing in the living room of Russell House, and I said, "I would love to own this house and live here someday." That moment is etched in my memory. I know Alice is trying to sell the property, but I don't think I could ever afford it.

July 20, 2014

I was visiting with Alice today, when she looked at me and said, "If you'll purchase Russell House, I'll carry back the loan for you." I was stunned! The love and the trust she must have for me, now, when my life is falling apart, was overwhelming. I gave it a three-second thought and said, "Yes! Yes, I will." We were hugging and sobbing.

July 26, 2014

Mother called to wish me a happy birthday and tell me how much she loves me. I said, "Mother, under the circumstances, I don't see how that can be possible." I felt sick and sad.

August 15, 2014

Darwin went back to Nevada to close out his house and get it rented. I'm staying on in Ashland because I'm closing on both properties. Flora came up for our annual vacation, and we're having a delightful time, even though I'm in the midst of making huge financial decisions. These are also huge emotional decisions. I'm a California girl through and through. I have a career that I love and fought so hard to achieve. And here I am retiring and moving to Oregon to take on running a bed-and-breakfast.

August 19, 2014

Flora and I were at the Britt Music & Arts Festival this evening, enjoying a glass of champagne and a cold salmon picnic, when Alice called to tell me the property was mine; we closed. Oh my God! I own Russell House!

August 30, 2014

For my seventieth birthday, I bought a townhouse and a bed-and-breakfast! I would have thought this whole thing would be scary, but it wasn't. Darwin and I are packing up what we need to finish out the season at Russell House. I have a house sitter for the LA house. I'll miss the kitties, but we'll bring them up soon.

September 1, 2014

I had an appointment with my attorney today. She told me that I needed to hire a forensic financial person and that her ex-husband would be perfect. I nearly cried when she told me he wanted $7,000 up front, but she insisted this would be necessary when we went to court. We needed to show that there was no financial abuse. So, I sucked it up and ran up another credit card. While I was sitting there, she called her ex to make arrangements. They were chatting, when all of a sudden she threw the phone across the room and shoved all the files off her desk, scattering them everywhere. I was aghast! I began to pick up the files, and she screamed, "Leave them alone!" I sat back down quietly while she attempted to compose herself, but I was too shaken up to remain there. I said, "Oh, goodness, look at the time. I'd better scoot," and quickly and quietly exited the office. Outside I called Darwin and said, "Meet me at Henry's," the nearest bar, where I downed two manhattans!

October 30, 2014

We finished our short two-month season at Russell House. I cannot believe all that I have done in the last few months. I own Russell House and a townhouse in Ashland. I withdrew a great deal of money from my retirement fund and am now feeling cash poor but property rich. I have retired from reporting and am now an innkeeper. It feels so strange to suddenly give up reporting. It was my life, and my identity in many ways. I struggled so hard and went through so much emotional trauma to pass that state exam. I can't believe it's in my past.

We rented the LA house, had movers pack us up, brought five indignant cats with us—I wasn't about to leave Papa Cat behind—and we're all settled in the townhouse. This major change in my life is serving me well during the process of this horrific lawsuit.

December 10, 2014

For the holidays, we've decorated Russell House to the nines. She is a regal beauty. I met a lovely woman at the Ashland Chamber of Commerce, and she and I put on a holiday tea. It was a huge success, and I made lots of wonderful new friends. Speaking of friends, Claudia and her husband bought a house in Ashland and moved up here. It's the best feeling to know one of my long-time friends is so close. And family too! Tony took a job in Eugene, so they'll be returning to the Northwest as well.

February 18, 2015

Mother called me yesterday on her birthday. I'm still pleading with her to settle the lawsuit. She said she told her attorney she wanted to drop it, but he told her he wouldn't allow her to do that because he needed to get paid. He's been working two years now without pay and fully intended to recapture his money from me.

February 26, 2015

Mother's attorney froze my government protected KEOGH account. That's all the money I have left, and freezing it without a court order is totally illegal. My attorney refused to take action, claiming I couldn't pay her, so I credit-carded another $20,000. Still, she said she'd have to go to court to get this undone and that would cost another $10,000. I was quite literally beside myself. I pulled out the age card, calling the attorney for the stockbroker, saying, "This is elder abuse! I'm reporting you to the bar association if you don't release my funds immediately. You did this on a good-ole-boy handshake, and it's illegal as all hell." He told me that it was only supposed to be temporary, and my funds would be available within the next twenty-four hours. I pulled that money out in cash faster than a speeding train. I told my mother what her attorney had done, and she said, "He wouldn't do anything so underhanded."

March 18, 2015

Mother's first attorney, who was sued along with me, got out of the case on a technicality. The best part is that Mother, Deedee, and Deedee's attorney have to pay her attorney's fees.

Speaking of Mother, she's on oxygen again.

May 5, 2015

My attorney called today and is dropping my case! How can she do that? Actually, she should have turned it over to another attorney last year. She has cancer, has lost fifty pounds, and is on strong medication—thus, her volatile mood swings. She told me I'd have to find a new attorney; she didn't know of anyone. I nearly threw up. I'm so scared. Her timing sucks! We're supposed to go to trial this month, and I haven't got an attorney. I can't afford to hire another attorney. Their retainers are astronomical—$50,000 up front. I decided to sit in on the court call when she went in to drop the case. Maybe the judge would be as appalled as I was that she would drop my case two weeks before trial. Darwin said she was a paper pusher and afraid to face Deedee's attorney in court. There's definitely some truth to that. I sat in on the court call and told the judge my situation. His response was, "I'm sorry, ma'am, but I can't force her to stay on your case."

May 15, 2015

I hired an attorney just to file a motion to extend the trial date. I sat in on this court call. I told the same judge my situation, "My attorney just dropped my case last week, and I need time to hire another attorney and get him or her up to speed. "

I felt like I'd been punched in the stomach when he said, "Ma'am, my courtroom will not be run by the timing of your attorneys. You have ten days." At which point Deedee's attorney said, "Actually, Your Honor, I will be out of the country and need an extension anyway." Upon which the judge declared, "Well, in that case, we'll continue until November 15. And, you, ma'am, just got very lucky."

I was lucky! But why did this judge hate me? As I was about to end the court call, I heard the judge say to Deedee's attorney, "Hey, my friend! I haven't seen you in months. Let's get lunch!"

July 26, 2015

I'm not spending twelve-hour days on reporting. I'm not sitting on the freeways for hours every day. It's time to begin writing again, and that's my birthday gift to myself this year. This horrible story needs to be told. I know from taking depositions that many other people have become entangled in family lawsuits as well. They and I need validation and allies. Today I began writing for a couple of hours after serving breakfast. It feels good—writing, that is, not serving breakfast!

Deedee

August 15, 2015

Leslie had to have used my mother's money for the townhouse and bed-and-breakfast she bought in Ashland. She's always crying poor, so I know she didn't have enough money to buy them. My attorney says this is good because we'll get those properties too. I am going to be so rich. I'll never have to work another day in my life. I'll be just like my friend Jessica. I'll get a facelift and buy some new designer clothes. I'll get another big diamond ring like Jessica's. Leslie rented my mother's house, and she's getting $3,000 a month in rent. I could kill that bitch. That's my money. Mother is still talking to Leslie, but it's okay. My attorney won't let my mother drop the case, and I hope she remembers our little kidnapping conversation. My mother said that Leslie said we should report him to the bar association. I sure can't let that happen. I told her, "I'll take care of it." She'll forget about it in a few days. I wish I could have been there for mother's deposition, but I'm running up my credit card and need to save some room on it for flying out for the trial. Ami's mother-in-law, Lil, took mother to the deposition. She said Leslie still looks like shit. She's put on a lot of weight. It's from all the wine she bought with my mother's money. Bitch. We can't afford wine. It's too expensive here. We drink martinis, and it's cheap vodka Conrad uses. Things will change when I get all my money. I'll buy the best again. No more cheap crap.

Leslie

September 15, 2015

I am completely and utterly depressed. How can we possibly go to court without an attorney? I am so scared. I'm going to lose everything and be homeless. Darwin is running the inn. I don't want to get out of bed. I play games on my iPad and read books all day to escape the madness.

October 1, 2015

I'm writing the story of the lawsuit. I need to make sense of it. It's developing into a play. To test my latent writing skills, I wrote a few pieces for the paper, which were a huge success. That and Darwin's encouragement have bolstered my confidence.

While I write the play, I am grieving. Tears saturate my laptop. I continue to call Mother and plead, "Please, let's settle this," but to no avail. I uncovered some letters Liam wrote and sent home from 'Nam. One was to Mother when she and Dad were in the throes of a legal battle. Liam told her, "I'm ashamed of you, Mother. Your anger and bitterness are eating you up. Now that you've remarried, I would think that you'd be looking to make your marriage a success rather than suing our father. You're ripping your so-called family to pieces. All we want is peace and harmony, and until you can manufacture that, there will be little, if any, correspondence from me because I'm disgusted with your behavior."

This was the last letter my brother wrote to my mother. She and Deedee were both on the outs with Liam when he was killed. I called Mother to read the letter to her. I was sure when she heard it, she would put an end to the lawsuit and all this horror. However, that was not to be. While I read the letter out loud, she screamed, "How can you be so mean as to call and torture me with that letter?"

October 25, 2015

We thought we'd have to go to trial on our own. I'd been trying to make sense out of boxes of documents my failed attorney sent me. I'd interviewed paralegals, called friends, and attorneys I've worked with. Everyone was so kind and tried to be helpful, but it amounted to naught. Darwin had been after me to make an appearance at Russell House. Guests were beginning to wonder if I existed. I showered, got dressed, put on makeup, and went over to make an attempt at being human. On the staircase I bumped into one of our guests, greeted her, and we began to chat. Before I knew it, I'd spilled out my nightmare story and was sobbing. She told me she was an attorney and said, "This is a clear-cut case of sibling vindictiveness." She nailed that down all right. She said, "I've retired, but my cousin is an attorney, and I think he could get this settled promptly." She gave me his telephone number and told me, "Call him." I didn't have any money. I was credit-carded to the roof. I put my Bay Area house on the market because I was scared to death that Deedee's attorney would put a lien on it and I'd lose my investment. It sold quickly, so I called my new friend's cousin, and he agreed to take the case for a $25,000 retainer. With the proceeds from the sale of the Bay Area property, I paid off all my credit-carded legal fees and was once again debt free, but it left me very little cash. My new attorney—my Atticus Finch— assured me he would settle this case for under the $25,000. A hundred pounds were lifted off my shoulders!

November 15, 2015

We traveled by car to LA for the trial. My lawyer, Darwin, and I are sure we'll win this hands down. I did tell my lawyer that I would like to petition for another judge because this one is clearly prejudiced against me, but he advised leaving him in place. I've spent weeks on a final plea to Mother. I was sure she would relent when I told her, "If you don't drop this lawsuit, you'll never see me or Rachael or the children again." She said, "This is just a little misunderstanding. Why wouldn't you see me?"

Darwin and I decided to make this as pleasant a trip as we possibly could. We stayed at the Hyatt in Sacramento on our way down and had drinks in the bar and enjoyed an outstanding dinner. It was bittersweet, though, because I thought of all the good times Mother and I had had there. In LA we stayed with Bernie and Andy, who eat out every night, so we got to explore new restaurants. Bernie and I have been friends for forty-five years. We've been through births and deaths, divorces, moves, and life-altering changes together. Staying with her fills me with comfort and love.

The trial was scheduled to go forward for a week. I was shocked. Again, we tried to settle, but they are determined to get their million as well as the house. I saw Mother in a wheelchair, and my first reaction was to jump up, give her a hug, and tell her how much I love her, but I couldn't make my feet move. Deedee was with her and had brought her friend, Jessica. They both looked beautiful! I felt like an old frump. My skirt was too tight, and my pallor was ashy. Deedee and Jessica took sexy stances and stared down at me like they were so much better than I was. My sister and my mother and I are in court. Mother and I were best friends. We did everything together. No one I know would ever have believed this could possibly happen. Why didn't Deedee and Mother choose to talk to me instead of suing me?

The judge made Deedee leave the courtroom on technicalities, but Jessica was allowed to stay. I can only imagine how angry Deedee was. She'd orchestrated this event for three years and couldn't attend her own party.

I forgot to mention that my failed attorney's financial forensic husband was supposed to provide us with documents showing that all financials were in order. I'd paid him $7,000 up front; however, during the last month, he kept upping his ante. I was held captive because I needed those documents. After paying him $18,000, the night before we left for the trial, he sent me a rough-draft document that would not be acceptable in court. I was so angry I could have killed the bastard!

Chapter Forty-One

Let It Be

Leslie

January 8, 2016

We've made four trips down to LA for extended trial dates. How many times can a person get beaten up and thrown back into the ring? We only have one more final appearance. Thank goodness!

February 16, 2016

Today was our final court appearance. All the testimony and evidence were in our favor. We were going to be celebrating tonight. We went out on recess feeling quite confident. We reconvened, and the judge said something I couldn't comprehend. My vision turned white, and there was a ringing in my ears. I gripped the arms of my chair, blinking my eyes and shaking my head. I had to snap out of this. My attorney leaned over to me and said, "We lost." I stared at him as he came into focus, and the ringing in my ears subsided. The judge was still speaking. He ruled that my mother was incapacitated from August of 2010, when she originally became ill, until August of 2012, when Deedee's attorney had his medical expert visit Mother and determine her sound of mind and capable of taking care of herself. The judge's decision went directly against Mother's testimony, which was "I was never out of it." It was ludicrous! Mother went to the beauty shop, out to dinner, spent holidays with Ami. She needed physical assistance, but she was never mentally incompetent. I will appeal!

February 18, 2016

We met with my attorney today and decided that appealing was out of the question—namely, it's far too expensive. I simply can't afford it.

My attorney said that there was a document in evidence that Mother had signed, disinheriting me. He told me that he was confident that she would not have signed that document and I should talk to her. Darwin and I stopped at the board and care, where I was told Deedee had moved my mother to another location and they did not know where. I called Mother's cell phone, and she answered. I asked, "Where did you move to and why?" She said, "Deedee thinks it's better if I'm in Santa Clarita, close to Ami." I replied, "Mother, that doesn't make sense. You were ten minutes away from Kaiser at the Encino board and care. Now you're an hour or longer away from medical attention." She answered, "I know. And I don't like it here as well as the place in Encino. The people are nice, but my room is small. My queen-size bed wouldn't fit in here. They had to get a twin bed. They could only fit in one very narrow dresser. And I have to share a bath. But it's only temporary. I'll be back home soon." My heart ached for her, but then I remembered that she was complicit. My mother had agreed to sue me. She could have said no.

I told her, "Mom, you signed a document disinheriting me." She said, "I did not. You know full well that I want everything to be equal between you and Deedee. That's why we filed the suit. Deedee said it was the only way." I said, "You did sign that document. It was entered into evidence. You might want to call your attorney and get it straightened out." She said, "My attorney wouldn't lie to me." I asked, "Do you think I'm a liar?" She said, "I'll call him." She called me back and said, "My attorney said you've already gotten your inheritance."

Deedee

February 18, 2016

I won! It won't be long before I get my money. My life will
be wonderful. Oh my God! I can hardly wait. Mother is
asking how soon before she can go home. I told her we'd have
to get the tenants out first. I'm not taking her home. I need the
money from the tenants. Ami says Grandma needs a lot of
help. The board and care is a lot cheaper than a caretaker. The
place I moved her into is $2000 a month cheaper than the one
Leslie had her in. She didn't need to be in such an expensive
place. Now I have an extra $2000 a month to spend.

Leslie

May 6, 2016

Last night I dreamed I was moving into an old Spanish-style
home in Santa Monica. There were moving boxes stacked on
the large covered front porch, and I was unpacking. A little
red truck with a Smiley Face logo and the words "Helicopter
Center" pulled up in the driveway on the side of the house.
My father came around to the front porch, looking as I
remember him from the '70s. He looked at me and said, "I
love you." I suddenly felt like I was in a bubble of love and
protection. It was miraculous! I woke up and still felt that love
surrounding me. I desperately wanted to go back to sleep and
into that dream.

May 8, 2016

It's Mother's Day! I miss my mother terribly! I thought she
might call. I won't call her. It's too painful. I have sent and
received many good wishes for the day and am grateful for
the love and support of family and friends.

The writing is coming along quite well. It's surprising how much I get accomplished by writing a couple of hours a day.

My weight is at an all-time high. I weighed eight pounds less than this when I delivered Rachael. It's depressing. I used to be so thin. I worked at it, but I also took it for granted. People said I looked good in anything I wore, and I was often asked to do modeling gigs for various benefits. Now I feel like a fat, dumpy, old lady, like the time I dreamed I was in Lil's body. I had her gray hair and no makeup, I was pudgy, and I wore a plain old dress. I was standing at a railroad station. People were walking by me, but nobody noticed me. It was the strangest sensation, being totally alone and unnoticed in a mass of people.

I am sad and scared. How do I come to terms with Mother and the lawsuit, learn to live with it, and move on? Deedee wasn't the only damaged child. Liam and I were damaged as well.

July 26, 2016

Mother called to wish me a happy birthday, saying, "I remember the day you were born. Your dad and I were so happy. It was the best day of my life." I cried. We spoke briefly. Then I said, "Mom, you were lied to about documents you signed. You couldn't read them. Why didn't you ask for an independent party to read them to you?" She said, "My attorney told me what they were." I said, "Well, he lied. Would you agree to have an ombudsman read the legal documents to you? It isn't too late to file a complaint against Deedee's attorney. If you remember, I always had an ombudsman read documents to you before you signed them when you were at the subacute nursing facility." She said, "Yes, I remember. Okay, let's do that."

It took me a couple of days to get all the documents in order. Then I called the facility to let them know I would be arriving the next day and meeting the ombudsman there, but I was told that was not possible. Deedee and her attorney had gotten a very fast guardian ad litem. The facility director said, "Deedee has instructed us not to allow you to see nor talk to your mother. We can give you no updates on the status of her health." My stomach roiled! I doubled over in pain, crying uncontrollably. When I was able to stand up and get ahold of myself, I realized how serious their lying and deception truly was to prevent my mother from having an ombudsman read documents to her and to keep me away so that I couldn't expose them. How much fear and anger must a person have to go to such lengths?

Deedee

August 6, 2016

I had a very close call. Thank God Mother tells me everything. She's so bored she's always dying to tell me the latest. Usually it's stupid stuff, so I almost didn't listen when she told me Leslie had arranged for an ombudsman to come out and read court documents to her. I hung up and called my attorney. He said he knew people and would rush through a guardian ad litem. He's so smart! Now I'm in charge of everything, so I told the facility not to give Leslie any information or let her near my mother, that she was a danger to herself and my mother, she was suicidal, and likely to harm my mother, plus she upset my mother.

Leslie

September 7, 2016

I am so upset about my tenant in the LA house being a backstabbing bitch. I'd given her notice that she would have to move out months ago, but she asked me for another month, and I agreed. Now Deedee's attorney has gotten to her, and she's refusing to pay me what she owes me and move out. I can't make the mortgage payment, which is going to kill my credit rating, and there's about $10,000 worth of my personal property there that I won't be able to recover. Damn it!

Deedee

September 15, 2016

Oh my God! I am so lucky! My attorney put pressure on the tenants in the property and they are now paying me instead of Leslie. I'm getting an extra $3000 a month, and I don't have to pay the mortgage because it's still in Leslie's name. I quit my job at the department store!

Leslie

October 3, 2016

October, my favorite month. The colors are in rapture. The air is brisk and fresh. I'm breathing! I'm alive! That is a miracle!

Subjects to discuss with my therapist today: 1) I'm desolate knowing my mother will die hating me; 2) I'm despondent that I won't spend these last years of my mother's life with her; 3) I'm hurt that Lil, Ami, Mel and others believe Deedee's tale that I stole Mother's money; and 4) I'm frightened that I will lose all that I have left and be homeless.

October 14, 2016

My attorney told me that I would have to file for Chapter 13 bankruptcy. I didn't understand. People file bankruptcy because they have a lot of debt. I have no debt. He told me that in order to save my Oregon properties, I must go under the protection of Chapter 13; otherwise, Deedee's attorney could put a lien on my properties and tie them up for years, even forcing me to sell. To complicate things, I was supposed to refinance and pay off my original mortgage with Alice this year, but I've been told I can't do that while I'm in Chapter 13, and I can't get out of Chapter 13 for three years. I'm going to try to get a refinance anyway, maybe a private lender.

Deedee

October 22, 2016

It's my birthday! With the $5000 I'm getting every month, I was okayed for another credit card, so I flew to San Diego to spend my birthday with Jessica. We're having a wonderful time shopping and drinking martinis and wonderful California wines—I must move back here—visiting the spa and working out at her club. Jessica is keeping an eye out for a nice house for me somewhere near her.

November 9, 2016

I lost out on getting any money from Leslie's Bay Area house. Now she's gone into Chapter 13, and we can't touch her Oregon houses. Fuck! We had to settle for $33,000. I expected to get over a million. I asked my attorney how soon I'd get a check for the $33,000. He told me I wouldn't get anything because the money goes to him, and Leslie's attorney, and court costs, and someone called a trustee. I'm a trustee, so I don't know who her trustee is and why I'm not getting paid. My attorney said not to worry. We're not done with Leslie.

Leslie

November 18, 2016

Deedee and I signed a settlement agreement, but somehow it doesn't feel done, perhaps because I'm tied up in Chapter 13. I was so worried about Deedee's attorney inserting a loophole in the agreement that I had three attorneys read it. They all think it's solid, but I know that any legal agreement can be broken and anyone can be sued for anything.

December 16, 2016

I'm drinking too much and doing stupid things. Since I can't talk to my mother or get any information about her, I called and pretended I was a friend of Mother's, asking after her health. I was told that Mother had gone into distress and was back at Kaiser. I immediately called Kaiser and said who I really was and inquired about Mom. They told me she was in critical condition and back on the ventilator. Oh my God! I had to go to her right now. Cautiously I asked, "Would you please ask my mother if she wants her daughter Leslie to be there with her?" They told me Mother said, "Yes, please." I told them I would be leaving soon and arrive first thing in the morning. I ran to pack my bag. I was all ready to go, but as I packed the car, I heard a voice in my head saying, "What are you doing?" I sat down and listened to that voice. This would be a repeat of former drama. Deedee and Ami would be there. Deedee had legal documents that would prevent me from seeing my mother. It would be humiliating and embarrassing. I had no rights, only that Mother wanted to see me, but with Deedee being guardian ad litem, she calls the shots, not Mother. There would be yelling and screaming. Mother would be in the middle of it. I would be hauled away by the police. I decided to wait until morning. I tossed and turned all night, getting little, if any, sleep.

The next morning, I called Kaiser and was told that Mother's condition had improved, and she'd been transferred to a subacute nursing facility in Santa Clarita, where she'd have to remain on the ventilator. I called the facility. They asked me who I was. When I told them, they said there was an order not to give me any information. I began crying. The nurse said, "I'm so sorry. I will tell you that your mother is alive and stable." I explained, "My mother asked for me last night, and I was planning on coming down." She said, "We can't allow you to see her." I begged her, "Please tell my mother that I can't come to be with her because Deedee has a court order preventing me, but that I love her so much." The nurse promised me that she would and repeated how very sorry she was.

I unpacked my bag and cried. I had a session with my therapist and cried. That night I took sleep meds my doctor had prescribed, finally getting some rest. The next morning, I sat down with my coffee and ruminated on all that has happened. I reread my play. I dozed off and woke up with clarity. My mother chose to sue me. She could have said no. She could have told me Deedee was pressing her to sue me, but she made the choice to move forward with it. I'd been thinking about Rachael. I couldn't burden her with this any longer. She hates trauma and drama. I hate it too. As long as I remained engaged with Mother and Deedee and my nieces, we would never have any peace. I had to let go. I'd sent Deedee, Ami, and Mel emails a few weeks ago, asking if we could, please, heal our family. Deedee never responded. Mel wrote back, "You're a fucking troll. Crawl back into your hole, bitch. You stole a million dollars and got away with it." Ami wrote, "Fuck off! You've ruined our lives."

My mother's abandonment of me has left a hole in my heart. I wish my brother were here. Thinking of his last letter home, I know he'd be appalled and just as heartbroken as I am.

For the sake of my sanity, my daughter and grandchildren, Darwin, and even Jacob, I let go. I meditated, doing positive affirmations. I once climbed to the top of Spanish Peak in Colorado and I imagined myself there now, allowing my mother, Deedee, Ami, and Mel to sail into the universe. I sent my love with them, permitting them to be free to be who they are without me. I'm free of my responsibility!

Chapter Forty-Two

Time Is on My Side

Leslie

January 1, 2017

Happy New Year! Another year has come and gone. We had dinner and danced the night away last night. It was a glorious evening with old friends and new. I wore my bridesmaid's dress from Deedee's fourth wedding, and, in spite of my extra weight, I looked pretty darn good.

All is well, except, of course, for being in Chapter 13 and worrying about a refinance, but we have a broker working on that. I went back to studying Italian and have met so many delightful new friends. I'm volunteering at the theater gift shop, and, as I once imagined, it's just plain fun. I meet so many people, and everyone is happy. I spend time at our local yarn shop. I work out at the Y, and I walk in the park where the sound of the creek and the smells of the woods feed my soul. I feel like I've come to Ashland for the summer and brought my home with me. I ought to send Deedee a thank-you note!

January 25, 2017

I'm at a resort in Mendocino, attending a writing retreat put on by Phyllis Theroux. This is an extraordinary experience. We attend a writing session in the morning, where Phyllis gives us prompts and we write. We take walks and write on our own in the afternoons. We come back together in the evenings for wine and reading out loud. Since Phyllis is a journalist, I threw a box of my journals in the car before I left home. I've been reading those at night and have decided to write a novel in diary format.

Deedee

February 12, 2017

Before Christmas Jessica and I flew to New York to go holiday shopping. I took my fur coat. It is wonderful, getting my life back! Five thousand a month isn't enough, though. I keep asking my attorney when I'll get the house, but he takes forever to get back to me, and when he does, it's the same old thing, he's working on it. I flew to LA and spent Christmas with Amiala. Meliza and I aren't on speaking terms. She's such a little tramp! I can't remember what our argument was about, but I'm not backing down. Denzel joined the navy and is stationed overseas. After Christmas I rented a car and drove down to Jessica's for New Year's. We bought slinky new evening gowns and went to a black-tie affair one of her friends put on. Conrad has been killing mad about the lawsuit and all the money we've spent. I thought I might have to fake a suicide attempt to get him to calm down, but I had a tantrum instead and he stopped complaining. I felt a little bit guilty, leaving him alone for the holidays, but he's always telling me we can't afford to fly the girls here so I said it would be cheaper to just buy my ticket. I told him I needed to spend time bonding with my girls. He's a big guy. He can take care of himself.

Leslie

April 19, 2017

I've arranged to have a reading of my play. I've hired some actors. We're going to use the back room at Liquid Assets and serve wine and appetizers. I'm worried, though, that I'll air my past family issues and embarrass myself. I think the play is a good, solid piece of work, but maybe others will think it's just plain stupid and self-serving.

April 25, 2017

My play reading seems to have been a success. I was overwhelmed with anticipation, and now it's all over. After the reading we had a lively discussion about the topics the play dealt with: caring for the elderly and the outrageous expense, wills and trusts, family lawsuits, and the flawed legal system. It was validating to hear other people's stories. I feel much less alone.

June 13, 2017

Alice died! I am devastated. I found out through a Facebook post her caretaker posted. I called Ellie, sobbing. Alice's daughter had moved her to a facility closer to where she lives in Washington, so I hadn't seen Alice for a few months. I can't believe she's dead. She was like a mother to me.

July 21, 2017

I wrote a piece about Alice that was published in the paper, and it received a wonderful reception. I was at a bar one night, and a lady asked me to sign her copy of the article. I've been working on my novel, but it's a slow process with everything else going on.

August 25, 2017

Rachael and Taylor were here for our annual girls' Ashland summer vacation. They bring me so much joy! When they left, I felt so sad and lonely and was reminded of my mother saying how empty her house felt when Rachael and I left. The tables have turned, and I am in the elder position. It's scary!

I spend hours in a day trying to talk to people about a refinance but to no avail. I'm told that they can't give me a refinance while I'm in Chapter 13, and I tell them my Chapter 13 plan calls for me to refinance before I can get out of

Chapter 13. I'm worried sick about it. Our only hope is a private lender, but the broker we have working on it doesn't seem to be getting anywhere either.

Chapter Forty-Three

Beyond the Sea

Leslie

January 1, 2018

A fabulous new year! We sent out 2017 with a bang! We had a big New Year's Eve party at Russell House. We played games. There was laughter and cheering. It made the house happy! Just before midnight, everyone gathered together to make a wish for the New Year, and then we toasted in 2018!

Deedee

January 12, 2018

I had a crappy Christmas and New Year's! I stayed home with Conrad and we did nothing! Boring! He's been killing mad about what I'm doing with the $5000 every month. I wanted to tell him it was none of his fucking business. I'm so tired of being ruled by men. When will I ever get my hands on that house? It's taking for-fucking-forever!

Leslie

February 22, 2018

A gentleman on Facebook who supposedly knew my brother said that my life was one of protected innocence. Really? Is that like when they ship your brother's body home from 'Nam and tell you, sorry, that was a war we shouldn't have been in, and he died for nothing, and you were damn lucky to get his body back? Or, I know, is that when your stepfather attempts to rape you and your mother says, "Oh, that was just a little misunderstanding"? Or is that like when your father blows his brains out and you're left to clean up the mess? Or is that like when your husband tells you he loves you, and he doesn't want a divorce, but he's having an affair with his cousin? Or is that like when your sister has been abusing her daughters, and you have to go to court to testify that she's an unfit mother in order to get the child off the streets? Or is that like when one of your best friends dies of breast cancer? Or is that like when you're left alone to raise your daughter, and instead of crying "victim," you educate yourself? Or is it like when you worked twice as hard as the men in your office and received half the pay? Or is it like when your boss patted your bottom, and you had to keep your mouth shut or lose your job? Protected innocence! What an asshole!

April 13, 2018

The costs of the townhouse and bed-and-breakfast combined are staggering, so we decided to remodel the bed-and-breakfast, move in, and rent the townhouse. Darwin is doing all the renovation by himself. I'm packing and slowly moving things over.

My broker isn't getting anywhere with a refinance, not even with a private lender. I'm anxious, nervous, and truly sick about this Chapter 13 plan. It requires us to refinance the bed-and-breakfast to pay the prior loan and court costs, but if you're in Chapter 13, nobody will loan you money. This plan is impossible. I believe that the judge, attorney, and trustee were not paying attention to the circumstances of my case, which are compound and complicated. They are professionals. They should have known that this plan they put me in was doomed to fail.

July 20, 2018

We didn't get moved into the bed-and-breakfast until June 15. We had guests during the move-in, which created a lot of comedy of errors because we had boxes and furniture all over the place, but generally speaking, people were very understanding and kind, even offering to help.

October 11, 2018

It's that time again! New Year's resolutions! This year Claudia and I decided to have a renewal day together and write out our resolutions. We went to the spa, sat in the hot tub, had massages, cleaned up, and while we sipped sake, we committed our resolutions to our journals. Mine are: lose twenty pounds, finish my novel, practice the piano more, study my Italian with intention, be on time, and get toned up.

October 31, 2018

It's Halloween! I still miss my mother, and I'm sure I always will. Sometimes I feel like I want to go back in time to be with her again. We had so much fun. And we were younger. My years of reporting and living in the Bay Area and LA were astounding, but these years are too. When I walk up the steps to our front porch or look out the windows of Russell House onto this magical city, my heart takes a leap. I can't believe I actually live here. I really should send Deedee a thank-you note!

December 17, 2018

I wake up in the middle of the night with nightmares about being homeless, and I'm afraid to go back to sleep. I wish I could refinance. I wish I were out of this Chapter 13 mess.

December 27, 2018

I love the holiday season. Right now, it's helping me forget my legal problems. We spent a fantastic Christmas at Rachael's. Jacob was there, and Christmas Eve Tony's parents put on a feast of delicious Italian dishes.

Taylor, Rachael, and I went shopping at the downtown mall, where the holiday decorations were spectacular, and the gaiety of the shoppers was intoxicating. Carolers were strolling along singing. The wine bar was filled, and the laughter lifted my spirits.

December 30, 2018

I am approaching 2019 with a great deal of excitement. I will turn seventy-five! I will get Russell House refinanced, and I will be free of the lawsuit. I'm healthy and happy. I will finish my novel, and I've already begun to lose weight.

Chapter Forty-Four

The Twist

Leslie

January 1, 2019

I'm beginning to put away the holiday decorations and thinking about how they are my history, as well as Rachael's. They bring me joy and nostalgia.

I like to dress to the nines and go out for a very festive New Year's Eve, but this year I have been under so much stress, I just wanted a quiet evening at home. I spent today reading and relaxing. It has been the perfect start to the new year.

There isn't a day I don't think of my mother. I feel the sting and pain of her abandonment, but I try to let that go and be in the moment. Deedee's attorney sued my mortgage company, but the loan remains in my name, and I can't make the payments without the rental income. This suit will go to court.

Deedee

January 1, 2019

Leslie won't sign the loan on the LA house over to me. The bitch! My attorney said he'd take care of it. He sent me copies of the settlement documents on the suit with the mortgage company and said it would be all right for me to sign Leslie's name to give the loan to me. He said they told her she wasn't a party to the lawsuit. She'll never find out what became of the loan, so it doesn't matter. My attorney is so smart.

Leslie

March 19, 2019

I went up to Portland to help celebrate Josh's thirteenth birthday. Wasn't it just Rachael's thirteenth birthday? It was nice to be together with Tony's family again. Family is important to them and makes me realize how much I miss my mom, sister, and nieces. I wonder if they're happy. I occasionally ask Rachael if she wouldn't like to get in touch with Ami; they were more like sisters than cousins. She says she just doesn't want to invite the drama back into her life.

Deedee

May 5, 2019

Oh my God! I'm so excited! The house is mine! My attorney got me a loan. I had to take out $300,000 to pay him. I thought that was way over the top, but Jessica says that's cheap for nine years of legal work. We settled with Leslie's mortgage company for $187,000. My mortgage payment is $3500 and I have to pay it. I didn't have to pay the mortgage while it was in the lawsuit. Fuck! This isn't so good! The mortgage Leslie had was only $1200. It isn't fair! And Mother is nagging me about going home. She said, "Leslie was going to take me home on the ventilator. You promised me if I went along with this lawsuit that you would take me home."

Leslie

May 20, 2019

As we get closer to the deadline for the Chapter 13 disaster, I'm getting more worried and anxious. Because I believe I was put in a plan doomed to fail, I contacted an attorney to get a legal opinion, and I got confirmation that, indeed, I was put in a plan doomed to fail. He said that the complications of the case were great and that the people managing it practiced in a small town and didn't have the experience or the expertise to deal with my case. Meanwhile, I put filing legal action on hold because I found an article in the *Wall Street Journal* concerning unorthodox mortgages and called one of the companies quoted by the journalist. They are looking at my situation. There is hope!

I found out that Deedee paid off the mortgage on the LA house, but I'm unable to find out any details of the settlement. I should, however, send Deedee a thank-you note because this will greatly improve my illegally damaged credit score.

Deedee

June 1, 2019

My fucking tenant moved out. The bastard owes me two months' rent. Amiala went to look at the house and said it's a mess. Fuck! I've got to get a tenant in there or I can't pay the house payment. Why does everything have to happen to me? My attorney promised me I'd get a million dollars and the LA house. Bastard! All I got was the house and a big fat house payment. And I hate that house. It's just a stupid tract house in a real crappy location.

Leslie

June 18, 2019

We were quite literally down to the last forty-eight hours before I would potentially lose both properties, and I was out of my mind with fear, when I received the email confirmation that I'd been approved for a loan. I began to cry. Nine devastatingly painful years are over. I have my life back! I'm the driver! This hateful, horrible part of my life is in my rearview mirror! Thank you, God and Universe, and the fabulous journalist for the *Wall Street Journal*!

June 22, 2019

I've been at Rachael's, celebrating her fiftieth birthday with her. We were reflecting on the differences and similarities on our fiftieth birthdays. She's the mother of two teenagers and a teacher. At fifty I was at the height of my reporting career and a card-carrying member of Sex in the City Over Fifty. For her fiftieth birthday I gave her the gift of a spa day. For my fiftieth birthday I received varied gifts, but my favorite was from Claudia, a subscription to *BBC Music Magazine* that came with a CD in it. Rachael's birthday dinner was at a bowling alley because Josh's baseball team had a party there. My fiftieth birthday dinner was with seven friends at Lulu's in San Francisco.

At every stage of my life, having Rachael for a daughter has made me a better person.

June 23, 2019

Today I saw my very talented Josh play baseball and thought how amazing it would be if my brother were here, sitting next to me, watching his great-nephew following in his footsteps. I felt someone sit down next to me, but when I turned to look, no one was there.

Deedee

June 28, 2019

I'm so stressed out I have a constant stomach ache, and my sore throat keeps coming back. Meliza said maybe I'm bulimic. That girl is dumber than a post. I told her, "So I throw up on occasion. That's how I maintain my weight. It's better than being fat. And I'm not bulimic." My mother is constantly nagging about going home, and Amiala is on the bandwagon too. She wants to take my mother home. She says she'll live with her and take care of her. She said, "If Aunt Leslie was going to take Grandma home on a ventilator, I can too." Fuck! I need a paying tenant in there, and I can't afford to pay a caretaker. My mother's income wouldn't begin to cover all the expenses. I can't take much more. Thank God I have guardian ad litem. My mother can't do a thing about going home without my saying so, and I'm not saying so.

July 1, 2019

Some asshole just served me papers. My mother and Amiala are suing me for elder abuse and claiming I illegally transferred the property to myself when it should have remained in the trust, that I forged Leslie's name on the loan docs, and that I made promises I didn't keep. This is un-fucking-believable. After all I've done for them! Those ungrateful bitches! That fucking Leslie must have somehow gotten to Mother. I told the people at the facility they couldn't let her anywhere near my mother. They screwed up! I can't afford an attorney. What am I going to do? I have to tell Conrad. Fuck! This can't be happening. I'm trapped.

Leslie

July 26, 2019

It's here, my seventy-fifth birthday! I feel so free! Tomorrow I begin a new chapter in my life, 365 days of blank pages to fill in as I choose. *The Diary of an Extraordinarily Ordinary Woman* has been sent to an editor, and I've lost twenty pounds. I've met my goals for this milestone year. But my greatest accomplishment is that I broke free from the mold of generational dysfunctionality that has encapsulated my family.

August 1, 2019

I received a Facebook message from a man who'd recently attended the yearly vets' conference. We exchanged emails, and he said that he was the man who found my brother's body. He told me he found Liam clutching his stomach where he'd been shot. He tried to close Liam's eyes but could not. He said Liam's face was dirty, so he took his bandanna, dampened it with water from his canteen and washed Liam's face. He stayed with my brother's body until morning when a helicopter flew them out. It's the most intimate story I've ever heard, and it gave me peace to know that my baby brother was protected until he was put on the plane for home.

Deedee

August 15, 2019

Mother and Amiala just have to drop this lawsuit. I'm desperate. I wanted to sell the LA house, but I couldn't because their attorney put a lien on it. Conrad and I are going to have to take a big loan against our house to pay for an attorney. We couldn't find a lawyer to take it on contingency like before. And the attorney I used to sue Leslie won't return my phone calls. Conrad is so mad he could kill me.

August 21, 2019

I'm going to attempt another suicide so that Mother and Amiala will feel guilty and drop this fucking lawsuit. I don't know any other way. Talking to them has gotten me nowhere, and we have no money to fight this case. I can't believe they're doing this to me, my own mother and daughter. I'm going to take a few pills. Conrad always gets home at five, and we always have martinis together. He'll take me to emergency to get my stomach pumped. I'll get a lot of attention, and this nightmare lawsuit will end.

Leslie

August 22, 2019

My sister's dead! I can't believe it! A friend from Georgia called me and then sent me a link to an article in their local newspaper. They say it was suicide, but I know Deedee wouldn't kill herself. She's too mean to take her own life. She would only attempt it to garner attention. Apparently, she took too many pills and sat down on a couch in their den, where she customarily sits that time of day to scan the latest fashion magazines while waiting to enjoy a martini with Conrad. The window was open. The neighbor was out in her garden and heard some low moaning as if someone was trying to call out. She was worried that perhaps someone in the house had fallen and been hurt, so she called 911. When the paramedics arrived, Conrad was casually drinking a martini and reading the paper. Another martini sat across from him on the bar. The police found Deedee too late to revive her. When Conrad was questioned, he said, "I thought Deedee took the golf cart over for a lesson and would be back soon. I didn't hear anything because I wasn't wearing my hearing aids."

The golf cart was still in the garage.

October 22, 2019

Today would have been Deedee's sixty-ninth birthday. Soon after her death, Conrad sent me her diaries. He said I'd know what to do with them.

Today I received six cases of my just-released novel, *The Diary of an Extraordinarily Ordinary Woman—and Her Rather Eccentric Sister.*

The End

BOOK GROUP DISCUSSION QUESTIONS

The Diary of an Extraordinarily Ordinary Woman and Her Rather Eccentric Sister is a work of fiction but feels so very real. Family members argue and reunite; tragedies and joys, big and small, affect family members directly and indirectly; and in the end, no one knows the full story—no one person can tell us the whole truth. In this novel and in real life, we're each left to fill in the gaps and come to our own understanding—and, hopefully, peace.

Connect this family history with your own life's story by musing on the following questions:

1) *The Diary of an Extraordinarily Ordinary Woman and Her Rather Eccentric Sister* is full of nostalgic detail. What tangible items—types of toys, styles of clothes, makes of cars, and so on—best call to mind your childhood, your young adulthood, your middle age, and your "third act" years?

2) This novel talks about generational trauma. Do you agree that inner generational trauma and behavior modeling is passed from parent to child? Are there any examples in your family? What are they?

3) Trauma may have familial connections, but it doesn't affect siblings in the same way. Leslie and Deedee responded to their environment in different ways. What differences, and similarities, do you see among members of the same generation in your family?

4) Leslie and Deedee often write very different diary entries about the same event. Think about an event, big or small, that you experienced with at least one other family member. How would each of you tell the story of that occasion?

5) Leslie writes in one entry about the 1989 Loma Prieta earthquake (chapter seventeen). She talks about fleeing her office building moments after the earthquake:

I jumped in my car and headed to the gate only to be confronted by the ticket taker. I was surprised that there would be someone checking tickets and collecting money moments after a major earthquake. I found myself asking him, "Do you know if the Bay Bridge is down?" He didn't know. I felt like an idiot for asking, yet as I approached the ramp for the Bay Bridge, a feeling just came over me that this may not be the best route home. Then I noticed that vehicles were at a standstill on the bridge, and people were getting out of their cars and walking around. I had to make a decision because it was getting more and more difficult to move off the ramp and back onto the freeway.

This one passage summarizes a lot of the novel: life going on amid chaos, the importance of last-minute decisions being made under pressure. What is an example of this in your life?

Made in the USA
Middletown, DE
24 January 2021